VULNERABILITY

By Robert T. Burson

ISBN: 1439268185
ISBN-13: 9781439268186

1

The saltwater turned to mist and sprayed in his face each time his catamaran hit the oncoming wave. Christakos had hiked out as far as he possibly could. He was completely extended out over the water; his feet wrapped around the rungs of the ladder allowing him to move the boat's center of gravity to maximize its speed. It was the final leg of the race with nothing more to be done to gain additional speed. He had fully extended the spinnaker and his boat cut through the water barely riding on one pontoon. His muscles strained to keep her from tipping. He would win the race or flip the *Egina* trying. His muscles screamed but he held on gaining on the boat in front. Looking back, he could barely see the third and fourth place vessels. Before the race he had judged these two had no real chance of winning. But they had obviously done their duty. He could never prove it nor would he try, but the captains of those boats had conspired to have him lose.

His muscles began to knot as he closed the gap. He was within meters of the lead boat and for the first time since the race had begun he could see its captain clearly. Through the spray of the ocean he could make out the determination on her face that somehow remarkably added to her beauty. As the *Egina* came abreast of her boat he could see the finish line marker buoys meters away. He was flying. A large gust of wind began to lift him and the *Egina* out of control. He tried to hike out even further but there was simply no place left for him to go. Still fighting for control of his catamaran he looked to the judge's boat and saw he had crossed the finish line first. But had he won? He quickly checked to see if there were any challenge flags flying from the lady's boat. There were none. He had won.

As Christakos brought the *Egina* back into the harbor he decided he needed to meet the mystery lady. She was beautiful and she could sail. What a tempting combination. The evening reception would be the ideal time to check her out.

2

Mike Williams put down his binoculars. "That was quite the race."

"I thought that Greek fellow, what's his name, would never win."

"Know what you mean. Philip, what are you still looking at?"

"Stop talking and take a look at the captain of the runner up boat." Philip Logan almost ordered.

I was not about to question that tone so I just brought the field glasses up and focused. "She's incredible."

"Now you can see what I was looking at."

"Do you know who she is?"

"Haven't a clue, but maybe I will put some effort into finding out."

"All you Brits think of yourselves as James Bond."

"Well at least we have a James Bond," Logan said. "All you Americans have is John Wayne. The Greek's name by the way is Christakos."

"Why does that name sound familiar?"

"He is one of the shipping magnates this country seems to specialize in of late."

Turning my back to the water and looking at Logan, I asked, "Why is it again we are going to the reception thing?"

"To meet women old boy," Logan responded. "What better way to spend your holiday?"

"Well all I know is that when we do these little party things you end up with someone beautiful and I get to tell myself that next time will be my turn."

"Then this will be the time, I can assure you," Logan offered.

"Okay, okay, what time does it start?"

"8:00 p.m. Do you want me to come by and pick you up?"

"No, I will take a cab and meet you here," I said. "Look I need to run a couple of errands. So I am going to take off. Is that a problem?"

Logan turned back to the sea and brought the binoculars up to his eyes, "Not at all. I think I will stay here a little while longer and check out the scenery."

3

I left Logan and headed up the stairs and into the main lobby. It amazed me how this place smelled of money and power. Only a dolt could miss it and they were prohibited from entry even through the servant's entrance. Of course, I don't belong here but I know it. How tonight is going to go will be - interesting, maybe that's the term. I figure there isn't a chance in hell I am going to meet anyone. I mean anyone within five years of my age, of the female persuasion, who will show the slightest amount of interest. I'll probably end up talking to Commodore and Mrs. Somebody listening to the trials and tribulations of life on the yacht and horse circuit. Still if it weren't for old Logan I'd never be able to attend the premier catamaran-racing event of the season. It is funny how a poor kid like me came to like yachting, but that's a story for another time.

4

"Hello, my name is Charalamambos Christakos." Christakos extended a hand to the mystery lady. "You are quite a sailor. I have not had such a tough race in a long time. I enjoyed it."

"It is nice to meet you." The mystery lady reached out to shake Christakos hand.

As he grasped her hand he noticed how fit she was. Tanned but not burned. Her natural skin tones obviously blended well with her nautical activities. She was wearing a black cocktail dress. He loved black cocktail dresses. They were designed to be just revealing enough to allow the imagination to have some fun. As he tracked towards her face he stopped to admire the swell of her firm and well-rounded breasts. He could see no obvious tan line there either. "I am Melina Fokina."

"I must compliment you on your skills. The way you handled the boat was quite impressive," Christakos said.

"Why thank you," She smiled, "you are most kind."

Christakos was stunned by the radiance she projected when she smiled.

"Ms. Fokina..."

"Please call me Melina."

"Melina I am just being truthful, really. Where did you learn to sail so well?"

"In Switzerland, on Lake Geneva."

"I see." Christakos was now gazing into Melina's eyes. There was a vague Eurasian look to them. Christakos wanted to keep the conversation light, but he was having a hard time concentrating. This mystery woman was one of the most beautiful he had ever seen. Her look, combining her eyes with her high cheek bones and dark hair was distracting even to a man who had as much experience with women as had Christakos. "I see your drink is low, may I get you another?"

"Why thank you. I would certainly appreciate that."

Christakos turned towards the bar and waved his hand slightly. He turned back to Fokina. Those gorgeous eyes now had a twinkle to them. "That was impressive."

"Thank you, you see I own this club."

"Well, it does certainly help to know the right people."

Christakos bowed his head slightly. It was then the waiter arrived with their drinks. He took hers from the tray and handed it to her. As he grabbed his drink he pointed towards the sun setting over the sea. "I love this time of the evening."

"So do I. Would you do me a favor?"

"Why certainly."

"Let's take a little walk. The club is crowded with too many eyes and ears."

Christakos nodded. This evening had all the potential he had hoped for.

5

"Well Philip, how did your trawling go this afternoon?"

"I was reconnoitering, tonight I will trawl."

"I see. What became of the mystery lady? I figured you were going after her."

"The truth be known I was, but it seems that Christakos fellow had the same thing in mind. They just headed out the back towards the water."

"Can't win them all."

"Mike I don't think in terms of winning and losing, just in terms of opportunities. And as a matter of fact I see a new opportunity standing at the bar. She looks like she is just there waiting for me. You don't mind if I go and introduce myself do you?"

Before I could say, "Of course not, what are friends for?" Philip was off in pursuit of the first runner up. As I suspected, this evening was going to be the usual disaster. It wasn't so much that I minded meeting new people, it was just they weren't the right people. Better head to the bar and get a drink. Boring people were more interesting that way.

"Scotch please," Mike told the bartender.

"Coming up."

As the bartender delivered my drink, I turned to face the growing crowd. Clearly, the face point game had begun. It didn't seem to matter what country or what social setting the game was there. A majority of the attendees were only intent on seeing and being seen.

A voice behind me asked, "Excuse me, are you American?"

Somewhat surprised, I turned to answer. Whoever this was, she was quite good-looking in an athletic sort of way. Maybe with luck this party would not be the complete disaster I had feared. "Yes, I am, is that a problem?"

Laughing she said "Oh no, nothing like that. I just sometimes like to talk to my fellow countryman that's all. Let me introduce myself, my name is Kate O'Hara."

I must have had a quizzical look on my face because she paused for a moment and then added, "My parents loved Gone with the Wind."

"Nice to meet you, my name is Mike Williams. My parents loved that movie too and had I been a girl they were going to name me Kate, which is a lovely name. Fortunately they didn't name me Rhett." She seemed pleased with my response. I hesitated. Should I? Why the hell not. Take a chance. "Well, Katie O'Hara, what is it that you do?" I asked in my finest Irish brogue, trying to sound like Scarlet O'Hara's father in the movie, whose name escapes me at the moment. I hope I don't offend her.

She had paused and then answered with a slight twinkle in her eye. "I am a financial reporter for the Washington Post. I am stationed in London. I am here getting background. I am doing a piece on the shipping business and Christakos."

"Did I say something funny?"

"No, actually it was what you didn't say. You see I was ready for the usual jokes about my name. Because of that I get a little self-conscious and have a set of traditional defensive responses lined up. But yours' was one I had never heard before. It was kind and funny and a little self-deprecating. I also like your Irish brogue or more accurately the noble attempt at you made at one. "And what do you do suh?"

I had to admit that her Southern drawl was much more convincing than my Irish accent. I usually lied at this point in the conversation. I had two standard stories. The one I chose was generally based upon whether or not I wanted to continue the conversation. I might say I was a U. S. government employee working with the state department. I had found over the years saying you were with the Foreign Service had the hint of travel and mystery, and as such, people stuck around to hear more. My other cover was that I was in the electronics industry and I would start talking like some kind of techno geek. Also over the years I had found that this drove people away faster than being seen with spinach hanging out from one's front teeth. Actually, both lies are easy because they are partially true. I have found the easiest lies are those that have more than a little element of truth in them. Working for the NSA, I am a government employee and because it was the NSA I was familiar with the sophisticated electronic gear.

"I work for the State Department."

6

"How is it you happen to be at this regatta?"

"Well, you see I was in need of a vacation and my friend, Philip, had an in here and so making a long story short I am here on vacation."

"Your friend, Philip?"

I laughed. Kate looked at me and waited. I realized she was trying to figure out whether I was gay or not. "I think he is around here somewhere." I looked around the room and found him standing at the bar, with what I might say was an impressive looking blond. Of course I do like blonds so I am a bit prejudiced that way. I pointed in the direction of the bar; "There he is, the tall paratrooper looking chap talking to the first runner up." Turning back to Kate, I could see the relief on her face. "Afraid I was gay when I said I was here with a man, huh?"

"Something like that. Not that I object, its just that I don't need any new "friends" if you know what I mean."

"I understand."

"What did you mean by first runner up?"

"Well my friend actually had set his sights on the lady who skippered the runner up catamaran. The rich Greek, what's his name...Christakos got there first."

"Imagine that, someone choosing an old rich guy over a young...?"

Kate paused and waited for me to fill in a little detail. I was beginning to like her but she was a reporter and she didn't need to know too much, at least not yet, "poor guy."

"You said you worked for the State Department. What do you do there?"

A partial truth was again the best answer. "I am in the communications section."

"I see. You carry the diplomatic pouch chained to your wrist and all that."

I answered "Something like that." I was really hoping she would change topics, but I could see she had a natural reporter's curiosity. So I decided to try and not to obviously change the topic. "You said you were a financial reporter. Now that it has been a few years, do you have any comments about the Gulf Wars, from a financial point of view?"

"From an economic point of view and from a personal one, I am glad it was short and sweet. Thank God we didn't lose very many soldiers. However, I am afraid that because of the inherent instability in Iraq in the long run nothing will have really changed."

"Kuwait is free isn't it?" I felt I needed to say something positive even though I tended to agree with her sentiments.

"Yes and once we get the oil fields back up to full production, the price of oil will settle down," Kate said.

"I thought they were back in business. Didn't we bring the fires under control within several months after the first war?"

I saw Kate was now in her reporter mode. "The fires were put out rather quickly, however, even today four years later, production hasn't gotten back to prewar levels."

What she said was true, though I was surprised she knew this information. Our government had gone to a great deal of effort to hide this fact. "I thought the fields were back in full production."

"Not really."

"How do you know this?" I asked.

"I have my sources," was all she said. I decided not to push it.

I could tell she knew a great deal about this subject. I had spent a lot of time in the Middle East in the last five or six years and had been curious about the effect of oil on the world economy. I decided to get a free education. "I was surprised to see how volatile the price of oil was during the entire crisis. I mean it isn't like we were going to lose to that Iraqi dictator or anything like that. And the world had to know we would never let anyone cut off the Saudi oil fields."

"That's true. But what causes prices to move so rapidly and to have such an impact on the world economy is the marginal supply of crude."

"Marginal?"

"Yes, the last barrel or barrels if you would. It's always the last of anything or the perception of the last of something that causes price swings. And we have seen some rather dramatic swings. Imagine what would happen if there was a perceived, not even actual, event associated with the availability of Saudi production or the stability of the Saudi royal family."

Not wanting to sound dumb but being a little lost, I simply responded, "bad?"

"I'm afraid bad would be putting it more than a little mildly."

Not that I completely understood but her analysis was consistent with what I had heard from briefings. I wanted to lighten the conversation as I had had enough heavy stuff for some time. "I am famished. Do you want to catch a bite?"

"I would love to, thanks."

7

"I always have trouble deciding where to eat when I am in an unfamiliar place."

"So do I. I don't what it is. Maybe I watch too many travel shows."

I was relieved with the way the conversation had gone so I suggested that we just eat in a little café I had seen across from the club. "I know. Those shows always show some average Joe from out of town who just happens to find a four star family restaurant with prices you could only find in Broken Bow, Kansas."

"And it seems I find the place that makes dinner at the Dorchester look cheap with the kind of service one can only find on an airplane."

I laughed at her reply and was more than pleased when she grabbed my arm and said, "Then let's go be disappointed together."

In fact we found the food to be quite good and service first rate. Before I could begin my string of questions to find out more about her, she asked me "So you work for the State Department?"

"I am stationed in Washington D.C."

"What desk?"

"I am attached to the Middle East desk at the moment." I again decided a partial truth would work best. "I am more a liaison really. I do a lot of traveling between Saudi Arabia, London and D.C." I thought it was a good time to find out more about her and less about me. In fact, I knew what I needed to know about me and I wasn't ready to share that with this lady, though I found her quite intriguing. "How long have you been in London?"

"It's been a couple of years now."

"Do you like it?"

"I love it. London is a great city. It isn't home of course, but it is a good second home."

"How did you end up here in Greece?"

"I'm doing a piece on Charalamambos Christakos and I'm doing some background work"

"But the club is private. How'd you get in?"

"That's easy, you'd be amazed what a press pass from the Washington Post will do for you."

Again I knew she was telling the truth. The pull of the press and particularly the Washington Post was enormous. In fact I had many friends and associates that hated the press for this very reason. I didn't fall into that group but there had been times the press had made my job more difficult and danger-ous. I called it the Anti-Watergate syndrome. Looking at Kate I could hardly be upset. "Care for more wine?"

8

Charalamambos Christakos breathed deeply, inhaling the sea air. He felt young and vital. He was fifty-four and but he had more energy than men ten years younger. The sea invigorated him; the smell of the salt air and the call of the seagulls made each day on or near it seem fresh and new. It had always been this way for him. His fondest memories of youth were sailing. He was proud of the fact he had learned young and had learned quickly. He could sail anything by the time he was sixteen, but more importantly he could sail it well; always winning when he raced. Unfortunately, work did not allow him enough time to sail as much as he would have liked. That was why he had of late, concentrated on sailing catamarans. He believed they were the fastest and trickiest boat to sail, vessels worthy of his time and effort.

He scanned the horizon thinking what would his life been like if he had been born in another place in time? He had graduated from university at twenty. He was gifted in math, but he liked the practical over the theoretical and so had studied marine engineering. He was grateful he had the skills he did. They made for a good fit. Upon graduation he had gone to work for his father, who had a small fleet of coastal tankers. His father's business delivered oil and other petroleum products to the Greek islands that dotted the Aegean. The business was small yet quite profitable. He had talent and soon Charalamambos, Charlie as his friends called him, was captaining a tanker. None of his fellow shipmates or the other captains ever used the word nepotism when they described his meteoric rise to commanding a ship. Both he and they knew he had earned the position. From his experience he could see that the world's demand for oil was insatiable and because of the demand future vessels would need to be larger and larger.

He remembered having his first, and possibly his only, argument with his father. He wanted the company to branch out into larger tankers. His father did not want the debt. His father had lived through hard times and to him debt was the death knell of a business. Therefore he initially refused to consider the idea. His father did suggest that it was time that Charlie began to learn the business side of tanker transportation. Maybe in two years time they would again visit the issue of growth. His father was not usually someone willing to compromise. This olive branch further confirmed to Charlie that he was right about the future. It also gave him the patience to wait. As it turned out this atypical bout of patience turned out to be most fortuitous.

Two years later, it was even clearer to Charlie that the future of the tanker industry was going to belong to those fleets that carried the most tonnage. Efficiency of transport was needed. Nothing was more efficient for moving crude than large vessels. Therefore, he decided to raise the issue again. He had expected his father to again deny his request. Rather, his father told him he could do as he wished, as the business would soon be his. It was then that he learned of the tumor that would kill his father. He did do as he pleased and soon the small coastal tanker fleet had grown into the world's largest ocean-going tanker fleet.

His fleet, the Hellenic Sea Lines, and it was his, there were no other owners, was now moving over one-half of the world's petroleum products. The last roughly twenty-five years had been on the whole good. He was now the richest man in Greece. He was also one of the richest in the world, if one were to believe *Forbes* magazine. But his success in business had not translated into his personal life. For this he had regrets. He had married twice and been divorced twice, but both times remained on good terms with his former wives. He had a son and daughter from his second marriage. He did not see them enough and this bothered him. Family was important and he wanted at least one of them to follow in his footsteps just as he had done. But neither one of them had shown any interest in his business. He had two chances and there would not be a third. After his second divorce he had decided marriage was too expensive a hobby. He would not make that mistake again, except that is also what he had told himself after the first divorce.

It seemed every time he sat in the captain's seat he would think of the past. But the past was the past and sitting high in the captain's chair of his new yacht he wanted to think only of the future. From his perch felt as if he could see the entire Aegean and it was beautiful. The sea was more beautiful than his new cruiser but only slightly so. The ship was state of the art. For that reason he needed only a small crew, a first mate and cook. His crew of many years was a married couple who had the good sense to stay below while he was entertaining. The owner of the world's largest oil tanker fleet was the master of his universe. From his vantage point he could see no other craft. He was strongly tempted to open the throttles wide and see just how fast his new craft could go even though he had been warned to wait until the engines had been properly broken in. He toyed with the lever and then decided to heed his marine architect's warnings, "pity." If he were on his cat he could have just gone for it. No engines to worry about, just him and the sea. On the other hand, if he were on his cat he would not have been able to devote enough attention to his guest. That would have been a shame.

He looked to the stern of the Helena and admired his latest traveling companion. He was thankful he had decided to sail at his club's catamaran regatta. He originally planned to miss it because of a business meeting. But for reasons he did not fully understand the meeting had been postponed. It annoyed him that he didn't know why the meeting had been cancelled, but he had met Melina at the race. She intrigued him and he figured he could live with not knowing everything. Melina was more exotic than most of the women he had known. When he questioned her about her past and where she had come from, she had been elusive. The best he could get was something about central Asia. But with a body and looks such as she had, who cared? She was, unlike his two wives, interested in his business. It seemed she always had questions. She did not ask questions about his money, but rather about barrels shipped, transit times and the ability of his competition to do the same. He saw her wave to him, topless of course. He waved to her and indicated to her to meet him below decks. It definitely was time to burn off a little of that extra energy or recharge the batteries.

As he went below decks to meet her, yesterday's meeting in Athens came to mind. Who would want to buy his fleet? The lawyer said he represented a wealthy family and that was all he said, rather vague and somewhat unsettling. The family had heard that he intended to retire. Retire, indeed. He would ask Melina whether or not he was ready for retirement. He had rather unceremoniously asked the man to leave. How odd, though. This was the third such inquiry about him selling his fleet. Every one of the potential buyers seemed to think he was in failing health. He reached the bottom of the gangway to his stateroom. As he opened the door he smiled. Melina was waiting for him holding two glasses of champagne and wearing something less than her fantail outfit. He had learned one thing for sure; he now knew why Melina had no tan lines.

9

I was a little down. I had really enjoyed meeting Kate O'Hara and even though we were together for just a short time I wished it could have been more. However, she suffered from GU, geographical unsuitability. I looked around my workstation wondering what I could do to pick myself up. I quickly gave up. This cubicle was part of the problem. I had often speculated that the committee members who designed them and advocated their use were made up of two kinds of people, old Soviet era apartment house designers and prison architects. Well at least I rated a window. Some of my more junior colleges didn't even have one of those. One thing was for certain working for the NSA. One's time was split between tasks that were mind numbingly boring or dangerously exciting. It had been awhile since I had the latter and in fact it seemed now all I was experiencing was the former. It was a dilemma, either being bored to death or scared to death. Maybe I should take up a line of honest work. At least that was what my mother advised on a least a weekly basis. It would have been more often but I only called her that often.

I looked my watch. Well at least I could make a call to England and talk to my old buddy Philip Logan. Philip and I had been friends over ten years. I had originally had met Logan when he was in the military. We had been assigned to a joint Anglo-American anti- terrorism task force. Logan was a Royal Marine. I was not. In my view he was a prototypical Marine. If you looked up the definition of Royal Marine in the dictionary one would have seen Logan's picture.

I began to dial. Talking to Logan was always a good pick-me-up. No one could deny it; the man had a positive attitude on life. As I heard the call begin to go through I began to anticipate catching up on how things were going in the Premiership, the season was only a few weeks old but it had all the promise of being a good one. The phone began to ring. Unfortunately the machine picked. It was one of those commercial I am not here leave a message, messages. I waited for the tone.

"Philip this is Mike, please give me a call when you have a minute. I need to know how Manchester United is doing." I put the instrument back on the cradle and swore under my breath, "Damn. Looks like no relief for the wicked."

10

Joann Davis looked down at her watch thinking it would be late in the day for any normal job, but the job of National Security Advisor was not a normal job. Her day had started early and promised to run late into the night. Being more tired than usual she wondered if she might be coming down with something. She had just returned from Berlin and London where she had met with her counterparts. It seemed about half the time she came down with something after one of her out of country adventures. She looked over and checked Jazel Hammiby, Under Secretary of State for Middle Eastern Affairs sitting across from her in the White House briefing room. To Davis' great relief Jazel looked as if she was about to fall asleep too. Maybe she wasn't sick maybe the briefing was just dull. With some hope in her heart she looked backed down at the briefing book and at the same time tuned back into the speaker.

Yes, it has to be him, Professor Samuel Mitchell, Chairman of the Petroleum Engineering Department at Texas A&M University. Davis thought to herself probably the smartest man in the country when it came to oil exploration and oil reserves but duller than the west Texas dirt of his birth.

Mitchell was pointing at some charts when Davis looked up. "The oil potential in the Caspian Sea basin and in Kazakhstan proper has always been enormous. The problem we have always had has been getting the product to market. That assumed, of course, that when the word "market" was used, it meant the United States. There were and are basically three options, all bad from the viewpoint of the market."

Davis could see Mitchell using a red laser pointer drawing a circle around Iran. "The oil could be sent by pipeline south to Iran. From the Iranian border the oil could be transferred into the Iranian pipeline system for delivery to their ports on the Persian Gulf. This approach is relatively easy and straightforward. The construction time and cost would be modest but the political costs if even payable are enormous."

"The second route has more potential choke points than a politician has excuses. First the oil has to be loaded onto tankers, small coastal ones, not the very large and ultra large ones that are common sights in the Persian Gulf, for shipment across the Caspian Sea to the Volga River. The vessels would then go up the Volga to the Volga-Donskoy Kanal. After going through the canal the tankers would enter the Don River. The ships would travel down the Don to the port of Rostov located on the Sea of Azov. The oil would then continue through the Sea of Azov around the Crimean Peninsula and into the Black Sea. Finally, these tankers would cross the Black Sea, pass through the Dardanelles and the Bosborus, and into the Mediterranean Sea. This is an interesting trip from a cruise-ship point of view but not very appealing for moving crude."

As Davis saw Mitchell smile, she rolled her eyes so only Hammiby could see her. The message was clear. Here was a guy who must have had his funny bone removed and now he trying to make jokes. Hammiby rolled her eyes in knowing response. Both administration officials turned back to the presenter and were pulled back into reality. The drone had begun again.

"There is a third choice. It again requires that oil be loaded onto tankers. However, this time the tankers would cross the Caspian Sea to Baku the capital of Azerbaijan. At which point the vessel would transfer the crude into a pipeline. It is anticipated that this pipeline would run from Baku southwest through Azerbaijan roughly following the 40th parallel to the Armenian border. The pipeline would then cross into Armenia, traverse that country, and enter Turkey." Only a few people knew and Davis was one of them that this third option was much more than theoretical. In fact much of it already existed. The Russians had almost had it completed just about the time the Soviet Union came apart about in 1989. As far as anyone knew it was just waiting there, rusting; waiting to be completed or junked. What she did not know was why it had been begun in the first place. But at this point in time the why was much less important than the where.

"Based upon the geo-political facts of life, it now turns out that from the point of view of America and the American oil companies, the least objectionable choice is third one. It has been and remains true today that the peoples of Armenia and Azerbaijan hate each other like only the Israelis and Arabs can hate each other. But the United States and therefore American oil companies have no grudge with either Armenia or Azerbaijan. Many believe that with enough money this hatred can be turned to mere disgust, making the pipeline a real option."

"In summation then, while the third choice is a potentiality the same cannot be said for choice one, the Iranian route. Equally problematical is the second choice. Even with the fall of the Soviet Union and our rapprochement with Russia and the Ukraine, it is unlikely that our government and our oil companies would consider using a route controlled by a former enemy for such a critical resource."

Davis rose immediately when Mitchell completed his presentation. She didn't want to take any chances and suffer through his response to a possible question. "Thank you for your presentation. I found it enlightening and I suspect the Undersecretary did also." Davis nodded in the direction of Hammiby.

Shaking Mitchell's hand Hammiby agreed, "Yes most helpful. Thank you again."

As he left, Davis turned to Hammiby and said, "Good stuff but he sure needs a personality transplant. Do you have anything else for me?"

"I do. I was waiting for Mr. Personality to leave. Hammiby turned to her aide and asked, "Please give me the Consortium Report."

The aide handed her a report. "Joann I want to show you something."

11

Davis and Hammiby retook their seats. Hammiby turned to everyone in the room and said, "Would you give us about five minutes alone please." She waited for everyone to depart and then began, "Several years ago, in fact right after the fall of the Soviet Union the various necessary departments of government had approved a consortium of Standard Oil of California, Exxon Mobil and Texaco to bring Caspian Basin oil and natural gas to market. The idea was to complete the pipeline begun by the Soviets. The departments of Defense, Commerce and Energy had encouraged the consortium of oil companies to start working even before all the necessary agreements had been finalized. The theory had been that by the time the necessary treaties were signed the only section of the pipeline that had not been reworked or completed would be somewhere near the Armenian-Azerbaijani border."

"So option three is very real."

"Indeed, but the problem is the theory."

"Of being able to work it out as the pipeline was being built?"

"Yes, it has proven to be more theoretical than practical."

"Meaning you can have two ends and not a middle?"

"Precisely. The Armenian government has been particularly recalcitrant in its negotiations. This obstruction has gotten worse after rumors of a Turkic economic league began to circulate. Centuries of hatred clearly dictated policy. The government in Yerevan wants its pound of flesh. Negotiating teams from America and the oil companies have been singularly unsuccessful."

"The dollar has been something less than almighty then?"

"To date. Without the proper treaties the work has stopped on the eastern portion of the pipeline. Meanwhile in Turkey a decision has been made to alter the original route of the pipeline. Rather than run slightly south of Yerevan, the capital of Armenia, the route was redirected to run through Nakhichen. This isolated portion of Azerbaijan is separated from the main part of Azerbaijan by Armenia. The decision was this time was based a little more on fact than just theory than fact."

"How is that?"

"The idea was that it would be easier to deal with the Armenians if the pipeline traversed a less populated region."

"You mean it was assumed that if the pipeline were out of sight it would also be out of mind."

"That is part of it. In addition the region Nakhichen is run, but not ruled, by a more pliant chieftain. One more who seems more approachable when it comes to the value of transit royalties."

"Go on," Davis said.

"Construction on the western portion of this missing section has therefore inched closer in geographical terms to completion. But politically there seems to be no hope. The closer the pipeline comes to completion, the harder the politicians negotiate. Materials and men have begun piling up at the western end as well as the eastern end. The oil companies know that if something does not happen soon progress will be delayed perhaps by years. Once the crews head to new projects it could take a long time to get going again.

"I see do you see any immediate movement?"

"Probably not, but you never know. I just wanted to bring you up to speed."

"Any more good news?"

"No. I don't have anything else for you right now."

"Okay then, I'm back to the wars, good evening." and with that Davis headed for her next appointment.

12

Kemal Kanuni could hear the call to prayers. It was the Sabbath and because of that it was very quiet. He stared again at the cable lying on his desk. Was it that cable or was it the gusting wind? Kanuni wasn't quite sure. Whatever it was he found himself thinking about his early days in London and how it was he had returned to his ancestral homeland Bir. As he thought back he marveled at what a difference location makes, Friday night here is certainly not a night for partying. London on the other hand was another story. On the whole, he preferred Friday nights in England. It was a time for making good contacts and of course having some fun, rather than following some ridiculous old superstitious customs.

London had been his home during the years right after his graduation from B school. While he was there he had worked for Goldman Sachs and Company. He had done the scene. He still could remember standing outside the club in Soho. In fact with little effort he could still clearly hear the music pounding in his head. He remembered pushing his way to the bar and ordering a double scotch neat. The bar was elevated and from that vantage point he could scan the club. It was always important to first check out the action and to examine the options. He knew he could always join up with his work associates but he wanted to see if there were any other choices. Careful clubbing was a great way to make contacts. Kemal had learned early on that contacts were essential for the things he wanted. Kemal knew what he wanted and it was power. From his vantage point the right contacts meant money. Money brought power, power in all forms. He wasn't naïve enough to think that money was all he needed. He knew he needed access to more than money. Still money was a start. He had done well manipulating futures contracts in his own account. He was quite wealthy considering his age and economic background. But it was not nearly enough for where he wanted to go. Thus, he knew he had to have access to more money and contacts. Once he could do this, power in all its forms would follow.

Before he had time to completely check out the scene he had felt his cell phone vibrate. To hear he had made his way across the floor and out to the terrace. He flipped open the phone to answer it and could immediately tell he was receiving an overseas call. He at first hesitated to answer it. He hoped that it wasn't the old bat from America wanting something. She always seemed to call late on Friday and as it turned out she couldn't do anything for him, no money and basically no contacts. The old lady was senile and no one under eighty would voluntarily listen to her. Had he known that he would have dumped the original call in the first place. Therefore he was grateful to hear his uncle come on the line. Briefly, his uncle told him of the union, the new council and most importantly that he was new chairman.

Kanuni could still hear his Uncle's voice as if it were yesterday. "I want you to come home. I need an assistant, an heir apparent," he added.

Of course he had told him he would come as soon as his could wind up his affairs. He remembered thinking this was his destiny. He had looked forward to his future and all its possibilities.

Starring at the cable again he wondered what Hans Schmidt really wanted. Schmidt was one of those contacts he had met while in London. In fact the club in Soho was where he had first met him. Over time they had developed a very profitable relationship. The last time he had seen the man was on one of the worst weather days ever in London. It was raw and it was raining. The calendar might have read May, the weather said January. A late season, very late, winter storm had unexpectedly blown in from the North Atlantic. A promising spring had vanished into winter. He had waited for Schmidt huddled against the side of a bus stop trying to stay dry. The wind was driving the rain almost horizontally. He was about to become thoroughly soaked when gratefully Schmidt's car pulled up and he got in.

Now many years later he had heard from Schmidt again, with a most intriguing opportunity.

13

This had to be a record. I thought as I pulled into my parking garage; went down one level and found my assigned parking place. Normally I would have bounded out of the car and headed for the elevator and up to my apartment. But not tonight, I just sat in the car thinking. I had just gotten home early, thank God, from another one-time date. Unfortunately it was getting to the point where I couldn't remember the last time I had gone out more than a once with someone. I really didn't believe my standards were too high. In fact if asked I would have told anyone who cared to listen that I had probably lowered my standards too many times and that was the real problem. I had really enjoyed the short time I had spent with Kate O'Hara but unfortunately she was GU, geographically unsuitable and therefore not an option. As I finally got out of the car, I told myself that I was just having bad luck.

Thankfully this deficiency was only occurring in my personal life. If I were this bad at making choices at work, I would have been transferred to the Fresno office years ago and there is no Fresno office of the NSA. I know it is true when I was younger my standards towards women were ridiculous and because of this I had missed the opportunity to get to know what I am sure today are some really nice women. Of course the job did not help but when push came to shove it was only an excuse. The plain truth was I was crappy at dating. I paused at the elevator door and reconsidered, actually I wasn't bad at dating, what I was really crappy at was dating the same person more than once. Ruefully I considered some other options, maybe

TV talk show testimonials or the priesthood. At least I would have some better failure excuses. Well tomorrow was another day. I was feeling a little better as I stepped off the elevator and entered my place. That was until I saw the light flashing on my answering machine. For me, a flashing light on Saturday night couldn't possibly be a good thing.

As I walked to the machine, I really hoped it was some kind of telemarketing call, but I doubted it. I hit the message retrieve button. "Mike, this is Bill. There have been some developments in the Middle East. I would like you at an 8:00 a.m. meeting tomorrow morning. I am sorry I know it is Sunday."

That was it. I had gotten a call from the Director of the National Security Agency. It had to be important. I rarely ever got my orders directly from William Brown though I had worked on his staff for the last couple of years. I decided to flip on CNN and see if I might learn something, better I have an idea than walking in to a meeting with God knows who, knowing nothing.

14

Abdul Aziz sat silently as he listened to those around him speak. He was waiting to be taped for an interview for one of the Sunday morning talk shows in the United States. It simply amazed him how people who knew so little could be sure of so many things. In this case it happened to be a television crew headed by the babe of the month female reporter from CBS. He smiled as they talked. With this group, creating a little bit or lot of disinformation would be easy.

"Mr. Aziz I see from your bio here you earned a college degree in petroleum engineering, graduating from the University of Texas at Austin. In addition to that technical degree it states you also attended the Wharton School of Business where you received an MBA.

"That is correct."

"So it seems that business of oil runs in your family."

"Yes you might be able to put it that way."

"For our viewers who are not aware Abdul Aziz is the son of the Senior Oil Minister of the Kingdom of Saudi Arabia who also happens to be serving as the Chairman of OPEC."

"Many Americans who I have talked to are concerned about our dependence on Saudi oil. How would you respond to this concern?"

"I want to assure your audience that the Kingdom of Saudi Arabia considers itself America's friend and ally. Secondly, while it is true we have a lot of oil the world is a big place that has changed from the oil embargo days. Even if we wanted to, we could not drastically affect the American economy. It is simply too large and diversified for that."

Looking at her notes the reporter continued. "The Kingdom does have a lot of its money invested in U.S. Treasuries does it not?"

"Yes it does and that is because it is a safe place to put our money. What could be safer especially in today's world?" Aziz smiled as he asked the question. "I can assure you the Saudi people and its Government would never do anything to place its investments at risk. That is why we are partners and good friends I might add."

"I understand that Muslim fundamentalism is on the rise in the Kingdom."

"This is really not true. Yes we have some followers of the prophet that wish us to reduce our ties to America. I can assure you this is a small not a very influential group. The overwhelming majority of the Royal Family and leading citizens support the U.S."

"Thank you Mr. Aziz. Is there anything you would like to add?"

"Yes. Please let your viewers know we are both good Moslems and good business partners with America."

15

As it turned out there was nothing on CNN and so I was going to go into the meeting a blank sheet which was sometimes good and sometimes very bad. Bad because I hadn't had time to mull over any potential options. I didn't like not having at least some kind of advanced preparation. I checked my watch to see if it wasn't too late. Eleven in the east was only eight in California. So I flipped off the tube and decided to make my weekly call home. I generally called on Sundays but I figured that wasn't a hard and fast rule and I might be tied up this Sunday anyway. Besides the calling home on the spur of the moment method sometimes worked. I should know. I had tried all other methods: the make a list method, the procrastination method and the regularly scheduled call method to me was the best.

I love my mother but as she has aged the infirmities of life have taken their toll. She does not feel well and is generally unhappy. This fact comes through on the phone all too obviously. I have tried to get her to move to Washington D.C. but she has so far refused saying her friends were all in the Bay Area. Unfortunately for her, her friends have now taken up this nasty habit of dying. There are so very few left now.

I dialed and the phone rang only once. She was probably watching TV with the phone sitting next to her. "Hi mom it's me." I had learned to never ask how it was going. If I did, she would complain and I would get frustrated and nothing constructive would be accomplished. "I have a funny date story to tell you. I figured a story of any kind would help lead me into the topic I had been reluctant to bring up again. Anyway I told her something light and pleasant about my date and then quickly changed the subject. "I was wondering if you would like to come and try living here in D. C. on a part time basis?" I was pleased she didn't automatically reject the idea. I decided that tonight had not turned out that badly after all.

16

The alarm woke me up. I hate getting up early on Sunday morning. It has become the one day of the week that I can lounge around at least a little while. But there was no value in complaining, there was no one to listen to my complaints and I already knew them. I showered and headed for the office. I arrived at exactly 8:00 a.m. Normally, I would feel good about this, considering the traffic around town, but as this was Sunday I couldn't give myself a little pat on the back. In fact, I was the last one there and that made me a little uncomfortable. I became a lot more uncomfortable when I looked around the conference and didn't recognize everyone there.

NSA Director Brown began the meeting. "Thank you all for coming on such short notice. As time is of the essence I will only make a partial list of introductions. Please if you would fill in your name and agency on the teepee card that can be found in the three-ring binder located at each of your places." I dutifully did as I was told. Looking around the room I could see we had a cross section of administration people and government career types. I knew I was classified as a career type even though I hadn't really intended to make this my life's work.

Director Brown waited for a couple of minutes until everyone was done before he concluded his brief introductions. "To my right is my boss National Security advisor Joann Davis. To my left is Jazel Hammiby, Under Secretary of State for Middle Eastern Affairs." No one else was introduced including the guy who listed his agency as the Library of Congress. I figured he had to be CIA because he was no more a librarian than I was the Pope of Rome. Director Brown sat down and turned to Ms. Davis and announced she would continue the presentation

"Thank you Director Brown. Within the last few months a new force has formed in the Middle East. It is ostensibly an economic league modeled after the early days of the European Common Market. This new organization is called The *League of the Bir* and it is comprised of the Turkic countries of the Middle East. The two key players are Hakan Kanuni and his nephew Kemal Kanuni."

I had no idea there were any more Turkic countries in the Middle East other than the obvious one called Turkey. I learned there were in fact several, most of the non-Russian Soviet States of Central Asia were Turkic countries. The largest and the richest was Kazakhstan but there were many more. I decided to remember them as the Stans. The National Security Director continued her presentation.

"…A council of countries has been formed. Each member country selects a minister to represent it. Each country was free to employ any method to select its representative to the new League, additionally it was announced the council would also always have a mullah as a member. The first name of the League, Osman, was chosen to honor the founder of the Ottoman Empire. The second name, Horde, refers to the historical power and glory of the Turkic People of Central Asia. Under Secretary Hammiby will continue the briefing."

"Thank you Director Davis. The only non-Turkic Country in this new alliance is Armenia. It appears it was persuaded to join up under the theory that it was better to join and prosper rather than be surrounded by enemies, including its age-old enemy Azerbaijan and many new Turkic ones."

The Under Secretary went on providing our group with more background information. From what I could tell so far there was no reason for us to be sitting here on Sunday morning. I mean who really cared if a group of countries had joined into a common market to make trading with each other easier, especially if they were halfway around the world? My smug viewpoint came crashing down when Bill Brown got up to complete the presentation.

"Normally we would not be much concerned about a group like this forming. As a matter of fact, it would be something we would welcome. However, we are unsure if it is something we should welcome or not. The reason for this is oil." My boss went on to explain about an almost completed pipeline and the substantial oil wealth of the region.

"In conclusion we are concerned about the influence another player might have on the world's energy situation in general and the United States' in particular. We don't know what the true intentions of the Kanuni's are. They may just be two businessmen or they may have political ambitions. It could be they envision this economic union as a first step to something as encompassing than the old Arab League; whose aim was to be the unifying force for all Moslem countries, from Morocco to Indonesia." As Brown spoke I began to realize I was the guy at the end of the food chain and if there was any onsite investigating that was going to be done I was the guy that was going to do it. "So in conclusion I would like all of you back here for a meeting on Wednesday at 1:00 p.m. at which time we will generate a specific course of action."

17

Chandler Wellington, President of the New York Mercantile Exchange, looked down from the window in his office onto to the usually chaotic trading floor and instantly knew something big had just happened. Controlled chaos was the usual form of business here, even on the weekend. Millions of futures and option contracts traded here daily. However, he could tell that the control half of the controlled chaos equation was missing. Chaos seemed to be ruling the floor. As he started to move to the telephone to find out what had happened, his secretary burst into his office. His usually calm secretary moved hurriedly to the television set in the corner of his spacious office and turned it to CNN.

"You must see this news report," she said.

Before he could speak he saw the Breaking News Headline streaming across the screen. A somber-faced news reporter was speaking.

"CNN has just received confirmed news coming out of Istanbul. The formation of a new economic union called Bir, meaning One in Turkish has been announced. This union is made up of Turkey and many of the former Soviet Union republics of Central Asia. The largest of which is Kazakhstan. Normally the formation a new common market particularly in this part of the world would not have a major impact in the West. However, this may not be the case of Bir. The reason is, concurrent with the formation announcement; the new league announced that it would complete a long delayed oil pipeline. This pipeline was first proposed by the Soviets. Before the pipeline was completed the Soviet Union disintegrated

leaving the central portion of the pipeline incomplete. The pipeline that was designed to bring oil from the oil rich region around the Caspian Sea to the West has remained undone due to age old political squabbling between two archenemies, Armenia and Azerbaijan. With the inclusion of both countries in the new economic union it is anticipated the completion of this pipeline will occur in the very near future. This also just in: Reuters has just reported what CNN has been reporting.

Chandler immediately clicked his computer screen to the oil-trading desk. The future price of crude had taken a very erratic turn. First it had begun to look like a rocket launch in the last five minutes. Then the price sank. It was apparent that the market was completely out of equilibrium. He knew he would have to decide within the next couple of minutes whether or not to halt trading in both oil futures and its options. He was hoping cooler heads would begin to prevail. The very idea of halting trading appalled him. However, he knew that when it came to volatility nothing could match the oil marketplace. This fact was caused by the obvious. Namely, the tremendous need for petroleum products by the industrialized West coupled with an equally enormous foreign dependency on this very same commodity from a very unstable region now with a potential new player on the block.

Chandler picked up the telephone and dialed the head of the Board of Governors of the Exchange. He preferred not to make this decision alone.

18

Bizhanov waited, he was dressed in black and he had darkened his face. This was the part that he both loved and hated about his chosen profession. He hated it because when the job was over a kind of sadness would overcome him. He would feel for a time as if something were missing in his life. He also loved it because when he had completed his mission he had that feeling of satisfaction of a job well done. He inwardly smiled. It was also true the money was nice. He had spent days tracking this man. Now within minutes the hours of tedious detail would bear fruit. Fortunately the man he waited for loved his routine. This was good because the man was well protected. If he had been more random in his movements Bizhanov knew he would have never been able to fulfill the contract. He did not need to know why this man was to die. He only needed to know who he was. However, if he were to venture a guess it would be that this dead man walking continued to object to the new economic union even after the deal had been ratified. Not only did he object he did so in a very public way.

The Turkish opposition leader came down this alley every Thursday evening. On Thursday's he would meet with his shadow cabinet at his favorite restaurant. The alley was the most direct route to his waiting car and the one least exposed. Bizhanov knew the route had been fairly well scouted but not by a professional. As such, one mistake had been made. At a point just before the street the alley narrowed so only one man could pass. It was there in the shadows that Bizhanov waited. His was a simple plan. He would let the lead guard pass, then step out and slit the throat of the victim. He would push the dead body back against the trailing guard then turn and shoot the lead guard with his silenced Lugar before he could get to the street and be seen by the waiting driver. It was all about timing. After killing the lead guard he would simply walk out of the alley and head for the garage where his ride was waiting. He would then go to the airport. He had an important meeting tomorrow night in Almaty. Bizhanov stole a quick look at his watch. It was time.

19

I thought it was more in-flight turbulence, but as I opened my eyes from yet another interrupted nap I found that the flight attendant was waking me for landing. I appreciated her thoughtfulness. However, what passes for service on an airplane really isn't much service at all. One was invariably awakened to be told that the plane was on final approach when there were at least another fifteen to thirty minutes left in the joy of modern air travel. Not to mention the time it took the plane to actually get to the gate. That was why when I flew I tried to take British Air whenever possible. It wasn't so much that I was an Anglophile as it was that I thought the service on British Air was better than most. It must have something to do with old world customs. Today or tonight, which ever it was, I was definitely not on BA.

As the plane descended I thought about how I had come to be on this flight. I had suspected it would come to this at last Sunday's meeting called by my boss Director William "Bill" Brown. I could tell I was the guy in the pecking order that was going to do some traveling but I had held out some hope that it would be someone else. Without much surprise that hope ended on Wednesday. When our little group met for the second time it was in the Situation Room in the White House, so I knew this new economic union had become high priority for the President. The basic and simple decision was to send a team to Turkey to meet with both Kanunis. For all kinds of complicated diplomatic reasons, ones I could never quite fathom, the group needed to be important enough so the new leaders would be happy to meet. While at the same time not being so important as to be considered as an new formal international entity, one meeting with the United States. As in all things governmental these days our little group received a mission statement for our trip. Again as things went these days I had to memorize the little gem.

> *The team's job is to explore the possibility of diplomatic recognition for the League of Turkic Countries. We are to gather information to be evaluated by senior officials in Washington. We are to convey this to the new league. We are to make no promises yet be friendly and supportive.*

My job, probably because I had spoken out against any recognition in our meetings was to check out its leaders. I knew my job was a loser. I was going to have just a few days to get into the head of the Chairman, Hakan Kanuni, and the temporary Vice-Chairman and maybe according to sources, de facto leader, his nephew Kemal Kanuni. It was a tall order in a short period of time. I hoped I wouldn't be wasting what little time I had on this Kemal Kanuni fellow in case he wasn't eventually chosen as Vice-Chairman. But if he wasn't chosen that would tell also tell me something. Unfortunately I knew trying to get into anyone's head was difficult, but it was especially difficult with Middle Eastern people. I had long contended that I could have made up a game *Who is more inscrutable*, the Chinese or the folks from Central Asia? If you could guess properly you got a trip to the city of you choice but not anywhere in Asia.

As the Wednesday meeting in the White House broke up I had been told my flight was leaving in three hours, from Andrews Air Force Base to Incirlik in Turkey, barely leaving me enough time to pack and phone mom to tell her I would be out of the country so she wouldn't worry if I missed calling her. The Air Force flight normally took ten hours, but because of bad weather it had taken an additional two. At least during the flight I had time to review the biographical information about Kemal Kanuni. It was evident from the organization of the material the information had been thrown together quickly. Kanuni's father died while he was relatively young and his Uncle Hakan had raised him.

The file noted before being taken in by his uncle, Kanuni's life had been a struggle. His father had been in poor health for years and his mother had died in the birth of his sister. He had to take care of both his father and his sister. Kanuni had worked but his working had only made the difference between being poor and poverty stricken.

His mother's family was from Turkey and they still lived there. Because they lived in Turkey, Kemal had had been to Istanbul. An editorial comment added that apparently Kanuni had been quite taken by the city. He had reveled in its past glories and its many modern marvels. Regarding his father, he was native to Kazakhstan. As far as the rest of his father's family, it was not numerous by local standards but it was old and cohesive. In fact he was descended from nomadic warriors who had once dominated central Asia.

There was no doubt this Kanuni fellow was smart. He father had been an economics professor at Al-Farabi State University. Kanuni had finished school early. And had received his undergraduate degree from Oxford and his graduate work had been at the London School of Economics. At both institutions he had been number one in his class. After school he had gone to work in the London office of Goldman Sachs and Company, though it appeared he had received offers from a number of the major financial houses in London.

From what I could see his Uncle seemed to be an interesting character, a true opportunist. The Uncle, Hakan, had no living sons. Based upon the notes and comments in the file, it seems that Hakan treated Kanuni as a son. Some had not adjusted well to the change in government when the Soviet Union fell. Not only had Hakan adjusted, he had prospered. Hakan Kanuni had been an official working in the Ministry of Oil under the old Soviet system. With the collapse of the Soviet Union in 1991, the new government of Kazakhstan needed to replace Russian officials with Kazaks. Hakan had become Interior Minister.

Physically Kanuni is tall and fairer than the average person in the region. These features reflect a mixed heritage. Though mostly Turkic, his blue eyes and height could be attributed to a German great grandmother and Russian grandmother. His family was Sunni Moslem, but like many in this part of the world was not fanatical about it.

I couldn't tell where this anecdotal information had come from, but if it was true it certainly revealed something about this man's character. I made a mental note to see if I could get an inkling of this aspect of the man when we met.

20

From the Air Force Base it had been decided that our team should be bused to Ankara for a two-hour flight to Istanbul. Since the Gulf Wars the region had been very unsettled. America is both loved and hated. Loved really was not the word, maybe appreciated was a better word. Many in the region were glad when we finally threw Saddam Hussein and his murderous family out of power but are still wary. Islamic fundamentalism at least on the surface seems to be growing stronger and stronger. Many more in the Middle East resent our presence more than the atrocities committed by their fellow Muslim. Anyway it had been decided by higher-ups that our American team needed to keep as low a profile as possible considering the current political climate in the region. Ruefully I knew low profile was a nice government term meaning inconvenience, delay and boredom. The Ambassador to Turkey, Paul Johnson, had sent his top aide to meet the team and further brief us as we bounced our way across the countryside.

During the lovely bus ride while we hovered between a state of conscious and unconscious, the aide briefed us and then told us he would not be accompanying us to Istanbul. He had explained that the diplomatic situation was very confused and it would be better if he and for that matter, the Ambassador, were not in attendance at the meetings. After we arrived at Ataturk International Airport, we made the final leg of the trip to the consulate in Istanbul in a diplomatic car, an unmarked yet very bulletproof Chevy Suburban. After arriving we were shown to our rooms and given the good news we would be meeting with the leagues representatives first thing the next morning.

21

The team gathered for breakfast the next morning. There were four of us: Alan Trimble worked at Treasury, Francine Holden was a Trade Representative and Oscar Valdez was with the State Department. As we chatted and got our bearings a Consular official told us we would meet with the League representatives that morning at the Inter Continental Hotel. We were all pretty tired but anxious to get going. We were told there would be six members of *Bir's* delegation not including interpreters. For that reason the consulate was going to assign us two additional diplomats to attend the meeting, something to do with protocol. It didn't make much sense to me but I was the spy in the group. I wondered who their spy was.

The meetings lasted three days and I during the entire time I couldn't figure out who their spy was. As a matter of fact I couldn't figure out why there were six members in the delegation. In reality they only needed two; well four since there were four of us. Hakan and Kemal Kanuni clearly controlled and spoke for their delegation. Also I was relieved that I hadn't wasted my time learning about Kemal Kanuni. He wouldn't be "acting" Vice-Chairman for long. In fact, if you asked me he would become the Chairman if and when anything happened to his Uncle.

As I sat in the meeting, only understanding a portion of the trade and economic issues, I decided the rest of the League team looked like mere mortals when compared to acting Vice-Chairman, Kemal Kanuni. In my opinion he had an amazing constitution. He seemed to be everywhere always saying the right thing. He was clearly brilliant. If I were to guess in public appearances he would most likely generate a kind of aura about him. There was something else about him; something I couldn't put my finger on. I would certainly put in my report that one needed to watch his actions first and listen to his words second.

After shaking hands and heading back to our respective headquarters I decided to make a change in plans. I had intended to return home and report to higher ups as soon as the meetings had ended. But to do the job right I needed to know about Kemal Kanuni and I figured that London was a good place to start. He had gone to school there and had taken a job there. It wasn't that long ago and I figured I could talk with his former classmates or co-workers. With luck they might provide me with some additional insight.

22

Kemal sat in his darkened office in Almaty, the former capital of Kazakhstan. He had recently returned from Istanbul. His meeting was scheduled after evening prayers as custom dictated. Finally, there was a knock at his private door. He rose and walked quickly to open it. Normally, his assistant would have handled this mundane task but not tonight. He opened the door and three people entered. They all wore customary loose clothing and as such they all seemed alike. They were dressed as travelers having in fact also just arrived from Istanbul. The small group consisted of two men and one woman.

Kemal greeted the men in the traditional manner and the woman in a way that would not have been approved of under Islamic custom. He then spoke. "Greetings, friends and fellow comrades, I am glad you have arrived." Indeed, they were friends or more accurately fellow travelers in the world of power and intrigue. The three knew each other well having served together on various missions in the past. That is why he had called them. He needed their special skills and talents.

"Akham, how long has it been?"

"Too long."

"Did you have any trouble in your last assignment?"

"Easier than I had expected," Akham Bizhanov said.

Kemal looked in the direction of the second man, Abdul Aziz, a distant cousin; "I saw your interview on CBS. I thought you did a good job. Just the right touch of bullshit"

Laughing Aziz responded, "That's my specialty, bullshit, at least for a while longer."

"Did the reporter have a clue about anything?" Kemal asked.

"Other than how to look good, I doubt it. So typical American, all flash and no substance," Aziz concluded.

Kemal nodded and then began, "I asked you to come so we could go over our plans one final time. Additionally, I want to make sure none of you had questions or had encountered any new problems. However, it is late and I need to talk with Melina first."

Kemal turned to Aziz and Bizhanov; "I will ring you in the morning. I have arranged suitable lodging for you upstairs."

Fokina and Kemal waited for the other two to leave.

"Melina you look wonderful. If it is possible you look better than when I first met you at Oxford."

"I looked pretty good when I was at Oxford but then I was younger."

"So was I."

"Have you made contact with Charalamambos Christakos?"

"You might say that. Let's say we have become very good friends."

"Does he trust you?"

"Yes, I think he is beginning to. I began by telling him about my early life. I could tell he appreciated my candor."

"What exactly did you say?"

"Just the usual, he required nothing special. I told him that my mother was from Egypt and my father was Turkish. And how, though not legally divorced, my parents hardly spoke to each other for years. I really played up the fact that because of that I had been shuttled off to boarding schools where rich girls were sent.

"Good. What else?"

"I told him I received my high school education in Switzerland and that was why I was so good with languages. I finished up the story by telling him how I went to University at Oxford and got my first job at Goldman Sachs."

"Did he like the business connection?"

"Yes it seemed to help. He's a sophisticated man. It is obvious he wants his women to be intelligent. I then sweetened the pot. I told him how I hated being taught by the nuns who believed fun was evil and that the only reason mankind was put on earth was to suffer for sins. I emphasized how much I liked to have fun and wanted to make up for lost time."

"Then you have become his companion?"

Melina replied, "Yes."

"Good. Without you, my love, my plan would never have gotten off the ground. I want to thank you."

"I thought you would bring up your gratitude and how you were going to say thank you."

Kemal took her gently by the hand and led her upstairs. "Remember Melina my love. Good things do come to those who wait."

23

There was no doubt about it I had mixed emotions. I had a lot of work to do when I got to England, but London has always been a fun place for me so I was torn. It reminds me of my hometown, San Francisco. Both cities have so much to offer in the way of culture, nightlife and wonderful neighborhood pubs. Of course the sports are different but I enjoy both kinds of football. As far as cricket goes I have been told that one has to experience it to understand it. In fact I did experience it with Philip. The game went on for hours and I couldn't begin to fathom what was going on. I will stick with the Giants. Actually, I knew work would win out and in a way I was happy, I guess it was my Catholic upbringing; lots of guilt about having fun and the joy of suffering.

The plane slowed as the engines roared. The British Air flight turned for its gate at Heathrow and came to a stop. I grabbed my bag out of the overhead compartment, exited the plane and headed for the underground. The trip to Piccadilly would take almost an hour but it was cheaper than a cab and by cab it would take almost that long. Thankfully I didn't have to wait. I entered a tube car that had to be older than I was. There were wood slats on the floor and the gum stuck under the seats had to be there since the fist conflict. The trip passed uneventfully; I exited the station and turned towards the Bull and Bear, which was just a short walk from the Underground Station.

I looked forward to seeing my buddy Philip again. I had arranged to meet him after work at one of my favorite places.

The Bull and the Bear is what any tourist would consider the quintessential English pub.

I entered the pub and peered through the cigarette haze and searched for Logan. Non- smoking sections have become standard in most American bars. The same cannot be said for England or for Europe for that matter. If there was such a section it was typically put in the back of the pub or restaurant just where the smoke was the heaviest.

Happily I saw he had managed to get a booth. "Good to see you Philip old boy," I said shaking his hand.

"Hello Michael. It is good to see you. I hope you don't mind but I took the liberty of ordering a Newcastle for you."

"Thanks I appreciate it."

Logan looked about and lowered his voice. "I got your phone message. I checked around the Yard and I believe I may have a few leads for you to follow."

"I hope my request didn't cause you any problems."

"None at all. The research section is used to me. It seems I am a regular at asking unusual questions."

Logan searched for the waitress, who was nowhere in sight. "Since I don't see our young barmaid, if you don't mind I think I will go to the bar and pick up our drinks."

"Mind? I don't want to die of thirst."

As Philip left to get our drinks, I got my luggage arranged and thought about how time flies. It hardly seems possible but I have been with the NSA for ten years, since 1985. I had torn my knee in a winter weather parachuting exercise and the NSA recruited me while I was in the hospital. The knee was fixed well enough for the NFL but certainly not for the Rangers. I met Logan on my first assignment with the Agency. I had been assigned to a joint British American terrorism task force. Obviously terrorism wasn't quite the issue that it had become since I was a rookie. At the time Philip was still a member of the Royal Marines. He hadn't left the military for Scotland Yard until after the Gulf Wars, just over four years ago.

Philip returned with our drinks. "Listen ole friend, I'm sorry but this just came up. I have to go out of town tomorrow and I will be gone at least a couple of days. Of course you can have free run of the flat and I should be back before you have to leave."

"I am sorry to hear that but I understand. What about the information?"

"Not to worry. I have enough to keep you busy. If by chance you need anything else, you can always contact my assistant, Maggie Smith and she can help you."

I appreciated what Logan had done to help me but I was still a little disappointed he would out of town. "So what will you be up to?" I asked. I figured if it was business he would give me some off the wall answer.

"My other job, didn't I mention it to you? Football scouting, the FA has asked me to do a survey on how to make the game more interesting to women. You see the new PC world has run head onto our old soccer world. It seems that someone thinks that the attendance at the matches should be about 50 percent men and 50 percent women."

"I thought it was 90 percent cretin and 10 percent normal."

"It may well be, but it seems that half the cretins have to be women."

"That *is* something to drink to."

24

The Ambassador to the new league from Azerbaijan, Dax Salyan, sat in his Istanbul office. Everyone upon seeing the view remarked how impressive it was. The office overlooked the Bosporus, that narrow stretch of water that separated the continent of Asia from that of Europe, East from West, Christianity from Islam and democracy from totalitarianism. It always amazed him that such a small thing could create such vast differences over time.

As he starred out the window he thought how his country was much like that narrow strip of water. It separated vastly different peoples and thus was vulnerable by its very location. To the south was the self-proclaimed Peoples Republic of Kurdistan, a no-man's land in the northern corner of Iran and the northern parts of Iraq. Farther south was the Shiite theocracy of Iran and the semi secular state of Iraq formerly ruled by Saddam Hussein, and now ruled by a revolving door of Shiite politicians. To the northwest was the country of Georgia, home of Joseph Stalin. It was amazing and a pity how the west chose to view recent history. The view was more of convenience rather than fact. As such, to them Adolph Hitler was the greatest villain and mass murderer of the twentieth century. They defeated this monster and, therefore, the world was saved and they could go back to the business of making money. While in fact, Joseph Stalin made Hitler look like a humanitarian and the world was anything but safe. Directly north of his little country was the largest country in the world, Russia. The Russian Bear was wounded and weakened but still very dangerous. But most pressing upon the Ambassador's mind was what was to the west and to the east. To the west lay Armenia an age-old enemy and a Christian island in the midst of an Islamic sea. Armenia was an ongoing concern but further west was the real problem, it was Turkey. By itself Turkey would not have presented much of a problem. But to the east beyond the Caspian Sea lay Kazakhstan, where the Kanuni's had always been powerful. Now their influence was being felt in Turkey. He could sense the danger. His country separated what could easily become two halves of one country dominated by a single family.

The intercom buzzed, shaking him from his thoughts. It was his assistant. "Mr. Ambassador, it is time to go to the meeting."

"Yes Hakim, I know," he responded tiredly. "I will be out shortly."

The Ambassador continued sit in his chair, though he knew he needed to go. He continued to ask himself just what he should do. The current president of his country was an old and tired man. He had served his nation well especially considering its turbulent history. It was now painfully obvious to all that he was no longer up to the task. In fact many of the country's leaders ranging from those in the military and commerce to religion had spoken to him about becoming the next leader of Azerbaijan. He knew that many considered him to be the only one who could lead the country. They had said so on more than one occasion. In their opinion he alone was the one person that could possibly maintain any semblance of real independence for his country. Almost overwhelmed Dax Salyan shook his head sadly, rose and left for the meeting.

25

As the acting Vice Chairman Kemal's office also overlooked the Bosporus. Within days the council was expected to name a permanent Vice-Chairman. Initially it had appeared he would be named to the post but after strong opposition from Dax Salyan, the representative from Azerbaijan, the council had chosen to select him on a temporary basis. In order to proceed with his plans, he needed the full support from the Council. He had spent hours with each delegate to the point where he knew he would be confirmed. However, he suspected that Dax Salyan might still prove to be a problem and Kemal needed a problem solver.

Kemal heard a knock at his door and then heard it open. There were only a few people allowed to enter in such a manner. He put down his cup of strong Turkish coffee and turned to his friend of many years, Akham Bizhanov. "Please come in and shut the door behind you." Bizhanov did as requested. "I may have a problem today. And I would like you to help me solve it."

"Of course. Tell me about your problem."

"Within just a few days the council will be asked to confirm me as Vice-Chairman. I would prefer that the selection be unanimous. However, I am afraid it will not be so. Dax Salyan will most likely vote no. Normally, I would wait to deal with such an offense, but in this case I am afraid that I can't wait. You see, Azerbaijan is critically important to the league. It is a choke point and I do not like to be choked."

"For the last several months I have been meeting with and talking to his assistant, Hakim Ton. I believe he is just our kind of man, ambitious yet weak. Based on what I have been told by my sources it is most likely that if something were to happen to the Ambassador, Mr. Ton would succeed him. I would like you to have a discussion with Mr. Ton."

"Yes, of course. I understand the importance of keeping your options open."

26

After Bizhanov left Kemal allowed himself a rare smile. Things were indeed coming together. He believed it now more than ever, he had a destiny. It was strange though how his life had come full circle. Before he had gone to England to further his education, Kemal had worked at the Kazakh Ministry of Natural Resources. Thanks to his uncle's patronage he had been allowed to intern at the highest levels of the ministry. He knew his land was rich in a wide variety of natural resources. However, one resource was paramount over all others. That resource was oil. Oil generated the hard currency his government so desperately needed. The Kazakh government needed a lot of money. The almost compulsive need to find more reserves drove the Ministry of Natural Resources to seek out any available source of crude almost regardless of the cost. For that reason the ministry could and maybe should have been renamed the Ministry of Oil and nothing would have been lost in the translation.

London, certainly more than New York, was the financial center of the new world order. Situated strategically in the world's time zones, early in the morning one could trade in Asia before those markets closed and by day's end one could transact business in New York. Billions of dollars, Euros and Yen moved around the world with the aid of only a few computer keystrokes. With his background it was natural for him to work in the commodities department. He had begun as a trader of oil futures, with Goldman Sachs and had ended as a currency trader. That was over four years ago. The hours were long and the pressures were brutal, particularly during the Gulf Wars. Many of his associates had burned out but he had thrived.

He saw his intercom line, light up. He pushed the button and heard his assistant. "It is time. The Council meeting is about to begin."

"Thank you." Kemal rose and headed out the door certain that bright things lay ahead.

27

I was awakened to the sound of a light rain. It was such a comforting sound. I wanted to roll over and wake up later, a lot later. Even though I had been in Europe for over a week I was still wiped out. Jet lag was a wonderful experience. Last night's reunion at the Bull and Bear had lasted only a few hours but I felt like I had been up all night. Philip was long gone by now, already on the way to Manchester. Since he had gone by train I was able to use his car.

I was uncomfortable with what I had seen of Kemal Kanuni while in Istanbul. His actions just didn't jibe with the reports I had read. The intelligence reports were also not consistent with the public press. This was not at all unusual, but usually there were at least some common threads. In this case there seemed to be none. In fact it was as if each person who described or assessed the man saw him differently. This made me more than a little uneasy. I had to complete my report. Washington had made it clear that it wanted it yesterday. But before I could finalize it I knew I had to resolve these differences. The report would be worthless unless I could provide a coherent picture of this man.

The dossier had provided me with some of the basics about Kemal Kanuni including extended family data, birth date and education. A starting point at least. One of things I found most interesting was that he was related to the Saudi Oil Minister on his mother's side. I made a mental note to check and see if Kemal had ever had any contact with Hazim Aziz or possibly his son Abdul who had also attended school in the UK.

I decided to drive up to Oxford where Kemal had gone to college. As much as I like England I hate driving here. Not only do they drive on the wrong side of the road they drive on the wrong side of the car. Every time I look in the rear view mirror I manage to get a glimpse of traffic coming right at me instead of the cars behind. If this isn't unsettling, then nothing is. I figured driving on the M-40 would be okay and that would cover most of the trip, but deep down I knew that eventually I would have to face the worst driving experience in the entire world namely, the backwards rotary--in my mind a near death experience if there was ever one. Of course, none of the driving could be done in anything but rain. And just to make things exciting one always needed to throw in the spray from lorries flying by at over seventy-five miles-per-hour.

28

I cheated the Grim Reaper and made it to Oxford alive, no thanks to the rain or the trucks. I started looking for a car park. Happily for me and no doubt more so for Philip I managed to find one and to park the car without incident. Without a great deal of effort I then was able to find the bus to the center of town. No mean feat for an American male who would rather be caught dead than be found riding a bus. Wasn't it our birthright to drive cars everywhere regardless of the consequences to the balance of payments or the effect on the environment?

My destination was the New College, founded 1379. I wondered what it took to be classified as an "old" college. I figured even though it had been a few years I could turn up someone who could enlighten me about Kemal Kanuni. I wanted to know more about the man, his character. I spent all morning at the college talking with educators and administrators. I learned nothing new other than everyone had an almost identical description. Kemal was a brilliant student. There seemed to be no subject that he could not do well in. Being an average student myself this kind of academic achievement was just short of disgusting. Maybe I just didn't trust Mensa-type guys.

It was getting to be time for lunch when I saw a pub aptly named the New Pub. Considering the relative historical time frame in England this place was probably founded just before Cromwell became Lord Protector. If the place had been called the "Old Pub" it had undoubtedly opened its doors in welcome to William the Conqueror. I stepped in or rather down into the pub. It was a typical English establishment. I managed to find a table near the fireplace. Within a couple of minutes a rather attractive thirty-something waitress who introduced herself as Lea came over to take my order. Several minutes later she returned with my fish and chips and a pint to help wash it down. Hoping for a change in luck, I decided to strike up a conversation with her.

"Hi, my name is Mike Williams. I am a writer for the *Los Angeles Times.* I am on assignment and I am gathering some background information. Do you have a minute to talk?"

She looked about the pub before she answered. "Certainly, I can spare a few minutes. What is your assignment?"

I hoped Lea didn't know much about L.A. since I was winging it. "We have a large Middle Eastern community in LA and my editors thought it would be a good idea to write a story about the new economic union in that region."

"I know less than nothing about economics, other than owning a pub is not the road to wealth. What can you learn here that you couldn't learn in London or the Middle East?"

"I was hoping to do a personal angle. The number two man in the new league attended Oxford."

"Who is that?"

"A fellow by the name of Kemal Kanuni," I replied.

"Don't think I've ever heard of him." I wasn't sure I believed her.

I pulled out a picture of Kanuni and showed it to her. "Maybe a picture will help?"

She took the picture and stared at it. It was obvious she knew him. "If you don't mind me saying it, it looks like you recognize him."

"I might say that," came her rather flat reply. "Kanuni was a regular while in school here."

"A regular? Do you mind if I take some notes?"

"As long as you don't directly quote me," Lea cautioned.

"No problem."

I started out with the obvious question, "I thought he was Moslem and didn't drink?"

"From what I could tell the only time he was a Moslem was when he had visitors from home."

Mike inquired. "How would you know when he had visitors?"

Lea responded, "Well, you see, we used to have a good time, if you get my drift, except when relatives came. Then you could count on finding him in the mosque on Friday nights as well as the usual praying bit."

"Did you ever ask him about this inconsistency in his behavior?"

"No, not really. There was no need to. He was a political animal. He was someone who could be anybody to anybody, a genuine face-point bloke."

"I gather you two had a falling out."

"No, not really. I always knew nothing would come of our relationship. I did think it would last a little longer than it did, that is all."

"What happened?"

"A kindred soul came along, that's what happened. A woman named Melina Fokson or Fokinal something like that. Not only was she beautiful, she was also a creature who loved power and politics. I didn't like or trust her. I believe she would have no problem selling her soul. Her only concern would be that it was sold for the highest possible price."

"Do you know what became of this woman? Or do you know of anyone who might know what became of her?"

"No, I assumed she got her degree and left to become a true predator in the world of business."

"So you lost contact with both of them?"

"Yes."

"I appreciate your time." I handed her a card. "Here is my local phone number. If you can think of anything or anyone who might help with my story, I'd really appreciate it. I'll be in London for the next couple of days before I head home."

I left the pub and headed back to the administration building. I thought I'd try and learn something about the Melina person.

29

Joann Davis looked across the desk at Jazel Hammiby and spoke. "The President wants to recognize the embryonic League of Turkic Nations tomorrow."

"Why isn't this premature? Mike Williams is still in London gathering more information for his report."

Davis spoke, "It's the President's view that our recognition will create a counterweight in the region. The league is weak, as it is only an association. Our policy towards the Middle East has been one of balancing off the different power bases in the region in an attempt to neutralize forces hostile to the USA. Since the end of the Gulf Wars and with the collapse of the Soviet Union, Iran has emerged as potentially too powerful an adversary. In particular the Iranian mullahs are gaining influence over the large Shiite majority in southern Iraq."

"But Saddam or one of his pathological sons will murder any of the locals if they get out of line."

Davis nodded, "But he can't kill them all and still pump the oil he needs."

"Sometimes I think he would be willing to try but, I agree with you."

NSA chief Davis continued, "It is more loosely organized than the EU. But it does exist and our recognition will add some creditability to it. We believe the leaders of the organization, Hakan and Kemal Kanuni, are people we can control. Besides if Williams finds anything substantial we can always quietly back away from situation."

"Control?" Hammiby asked. "Is it really possible to control anyone? Besides aren't we bothered that this new League recreates in a lesser form the Ottoman Empire?"

"I have mentioned your concerns to the President but he is intrigued with the possibility of a new source of oil. Kazakhstan and the region around the Caspian Sea contain a substantial amount of oil. The region quite possibly contains the second-largest known oil reserves in the world, second only to those found in the Persian Gulf region. With a cohesive political unit in the region, another practical source of oil becomes available. Within a single economic unit oil can be pumped from the Caspian Sea region, put on tankers and moved to Azerbajan, where the oil can be off-loaded into a pipeline for transit to Turkey. Besides informally the Kanuni leadership has assured us that our oil and engineering companies will be used in the final completion of the construction of the pipeline."

"I thought it was almost completed," Hammiby asked.

"It is. But from what I understand maintenance will be an issue and we are in line for that. There is more. Just to let you know, the President agrees with your worries about the long run stability in Saudi Arabia. If any problems develop there America will have another non-Persian Gulf source of energy. As the world's largest consumer of petroleum products we will be able to play our sources off against one another."

30

"My fellow council members, I have important news. The United States will soon announce recognition of our organization," Hakan Kanuni declared. The full council had been called into special session. Up until this moment many had wondered why. Hakan continued his speech. "This is truly a great day for our people. It could not have happened without the tireless work of my nephew, Kemal. In recognition of his efforts it is now time to make his selection to the office of Vice-Chairman permanent." Taken more by surprise than trying to maintain a sense of decorum, most of the council members simply sat quietly around the table.

The Turkish representative rose to speak, "My fellow patriots, I agree with Chairman Kanuni. It is an appropriate request. If no one objects, I move that we choose Kemal Kanuni as our Vice-Chairman."

Chairman Hakan Kanuni looked about the table. He had seen Dax Salyan seek recognition. He wanted to avoid recognizing him. The Chair knew the Azerbaijani wasn't going to be the second he was looking for. Unfortunately, no one had responded with an immediate second. Barely able to conceal his disgust, but at the same time knowing in what high regard the ambassador was held by the council, Kanuni turned to Salyan and said, "The Chair recognizes the distinguished Ambassador from Azerbaijan.

Inclining his head in the direction of the Chair, Salyan began to speak. "I wish to thank the Chair for recognizing me, though I suspect he will not be happy with what I have to say.

I have an objection and would like to make a point of order. Gentlemen of the Council it does not surprise me that the Turkish representative wants this result. As you all know he is a member of the Kanuni clan. He would most certainly want to secure this position for a family member. My country would be most uncomfortable with this decision."

The council sat in stunned silence. Even the Ambassador's deputy could not believe his ears. He, of course, knew that Azerbaijan would sit between the two halves of the Kanuni family, one in Turkey and the other in Kazakhstan. He, however, subscribed to the theory his country was best served by joining rather than fighting this Turkic organization. Weren't they all Turkic and Moslem? In addition, the economic opportunities were enormous. Trade between central Asia and Turkey and, for that matter, the rest of the world, would have to go through his country. It was all but certain that an oil pipeline would follow. The American oil companies would be sure to invest now that diplomatic recognition had been attained.

Chairman Kanuni looked at the rest of the group, all except the Azerbaijani, in that he was no longer able to hide his irritation. "Any further points of order?" He could see that no one else wished or dared to be heard. In fact he suspected that at least some wanted to get out of the chamber as soon as possible. "Good. I will take your silence as a second? We will proceed to the vote."

There was no surprise when the final vote was tallied. But what was a surprise was the number of delegates swayed by the presence of Ambassador Salyan.

31

Dax Salyan did not wait to mingle with the other representatives after the fateful meeting. As he expected, the Istanbul conference had confirmed Kemal Kanuni Vice-Chairman of the League. He now believed this was but the first step on the road to unification under the Kanunis. Why the others did not see this danger he could not fathom. Today they might be a common market; tomorrow, the individual countries would be relegated to the role of a province within a single country. This country would stretch from Turkey to Kazakhstan. While he personally saw a great advantage to the concept of a Turkic league of countries, especially for Azerbaijan, he saw a great danger in the concept of a single country.

Dax suspected that Kemal Kanuni was ambitious, very ambitious. While his Uncle Hakan was something of an idealist and therefore somewhat constrained, Dax knew that Kemal was not. He would have to watch this man very closely. He would have to follow the old saying keep your friends close but your enemies closer.

He needed to get home quickly. He had to shore up the support for his position or he would be left to dangle in the prevailing political winds. He had chosen to take on young Kemal and he wanted to do more than just live to talk about it. Rumors persisted that people who had gotten in young Kanuni's way had a habit of becoming involved in accidents. He assumed that by leaving quickly, there would be no time to stage such an accident.

He had calls to make, and quickly. He needed to have his private jet ready to take him home. He had to call his office. There were papers in his briefcase that he needed. He would ask his assistant Hakim to bring the papers directly to the airport. He did not want to take the time to go back to his office. Dax did indeed respect the reach of the young Kemal. As he left the parliament building, he signaled for his driver to pick him up. From the back of the stretch Mercedes limo he made the necessary calls. The car sped through traffic to the Ataturk International Airport. One of the perks of his office was the use of diplomatic license plates. With them he could go directly to his private jet without going through the main terminal. He estimated he could be airborne in about thirty minutes. He assumed it would take Hakim almost that long to get to the airport from the embassy. There was nothing he could do about it. He did not like the idea of having to wait for those papers. But he had to have them.

As his vehicle approached his private plane there standing on the tarmac was his assistant. This was a surprise. Not only was Hakim waiting for him he had the briefcase he had requested in hand. What good fortune Salyan thought, less time on the ground for Kanuni mischief.

The car pulled to a stop in front of his assistant and the Ambassador exited the vehicle. "Hakim, it is good to see you."

"Thank you, minister. I have the papers just as you requested."

"How did you get here so quickly? I thought it would have taken you longer considering the traffic."

"I knew how much you needed these documents, so I took alternate transportation." He pointed to a nearby motorcycle.

"I commend you on your resourcefulness, but I did not know you knew how use one of those."

"I don't I had to use a driver."

"I see. Well, thank you. I need to be going. I will call you from the capital as soon as I touch down. Stay in the embassy until I call. I may have another job for you."

"Yes, Excellency. I will do as you request."

Dax took the briefcase and boarded the Lear 45. While the Lear was a modest-sized business jet with a cabin built to hold eight passengers, it was a luxury for a small country such as his. The plane had a galley and a full lavatory, creature comforts Dax was oblivious to, his mind concentrating only on the danger to his country and to himself. As soon as he entered the plane, the aircraft began to taxi for take-off as the pilots had the engines turning over from the time they saw his car arrive. The flying distance from Istanbul to Baku was about eleven hundred miles. The plane was given immediate clearance for take-off, bumping a British Air 747 bound for Heathrow, another perk. Dax estimated the flying time to Baku International Airport would be no more than two hours and thirty minutes or so. Surely his quick departure had left him enough time to stay ahead of Kemal. The Lear roared down the runway and was quickly airborne.

Dax settled back into his chair. In two hours or so he would be home. The papers in his briefcase would be all the proof that he needed to save his country from being swallowed whole by the Kanunis. The plane had cleared Istanbul and was winging its way home. Its route was the usual one. He was soon over the Black Sea. The flight would cross the Republic of Georgia and finally swing southeast to Azerbaijan.

Salyan looked at his briefcase. He would have to get back to work. But first he needed a breather. A couple of minutes wouldn't make any difference. He sat in the plane trying to calm down, to relax. Eventually he succeeded. With that Dax at last reached for his briefcase. He wanted to make sure the papers were in order and that his presentation to the President was concise and to the point. As he opened the case he noticed there were three cigar-sized cylinders at the bottom of the bag. He knew he had been betrayed.

32

Hakim waited sixty-five minutes, he knew from his calculations that after this amount of time there was no way on earth the plane could return. There would have to be an accident report but undoubtedly it would be brief. In dry technical terms all it would say was as air traffic in Turkey was getting ready to hand the plane off to the controllers in Georgia, and as the controllers confirmed to each other that they had the plane on their radarscopes, the plane simply vanished from their screens. The hand off would have occurred over the eastern Black Sea. Thus there would be no wreckage or any hope of ever finding any wreckage, the water was simply too deep there. Finally the report would confirm what the controllers immediately surmised. Not only was the plane lost – there was no hope of finding any survivors.

He had taken a calculated risk, of that there was no doubt, but the rewards would be worth it. Of course he had known nothing about building a device. However, Bizhanov had solved that problem. Certain the job was finished Hakim reached for his cell phone and spoke quickly, "it is done."

33

Chairman Hakan Kanuni sat in his office just off the council chambers sipping his afternoon tea. He enjoyed this time, a quiet time to think and meditate. He could not make time for his tea everyday but that was his goal. He asked himself, why couldn't he as the leader of his people have his way in this small thing? As he contemplated this question, really one of balance of power and duty, he heard a light knock at his private entrance and his nephew Kemal entered the room.

Motioning to a chair "Please sit down. I wanted to talk before the upcoming council meeting. As you know, we serve at the discretion of the council for a limited time. This fact makes both of our positions weak. We are merely managers of the council. We have the power to set the agenda, but little else. The council members serve at the whim of their individual governments. They are in general weak bureaucrats who enjoy the title and prestige of being ministers but want none of the decision-making that goes with the job. Furthermore as I am sure you recall our compact requires the council to support all major decisions by a super majority. The things that should and need to be done are constantly being referred to one endless committee after another. This system limits our ability to achieve our goals and of course the goals of our people."

"I know all of this, Uncle. The council is where a thousand indecisions are made. What do you have in mind?"

"I think it is time to make our positions stronger. We need an election. Everyone in the league should be given the opportunity to vote on our positions. After this election our power would then flow from all the people rather than the Council or the League's individual governments."

"Yes, Uncle, I agree that an election would give us the necessary power to achieve our goals or to at least make them easier to obtain. The Council will be hard pressed not to approve of such a vote, particularly now with that troublesome Salyan gone. But is the time right and are the issues right?"

"Though I was sorry to hear of his death; his passing will make our lives easier. Allah does seem to work in mysterious ways. The time couldn't be better and we will control the agenda. We will win impressively," Hakan said.

"Uncle, then let's go to the council meeting and tell members of their insightful and momentous decision."

34

Chairman Hakan Kanuni entered the council chambers followed by Vice-Chairman Kemal Kanuni. All the ministers rose to greet them. Both men acknowledged the fact that the others had risen when they entered. They moved to their respective places at the head and the foot of the council table.

"I thank you all for being present." The Chairman knew that only a great illness or death would have prevented all the original ministers from being present. "I would like us all to welcome our newest member." He pointed to Hakim who had until recently been the former ambassador's chief assistant. "It is sad that this fine man has been elevated by tragedy. The recent accident that took our beloved friend Dax Salyan will always sadden us. But I am sure that Ambassador Salyan would have wanted us to press ahead with the great tasks that remain in front of us. Please welcome our new Ambassador." With that everyone rose in applause.

Having been told in advance to keep it short Hakim rose and spoke briefly. "It is not the time for me to say anything other than to thank you for your condolences to the Ambassador's family. I also promise to you that I will try and fill his great shoes as best as I am able." With that Hakim sat down and looked to the Chairman.

"Thank you Mr. Ambassador." The Chairman knew things were now in place. He had a lap dog where a tiger used to reside. What a fortunate accident. The Chairman continued his opening remarks. "May the peace of Allah be with us. My fellow ministers our League is new and has taken its first small steps like a young child and must now take larger steps. I want the world to know that we are peace-loving people who believe in the tenants of Mohamed. The Great Prophet should be our guide. For this reason I believe it is necessary that we allow all our people to decide. I think it is important for the future that our people to affirm your decisions to select me Chairman and my nephew Vice-Chairman of this great Council."

There was a murmur among the ministers. They looked at one another and at the Kanunis. This was something none of them had anticipated. Finally, the oldest minister, the one from Turkmenistan, spoke. He was the exception to the rule, not a typical bureaucrat or politician, but rather, a man of great intellect who had survived many years under the Soviet rule. He himself had been a freedom fighter in his youth. For this among other reasons what he said carried a great deal of weight at the council, second only to the Kanunis now that Dax Salyan was no longer with them.

Befitting his age he slowly rose to speak. He was old and frail but his voice was strong. He began slowly. "If we are to be able to spread the word of Allah, we must be strong. Let the Koran be our guide. Did not all defer to Mohamed? It is time again for a strong leader. We must preserve the teachings of our beloved religion. We must be strong to ward off the dangers of the West and its secular society. We must in peace go forward. I concur with the Chairman. It is time for the people to approve our choice of leader. I move we agree unanimously there be an election as requested by our Chairman."

Kemal smiled as the entire process unfolded. As he knew they would the Council agreed in unanimity to hold an election

A plebiscite was to be scheduled in three months' time. No one at the table seriously doubted the outcome.

35

I had arrived back late from Oxford. But before I went to bed, I emailed Washington to see what, if anything, Research might have on this Melina person, the Saudi Oil Minister and his son and of course the Kanuni's. If there was one thing you could count on was the eavesdropping ability of the NSA. The computers there were unbelievable. If they bugged a bedroom those computers could tell the difference between yes and yes. I had made some headway, but time was short, little did I know how short. I learned as soon as I flipped on the television to B Sky B and saw much to my surprise that Washington had just recognized the League. I didn't know if that meant I should return home or what so I checked my email.

You would have thought I hadn't checked my messages for weeks the way they rolled by. After they stopped I scanned them until I found one from Jazel Hammiby.

> "Mike I suspect you have seen the news regarding the recognition of the League. The President was under a lot of pressure and felt it was necessary to do it. In line with administration policy, it's his view that our recognition will create a semblance of a counterweight in the region."

> "You are to continue your investigation. The priority status has been upgraded to IA."

> "Best of Luck."

> "J H"

I starred at the message with a sinking feeling. The pressure was now on not to embarrass the President. So as not to embarrass him I had to move quickly. Well at least I could ask for almost anything from Washington and be assured of getting it pdq.

With a renewed, almost overwhelming, sense of urgency I began to scan the rest of my messages. I had to remind myself as I went through the more promising ones that it would take some time to properly conduct my investigation. No matter what had happened beyond my control, research and analysis took time and in many cases could simply not be rushed. The research branch had a policy to send out messages as information became available. Therefore it was not unusual to have a whole string of short messages as compared to one lengthy one.

Sorting through the most promising yielded some very interesting background information.

"The head of the State Police in Kazakhstan and the Chief of Staff of the Turkish Army are related to the Kanuni's and have expressed strong support for the League Both branches of the family are nominally Sunni-Moslem. Military intelligence believes the Army Chief to be a strong nationalist with expansionist dreams. He has been actively involved in the suppression of the Kurdish minority (see related email) as both an implementer of policy as well as an advocate."

I toggled down to the "Kurds" email.

"The Kurds, a separate ethnic and linguistic group of people, have been struggling for centuries to establish a homeland. They live in the Taurus Mountain of eastern Anatolia (Turkey), northern Syria, and the Zagros Mountains of western Iran and northern Iraq. Though the governments in the region can't agree on much, they all are in agreement in actively suppressing Kurdish separatism. The region is generally referred to as Kurdistan. The oil fields of northern Iraq are located in a Kurdish region. Since the Gulf Wars, the area has only nominally been controlled by Baghdad. Except for the oil resources the area's main economic asset is its location as a land bridge between various regional market centers."

I scanned through the rest of my messages but they yielded nothing of significance. I had hoped they had come up with something on this Melina person but nothing yet. I checked my watch, as I didn't want to be late for a morning appointment with the manager at the London office of Goldman Sachs and Co. Kemal Kanuni had gone to work there after his graduate work at the London School of Economics. I had given the receptionist my usual journalist cover. However I was a bit worried whether or it would hold up. There may actually be some employees there who were familiar with the L A *Times* and might wonder if I actually worked there. As I headed out the door I figured if I was questioned too extensively I could always say I was new to the paper and then act a little eccentric.

36

Because the day was so nice I decided to take a taxi. It was more expensive for the American taxpayer but since I got to see the sun and it would improve my work efficiency it seemed to be a fair trade off all and all. I arrived at the Goldman Sachs office about eleven in the morning and introduced myself to the rather attractive receptionist as a reporter for the Los Angeles *Times* financial page.

Thankfully the wait was only a few minutes. For some reason, obviously a character flaw, I had never been able to completely train the impatience out of myself for waiting around. Before long a tall and rather slender man of about fifty-five approached me.

"Hello, Mr. Williams. I am Nigel Jones. How can I help you?" As soon as the manager said hello I figured I had lucked out again. A proper British accent was readily apparent. This would mean that the only *Times* that meant anything to Nigel would be the London *Times*. He probably didn't know there was another *Times* and in, of all places, Los Angeles, California.

"Mr. Jones, I want to thank you for allowing me a few minutes of your time. You see, my newspaper, the Los Angeles *Times* has assigned me to write an article on the oil industry. I have been in the Gulf where I looked at the usual things, such as production facilities, oil terminals and the effect of the Gulf Wars on the region. I was scheduled to lay over in London when I decided a foreign financial point of view might provide a new and different angle that might grab an audience. In Kuwait and Saudi Arabia I was told that London has become the main market for oil related financial products, you know, things like options and futures contracts. As you can imagine the price of oil is certainly important to our readers back home."

"Yes, I can see that with all the cars and freeways you have there, petrol would be of interest. Please come to my office where we can talk for a few moments."

I followed Nigel Jones into his corner office. I immediately noticed that the view from his office was impressive, particularly on such a beautiful day. The office looked east across the Thames toward Whitehall. I could see Westminster, Big Ben and the Houses of Parliament. Further down the Thames I even could make out the Tower of London and the Millennium Dome at Greenwich. "Mr. Jones, your view is outstanding."

"Yes, quite. I suppose that it is." I thought there is typical British understatement. "Please have a seat."

"Thank you. In Los Angeles the price of gasoline is a major topic of conversation. But it is a fact that the general public doesn't know the first thing about the finances associated with the oil industry. I would appreciate it if you could give me a general description of the process and then how specific options and contracts are handled in this office."

"Very well, you know I began my career here at the oil desk."

"I will be sure and mention in my article." I made a note on my pad. I really wanted to say big ego, but I contained myself.

"The oil world is basically divided into groupings with competing needs and resources," Nigel began. "The first group is the producer countries. This group can be further divided into OPEC producers and non-OPEC producer countries. The members of OPEC are Iran, Iraq, Kuwait, Saudi Arabia, Qatar, The United Arab Emirates, Venezuela, Libya, Algeria, Indonesia, Nigeria, Ecuador and Gabon. As a group their oil reserves represent two-thirds of worldwide-discovered reserves. The Kingdom of Saudi Arabia reserves alone account for about twenty-five percent of the world's reserves or about thirty-seven percent of OPEC's. All other producer countries make up the rest. These are principally, Mexico, the countries of the former Soviet Union, Canada, the United States, Great Britain and Norway." I was taking notes as Nigel continued speaking in his professorial style.

"The second group of players in the oil game is the consumer nations of the world. These are basically all the countries of the world, but are dominated by the G-7 nations. The International Energy Agency is the multinational organization that represents these consumer countries."

"How is the price of oil set?" I asked.

"Very good question. The pricing system is market-driven in the macro sense. But in the micro sense it is not. The easy answer is that the Oil Ministry of the Kingdom of Saudi Arabia sets the price. However, market conditions will dictate whether or not this benchmark price will hold."

"I don't understand," I responded.

Nigel began to explain. "The laws of supply and demand govern the oil market; any market, for that matter. The supply of oil is determined by a number of factors in the various producing countries, for example, its oil reserves, population size, economic status and condition and its politics. The demand for oil is governed by the economic expansion or contraction of the consuming country, its politics and weather conditions."

This made sense so I reviewed my notes to see what, if any, additional questions I might have. "What are the roles of the oil companies, etc.?"

"The oil companies basically contract with producer countries to acquire the raw material petroleum. They then contract with transportation companies to move the product to their sources of refining. The transportation companies may be wholly owned subsidiaries or they may be independent contractors. A large independent contractor, for example, would be the Hellenic Sea Lines. This Greek owned tanker line moves much of the non-OPEC oil in the world. The oil companies will then refine their petroleum into various products. These products are then put into the final distribution chain which moves products to the ultimate customer."

Thinking about the Aziz family I wanted to know more about Saudi Arabia. "The Saudi's seem to have the ability to heavily influence the market. Can they control the market?"

Nigel reflected for a few moments and then responded, "Not by themselves alone, no. It would be possible for a group of players to control the market. But remember, in the past there has never been enough unity long enough on the part of the suppliers to control the market. Given the assumption that enough producers could cooperate long enough, there is the possibility of an effective cartel. I also think the producers would need to control a portion of the oil transportation network."

"Why would that be?" I asked.

"Well, you would want to have some control over the producer countries not in your cartel."

"I can see your point. I only have a few more questions. What is the role of the oil futures and options market?"

"The oil futures market is the financial mechanism for the market to influence the basic price of oil established by Saudi Arabia. That is, say the Saudis establish a price of $25.00 per barrel. The $25.00 should hold providing that the price was established when the market was in equilibrium. But let us say that the winter in North America is unusually cold. The demand side of the market will force up prices, and the futures market reflects that demand. As another example, suppose a producer country such as Russia needs foreign exchange badly. It will increase production, thus pushing the market out of balance by increasing supply. All things being equal, the price of crude will fall and the market will reflect this economic fact."

"Can a lot of money be made in this market?"

"Yes and quite a lot can be lost. Violent swings in supply and demand can create great economic dislocations."

"Thanks your explanations have been most helpful. I would you mind if I changed course a bit?" Obviously flattered Jones said, "No not at all."

"What is the role a brokerage house such as Goldman Sachs might play in this process?"

"Goldman Sachs and the other major global brokerage and investment houses make the market in the oil futures market."

"Make the market in oil futures?" I asked.

"Sorry, it is a term of art. Goldman Sachs and the like create the market for the buyers and sellers of barrels of oil. We write futures contracts and options on those contracts. We will hold these contracts to allow the easy transfer of them between buyers and sellers. In addition, we will invest in the contracts themselves for our company or clients or just as a method of creating market equilibrium."

"This market making process sounds as if it could be terribly risky." I added.

"It could be if the market was affected by several unforeseen events," Jones responded.

I was a bit taken aback. "Aren't all events unforeseen?"

"Yes, in some sense they are but not in the market sense. We know natural disasters take place. We generally know where and the kind that occur in a given area. With this kind of information we can run sophisticated computer models that allow us to price these kinds of risks. We can also run models that can accommodate an unknown risk."

"An unknown risk?"

"We have the ability to quantify the risk of sabotage or a coup, something like that."

I was impressed, but something stuck in my mind. "What happens if multiple unknown events occur?"

Jones smiled and said, "In that case as you Americans would say we would be shit out of luck."

We both had a good chuckle. "Thank you for your time. I just have a couple of more questions. Is the trading desk here the main one for the company?"

"Yes it is As a matter of fact a few years ago we had Abdul Aziz, the son of a then Senior Oil Minister of the Kingdom of Saudi Arabia working here at our desk. Quite a coup, wouldn't you say? By the way, his father is now serving his as the Chairman of OPEC".

I already had that information but continued to takes notes. "Well, that is something indeed," I continued. "I understand that Kemal Kanuni also worked here."

"Yes, I believe you are correct. However, I can't tell you much about him. You see I was working in Hong Kong during the time that both Mr. Kanuni and Mr. Aziz worked here. You see I took over as manager about the time they left the firm. The former manager died unexpectedly from a stroke. I was called home after that."

I could tell Jones was anxious to get back to work and I didn't want to wear out my welcome, so I decided to wrap up the interview. "Well again, thank you for your time. I appreciate it. It was a pleasure." One last question, "Would you mind being quoted in my story?" I rarely heard anyone say no to this last question. But even if the answer was no, the interviewee was flattered and was generally available for any further questions I or rather the NSA might have.

"Why no, no not at all. It was a pleasure for me also," was Nigel's response.

I rose and left his office hoping to catch a glimpse of the young thing in the lobby. But unfortunately, it was lunchtime and she had apparently had taken her break. In her place was a more seasoned lady who nodded rather curtly as I left. I was certainly glad she had not been manning the gates when I had arrived.

37

As I headed pack to the flat I was looking forward to visiting with Philip. He was due back from his trip. As I headed down the tube steps I thought I noticed someone familiar looking. Not in the sense of knowing someone rather in the sense that I had seen him earlier in the day. I was probably wrong. It was more than a little unsettling to think I could have attracted someone's attention here in London. I made a mental note to be more observant. The remainder of my trip back to Earl's Court and Philip's flat was uneventful.

My host had not yet returned so I had time to log on to my computer to see if Research had come up with any additional information. There were only three documents, one was background information and could wait. The second was curious. It was a request from the state department that I attend an embassy function this evening. I didn't know why but I had long since learned not to worry about the logic of some things our government did.

The final file was the one for which I had been waiting. It seems the identification section had had some luck with finding Melina, including a picture. I clicked on the email picture. To my surprise this Melina person was the same one that Philip and I saw at the Yacht club doing all she could to ingratiate herself to the Greek shipping magnate. Included with the picture was a very brief biography.

It seemed she had attended Oxford at the same time as Kemal Kanuni. Before that she had been shipped by her estranged parents to a very exclusive Swiss nun run boarding school.

My head was spinning, it could have been a coincidence but I just didn't believe in coincidences this large. There had to be some kind of connection between these people. I just needed to figure it out.

I turned to the other more mundane message. The file contained more background information. This time on Kazakhstan for which I was grateful as I knew next to nothing about the country. The report indicated that the country is nominally a democracy but the people are not politically aware. So in reality it was run by a small number of well-connected families; the situation being similar to most all of the countries in the region. I assumed the Kanuni's were one of the players even before their name was listed. The name was first on the list.

I needed to get a report off to Washington. I finally felt I had pulled together enough information to send something of value to Washington. There was more to the Kanuni's, particularly Kemal, than met the eye of that there was no doubt. Of course this was common for people in positions of power. It was a character issue plain simple. I didn't really have enough data yet but I didn't trust him. I knew Washington would take that kind of analysis and place it in the file directly above the round file, one step from oblivion. But at least now I had enough concrete data to suggest that extreme caution be exercised when dealing these people while at the same time justify a continuing investigation.

I began my report, hoping it wouldn't be buried because of the President's new policy.

"I was asked to go to Istanbul as observer, with a small group that was sent to review the issue of recognition of the League of Turkic (Islamic) Nations. A major component of my assignment was to develop an understanding of the Kanuni family. This report is a synthesis of my observations and information provided by the NSA research department. Kemal Kanuni is approximately six-foot-two inches tall, rather large for this part of the world. He is physically fit. I would estimate that he weighs no more than 190 pounds. His features reflect a mixed heritage. Though mostly Turkic, his blue eyes and height can be attributed to a German great grandmother and a Russian grandmother. He is ostensibly Sunni Moslem but he does not appear to have any fundamental religious convictions. His mother, now deceased, was from Turkey. His father's family was descended from nomadic wanderers who had populated central Asia for centuries. His father is also dead. Though not large in number, the family is influential or at least appears to have good friends in important places. Kemal is the second most important family member after his Uncle Hakan. Hakan was the founder and is the first chairman of the League of Turkic (Islamic) Nations."

"The stated purpose of the League can be compared to the early European Common Market. The member states wish to improve the economic lives of their citizens. The League's charter emphasizes the peaceful intent of the member nation states as well as the League itself. As you might expect there is a strong influence of Moslem thought contained throughout their charter. However, our experience has shown that the Sunni Moslems of the entire region are among that religion's least dogmatic followers. I caution you though; we should not discount the influence of religion on this League or its member states. There are fundamentalist forces at work in the region that appear to be growing in strength. I refer you to file CIA-MW, prepared by the CIA regarding the issue of Moslem fundamentalism.

"My observation of Vice-Chairman Kanuni is that he is quite bright. He was educated both at Oxford and the London School of Economics. More than intelligent, I observe that he is a dynamic leader. He is forceful, charming and magnetic. Undoubtedly, he has the potential to be a great and continuing influence in central Asia, possibly the entire Islamic world. There is no question that he will be a player we will have to deal with now and in the future.

"As part of my assignment I did an initial background check of Mr. Kemal Kanuni's life in the United Kingdom. In summary, I found that he was like many young men from the Islamic world permitted the freedom of the Western world. He indulged in many of the pleasures prohibited by the Koran. This in and of itself is not unusual or uncommon. What however, does appear to be different is his attitude toward life. Many of the young men from that part of the world rather quickly show remorse for having violated the Koran, particularly once the novelty of the West and its attractions wear off. For him, this appears not to be the case. My limited research shows that he was cold and calculating about all his aspects of life including religion. I have found this is unusual for most Moslems. As a caveat, these are my tentative and preliminary conclusions/observations

I re-read the report and was happy with it as a starting point. I just hoped we weren't so far down the road that my starting point was useless.

38

I heard Philip enter the flat. "Hey Philip come on in here I want to show you a picture."

"What? No hello, how are you doing?"

"No just get your ass in here," I responded.

Philip entered the room I had set up in. I pointed to the computer screen. "Look who turned up."

"It's the babe from the yacht club."

"Yes it is. Her name is Melina Fokina. She attended Oxford and apparently she knew the guy I was assigned to investigate."

"Knew as in knew?" Philip starred at the picture. "She is really good looking. Isn't she?"

"Yes in an exotic sort of way and yes, apparently so, to your first question. It looks like I need to learn a lot more about her and Kanuni. Question, do you think there was anything with her and Christakos?"

Philip thought for a moment. "Nothing off the top of my head but I can check around. I do have something about Christakos though. Let me go pull some of my notes." While I heard Philip rummage through his file cabinet I started to change. I needed to find something appropriate in my limited travel wardrobe, something dull with shades of gray.

Philip returned holding several pieces of paper. "Here it is. As I remember, quite a story, though I'm not sure how useful it will be."

"Great," I said, "you can tell me as I get ready."

Philip began to tell me a story.

"Athos Christakos was in the lounge of the Hotel Monte Rosa, a must when in Zermatt."

"Before you go any further who is Athos Christakos?"

"Christakos only son. With him were the members of his climbing team, all familiar faces except for a Russian by the name of Alexander Yeltsin. None of his group knew this new man. He had replaced Jim Smith, an American, who had torn his ACL in a pick up soccer game just before he was to come to Switzerland. From discussions I have had any mountaineer would not have liked the idea of having a new player involved, but apparently their time frame left the team no choice. Alexander certainly had the credentials to be a team member. Reportedly he was the team member with the most Himalayan experience having already made a successful ascent of Mount Everest and K-2, a truly remarkable feat, I might add. The team was to make a practice ascent of the north face of the Matterhorn in preparation for their August assault on Mount Everest.

Teams needed more than just experience and again it appears this was something that concerned Athos. All the team members agreed it seemed strange that Jim had had an accident. Jim did love football, soccer in America, but as a rule he would enter into a regimen at least six weeks before any climb. Before his accident he had never let any outside activity break his routine of diet and fitness training. Athos and Jim had climbed together on four other ascents." Philip paused for a moment and shuffled through his notes. "Yes, here it is. In retrospect the way the team had been informed of the injury was strange and as you will find out more than somewhat disconcerting."

"What happened?"

"They got a last minute telegram of Jim's injury. Several team members tried on several occasions to phone him with no luck. Also included in the telegram was the recommendation that Alexander, Alex, be his replacement. Because of the timing the team had had only one "bonding" session on the day before the climb."

"Did anything unusual happen the night before the climb?" I asked.

"It seems Athos got lucky. He ran into a gorgeous auburn haired creature at the bar. This was not an uncommon experience for him. It appears that good looking women often sought him out."

"The same with me."

Philip rolled his eyes and continued. "Upon meeting, these women would soon learn he was single and rich. The only son of the Greek shipping magnate, money and power came easily and early to him."

"Quite the aphrodisiac, "

"Quite."

"The next day the wind was howling. A late season storm had attacked the north face of the Matterhorn. Athos, as team leader, had wanted to call off the ascent until the storm had passed. However, Alexander had encouraged the team, dared them would have been a better word, to go ahead and make the climb. He said the storm conditions would better prepare them for Everest. The team had voted to go and Athos had gone along, team spirit and all that. Of course to someone who had other options team spirit might seem like a poor reason, considering the weather and all."

"What was her name?"

Philip looked through his notes, "Let's see. Lady Jane Blair, the Countess of somewhere, apparently no one could exactly remember where or of what."

"I always thought that to qualify to be a countess one had to be a member of the blue haired lady set."

"Generally you are correct. It appears our Lady Jane was the exception to the rule."

"Do you think this person was really a Countess?"

"I don't, as a matter of fact I don't even think she was even English."

I nodded and then motioned Philip to continue, I was starting to run out of time and was having difficulty finding a pair of socks

"The conditions were harsh. Ice and snow driven by strong winds had come up and cut visibility to almost nothing. Athos as team leader was first by about twenty feet above Alex but was at the point of the ascent where Alex was to take over. The plan was to have Alex come up and scout the best route to the first base camp, a wide ledge sheltered from the weather. The ledge had been chosen because it was wide enough to set up two tents, a luxury for a mountain climb. The plan was to push to the top of the mountain the next morning.

From below the rest of the team saw Alex reach the change over point. This was a rather tricky maneuver but nothing too difficult for a pair of experienced climbers. They clung to the side of the mountain apparently discussing the final push to the ledge. Once the two of them reached the ledge; the rest of the team would follow. As Athos waited, Alex pulled himself higher and higher driving in one piton after another, eventually moving out of sight. It seemed to take longer than expected for Alex to give the signal to come up. By then everyone was quite tired and was looking forward to a break. Finally, it came. Athos began moving up the lines, hand over hand. He moved along the line anchored by the pitons driven by Alex

Slowly, ever so slowly, the team below saw him move up the face. At this time of the day and this part of the climb any experienced person would tell you that one sucked air like the morning after a major hangover. The plan was to have Alex safely stand on the ledge while at the same time anchor the line for Athos. It was then that things starting going wrong. The rope was whipping around. It had too much slack, almost immediately the line gave way. Athos started sliding down the face. There was nothing anyone below could do. The safety pitons started pulling out one by one, falling like dominos. Then at last one held.

The line jerked tight. Athos bounced up five feet. He immediately settled back, the wind knocked out of him. He hung in space trying to catch his breath, swinging back and forth. Everyone stopped; stunned. He began call to his partners below. If they could come up quickly, he could be saved. Unfortunately just as help started to come the last piton gave way and with it the entire line.

The team members did not hear him scream. What they saw and just for an instant was Athos sliding down the rest of the face of the mountain. There was a look of puzzlement on his face as he disappeared down the mountain. They were stunned. Athos, the expert mountaineer, was gone, quickly and quietly. When they re-gathered at base camp, they asked Alex what had happened. All Alex said was that he had never seen Athos after he had taken the lead about thirty feet below the ledge. He merely could speculate; maybe the line had given way or maybe he had simply slipped in the cold and snow. He just did not know."

"That is quite a tale," I said.

"There is more. Alexander Yeltsin's real name is Akham Bizhanov. The source of this story was one of the team members. I can't tell you anything more."

"Akham Bizhanov, now there is a name I haven't heard in a while."

"I thought you might find that interesting," Philip said. "By the way, why are you getting dressed up?"

I briefly pondered what I had heard, making some additional mental notes. I then told Philip about my Embassy duty. His only response was, "I'm glad it's you and not me." I could only agree.

39

Kate O'Hara wondered why there was a phone ringing. It made no sense. How could there be a phone on this river trip? That was exactly why she had chosen this vacation. The only way of contacting or being contracted by the outside world was by radiotelephone. But radiophones never ever rang, and this one just kept ringing. As the fog of sleep lifted, Kate finally realized that unfortunately she had not been on a river trip. She had been really out of it, dreaming about one of her favorite vacations, river rafting. The telephone, it seemed, was incessantly ringing. These damned European phones rang twice as often as the damned American ones. Rolling over, she fumbled around grabbing for the receiver and at the same time wondering what time it was.

Reality came flooding back to her as she heard the voice of her editor at the other end of the line. "Katie, my girl." Anyone other than Jamie O'Doul talking to her like this would have really tightened her jaw, but he was just too lovable. Jamie was a native of Dublin and it seemed had worked at every level and office ever created by the Washington *Post*. Though no one really knew for certain how old Jamie was, she wouldn't have been a bit surprised if his first assignment as a cub reporter was to interview Daniel O'Connell about being the first Irishman to serve in the British Parliament. "Are you okay, my darlin'?"

"Jamie, I'm fine. Why do you ask?"

"Well for one thing, you haven't been to work for two days and that is just not like you."

"What? What day is it? What time is it?"

"Half-nine, Tuesday morning."

"Wow, I must have been tired. I was doing some research out of town over the weekend till very late on Sunday, really quite early on Monday morning. I traveled back on Monday. When I got back to my place I lay down to get some rest. It sure looks like I got some rest. I slept till Tuesday. Boy I haven't done that years."

"Well, I hope you are refreshed because I need you to attend a party at the U.S. Embassy."

"Why do you need me to go? Can't the society editor do it?"

"This is not a society party."

"They are all society parties."

"Well, that is true, but in this case the usual list of attendees is just different enough to think that you might learn something useful."

"You mean something other than who is doing who and what flavor they are doing it in."

"Yes, well, maybe a little of that, too. Just trust me, I have a feeling about this. It may be nothing but I have, as you are so willin' to point out, been 'round for a while. Experience in our business does count for something. Besides, I've covered for you the last couple of days and other times before that."

"Okay, but only because of you."

"And my ability to twist your arm with such ease."

"Yes, and because of that. What time and what is the dress code?"

40

Kate hated these Embassy parties. It seemed there were more pretentious people per square inch here than any other place on the planet except maybe any run-of-the-mill Washington D.C. cocktail party.

But in this case maybe Jamie was on to something. If he were, it would be worth putting up with the usual overage gropers. She drifted back to her conversation with him.

"What is different about the guest list?"

"Well, for one, there is a newcomer, a Mike Williams."

Momentarily She wondered if was it was the same person she had met when she was in Greece. Well to find out would at least create something of interest for her.

Kate wondered how Jamie O'Doul knew who was on the guest list. But she also wondered how a man of his years could possibly still be called Jamie. Maybe the Ambassador checked with Jamie before he invited anyone, for all she knew. "What's so important about Mike Williams?"

"Well, my dear, I think he is a spook."

"Jamie, you think everyone one is a spy."

"Well, aren't they?"

"In a sense, you are a spy, only you like to call yourself a reporter."

She was fond of Jamie but when he began into his conspiracy theory she knew she needed to cut him off. It was not so much that she thought he was full of shit, rather it was just that she had heard his speech so many times she could repeat it verbatim. "So you want me to meet this guy? And when I do what do you want me to find out? Like, he is going to tell me anything useful if he is a spy."

"I want you to see if he knows, or if anybody he knows, knows something about Kemal Kanuni."

She was stunned. What did Jamie know about Kemal Kanuni?

"Kemal Kanuni?" she queried guardedly.

"Yes, you must know him, the young Vice-Chairman of that new Turkish economic league."

"Why would you care about him, he isn't the President for Life in the latest central Asian country?"

"That is true but I listened to his latest speech on the short wave and I think we should find out something more about this character. The way he delivers his speeches as well as their contents reminds of the way some of our rather more disagreeable characters from our not so distant past began."

Kate relaxed. "Okay, I'll see what I can do. What time should I be at the Embassy?"

"The usual time, my Darlin, the usual time," Jamie replied.

41

It was slightly after 8:00 p.m. by the time I arrived at the U. S Embassy in Grosvenor Square, home to what had to be the ugliest embassy building in all London. I hoped I had waited long enough to be fashionably late, or if not fashionable, at least late enough to the reception so as not to be the first one there. I generally, which was a nice way of saying all the time, really didn't like attending official government social functions. I had learned to my prior great regret punctuality at these events was a vice, not a virtue. The worst time I could ever remember was one party at the Saudi Arabian embassy in Washington. I swear to this day I had to have been not only the first American to arrive, but the very first person of any nationality to arrive except the staff and of course, the Saudi Ambassador. So there I was alone trying to make light conversation without the benefit of a drink of any sort. Fortunate for all, I didn't start a war. My real problem of course was a bad sense of social timing.

I dutifully went and stood in the security line. Ever since the Gulf Wars the embassy had been fortified with additional barricades with additional security guards inside and out and metal detectors. Of course the massive fencing around the building only added to the look, I call prison modern. Everyone in line had an invitation. I had none, and maybe with some luck the guards wouldn't let me pass. Unfortunately that wasn't the case. I showed my id and was waved through. Hoping to buy some more time to avoid having to make meaningless conversation for as long as possible, I chose not to stand in the receiving line and instead headed straight for the bar, where I hoped they would serve me even though I had been a boor. "Scotch please," I told the bartender.

"Coming up."

As the bartender delivered my drink, I turned to face the growing crowd. It was then that I heard a voice behind me ask, "Excuse me, Mike, I don't know if you remember me."

I was more than a little surprised to hear my name, I turned to answer and standing in front of me was Kate O'Hara.

"I certainly do remember you. How are you doing? Or more exactly what are you doing here?" I know I was starring but here was the exception to the rule of embassy parties. I had enjoyed being with her for that short time in Greece. She wasn't drop-dead gorgeous but neither was she a member of the kennel corp. In fact, she was quite good-looking in an athletic sort of way. I smiled broadly. If she was alone for whatever reason I was lucky. This party would not be the complete disaster I had feared.

42

"My editor, Jamie O'Doul, asked me to attend. Do you know him?"

"Can't say that I do."

"Well he seems to know you. He thinks you are a spy."

I paused before answering. I wasn't quite sure how to proceed. Then I decided to go with it. "He does?"

"Yes, but of course he sees conspiracies everywhere. By the way, are you licensed to kill?"

Kate O'Hara was not only good looking but seemed to have a quirky sense of humor. I liked that. Responding now in my best British accent, "Yes, but only if I use my Walther PBK." Kate laughed and I liked the sound of it. All of this made me a bit nervous. Unlike James Bond I did not find it that easy to meet and talk with attractive women. I figured it was all the years of training under the nuns in grade school. Of course it had been years since anyone had used a ruler across my knuckles to straighten up my thinking, but childhood memories are some of the most powerful.

I took a sip and noticed I could use a refill. "I'm about out." I lifted my glass to show her. "Can I get you a refill?"

"Thanks, that would be nice."

"What are you having?"

"A little white wine would be nice. I wouldn't want you taking advantage of me, being a man of the world and all." The Southern drawl was apparent again.

I returned and handed her the drink. I wanted to learn more about her and get the conversation away from what I did for work. "I remember you told me you were stationed in London, how did that come to be?"

"I don't want to bore you."

"You won't bore me. Give me the long version if you like," I responded. I figured that boring from Kate couldn't be any worse than this event would have been without her.

Kate began. "My great-grandparents came to America from Ireland at the time of the famine. They were farmers in the area just south of Limerick. After the blight hit, they gathered up their few worldly possessions and managed to buy two tickets for America. They left from Cork and came to Boston "No Irish need apply" caused my great-grandfather to seek employment in the Navy. And it was the Navy that had brought my mother and father to San Diego.

My great-grandfather and grandfather had been enlisted men. A standing family story had my great grandfather telling my grandfather that in his day the Navy was made up of iron men and wooden ships while it was now made up of iron ships and wooden men. My father, as his father and his grandfather had done, entered the navy as an enlisted man. He saw action in Korea and decided to make the Navy his career. The Navy had offered him the opportunity to attend college, which he quickly accepted. Upon graduation he had made the jump from the enlisted ranks to officer status. As the world's oldest ensign he was sent to Vietnam, again seeing action. Before and after his tours of duty he had been assigned to North Island. So San Diego, more specifically Coronado, became home.

I lived in Navy housing. The Navy decided that cable TV was an unnecessary luxury. Consequently, my television viewing choices were rather limited, so to increase my choices I began watching programs from Mexico. To my mother's surprise, she found I had learned Spanish while viewing TV. It seems I had some natural ability in languages. It was this talent that led me to minor in languages."

I had not grown bored listening to her; in fact I wanted to learn more. "A minor, I would have thought you would have majored in it."

"My father insisted I get a practical degree, the business school at San Diego State had, and for that matter still has, a very fine reputation. I chose accounting and for reasons that still eluded me, chose to take the CPA exam. I passed but then I drew the line. I knew I wasn't cut out to work in public accounting I don't have the personality for it. I would have been a round peg in a square hole. At least, however, my father was mollified. Besides I'll bet I have the most unusual major/ minor combination in the history of San Diego State University. I had also always enjoyed writing, so I decided to try playing journalist before getting a real job as my dad would say."

"Well it looks like you are still playing journalist," I said.

"True. My language talent, on top of my business acumen has led to numerous opportunities. I've worked for The Wall Street Journal in New York and in Frankfurt. I spent a couple of years in L.A. and had extended stays in Paris, Milan and the most exotic, Istanbul."

I was impressed and was about to ask her another question when she spoke up. "Enough of me, tell me something about you."

"Well you know everything. I am a spy and if I tell you any more I will be forced to kill you." She looked at me and laughed. I continued, "My grades in high school and SAT scores pointed me to a premier institution of higher learning. Most of my friends were attending the University of San Francisco and that's where I wanted to go. However my pocketbook had the last say, so I crossed the bay to Cal Berkley. Even going to a U.C. school stretched me pretty well financially. To help pay for school, I joined ROTC." Kate looked at me with a look of some horror on her face. I continued, "No it was okay. When I joined it was merely unpopular, not hated, not like in the Mario Savio years. After graduation I joined the Army as a second lieutenant. At Cal I majored in computer science. Because of this and my test scores, the Army had assigned me to the Pentagon to work in the intelligence section. I worked there two very long years. I found the work easy but somewhat boring. You see I really wasn't an "inside" person. I requested and got a transfer to the Ranger school. I am sure my superiors must have thought I was crazy asking to leave the Pentagon to jump out of airplanes."

I was about to continue when the announcement was made that it was time for dinner. Everyone was asked to proceed to the dining room within five minutes. Kate leaned towards me and said these little warnings were meant to give everyone time to go to the bathroom. Apparently it would be truly bad form to have to get up to go to the loo just after everyone was seated. She then asked, "Do you know where you are sitting?"

"No, not really" was my reply. "I didn't bother to check."

"I can arrange for us to sit together if you don't mind?"

"Thanks. I would like that."

"Good. I will be back in a couple of minutes. I just need to arrange it. Please wait here for me, okay?" Before I could reply, Kate had hurried off and was soon lost in the midst of all the guests.

It was certainly not everyday that I had dinner with an attractive woman. While she was gone I watched as the guests made their pre-dinner preparations. Some went off to answer the call of nature. Some downed the last of their drinks and moved toward the dining room. There were more than a few who reached for their cell phones. I view those phones as a great tool, but I think many people see them as a symbol of personnel importance. They apparently think they are so important that their pearls of wisdom are needed twenty-four hours a day, seven days a week. I think the opposite. Basically, if one is really that important you don't need to be tied to an electronic leash.

I saw a small group which I believed to be the veterans of the embassy party circuit head to the bar for another round. I could not think of a good reason not to follow the example of those more experienced than I, so I headed toward the bar to get Kate and myself a drink. Just as the bartender handed me the two glasses, Kate reappeared, seemingly out of nowhere.

"I ordered you a drink for the road," handing her a glass of white wine.

"Thanks. I would hate to get thirsty between here and the dining room," Kate responded.

"Well, you know how dry some conversations can be."

"Well, I arranged for us to be seated as far from the Ambassador and his table as possible. I don't know anyone else at the table but I thought distance was more important than familiarity. So if the conversation is dry, you will have no one to blame but yourself."

"Well, I guess I will have to be my usual suave and debonair self."

"Yes, I forgot. Is suave and debonair the first thing they teach you in spy school?"

"No, the first thing they teach is how to chase down the bad guy wearing a coat and tie, never once mussing your clothes."

I appreciated the quick repartee and banter. It was obvious only someone who was intelligent could keep up as well as she was, so I figured she wasn't lying about her academic success.

Kate started walking towards the dinning room and as she went she said. "We had better head to dinner. It's a tradition here that the Ambassador asks the last one to sit to lead the group in some kind of dinner invocation. The Ambassador has found that this little trick gets everyone in and seated very quickly. I would guess that you aren't much for leading a group in a pre-dinner prayer. And I would insist that you seat me."

"I was unaware of this motivational strategy. We better run then. With luck we can knock down one of the older couples on our way in. Then for sure we, rather I, won't have to lead the group in singing *Kumbaya* before the meal."

Kate laughed as we headed into the dining room.

I seated Kate and, sure enough, our table was in the boondocks. Most people would have been disappointed to be located so far from the action. I was glad I was not one of them. There was actually the possibility that I could continue my conversation with her. Strange how things work out, I was really glad that I had been forced to attend this dinner.

It was almost 11:00 pm and the dinner was almost over. Kate and I had spent the entire meal talking basically only to each other. I knew it was rude to the other guests but I really didn't care. I was having fun, a lot more fun than I had had in a long time and did not want to ruin it. Shortly the Ambassador would give the perfunctory after dinner speech and then everyone would be free to leave. If this were San Francisco or Washington, the power couples would repair to the latest "hot" lounge for a late evening discussion. But this was London and last call was 11:00 pm and here they meant last call. Since it was nearly 11:00 pm I assumed most people would just go home. I wanted to bring Kate to my place but since I had no place I figured that wouldn't work. I could always see if the Ambassador could loan me a room but then again the ambassador might not approve. Bad form and all to have the Ambassador phone the National Security Advisor and ask what kind of person he had sent over here.

I saw Kate glance at her watch. I figured I had had more fun than she and that she wanted a way to get out. I began to speak when the room became silent.

"...and so my dinner companions, I wish you a good evening and a bright tomorrow," the Ambassador had concluded his benediction.

I turned to Kate. "I enjoyed meeting you. I rarely attend functions like this and when I do I am reminded as to why I don't go to them very often."

"You mean that no one ever invites you?"

"Well, yes, that and they are usually the most boring things on earth. Birthday dinner with the in-laws is positively light and airy by comparison." I saw Kate's expression change. She took my light joke about in-laws the wrong way. However, it was nice to know that her quick watch check was just a check to see what time it was and that she was interested in me. I continued, "Not that I have any in-laws; just experience with my brother's in-laws." Kate's face softened perceptively. Seizing the moment, "Would you like to have lunch tomorrow?"

"Yes, I would like that a lot." Kate responded.

"Why don't you pick the place? I can meet you there."

"Okay. Do you want bad English food or worse English food?" Kate laughed as she asked.

"How about a place where we could get some fish and chips? I like fish and chips well enough, but fish and chips is really a great excuse for a pint," I played along.

"Then let's meet at Jonathon's. It is right off Piccadilly near Lilywhites. Say at 1:30 or, as they say here half-one."

"Sounds great. I will see you there."

43

Abdul Aziz waited until all the other passengers had cleared the plane. The first class cabin flight attendant looked at him. Abdul could see a question in the man's eyes. He knew that most first class passengers deplaned quickly before the usual crush from the main cabin occurred. His slow departure was indeed a bit unusual. He was pretty sure that the flight crewmember wondered why anyone who could avoid it would want to get caught in the traditionally long lines in customs. Of course, this was exactly why he had waited.

The data files located on hard drive of his laptop computer consisted of sensitive econometric models, oil production and banking reserve figures. This information was so sensitive that he would not want to explain to some members of the government how he came to have such data. For that reason he wanted to wait to go through customs until the crowds were at their greatest and the inspectors' interest was limited to the obvious and regular type customs infractions such as bringing alcohol into the country or banned videos or music cd's.

As planned, the crowds were large and lines were long. It was Monday night in Riyadh and two other international flights, one from Zurich and another from London, had landed at approximately the same time as his. It was no coincidence that he had chosen his flight from Istanbul to coincide with these other flights. As he approached the lines at customs he looked to see which inspector seemed the most bored. He made his choice and waited patiently in that line. Finally it was his turn to go to the inspection station. The customs inspector asked if he had anything to declare, which of course he did not. Prior to arriving at the inspector's station Aziz had made sure to warm up his computer. In that way he would be ready when the customs agent asked about it; the less time to think the better. As requested Aziz flipped open the screen and showed the man the main menu. The inspector scanned the menu and then asked that Aziz show him a few files. Once that was done to the guard's satisfaction Aziz was waved through.

He moved with the crowds to the transportation area where a ride would be awaiting. There to his right, near the cabstand, was the white Audi he was expecting. The trip to the Inter-Continental Hotel would take no more than thirty-five minutes. The meeting with his father, the Senior Oil Minister of the Kingdom of Saudi Arabia wouldn't take that long. The vehicle pulled up to the hotel. Abdul got out quickly; declining any help from the doorman entered the lobby and headed for the elevator bank.

44

Fahad Amani was just about to end his shift. He had been called to the airport by the airport security office. A suspicious-looking shipment had come in from Damascus, Syria. The airport police had shown him the crate that had been delivered by Turkish Air. Fahad knew airport security had been justified in their concerns. It was a rare day when Syrian goods were shipped anywhere on a Turkish airline. The crate had been isolated in a storage warehouse the farthest from anything that might be damaged if there was an unexpected explosion.

Fortunately the explosives team had gotten the shipping crate open without incident. He and the head of airport security then had gone to investigate the contents of the box. It was at that point that Fahad relaxed and knew his long workday would not be any longer. The contents of the box were as the shipping manifest had stated -- dried dates. Both Fahad and the Chief of Security knew it was reasonable to ship perishable goods by air and by the fastest means available. Apparently in this case it was a Turkish air flight.

Fahad turned to the chief, "Well it looks as if everything is okay. I appreciate your efforts."

"I am terribly sorry for having extended your day. I know it is late and I have made it even longer."

"Don't be concerned about the time. Your help will be highlighted in my report."

As Fahad was walking back through the airport's main lobby to retrieve his vehicle he thought he recognized Abdul Aziz. It seemed odd to him that such an important man was carrying his own luggage and was without escort. Fahad decided to follow Abdul Aziz. He would do so at a distance and with great caution. There was no point in letting curiosity get him in trouble with so powerful a man as the Chief Oil Minister of the country.

Fahad followed him outside. Aziz walked towards a white Audi. Fahad was fortunate to have parked in a temporary space in front of the airport so he was ready to pull out quickly. Aziz got in the Audi, which was surely a government car with a government driver. The vehicle traveled to the Inter-Continental Hotel where Abdul got quickly out of the car. Actually, quickly was understating it; he practically ran from the car into the lobby ignoring the doorman's offer of help. This was a very unusual course of action for a person of importance. Fahad again parked his car in a temporary space and entered the hotel lobby just in time to see Abdul look around and enter the elevator. Fahad watched as the elevator went all the way to the top floor.

45

The elevator stopped. Abdul took out a key, inserted it into the lock, turned it, and the elevator's security system released the door to this exclusive floor. Abdul walked to the suite at the end of the floor. The door swung open revealing a suite as opulent as any in the world. Striding across the lobby ready to embrace his son was Hazim Aziz, the Senior Oil Minister of the Kingdom of Saudi Arabia and for this year, the Chairman of OPEC.

"My son, it is good to see you."

"And it is good to see you father," replied Abdul.

"Please come and sit," said Hazim Aziz.

"Has the King's health improved any?" Abdul asked.

"The Monarch is not aging well. He is growing more infirm as the days go by. The Crown Prince runs the country in his name. That works for daily issues but it does nothing for the larger issues affecting us. There is a battle in the Royal family. Some want the country to become an Islamic state others do not."

"Where does the Crown Prince stand?"

"He tries to appease both sides."

"Does this work?"

"The Prince is a remarkable man. Yes it has worked and as long as he remains in power that fact will probably remain the case."

"And you how does this rift affect you?"

"My oil policy suggestions are constantly being second-guessed, debated and overruled in the name of family appeasement. Inaction over action is the current state of affairs."

"That means the Royal Family remains tied to the United States." Aziz said.

"The memories of the Gulf Wars remain strong."

"Yes father but the United States saved us for its own benefit, not ours."

"Not all in the Royal Family would agree with that analysis."

"There are others outside the Royal Family that would agree with me."

"What you say is true but dangerous to speak aloud. Have you, as I asked, talked to your Cousin Kemal?"

"Yes, I have. He is ready for us to move forward with our portion of the plan."

"That is good, very good. Shortly we will be able to throw off the control the Americans assert over our lives and our destiny. Please review these papers and I will tell you how we shall begin."

Abdul Aziz scanned the papers his father gave him. The plan was brilliant. The beauty of this plan was it attacked America in more than one way. He smiled, before long America would be challenged on many fronts. Abdul knew it was important to have a multi-faceted plan. In the past, failure had always come because any attacks on America were singularly dimensional.

"Father, I am impressed."

"My son, I am glad you are. Soon, very soon those godless Americans will come to us and it will be us who make the rules, not the other way around. It is essential that Kemal Kanuni follow through with his side of the bargain."

"I know that father. He will do it because it is in his interest to do it." Abdul answered.

"Good point. Here, I have some other things you will need." Hazim opened a special briefcase. "This is a secure cell phone. You can reach me from anywhere in the world. The special encryption device prevents anyone from tracing your call. It can also be hooked to any standard fax machine and will be equally secure. As you know, we will need to keep in close contact over the next several months to make this plan work."

"Indeed, father." Abdul looked at his watch. "I must go. My flight will be leaving shortly. I will contact you again when I get to London and get my new office set up."

"Go with Allah, my son."

46

Fahad Amani decided to wait at the hotel and see if anything happened. Seeing the son of the Oil Minister basically sneak into the country deserved at least some of his attention. He decided to go to the gift shop in the lobby and purchase a newspaper. About twenty minutes had passed on his stakeout when his cell phone rang. He checked the incoming number. It had to be Mustafa Zell. Mustafa's shift followed his. Fahad realized he had completely forgotten to phone in to headquarters.

Fahad flipped the phone and answered.

"Fahad, this is Mustafa. Are you all right? I expected to see you when I came in."

"Thank you for asking. Yes I am fine."

"Where are you?"

"I am in the lobby of the Intercontinental Hotel." Considering all things Fahad decided a little backup might not be a bad thing. "I think you should come over here. I was at the airport about ready to return to headquarters when I noticed Abdul Aziz in the airport. He was acting a little strangely so I decided to follow him."

"Certainly I will come right away, but when you say strangely, what do you mean?" Zell asked.

"Well, he was acting like an average business man. You know, none of the trappings of someone important. "Do you know the man?" Fahad asked.

"Yes I do. I have never known him not to travel with an entourage." Zell said in agreement. "What happened next?"

"I followed him to the hotel. Again he did everything possible to avoid drawing attention to himself."

"Maybe he is meeting a lover".

"Maybe, but I don't think so. If it were a lover, the lover would have gone to meet him. No one thinks of coming to Saudi Arabia to fool around. The penalties for getting caught are just too high here."

"I see what you mean."

"I have this gut feeling that it might be something else."

"Your famous intuition?" Zell said.

"Yes, I have to go. But call me when you get to the hotel. Don't come in just wait in the car."

"No problem. I will be there shortly."

"Thank you." Fahad went back to pretending to read his newspaper.

47

Fifteen minutes had passed since his initial conversation with Mustafa when his cell phone buzzed in his pocket again.

"I am here. What do you want me to do?"

"I want you to follow Abdul Aziz when he comes out of the hotel."

"If he comes out. What are you going to do?"

"Correct, if he comes out. I will wait here and see if anything happens. I will call you when he is in the lobby."

Fahad Amani sat patiently reading his newspaper when saw Abdul get off an elevator and enter the lobby. Fahad hit the send button of his phone having previously dialed the number.

"Yes," Mustafa answered.

"Get ready. He will be out the doors in just a moment."

"I see him. He is getting into a white Audi."

"It must be the same car he came in. I followed him in a white Audi to this hotel. Call me after he gets to his destination."

"Okay."

Enough time had passed that he found he actually had read most of the paper when Hazim Aziz exited the elevator. To the trained eye the disguise was not very good, but to the mostly foreign staff of the hotel it was good enough. What was unusual was that only one other person got off the elevator with him. Fahad knew that person was his bodyguard. He too was disguised or at least had made an attempt at deception. It was hard to look inconspicuous when you looked like an American football player in a country of soccer players. In addition, there didn't seem to be a tailor in the world who could with any degree of success hide the bulge of a firearm worn under a suit coat.

The senior Oil Minister who was wearing sunglasses did not look around as he walked quickly but not too quickly across the lobby in the direction of the side entrance. Fahad quietly put down his paper and moved slowly behind the minister and his guard so as not to arouse anyone's attention. He remained hidden to them as they left the hotel and indeed there was a car waiting for them. However, it was not the minister's regular Mercedes; rather it was a white Audi. He saw both the minister and his bodyguard get into the car and speed quickly away as he exited the building. Fahad knew he would never be able to catch up with them; his car was on the other side of the building. All he could do now was to wait for Mustafa's call.

48

How strange, Fahad Amani mused as he walked back to his car. He had just witnessed what appeared to be a clandestine get together between Hazim Aziz and his son Abdul Aziz. Why would the arguably second most powerful man in the country need to visit secretly with his son? Fahad racked his brain but could think of no other explanation other than it had to be a secret meeting. The Oil Minister had apparently traveled to this parley in a white Audi. Senior government ministers never traveled in anything less than a 700 class Mercedes. Could he have just been sacked and I've just not heard about it yet? That would be an explanation of the vehicle downgrade but he doubted the Oil Minister had been fired Almost Fahad immediately rejected the thought. If Aziz had been just been fired there would have been no way that his son could have had enough time to fly in.

As Fahad approached his car he noticed the air was cooler now. The sun had set and with it some of the heat. He hoped Mustafa would call soon, but most of all he hoped Mustafa had learned something to help explain away this strange situation. He had just settled into his car when his cell phone rang.

"Hello? This is Fahad Amani."

"Fahad, this is Mustafa."

"Yes, Mustafa, what did you find?"

"I followed our man directly back to the airport." Zell began.

"How did he behave?"

"Like a businessman taking a business trip. "He went directly to the business class lounge and then caught his flight.

"Nothing more?"

"No, nothing more."

"Where did he go?" Fahad asked

"It appears he flew on British Air."

"Could you tell what the destination was?"

There were a number of departures at this time of the day. But the flight looks like its ultimate destination is London." Zell said.

"And no one looked at him twice?"

"No, the desk at this particular time of day is manned by an all British crew. They check in the passengers and then become passengers themselves as they catch the flight home."

Fahad was growing wary. It was apparent that Mustafa did not want to be too specific. His assumption was that Zell was concerned that someone might be eavesdropping on their conversation. He admired Mustafa's caution; he showed initiative beyond his years.

"I see. It appears our friend got lucky with his choice of flight time."

"Yes indeed, it does seem that way."

"Thank you for your help. I'm going to go home now. Can you come in a few minutes early so we can compare notes?"

"No problem, I'll see you tomorrow. Good night."

49

Hazim sat in the back seat of his Mercedes as it sped to the Oil Ministry. If his driver had bothered to look back at his passenger he would not have noticed anything out of the norm. The Oil Minister as usual was spending his time studying various reports. In fact the reports Hazim were reviewing were not his normal ministry reports. The reports from his source at the Finance Ministry showed he had been more successful than he could have imagined with his manipulations in the market. He now had amassed enough money to implement his plan.

He needed to act quickly. If he did not he was certain that some young buck reporter or worse yet, some liberated female reporter, would stumble across the fact that Saudi Arabia was not paying its bills. Over the last several years he had systematically caused the Government to reduce it bill-paying timeliness. If it were not for the country's reputation he could understand why no one would do consider doing business with them. Every plan had its vulnerable side and this was his plan's Achilles heel. That is why he had waited to the last possible moment to implement this stage. He knew that once he had committed to this action, there would be no turning back. As they say, he would have crossed the proverbial Rubicon. If he were discovered after the King was dead, it would not matter, for he would be the president of the newly founded Islamic Republic of Saudi Arabia. He would be a hero because of his actions. If he were discovered before the assassination, hopefully he would have time to arrange for an accident.

A great risk, but again the reward was also great. There were many levels of risk. Even if the original plan went smoothly, he did not trust Kemal Kanuni, or rather he trusted him completely; completely enough to know that Kemal would kill him and Abdul at his first opportunity. However, he had known this from the beginning. He just hoped that the precautions he had taken would work out as well as his financial dealings. He had done his best. It was up to Allah now. The car slowed as it approached the Ministry Building. It was time to gather his thoughts for the day.

50

Kemal Kanuni sat, in traditional garb, under the blazing television lights trying not to rub off his makeup. Thirty seconds to broadcast. The producer of the Istanbul radio and television studio indicated that everything was ready to go. He looked again and the producer was showing with his fingers three, two, and one pointed at him. The camera light came on. It was time to begin.

The television and radio broadcast was about to be transmitted to the entire Islamic world, not just the countries in the League. Significantly, both CNN and BBC were picking up the feed live.

"I have the saddest news to report. Our great leader, Hakan Kanuni, the founder of our League, a man without whom we would never had had the opportunities we see today; has suffered a most serious stroke. Twelve hours ago our beloved Chairman fell ill. As all of you know this is also a personal tragedy for me. Not only was Hakan Kanuni our guiding light he is my uncle, more than an uncle, almost a father. When I was but a young man my father died and Uncle Hakan took me and raised me. He made me what I am today."

"It doesn't seem possible this has happened. It was just a few short weeks ago that he and I addressed you in what had to be his finest hour, his and my overwhelming affirmation by you of our roles as Chairman and Vice-Chairman of our new League. "

"Therefore it is with a very heavy heart I have agreed to accept our Council's request to take up his mantel of leadership. I know you all join me in hoping my duties will only be temporary, until our beloved leader returns to us in complete health by the will of Allah. I pledge to follow my uncle's policy of peace and prosperity. My desire and hope is to fulfill the word of Allah in all my dealings. I will remain as he, your humble servant. Peace to you all."

The camera light went off. The studio lights returned to normal. There was one more addition task. He needed to make sure the Western countries were comfortable with this sudden change in leadership. To alleviate as many concerns as possible he had scheduled key interviews with CNN and BBC.

51

"Jamie, I have a great idea for a series of articles."

"What is it?"

"Before I tell you I want you to promise that if you like the idea you will let me do the series. I don't want you handing it off to senior Sam just because he has been here for 100 hundred years."

Jamie O'Doul laughed, "A little competitive today?"

"Not just today. I want you to promise." Kate knew that O'Doul was crusty on the outside but was basically soft hearted and with a little pushing would grant her, her wish.

O'Doul sighed. "Okay, if I like your idea, you can do it all."

"As you might remember I recently went to Turkey."

"Yes as I recall you did a series of stories on the unique situation that Turkey finds itself in today."

"I'm glad you remembered," Kate said.

"Oh I remember quite well. You compared Turkey and Russia as being lands comprised of a series of contradictions. Turkey is Islamic but not Arabic. It is a democracy but with a very influential military. In addition there is a strong undercurrent of Islamic fundamentalism running through the country while it is officially nonsectarian.

You went on to point out with associated details that only Russia and Turkey are the two countries in the world that occupy two continents. Also like Russia it is culturally both Western and Eastern in nature. Furthermore you pointed out that Turkey is a member of NATO but can't seem to break into European Union."

"I guess you do read my stuff."

"I read everyone's stuff; it's only the better stuff I remember."

"Thank you."

"What's your idea?"

"I want to do a series on the new economic League founded by the Hakan Kanuni. I want to approach the stories from both an economic and historic point of view. I think given the right set of circumstances the League could become a country, a union of Turkic Countries."

O'Doul asked, "You mean a possible second coming of the Ottoman Empire."

"Yes something like that. Plus with the unexpected passing of Hakan Kanuni, Kemal Kanuni has ascended to the Chairmanship. I think he has personality appeal. He is handsome and mysterious. Readers love that kind of stuff."

"Sounds interesting, what did you specifically have in mind?"

"I thought I could run four or five articles. The first couple of articles would lay the groundwork for the next three. The first would be on Hakan Kanuni and his role as founder of the new League. The next would be about the countries comprising the league, their histories and cultural composition. These stories would lead to the meat of her investigation. The third story would be about the new leader, Kemal Kanuni. The following story would be about the current economic opportunities of the League, primarily its oil production potential. The last article would be a speculative article about the future of the League and its leader."

"How much time do you think this will take?"

"Well I have done some preliminary research already, enough material for the first two pieces and probably the fourth. The last will fall out of the first four. I don't have much if anything on Kemal Kanuni. I know he was educated in England and had worked in London before returning to Kazakhstan and then eventually Istanbul. I thought I would begin by going to Oxford and see if I can find anyone who knew him in his University days. But to give you a specific time frame, two or three weeks."

O'Doul nodded and said simply, "Have at it."

52

Chairman Kemal Kanuni entered the League's new Council Chambers. The delegates now designated as ministers by their respective countries rose to greet him. Kemal returned their greetings, waving his hand and saying, "May Allah be praised. Please be seated." The ministers moved to their designated places and waited for Kemal to call the meeting to order. The agenda was brief but extremely important.

"However before I begin I would like to report on a particularly important item. No discussion is necessary this is for information purposes only. Turkey is prepared to recognize Kurdistan. With this recognition the Turkish-Azerbaijani Consortium, which was ready to put its operations in mothballs and reassign its crews, is now ready to connect the two ends of the pipeline through Kurdistan. Concessions from our League were instrumental in this recognition. In addition, Turkey has promised to provide protection to the consortium and its workers. As a part of NATO the Turkish Air Force is a formidable weapon of protection in the region. The League will ensure the pipeline is completed as fast as possible. With its completion we will have the hard currency to do the things that need to be done, the things we have talked about for so long."

"The first item of our meeting is the selection of a new Vice-Chairman. The sad and untimely death of my uncle necessitates that we choose someone to take my former position. I would like to put the name of Hakim Ton into nomination. He too recently experienced an enormous personal tragedy, the death of our great friend and counselor, Dax Salyan. I am firmly convinced that he will be an outstanding Vice-Chairman for our Council. He will strengthen us in ways as no one else could. Do I hear a second?"

There were several cries of second, as it seemed that all wanted to second the nomination.

"Thank you. Does anyone else want to add another nominee?" There was total silence. "I gather that Hakim Ton has your unanimous support. Therefore, I declare him the Vice-Chairman of the Council. Hakim, please, if you will take the Vice-Chairman's place at the foot of this council table. Thank you.

"The next item I feel needs some explanation. For many years our Islamic world has not worked well together. Establishment of common goals and strategies among our many peoples has been insufficient. There have been many reasons for this. I don't want to dwell on what hasn't worked. It is simply my intent to change all of this. We all know of our great potential. We must reach that potential. We should be ashamed that we have not done better for our peoples. We have allowed our enormous assets, our national treasures to go to waste, to be controlled by the West. This must end. To do this we must improve the communication among the Islamic peoples. We cannot and will not continue to work in isolation from other oil- producing countries, the greatest of which, we all know, is Saudi Arabia. It is a fact that if you add our readily obtainable reserves to theirs, over 65% of the world's accessible supply of oil can be accounted for. For that reason I would like you to accept my recommendation that we grant full voting status in our council to Abdul Aziz."

Even though the council members knew of this agenda item they still sat in silence after Kemal's speech. Kemal began to speak again. I know what you are all thinking. You are asking the question, are we moving too fast? I will answer that question. Unequivocally No! This move makes good sense and it is not too soon." Kemal stopped speaking and looked at the delegates, waiting to hear any opposition. Almost as if on cue he heard clapping. Hakim Ton was clapping loudly and praising the requested action. Kemal turned and acknowledged his reaction, within seconds the remaining delegates all joined in.

"Thank you, fellow members of our Council. I will inform Abdul Aziz of your generous and gracious decision. Now to the last item."

"Our League needs a revised charter. Recent events have raised the level of our power in and responsibility to our member countries. Our old charter is inadequate. While this is truly a momentous step we can lose site of our direction in bureaucratic haggling for that reason I took the liberty of drafting such a statement for each of you to review. It can be found in the folders at each of your places."

The ministers in unison opened their folders, which contained a single sheet of paper. On that paper were the following words:

> The Turkic people, wishing to live in peace and harmony with the other people of the world, wish to unite to bring economic prosperity to our children and ourselves. We ask guidance from Allah in all our endeavors.

They all stared transfixed by the words in front of them. Silence filled the room for it seemed the longest time.

Then quietly, almost in a whisper, Kemal spoke. "Does anyone see the need for any changes?"

Hakim's voice filled the emptiness. "I believe this to be a magical statement. It represents our goals exactly. I know you are a man of low ambition, whose only desire is to see this charter fulfilled. I move to accept this document as written."

"Thank you for your support, Mr. Vice-Chairman. Does anyone object?" Kemal stood and looked around the table. "I see no objection. I want to thank you for your support. Over the next several months and years I will be working hard to fulfill the hopes and aspirations that you have placed in me." Still standing Kemal lifted his gavel and struck it, "I must prepare for the rally. This meeting is adjourned."

53

It was late in the afternoon. The rally had been scheduled to coincide with the cooling of the day and not conflict with evening prayers. But it did not matter, for today the heat and humidity hung in the stadium like an oppressive blanket. The national soccer stadium was packed to over capacity, filled with 100,000 men, women and children waiting to hear their new leader, Kemal Kanuni. The crowd sat in hushed anticipation as the hour of the speech approached. Kevin Law, the NSA station chief from the United States embassy and his counter part from the United Kingdom legation, Reginald Blaire, sat together in a small section reserved for the diplomatic corps. It seemed that they had drawn the rather undesirable assignment of having to sit through the new chairman's speech. Both men knew these speeches were usually long and always boring.

"Well, Reggie, I see you drew the short straw," Kevin said to his friend.

"I say there, Kev old boy, I don't see you off partying, do I?"

"Why, anytime we are together it is a party. You know at times like this I wished I had never learned the language. Do you know what we can expect today?"

"No, not really, but from what I hear we may actually find this entertaining. Rumor has it that this Kemal fellow is quite the orator."

"I have heard the same thing. But you know the people here don't get out much so it's hard to really judge what they say."

The sun had fallen behind the stage from which Kemal was to speak. A kind of anticipatory music began to play. Then the rumble began. First it was the music but soon it was evident that it was the crowd. Just as it seemed that the crowd reached the height of frenzy, doves were released and trumpets blared. Kemal Kanuni stepped out onto the dais. The sun shone behind and he appeared to radiate. He walked slowly and majestically to the microphone. As his speech began he spoke slowly and softly. Law saw the crowd strain to hear his every word. Then gradually he spoke louder and more quickly. Kemal Kanuni began to talk of the former greatness of the Turkic people and their future potential.

"This League will be greater than the sum of our parts. This League will build on our former greatness and it will take us to a new prominence in the World. The West will now listen to us, not the other way around. The West will come to us. Allah will make it so. Our oil wealth, our talents and most importantly our moral vision will lead us."

His impassioned speech had captured the crowd. As he raised his arms the entire stadium rose in unison. Law saw the crowd had begun to follow his every move, completely wrapped up in his words. Kanuni's speech ended and with it a total silence fell upon the crowd for a moment. Then as if a volcano had sprung to life, the crowd screamed and cheered. At that point there was no doubt that everyone, man, woman and child, would have done anything he asked.

Law turned to his associate. "Reggie, even if I didn't understand him, I think this crowd would have followed him anywhere. And I would have joined them!"

"I know what you mean. Does he remind you of someone?"

"I am afraid so. I know we usually stop for a pint after these affairs but I really must get my report on the wire home."

"Agreed, we will do it the next time."

54

I wasn't in London on holiday, far from it, but that didn't mean I wasn't flat-out tired. I needed some time to recharge my batteries. If I didn't get a break soon, I was afraid I would lose my effectiveness. In my line of work, all work and no play did really make you a dull boy. Many times a dull boy was a dead boy and that was something I didn't particularly want to be. I hoped taking some personal time today including my lunch date with Kate O'Hara would help. Normally, I would have taken the tube to Piccadilly Circus, but because the day was so nice I decided to walk. There was nothing like walking in London, unless it was walking in London on a sunny day. I planned to stop at Lilywhites and check out the latest sporting gear. As a rule I hated shopping, and to each rule there was an exception. In my case it was sporting goods stores. Lilywhites was the Cadillac, or rather the Rolls Royce, of sporting goods stores so I rarely if ever missed going there when in London.

Normally I could spend several hours looking at all the sports equipment. Today I was a little bit distracted, though, and I finished looking at the golf and soccer equipment early. I probably didn't want to admit it to myself, but I was excited about my lunch date. I was too old to act like a teenager, but the anticipation of seeing Kate again was a nice feeling. I had to also admit to myself it was one I hadn't had in quite some time. I was still running a little early so I stopped at a newsstand and purchased a paper. I love reading the London tabloids, not much news, but a lot of entertainment value. As I looked over all the choices there was a headline about the coming of an

Islamic Messiah. I couldn't resist. I purchased the paper and headed to Jonathon's to wait for Kate.

The story talked about the League, now officially named Bir. It described the historical significance of the name. How Osman referred to the original founder of the Ottoman Empire, a tall man with a charismatic personality. It went on to say how the term horde referred to the ancient organization of the Turkic people in Central Asia. How it was the intent of the League's founder Hakan Kanuni to link all Turkic people into a single economic unit like the current European Union. Lastly the article went on to describe Kemal Kanuni and how he just recently had become Chairman. The piece was flattering to him describing him as a little known but emerging world leader.

About 1:15 pm Kate arrived. By then I had finished the newspaper article, "Hi," I said as Kate sat at the table. "You're early."

"Hi yourself. I know. Is that a problem?"

"No, not at all. In fact, I'm glad," folding the paper and putting it on the table.

Kate glanced at a banner of the paper as I put it down. "You're reading that thing. I don't think it even qualifies as bird-cage-bottom material."

"Professional jealousy?" I retorted. I could see Kate was about to respond when her eyes drifted to the article on Kemal Kanuni. Without speaking, she reached across the table and grabbed the paper and began to read the article. I was surprised at the change in her. One minute she had been sitting down joking the next minute she had drifted off to another world. Within minutes she had read the article and as if coming out of a trance began to speak as if nothing had happened.

"Hardly. I just hate to see trees wasted."

"That was a nice trick. How do you do it?" I asked.

"What do you mean?"

"Well, you start to respond, drift off into the paper and pick up our conversation as if nothing happened."

"I'm sorry. You see, I saw the lead article and I was curious as to what it said."

"Really? Why's that?"

I could see she was ready to respond but then hesitated and said nothing. Without knowing it just occurred to me that I might have accidentally moved our embryonic relationship to another level. I waited to see what she would say or if she would say anything at all not so much out of some insight into female behavior but total ignorance. Compounding ignorance with action I decided it was time for a tactical retreat. "Earth to Kate, earth to Kate," I joked. "You drifted again. Are you sure you feel okay?"

"Yes, I'm sorry I did sort of leave didn't I?"

"Yes, but it's okay."

"I was surprised at the article. You see I just pitched my editor about a new writing assignment. He gave me the go ahead and..."

"...And part of if had to do with this Kemal Kanuni guy," I finished her sentence; again immediately concerned I had overstepped my bounds. To my relief I saw she wasn't upset, she looked relieved actually.

"Exactly and when I saw the story, I figured someone had beaten me to the idea. But I don't feel so bad after reading it. The stuff was softball material. I plan to be much more in-depth particularly the financial aspects. On reflection, I think this is really pretty good. This article means there may be more interest in the subject than I had originally thought."

I respond again without thinking, "So more people will read your stuff and you will move a step closer to the Pulitzer Prize."

"That's it exactly. Come to think, this is better than pretty good, this is great!"

I was relieved to see she hadn't minded my interruptions. She had gone with them and for me that was really good. Usually I can get off on the wrong foot when I make some unsolicited comments. Hoping not to break my lucky streak, I changed the topic.

"I assume you live in London proper."

"I do, I thought about living out of the city, because of costs and all but I just couldn't do it."

"Why is that?"

"Too much going on professionally for one," she responded. "Besides I got lucky and managed to find some roommates with whom I could share costs."

"Where do you live?"

"Half way between Kensington and Earl's Court. I share a flat with two other working class girls, June and Maureen."

"Working class?"

"Yea, we have to work to live, weren't born to the right parents."

I laughed. "I am very familiar with that status. Are they locals?"

"No, June is Canadian from Vancouver and Maureen is from Australia."

"Quite impressive, truly an international household."

"It would be more impressive if we actually did things together. Our schedules are so out of sync we seldom even see each other. Though we do schedule a regular monthly work party."

"Work party?" I asked. Kate laughed. I liked the way her eyes twinkled when she did.

"Yes once a month we meet to clean the place. We order pizza and wine."

"Doesn't sound like much gets cleaned," I said

"You are right, but we sure have fun... And it gives us the excuse to meet the following month because we know the place will really need to be cleaned by then." With that Kate grabbed the menu and said, "I am hungry. Let's order."

I'm hungry too and pleased. I can see Kate is the kind of lady who actually wants to eat and won't order wood chips unsweetened with a side of water.

Kate looked at me after our lunches came. "Hey! You've asked all the questions now it's my turn. We've established that you work for the State department, right?"

"We have. I'm a trouble shooter." I responded.

"A trouble shooter?" She looked at me quizzically.

"There are times when there are conflicts in the information the Department receives. The information is what the Department uses to help make policy. My job is to clarify and resolve those differences."

"So you are sort of a modern day Solomon?"

"In a sense yes, I gather information and then make certain recommendations. The higher ups then choose to use or not use the data I give them." I filled in a few more details of my personal history that we hadn't talked about before. She seemed to be genuinely interested.

"I've done a lot of talking for me. I have some questions too." She smiled.

"Good. But I've got to get back to work. Why don't you save them until we get meet again?"

This was the first time in my entire life; at least since the second grade that I had been asked out on a date. Being asked sure took a lot of stress out of things. "Did you just ask me out?" I asked.

"It seems I did. I've never done that before but yes I did. Is it a problem?"

"Not at all. It's just the first time for me too."

55

Akam Bizhanov did not know why nor did he care. All that was important was he had a job to do. He considered himself a professional and he meant to do this job professionally. He had been following Lydia Christakos now for over a week waiting for just the right time. The right time had arrived.

From what he had observed she was the perfect candidate for the accident he had planned. She was young, privileged, attractive and best of all, headstrong. It took little effort to intercept her phone calls; because of this he knew she was going back to London this afternoon. A new Andrew Lloyd Webber play was casting and she wanted desperately to be in it. Bizhanov did not know if her new boyfriend, *Randolph upper crust* would go back with her. It really didn't matter; two would be as easy as one.

As the day wore on the weather turned unrepentantly bad; a particularly nasty storm had angrily blustered in from the North Atlantic. It was slightly less than one hundred kilometers back to her place in So-Ho. Bizhanov knew regardless of the route she chose the first twenty five kilometers would be covered using two lane country roads; after that it would be the M-I back to London.

Bizhanov had parked just off the road leading to where Lydia had spent the weekend. He had a clear view of its front and her car, a green BMW convertible. It was common for day-hikers to leave their cars on the side of the rode, so it was most unlikely anyone would take notice of him. It was mid afternoon when she came out of the front door, with her luggage.

It appeared that she and her boyfriend were arguing. She was waving her arms and walking back and forth. He was pointing at the car and was trying to stop her pacing. This went on for several minutes until she threw her bag into the trunk. She got in the car slammed the door, and spun the wheels as she flew down the driveway. She hardly hesitated at the main road before turning right and accelerating away.

Bizhanov was grateful he had taken the precaution of starting his motor. If he hadn't it was conceivable she could have gotten away from him. He followed her down the main road. She was driving like a woman possessed. As he reached for his cell phone he hoped he wouldn't get killed as he was moved wildly back and forth across the road trying to keep up with her. He hit the programmed number, spoke briefly and hung up.

It was beginning to rain hard dropping the visibility. With the rain she had at least slowed down enough to stay on her side of the road. Bizhanov had dropped back about fifty meters. The time was right. As she rounded a turn she came upon a couple of lorries. The trucks were running two abreast effectively blocking the entire road forcing her to slow down. She was very near getting on to the motorway, but rather than waiting for the road to widen, she pressed up on the truck in her lane, flashing her lights and blowing her horn, gesturing for the drivers to move so she could pass. As a common courtesy most all truck drivers would have made an effort to do this for a pretty lady in a fancy car.

This time was different. Rather than moving the two trucks sped up in unison, with the truck in the opposite lane falling back slightly so as to be parallel with Christakos. While this was happening Bizhanov had closed up behind her. She was effectively boxed in and trapped by the movements of the other three vehicles. The convoy began to accelerate. The truck in the outside lane began to move over forcing her closer and closer to the edge of the road. Her road visibility consisted of nothing more than the back of and the sides of the two trucks. She began to slow and as she did Bizhanov came up from behind and bumped her car. It was a gentle nudge, but was enough to force her to accelerate to keep up with the lead vehicle.

Bizhanov had her just where he wanted and gave the truckers their final signal by flashing his lights. The outside truck moved slightly away from Christako's BMW allowing her to move slightly away from the road's edge. With that final move all her momentum was straight ahead. As this happened Bizhanov dropped back to make room for the truck that had been running next to Christakos' car. Meanwhile the lead truck pulled away, waited to the last possible moment and then followed the road, which turned dramatically to the left. It was unlikely that Christakos had the driving skills to follow the road but even if she did she certainly did not have the time. Her BMW continued in her original direction straight into a five-foot high stonewall surrounding a cemetery. Bizhanov watched in his review mirror as the car disintegrated upon impact and burst into flames.

Bizhanov smiled as he got on the M-I. Later when he checked the newspapers he would see the police had determined that she had left the road at approximately one hundred kilometers per hour. They could find no apparent mechanical reason for the incident and thus had attributed it to poor weather and poorer driving.

56

Abdul Aziz stared out the first-class window of his British Air flight as it made its way to London. Had there been something to see it did would not have mattered for he was lost in thought. His father's plan was brilliant. If there was ever an opportunity to put that godless country in its place, this plan was it. The Islamic people would regain their rightful place in the world order and he and his family would be one of the main reasons. He checked his watch. In just a few hours the plane would be landing and he would make his way to the offices of Winslow and Sons Ltd. Investment Bankers.

Winslow and Sons Ltd. Investment Bankers was a small investment company founded in 1875. His father had acquired the firm about fifteen years earlier when the last of the "Sons" had died and there were no family members left to run the company. Actually Trafalgar Overseas Ltd., a Netherlands Antilles corporation, had acquired one hundred percent of the stock of the investment firm. His father controlled the trust that owned this Caribbean-based shell corporation. Abdul knew it was virtually impossible for anyone to find out the true ownership of the investment company. Success of the plan demanded this secrecy.

Hans Schmidt was the President of the company and to the entire world, the owner. Originally an East German communist rehabilitated after the Wall fell, Hans was just the kind of man for their purposes. In actuality, his only rehabilitation had been the price for which he would steal. He did, however, have one other endearing quality, his hatred of the United States of

America. To him, America had caused his country to cease to exist. Hans thought himself a patriot. So even though he felt no remorse and was happy to cheat and steal from his fellow East Germany citizens while the communists were in power, he was outraged when this opportunity was denied him upon reunification. Abdul thought this a strange personality quirk considering that in his new role he could make substantially more money than under the regime of the German Democratic Republic. Abdul believed that Herr Schmidt would do anything to seek revenge on the United States. Nonetheless he wanted to make sure there was no confusion when it came to implementing his father's options programs. Abdul closed his eyes to get a little rest, knowing it would do no good to be tired before the process began, for this task would be a marathon, not a sprint.

57

Kemal allowed himself to be pleased with the progress of his plans. He knew there was always danger congratulating oneself too soon, but even he had to admit things were going well. His margin of victory in the recent election was overwhelming. He was the most popular man in the Turkic world. Along with his popularity he had garnered a great deal of power. He had become de facto leader over all the countries in the league. The West, in particular America, viewed him as a progressive man of peace.

He was back in Istanbul, his new home base, to begin the second and final phase of his plan. Today was Friday and soon he was expected to be at evening prayers. He had chosen a nearby mosque this week as part of his new tradition of attending local religious services. He knew the people loved that he attended services at a different neighborhood mosque each week. It did not matter which country he was in at the time, all that mattered was that he was there, a religious man who was in touch with the common man. As the leader he was allowed the privilege of interpreting the Koran for those attending services. This privilege was proving invaluable to his plans.

All successes have unintended consequences, in his case it was the loss of personal time. It was becoming harder and harder to take time off. Kemal heard the rustling of bed sheets. He looked over and saw two of the advantages of having some time off. Two lovely young women were waiting for him. He knew little about them and did not care. They were Russian or Romanian, not locals and that is all that matter. Even if they could talk no one would understand them. It was obvious they needed money and how they got it mattered little. They were willing and that was all that mattered. They were willing in the way he had grown so fond. He had first tried the *ménage a trios* while at Oxford. He had found that he had exceptional stamina and satisfying more than one lady proved not to be difficult. He motioned for them to come to him. He loved for the two of them to explore each other while they undressed him. They came to him their bodies flushed and nipples hard. As they approached he glanced at the clock on the nightstand. He had given orders to his staff not to be disturbed. On prior Friday afternoons he had hinted to his staff that he used this time to prepare for the night's Koran teaching. While he believed his orders would be followed without question or hesitation, providing a religious reason would ensure a bit of added incentive in an uncertain world.

58

Hazim Aziz sat in the backseat of his limousine with the privacy glass fully up as his driver took him back to the Oil Ministry Building from his regular Wednesday meeting with the old King and the Crown Prince. From memory he dialed his son's phone number on his encrypted cell phone.

"How did your meeting go," Abdul asked?

"It is not over. The King was very weak today. The Crown Prince asked that I return later after the King had had time to rest. But to answer your question, the King liked my suggestion, better yet so did the Crown Prince."

"Won't the Foreign Minister be upset about you stepping into his territory?"

"A little maybe but I don't think enough to cause any problems. I pointed out that since the Gulf I we have been supplying all of Jordan's oil at substantially below market prices. I then indicated that because of this fact it was an issue upon which the Oil Ministry needed to take the lead. I also assured the Royal Highness that I would contact the Foreign Minister to co-ordinate the meeting."

"Did they bring up any issues with the Jordanian government of which you were unaware?"

"None, even if they had I would have turned it aside invoking national pride and our petro-power."

"An intoxicating combination indeed. Very good, I will continue coordinating things on this end," Abdul said.

"Good. I believe everyone will accept my proposed timing of the summit. The King is scheduled for his annual checkup in London. From my sources in Jordan we know that about the same time their King is to be there for a cancer follow up visit." Hazim said. "I am almost back to the office. I will call you again as soon as I have anything. Good-bye my son."

"Good-bye, father."

59

"Majesty, Crown Prince, I would like to begin our discussion with the status of our current accounts." Hazim Aziz began as the Wednesday meeting resumed. "I would like to say your Highness looks much better after your rest. I hope you feel as well."

"Thank you, yes I feel much better, please continue with your report." The King answered.

"As you are well aware, only you, the Crown Prince and a few senior ministers of both the oil and finance ministries know that the Kingdom lives hand-to-mouth economically. As great as the cash flows are coming into the country, they are equally great going out."

The Prince spoke, "So in essence the current accounts of our country regularly hover at or near zero. What about the international finance experts? Do you think they suspect this is the case?"

"Yes I do. They are not stupid, but I doubt they have any idea as to its extent." The Oil Minister responded.

The King struggled to speak. "We are not an economic basket case. Let us increase our cash flow by increasing oil production."

Aziz responded, "Increasing production does not, however, come without certain consequences."

"Yes, yes I know but the Royal Family is willing to live with those consequences. As you know, America has been urging us to increase our oil production."

"Of that I am aware." Aziz answered.

"I had a telephone conference call with the American secretaries of Treasury and Commerce yesterday," the Crown Prince said. "They again requested that the Kingdom increase its oil production."

Aziz paused before he spoke again. "I suppose it was a typical request. From my experience they can't seem to understand that what is good for them or what they think is good for them is not necessarily best for us."

"Agreed Minister, I am never quite certain whether these Americans are ignorant or arrogant."

"Basically, sir, I think they are easy to understand if you think of them as the spoiled teenagers of the world."

"Good point."

"As you know, your Highness, we do not normally just agree to do what they want. However, this time I suggest that we have an exception to the rule. Our interests and America's interest seem to be the same at this time. Our cash flow situation demands that we increase our production."

"What of our OPEC friends?"

"Sire, cheating within OPEC is as expected as a camel's foul temper. The key to getting along within OPEC is simply not to cheat more than one's fair share. The Kingdom has maintained its production quotas longer than any other member state. Actually, it is our turn to bend the rules."

"Are there any other reasons to or not to increase production?"

"Actually, there is a very good reason to increase our production."

"What is that, Hazim?"

"My intelligence sources have informed me the new Turkic League in central Asia is about to become a player in the market place. It seems its years of potential will actually be realized and quite soon."

The Crown Prince looked at his brother and the Oil Minister. "Then we would have a difficult competitor for the American market."

The King nodded and spoke softly. "I would like to prevent America from looking into this option. America is like an oil junky. I want to keep them *our* oil junky."

The Prince spoke to his brother, "Your points are well-made." Turing to Aziz, "Please do what is necessary."

"One more thing."

"What might that be?"

"I want to cover our tracks. Though cheating is expected among our fellow OPEC members, subtlety is also expected."

"Do you have a plan?"

"Yes, your Highness. I would like to broker this *excess* production through a shell company located in London. The use of this shell company will give us plausible deniability."

"You have thought this through, minister."

"I have contacts with Winslow and Sons Ltd., a small but respected investment banker. With your permission I will use them for these transactions and any others necessary to obscure our actions."

"You have it, Minister. Please proceed as you see fit."

"Aziz turned toward the King and then his brother. "Thank you, your Majesty, your Highness."

60

"One of the things I really liked about my job is being able to work at home. I find that to be a real perk." Kate was telling me over coffee after dinner. "I believe I do some of my most creative work there. I find the peace and quiet help my creative thinking. I don't usually do my writing there but I do my research and organization there."

"So you do your writing in the office?" I asked.

"Yes generally, unless I am in the field. In a kind of juxta-position, I find the hustle and bustle of the staff room better for writing. I guess it must be the energy and vitality of the place."

I poured some cream into my cup. This relationship was becoming complicated. I really liked Kate on a personal level. On a professional level I needed to get all the information I could from her on Kemal. I of course had lied to her about what I did for a living, clearly not a strong foundation for a personal relationship. I was trying to figure a way out of this box. I saw nothing but bad coming from the direction I was go-ing, a Gordian Knot if there ever was one. "When we met you told me you were doing a piece on the shipping industry. I have looked for it since then but haven't seen it. Did I miss it?

"You haven't missed it. Recent events have delayed it. I find this a bit frustrating but it is the nature of the kind of journal-ism I do. The delay is a problem but what really concerns me I that I begin to forget the small points of the research I have done. Many times it is in the small points where I fund a lively personal angle. I do make extensive notes, but notes are dry and that is what concerns me the most when I have a project delayed."

Still trying to figure a way out of the box I found myself in I ask another question. Easier to question than be questioned I have found. "If you don't mind me asking what caused the delay?"

"Oh, it was me. I came up with a new and a more time sensitive idea. I've mentioned it. It is the multi part piece I am doing on the new Turkic Economic League. The first two parts are done, they were easy to research and write. The final two articles are also pretty well along. Funny it is the third one that is causing me problems. If I can't make headway on that one nothing gets run. As part of the deal my editor insisted that all five of the articles be completed before anything was run. I wasn't totally happy with the delay but at this point I am grateful. It would be super embarrassing to start a series of five articles, run two under your byline and then have to stop. I could just imagine the jokes that would have come from such a screw-up."

"Maybe I can help," I offered.

"Well I don't know..." she began and then hesitated.

"Look give me a shot and if things don't work out or you become uncomfortable tell me and I'll back off."

She smiled. "I'd hate to screw up anything we might have going over this."

"I have pretty thick skin. It won't hurt my feelings if you tell me to buzz off." It was a good line but not the truth. I would really hate to have her tell me to get lost once we collaborated. "The third article was going to be about Kemal as I recall. Is that correct?"

"You remember correctly. It isn't that I don't have enough information about Kemal Kanuni. That's hardly the case. It's that so much of it just doesn't make much sense. The sum of the parts don't add up to the whole and vice-versa. To clear up some of these conflicts I went to Oxford. Up there I got lucky and actually found some people who had known him from his university days. One person, an Eileen Wright in particular, was most helpful."

"How did you find this person?"

I ran the names of those who had attended class at the same time as Kemal against employment records in the local area. Lucky for me, Eileen had stayed on at Oxford to teach. It turned out that Eileen had been somewhat of a party girl during her younger years. During those days of liberation she and another student at university, a Katrina Fokina, had partied with Kemal, sometimes alone and sometimes it seems together."

"I take it that the term *party* meant something more than drinking and dancing in this case?"

Kate continued. "Exactly, however, as graduation approached Eileen's Protestant upbringing seemed to reassert itself and she had ceased seeing both Kemal and Katrina. According to Eileen, Kemal and Katrina were made for each other. Their moral philosophy or actually as Eileen put it, their lack of moral philosophy, was identical. She was careful to say that they were not immoral but actually amoral. After one particularly long interview Eileen had confided to me that she thought they were both driven by a lust for money and power, power in particular. She believed they were the kind to say or do anything to have and to hold onto power."

"Do you think what she said was true or was it just sour grapes from a jilted lover?"

"I'm not totally sure if the statements given by Eileen were objectively accurate," Kate replied. "What I am sure of is they were true in her mind. There had to be some accuracy to her description. And yes, she is bitter still to this day, no doubt about it."

This information was great. Kate had just confirmed what I had learned about Kemal.   Today it appeared that religion was integral to his persona. Whether or not actually he believed any of it is something I would have to find out. Certainly in the past he wasn't the best practicing Moslem ever, but that was quite common here in the U.K particularly among the University set. I also knew that some people changed as they grew older. In my gut I felt he wasn't one of them. "Did you find out anything about Katrina Fokina?"

"Only a little, while Eileen was reasonably attractive apparently this Katrina was stunning. Eileen had wanted Kemal and Kemal had wanted Katrina."

"Have you gotten a picture or seen a picture of this Katrina person," I asked.

"Not really. Besides this is great stuff but if I can't confirm it, I can't run anything."

Here was a little opening for me, a partial bit of the truth. Security concerns were paramount. I had had Kate checked out and as far as anyone knew she wasn't a subversive or a security risk. But being neither of these didn't mean she was cleared for top-secret information either. "I can corroborate the information." I said simply

Kate looked at me surprised and confused. "You remember I told you I was a trouble shooter for the government?"

"Yes"

"Well I wasn't being completely open with you, for security reasons. I don't work for the State Department."

"Well who do you work for?" was her almost instantaneous reply.

"The NSA."

"Oh great, you are a spy. I have a great story with a confirmation that I can't use because my source is a government spy"

"Look, I can't tell you a lot but if you trust me, you will be able to run your story and it will be timely as hell. I am putting a report together on Kemal Kanuni. I think we can help each other if we work together. Will you trust me?"

Our coffee went from lukewarm to ice cold as she sat in silence. I could see her expression shift with each new thought. Finally she looked at me and simply said, "Yes".

61

It was mid-afternoon I was back in Philip's apartment semi watching CNN International but mostly think about how far Kate and I had come in such a short time. Field agents always had some flexibility about bringing non-agents into their confidence. I hadn't gotten to the edge of the flexibility yet but I could see it from there. I had sent Washington a number of reports already each one requiring I gather more and more information. My superiors were happy with what I had sent, but I was not. I just had the feeling the something was up and time was short. I had conveyed this verbally to Jazel Hammiby and to my satisfaction and dread she agreed with me.

The special report logo had come up on the screen. This caught my attention. The reporter was standing with an obviously wind blown desolate landscape behind him. He was obviously in some high desert location.

"It is cold here; it seems to be cold all the time. That is life in the Zagros Mountains. Kural standing next to me has been a Kurdish freedom fighter just as his father was. Now it seems that the impossible is about to happen -- his people are to have a homeland. The Kurdish Council will decide tonight and if the rumors are correct The Council will vote to accept the proposal from Ankara."

"Kural there had been rumors for months. Are you surprised?"

"Yes, it hardly seems possible. What began as a whisper, like a light breeze here in my beloved mountains has grown into a roar, a storm of change has happened. My people will now have a fresh start, a new beginning. I believe the new League has made all of this possible. My Kurdish people owe a great deal to Kemal Kanuni, he made this possible."

"Thank you Kural, a poet and a freedom fighter. To the outside world it would seem that justice has finally prevailed. After years of fighting them, the Turkish government has decided to change directions. It has agreed to recognize a semi- autonomous Kurdistan with it as its international protector. Turkey has also said it will support the Kurd's territorial rights in Iraq and Iran. Essentially the Kurdish people will have a new country. The new border of Kurdistan will run from the border of Turkey all the way to Azerbaijan proper. Along with this news we have learned Kurdistan will have full status at the League of Turkic nations.

"...And now to Hugh Evans somewhere in Azerbaijan," the reporter concluded.

"Thank you Sanjeep"

I am standing where the two ends of the pipeline from Baku and the Black Sea will be joined within a few short hours. It is hotter and drier, and if possible, windier here than out in Midland/Odessa, where Steve Ross, Tex to his friends and co-workers, calls home. In fact home is anywhere in the world where oil well and oil pipeline work is being done. Steve I find it amazing this pipeline which for so many was nothing more than a dream is almost done."

"Hugh, you and me both, this place is one of the toughest I've ever had to work in. If God had created hell on earth, this spot is surely in the running."

"This job was completed in record time wasn't it?"

"Yes, it never ceases to amaze me how fast something can get done if a government wants it done."

"And vice versa?"

"And vice versa. There are times it seems the sole job of government is to impede progress. This is particularly the case in the United States. It doesn't make any sense to this oilman. Why in the world would the U.S. government want to make it so hard to produce domestic oil? It makes no sense to me as to why it would want to allow us to become dependent on foreigners for such an important commodity."

"Steve your complaints are commonly heard in the oil patch. Isn't the environment important?"

"Of course it is and every real oilman respects the environment. But remember the environment applies to the entire world not just in our own backyard. Poor environmental policies in a place like this will eventually affect all of us."

"Are you saying this pipeline has environmental issues?"

"Let's just say the rules are different here." The squeal of the radio interrupts the interview. "I have to go now."

"Thank you Steve. My sources in Baku tell me they are ready to start pumping as soon as the pipeline is complete. Now back to the studio."

As the program host returned it occurred to me that for a region where for much of history progress took decades things indeed were moving very quickly.

62

I had agreed to accompany Kate on a trip to Harrods. Apparently she had procrastinated as long as she dared at finding a gift for her mother for Mother's day. We agreed to meet at the South Kensington Underground Station.

"How is my favorite spy?"

I laughed, "Fine. You know I'm not a shopper. I'm a buyer. Catalog shopping was made for me."

"Good, I was hoping you were a buyer. Hopefully you can help me pick something out for someone who has everything they want or need and has an interest in nothing else."

"I would say this is a truly a challenge. How about something small, something with a Harrods logo for example? I find little things make the best gifts sometimes. I got a lighted key chain once, didn't seem like much at the time but I use it everyday and it is great. I don't have to fumble around in the dark trying to open or unlock a door."

"Hey, that's a good idea. See you are just the person I need for this project." Kate said as she took my arm as we headed off to Harrods. It was too nice a day in London to waste inside shopping but her companionship made it worthwhile. So off to the world famous store we went. I was glad to be with Kate but hated the idea of shopping. "Maybe we should wait until tomorrow. There aren't enough nice days in London to waste one inside."

"Normally I would agree with you. But it's too bad. You are just going to have to come along like it or not."

We first browsed the wine department, looking a little at the wine and a lot at our fellow shoppers. One in particular, a distinguished gentleman caught my attention. He seemed vaguely familiar, Mediterranean if I were to guess. The man was there with a buyer. He was obviously a regular and seemed to be ordering for more than this weekend. "Kate do you recognize that man over there?" I pointed in the customer's general direction.

"Sure he was our host when we first met. That man is Charalamambos Christakos, the Greek shipping tycoon. Last time I checked."

"Which wasn't that long ago," I joked.

Feigning annoyance Kate continued, "He owns one of the largest if not *the* largest oil tanker fleets in the world. Besides the fleet he also owns a Greek island, a larger one than those usually owned."

"And a yacht club," I added.

"A sailing club and numerous properties throughout Europe. I understand he is also quite the lady's man."

"Yes, as I recall he and a remarkably attractive lady seemed to hit it off quite well. Do you remember?"

"Yes, I recall she also happened to be one of the race's contestants."

"Do you know who she was?" I asked. "The lady was really good looking."

Kate looked at me in a funny way and said, "You don't get around much do you? Her name is I mean rather was Melina Fokina. Now she is the second Mrs. Charalamambos Christakos. Their wedding made the society pages everywhere. The gossipmongers had a field day. Apparently in the past our friend the tycoon had vowed never to marry again."

"Messy first divorce?" I asked.

"As messy as they come," was Kate's reply.

In the most male chauvinist response I could muster I said, "Maybe this one was worth it. She is a twelve on a ten point scale." Kate proceeded to slug me and dutifully I shut up. She finally settled on a bottle of French Merlot. The clerk had informed her that the vintage was acceptable. She bought it and made her way to the side exit of the store.

"How are you going to get that to your mother? You can't ship wine through the mails."

"You can if you call it olive oil," was her response.

"I see," was all I said.

We finally emerged from the store at dusk and turned right toward Old Brompton Road. She had suggested this exit because it was less crowded. As we stepped out onto the sidewalk I noticed a number of limousines waiting in the street. I was about to ask Kate a question when Christakos emerged from the store.

Kate started looking around. "He is looking for someone, I wonder who it is? Kate nudged me and pointed, "Look someone is waving to him."

Christakos had also seen the woman. He waved back in recognition. She was obviously beckoning to him, motioning for him to come to her. The woman waving was a strikingly beautiful Eurasian. I then thought I recognized her as the same lady from the yacht club; the shipping magnate's new wife.

As Christakos stepped off the curb to go to her, things seemed to go into slow motion. The first car jumped forward, cutting off pedestrian traffic from the street. The back car leapt backward. It blocked nearly the entire street from traffic moving toward Old Brompton Road. The woman continued to wave enticingly and Christakos continued across the street to meet her. It was then a black Mercedes flew around the corner. Charalamambos Christakos had no chance. The car struck him going at least 30 miles per hour. He flew over the car like a mannequin. He was dead before he hit the pavement. The black Mercedes continued down the street, squeezing through the space left by the back limousine.

Immediately after Christakos was run down, the woman who had been waving to him was quickly escorted by what appeared to be a security guard to the backseat of one of the awaiting cars. I don't know why but for some reason I noticed all the cars on the scene were black Mercedes and were all leaving at once. Amazingly in less than 40 seconds all the cars had sped off. For few more short seconds it was eerily quiet. A lifeless body lay awkwardly in the street, blood flowing from his mouth and ears. Shoppers and other passer-byes appeared stunned into silence. Then chaos broke out. People were screaming, cars honking and then the distinctive sound of a police siren wailing could be heard in the distance coming closer.

63

I could see Kate was stunned, I wasn't much better. Even though I had seen people killed before. Charalamambos Christakos lay dead in the street in front of us. If the police found us we would be material witnesses to the accident. I for one didn't have time to get caught up in a police investigation.

"Kate we need to leave." She looked at me her eyes glazed over.

"What did you say?"

"We need to go, NOW!"

"Why? Don't we need to talk to the police?"

"Kate, we will talk to the police but not now. We need to leave. Please come with me." I gently pulled her arm. "Come with me!" She slowly started to respond. "Kate please show me the quickest way out of here." She had finally regained her composure.

"Follow me, I think I know a fast way out." We re-entered the store and moved quickly across the front of the store to the opposite exit. I took her hand as we walked outside and headed down the street away from the store. I hailed the first available cab. We got in. I looked at her and asked, "Where do you want to go?" I waited for her to decide where we were going to go. After a slight hesitation she told the driver to take us to her office, the London office of the Washington *Post*.

She looked at me and said, "I want to check some things out before we go back to my flat. As we sat back in the cab I looked at her amazed. Just a few short minutes ago she was almost in shock. Now she had regained enough of her composure to begin acting like a reporter. I found her a very interesting person.

64

We moved quickly into the lobby. "I need to check something out and it can't wait." The guard was sitting at a desk in the center of the lobby, American style. He looked up and greeted her.

He appeared to immediately recognize her. "Well hello, I haven't seen you in quite some time. Too good for us common folk?" he joked. Kate whispered to me, "When I first got to London I used to work a lot of nights. However, as I developed some seniority I was able to work a more standard schedule. Now I am only a semi- regular at night." "Hi to you. How are you doing?"

"Can't complain, of course it wouldn't do any good if I did. I see you have a friend with you."

She appeared to be trying to prevent the conversation from progressing. She was extending her hand so the guard could give her a night swipe card to be used to operate the elevators. "Not a friend, a relative from America, sorry but we have to run." She gave me a slight shove in the direction of the elevators and walked rapidly to that direction with me following. She pushed the call button and swiped the security card at the same time. Since practically no one was at work even early on Saturday night, an elevator was immediately available, the doors opened and we ducked in.

"I am glad the lift came so quickly. I usually find these security measures to be a complete time-wasting nuisance, however, tonight considering everything I am grateful they are in place."

I hadn't said much. My training had suggested that it was usually best at times like this to let "civilians" talk things out.

Kate continued. "The old timers told me that in the old days, there was no security and no need for security. That all changed during the Israeli occupation of southern Lebanon. Terrorism came to London. Many subtle and a few not so subtle disruptions have crept into everyone's daily lives." The elevator rose quickly to the twenty-fourth floor, tall for London. We stepped off the elevator. I looked around. The offices looked to be mostly vacant.

"Not many here," I commented.

"Only a skeleton crew is on duty. Saturday night in London means Saturday evening on the East Coast and Sunday morning in Asia. It seems that very little happens during the weekend." Kate said. "It appears America's obsession with playing on the weekend has gone global. It is tough to have a coup when the generals are out on the golf course and the soldiers are at the soccer match."

I followed Kate as she continued to her office; actually, it was more a workstation in a cubicle. Kate took off her coat and said, "It isn't much but I have one thing the others would practically die for, it does has a view." She rolled her chair back so I could actually see a small corner of the Thames. She sat down and turned on her computer. As it booted up she pointed to a nearby chair and indicated I should bring it over next to her machine. It seemed to take forever for the machine to come up but we were in a hurry and time does act strangely when one wants something quickly. Finally the screen prompted her for her log in code which she typed in.

"What are you looking for?"

"There is something niggling at the back of my mind. I just can't quite put my finger on it." I could see she had started searching. I read over her shoulder as she began by reviewing the *London Financial Times.* Charalamambos Christakos name appeared frequently. I could see that the Hellenic Sea Lines moved a lot of world's oil. I couldn't see how much but it was obviously it was a lot. The tanker line had originally been headquartered in Athens, but a succession of socialist governments had driven him to locate his official headquarters to the Netherlands Antilles, his ships registry to Panama. He seemed to have two personal residences, his luxury yacht, The Medusa and a flat in Chelsea. According to the articles she was scanning I could see he claimed he could run his entire shipping empire from either location. He had all the necessary electronics to monitor operations from either spot.

Kate next moved her search from the staid *Times* to the more flamboyant *Sun*. It was obvious Christakos was a favorite of the tabloids. Kate pointed out wedding pictures taken at his third wedding by the local paparazzi. "The guy has been married three times, I see."

"Yes he has. From what I have read one of the divorces was fairly amicable and the other was the complete opposite" Together we scanned his biographical data. He had two children who could not have been less interested in the shipping business. His daughter had taken to the theatre here in London; she also seemed to like fast cars and older men. The son was an outdoor enthusiast. His favorite sports appeared to be in no particular order women and mountain climbing.

"Haven't found what you were looking for?"

"Not yet, but I have one more thought." I could see Kate fingers fly across the keyboard. As she typed I got up and went to the window. Night had fallen and London looked beautiful.

"I got it!" I heard Kate exclaim.

"What is it?" I asked.

"Come here and look at this picture."

I walked over to the computer and saw a picture of Melina Christakos. Only the picture was several years old as I could see she was younger, but no less attractive.

65

"Where did you find this?" I asked.

"I accessed the administration department at Oxford."

"Besides a journalist you're a computer hacker also?"

"Don't worry so I far these records I have searched are public information," was her reply. "Their records have her listed as Katrina Fokina."

I had retaken a seat and said nothing. I had unexpectedly reached the crossroads with Kate, much earlier than I had wanted or hoped. I knew we had inadvertently stumbled upon some very interesting information. I also knew I was the only one that knew it. Eventually Kate would find out about it, of that I had no doubt. As the saying goes it was time to fish or cut bait. "Mike, are you okay?"

"Fine, just thinking. Kate I've told you I work for the NSA." She nodded. "I have told you my job is to sort out information conflicts."

"You lied to me?'

"No, I didn't my job is to resolve conflicts in conflicting information we receive at the NSA. From time to time I also go in the field to gather information personally. What I haven't told you is that is the case now. I am on an assignment. I have to report back to Washington shortly and that report will be Top Secret. I answer directly to the director of the NSA."

"What is your assignment?"

"I am to gather information on Kemal Kanuni," I replied.

"Why is that?" she asked. I think to test me more than anything else. "I can't say." There was no reaction to my answer, so I think my guess was correct. "I think we can work together."

"How is that?" she asked somewhat warily. "How can the press and the government work together?"

"I think if you are willing it can work this way. You help me with my report first. In the process I will undoubtedly reveal information to you that either you would never find or take so long to find there would be no value in that information."

"And…"

"And once my report goes to Washington, you finish your series and run your articles. You will still have an exclusive of a very timely story."

It was Kate's turn to think, so I sat there and said and did nothing. "I think I can live with what you propose."

"Good" I was really glad because I had become very excited about the possibility of working closely with this lady. Right or wrong I had developed higher aspirations for our relationship. No doubt the next several weeks would tell a lot. "Let's see if we can dig up some more information about our lady friend."

It was nearly two hours later and we had turned up nothing. It wasn't as if Melina Christakos had sprung to life on the day she was married to Charalamambos Christakos, but it was close to it. Kate had checked birth and passport records of here in the United Kingdom, Greece and Turkey. All that she could find was that she had been educated at boarding schools in Switzerland prior to attending University in England. "My guess is that she had wealthy but disinterested parents."

"I agree. I'm speculating that neither one cared too much for parenting so she was pretty much left on her own. I don't know if that makes any difference but I think it is something we may want to keep in the back of our minds."

Kate looked up from the screen. "I can't find anything else, zip nada."

"That's okay," I said "I can add some details. For one she and Kemal Kanuni were more than just friends at Oxford."

Kate looked tired but this news perked her right up. "That is interesting."

"I thought you might think that. Before we call it a night, I need to know a little more about Christakos, businesses and his family."

66

Kate swung around and starting pounding away on the keyboard. There were volumes of data available on Charalamambos Christakos. There was little meaningful data on the women in his life. It wasn't that women weren't mentioned in connection with Christakos. In fact, it was quite the opposite. It was just that the information was useless. All kinds of women were mentioned in all kinds of situations. I could see it would have been easy to get bogged down in the more lurid details of the man's life. It seemed that only sensational stories were available when it came to women in his life.

"Kate please pull-up some financial data if you would." I hoped her background would be useful.

"There is a lot here," Kate said. "This is a 10-K report."

"10-what report?" I asked

"It is a financial report prepared by a company listed on a United States stock exchange and filed with the Securities and Exchange Commission."

"I knew I brought you along for a reason." was my only comment.

She smiled and kept talking. "This 10-k report is for an American subsidiary of the Hellenic Holding Company Ltd. The Hellenic Holding Company Ltd is the Holding company for the Christakos financial empire. The Hellenic Sea Lines is a subsidiary of this holding company."

"How did the company do?"

"Great, it makes a lot of money," she said without looking up.

A thought struck me. "Hey I thought all these Greek shipping magnates had private companies. Why would this guy have public one?"

"Remember it is a public subsidiary. The parent is a private company, but to answer your questions, most likely to get cheaper capital. Control is maintained up stream at the parent but money can be raised in the stock market. In my opinion it was kinda ingenious of him."

"Who's on the board?"

"Good question, give me a minute." She typed away and within seconds she had come up with a list. "Last year's report listed Athos Christakos and Lydia Christakos as well as Christakos and a man name Khahl Hrawi."

"Where can we find this Khahl Hrawi?"

She typed some more. "Here in London," was her answer.

Bells were going off in my head, but I wanted to remain calm at least for a little while longer. "Let me know what you can find about Lydia Christakos."

Again she went to work on the computer. I was intently looking over her shoulder when a picture of Lydia Christakos appeared on the screen. She was quite young and pretty. And quite dead.

67

Kate sat there stunned, as was I. We quickly scanned the newspaper articles. Lydia had died in an auto accident. The story was written to lead one to conclude she had been driving too fast in the rain with her fancy car and that accidents of this kind happen, particularly to spoiled rich girls.

"This is amazing." was all Kate said. "Let me check on her brother Athos."

I said, "Don't bother."

"Why is that?"

"Here is another tidbit. He is dead too."

"What?" she practically screamed.

"The public story is that he died in a Swiss climbing accident. He was an avid and successful mountaineer."

"Apparently not successful enough," she retorted.

"What I am about to tell you is off the record, is that okay?"

Not hesitating, "Yes."

"I have it on very good authority that the accident was likely not an accident. It seems a paid assassin was involved in the climb. The testimony of the other climbers can neither prove nor disprove whether Athos' fall was a mishap or not."

"Wow"

"Let me ask you another question. With both his kids dead, who runs the company?"

"I don't know. We will have to do some more digging."

"I think we need to make a call on Khahl Hrawi," I said.

68

Fahad Amani had not slept well. He could not get yesterday's surprise out of his mind. Why would the country's Senior Oil Minister need to meet in secret with his son? He had asked himself this question over and over all night. Now he had started the new day with this same troubling question. Not sleeping, he decided to get to work early. There was something he could not put his finger on rolling around in the recesses of his mind. He needed quiet time in the archives. Also it would be easier to do a little investigating before everyone arrived for work. The fewer people around, the fewer questions he needed to answer.

He hoped getting into work early would give him extra time with Mustafa Zell. He knew he could trust Mustafa. Discretion was certainly essential anytime his kind of work involved the upper echelons of government.

Fahad headed to the stairwell as he took his usual route to the fifth floor where his department was located. On the way up he decided to go directly to Mustafa's cubicle rather than go to archives.

"You are in early," Zell said as Fahad entered his cubicle.

"I know. I could not sleep. I found our little unexpected encounter yesterday at the Inter-Continental Hotel to be most unsettling."

"I know what you mean," Zell concurred.

"We must be very cautious and very thorough. If it turns out that we find something, General Gahmill will insist upon an airtight case. Did you find anything?" Fahad asked.

"Possibly. After you went home last night I decided to make some calls on some of our usual suspects."

"And?"

"You remember Abdul Yunni? I contacted him."

"Yes, isn't he, rather *wasn't* he the editor of the *Islamic News?*"

"Correct."

"What happened to the paper?"

"It was one of several the government shut down for subversive activities," Zell said.

"Oh yes, I remember now, that was several years ago, wasn't it. He and the paper were accused of supporting the United Islamic Front. Did he go to jail?" Amani asked.

"He did not. He's been under what amounts to house arrest, which is strange for supporting an organization dedicated to replacing the present Saudi Government." Zell said.

"As I recall, the organization did not advocate violence. It advocated a peaceful transition to an Islamic Republic; maybe that would explain it, but I doubt it. What did he say?"

"It is not so much what he said but rather what he did not say." Zell said. "I left our little meeting with the distinct impression that he had a benefactor in high places. That's what kept him out of prison."

"That makes sense. At least at home one's life expectancy is much better. Did you get a sense as to who his supporter might be?" Amani asked.

Before Zell answered he got up and looked around the office. In a soft voice he spoke. "No, but if I were to guess, Hazim Aziz would be my first choice."

Amani nodded. "A logical deduction, he is the highest ranking member of Government who is not a member of the Royal Family. I appreciate your help. Let us keep this between us. "I am going to Archives. There is something I need to check out."

"Good luck let me know if you need anything else."

69

I had escorted Kate out of her building. "Want to get a drink?"

"Thanks, but the day has caught up with me, I think I should just go home. Do you mind?' What a question, of course I minded. I liked being with her and now I had been rejected at least a little. "Of course not, I understand." Bullshit, I couldn't possibly understand, but at least I knew what to say. I wanted to ask if she was doing anything tomorrow, but then again maybe I was pushing too hard. I wasn't real good at this game so I decided to be safe rather than sorry.

"Why don't I come by your place first thing Monday? I think we would be most successful if you made an appointment as a financial reporter to have an interview with Khahl Hrawi first thing Monday, if possible."

"Okay, I can try. I suspect considering all that has gone on he would be willing to talk to the press. But who are you?"

"Your associate and gofer, do you think it will fly?"

"I'll try. See you Monday then." She waved and walked into the tube station. I waited for her to disappear and rather dejectedly hailed a cab.

70

It was the first time I had been in Kate's flat. We had agreed to meet first thing Monday morning. I would have liked to spend Sunday with her but, I didn't and there was nothing much more to be said. "Did you get an interview?"

"Sure did. We need to leave now to see Mr. Hrawi."

As we walked out the door, I decided to ask her how her Sunday had been. "Did you have a good day yesterday?"

"Yes, my roommates and I had our monthly flat cleaning party. I don't know if I told you but we schedule a time to clean the flat and come hell or high water we hold that day open."

I was relieved to hear this. "I do recall."

"I wanted to invite you over but you probably wouldn't have enjoyed it and the crap we both would have gotten would have been enormous."

I believed her. "I hear you."

"What did you do?" she asked breezily. I hoped over breezily but I wasn't totally sure.

"I dispatched a report to Washington and brought them up to speed on Melina. Then went to a pub and watched a soccer match, Chelsea versus Arsenal."

"Ha, a London derby. Was it a good game?"

It was good to hear Kate knew something about soccer. "It was great Chelsea won in added time, 3 to 2."

By now we had gotten to the corner where I hailed a cab.

We arrived in front of one of those stately Georgian style buildings so prevalent in London. We walked up the steps and entered the building. The contrast couldn't have been greater, eighteenth Century on the outside and twenty-first Century on the inside. We walked across the lobby to the reception desk, a smoked-glass topped table with only a computer and phone on it. Behind the desk sat a woman of indeterminate age. Behind her were double darkened glass doors which most likely lead to the company's private offices

"May I help you?'

Yes, I'm Kate O'Hara, with the Washington Post." She handed the receptionist her card. This is my associate, Mr. Williams. We have an appointment to see Mr. Hrawi."

"Please take a seat and I'll let Mr. Hrawi know you are here." Five minutes later, a gentleman of about forty-five came over to us.

"Good morning, I'm Keith Brown, Mr. Hrawi's assistant. Mr. Hrawi is able to see you now. Please follow me." We followed Brown to a small conference room containing a round table with four chairs. The office had no window but it did have a large painting of what must have been the flagship of Christakos line.

"Please make yourselves comfortable Mr. Hrawi will be with you in a moment."

With that Brown closed the door and left. I indicated to Kate to be silent, pointing to the walls, then my ears.

"I'm really looking forward to this interview," Kate said. "I think this will give me a fresh angle for my articles. Remember you are here as a favor to Jamie O'Doul so the less you say the better, in fact saying nothing would be the best."

Hrawi entered minutes later, extending his hand first to Kate and then to me, "I'm Khahl Hrawi, Vice-Chairman of Hellenic Sea Lines. Please take a seat."

Kate opened her note pad and began. "Mr. Hrawi please let me thank you again for accepting this interview," Kate said. "And please let me begin by offering you our condolences over Mr. Christakos' recent death."

I watched Hrawi. He said "thank you" and nothing more. His face showed no sign of emotion. He simply raised his hand indicating that Kate should continue.

"What, if anything, has been the immediate impact of Mr. Christakos death?"

"The day-to-day operations of the company have been unaffected by the recent tragedies. Charalamambos Christakos had turned the daily running of the company over to subordinates. He wanted the company to survive himself. He had thought that the best way of doing this was to allow others the opportunity to succeed and fail while he was still alive. This insightfulness has allowed the company to continue normal operations."

"You used the word tragedies. Is there something else?"

"Yes, I assumed you knew. It is of course public record. Mr. Christakos' children both died rather unexpectedly. His son in a mountain climbing mishap several months ago and his daughter recently lost her life in an automobile accident."

"My goodness, how sad."

"Yes, it has been quite unsettling, but the company remains today as strong as ever. We have a strong and experienced board."

"Why don't you tell me a little about yourself," I broke in.

"Of course," he cleared his throat. "I have been with the company for over twenty years. At present I am acting board Chairman until the board meets and settles on a permanent Chair. I am an engineer by training."

Kate picked up the theme. "A little personal background would put a human touch on my story."

"Yes, well let me see. I am Lebanese, a Maronite Christian. My wife has passed away but I have two daughters both married who live here in London." Kate smiled and nodded at this, writing in her notepad. "I am fluent in several languages including Greek, English, French and Arabic."

"Mr. Hrawi your background is impressive," I broke in again. Thought it would help to keep the act going just a little longer. Kate immediately began speaking. I could see Hrawi was enjoying our competition.

"The daily operations are running smoothly what though of strategic items?"

"I am glad you asked," the Vice Chairman said. I thought of course you are. That was why you accepted the interview. You wanted to assure the world that everything was hunky-dory at oil-movers-r-us. "Our Board has met a number of times since the accident. We have agreed to push forward with all the initiatives previously approved. You see Mr. Christakos will continue to be with us in spirit for a number of years to come."

"I am sure my readers will be pleased to hear this," Kate spoke while writing. Without looking up she asked, "Who owns the company now?" It was my turn to observe. Hrawi didn't flush or hesitate. "With both of his children dead and since they had no heirs, the stock of the Hellenic Sea Lines as well as all of Mr. Christakos assets are now controlled by the Christakos Foundation."

Kate continued. "Let me confirm this with you Mr. Hrawi, Mr. Christakos estate is controlled by a charitable foundation?"

"Yes it is a charitable foundation formed in the Netherlands Antilles. Mr. Christakos wished the income from his many business ventures be used for the good of mankind. He had a wide variety of interests that were specified in his will. I can't divulge them to you now, of course."

Kate nodded like she understood, "Of course. But we will have an idea some time soon won't we?"

"Yes, once all the legal paperwork is resolved most assuredly."

I broke in for what I had planned to be the last time. "Won't it take some time to clear up legal matters?"

"I would anticipate a couple of years. Mr. Christakos was a very wealthy man with many assets, that need to inventoried and otherwise accounted for."

Kate spoke, "Mr. Hrawi, I am almost done. I just want to make sure I understand this information."

"Continue"

"The Foundation will control the company's board, thus really controlling the Hellenic Sea Lines."

"Yes"

"Who is on the foundation's board?"

"Currently there is only one person."

"One person, isn't that unusual?"

"No, not really, you see the foundation was just recently formed and Mr. Christakos only had chosen the Chairman and Vice-Chairman. He was a very busy man and had not yet had time to select the others he wanted on the board with him."

"How recently?"

I hoped Hrawi would answer Kate's question.

Hrawi paused. I think he was unsure as to what to say. Kate gave him a smile. "I know this is hard, but I'm sure the financial community would like some reassurance."

That seemed to decide it. "Just shortly after Lydia's, his daughter's, death."

Kate made a note and then spoke "Of course how reasonable" I could see Hrawi relax a little. Kate continued. "I presume Mr. Christakos was the Chairman." Hrawi nodded. "Who was the Vice Chairman?"

"Why Mrs. Christakos of course."

71

The Ministry's records were stored in the building's two basements. The only access to that part of the building was by means of a secure elevator. Fortunately for Fahad Amani, his security clearance was such that he did not have to get permission to wander about in the stacks or computer records.

The elevator doors slid open and for as far as the eye could see were shelves lined with files illuminated by the harsh fluorescent light. In front, guarding these papers was a grizzled old army sergeant sitting behind a metal desk. To his right and to the guard's left was the computer research terminal. He knew it was ministry policy for security reasons to use non-ministry employees to guard certain installations. The Archives were one of these installations.

Amani approached the front desk. "Sergeant, my name is Fahad Amani. I need to look in the records. Here is my security clearance card." Fahad removed his identification card from around his neck. The sergeant took the card from Fahad and swiped the card through the magnetic reader.

"Please put your right thumb on the screen." The guard pointed to a small screen that lay flat on the desk

Fahad did as instructed and waited.

The security officer watched his computer screen and waited for clearance to be granted or rejected. As he waited, his right hand was poised to push a button hidden under the desk. He would immediately push the button if clearance were denied. However, within less than ten seconds clearance was granted.

"Everything appears to be in order sir. Please sign in."

Fahad signed in and then walked to the research terminal. "Has it been busy, sergeant?"

"It has been quiet all week. You are my first visitor today," was his reply.

"Well then, it is good for you that your pay is the same with or without visitors." Fahad spoke as he sat at the computer terminal.

Fahad began typing. The cataloging program was a newly installed state-of-the-art program based upon key word use. He typed in the words Islamic Fundamentalism, United Islamic Front, Abdul Yunni and Hazim Aziz and hit enter. Within seconds four references were listed. Every report written for the agency was required to have a computerized head note. This head note was accessed by the system. In addition to the head note, the system provided the date that the files were generated. He could see from the dates listed that the references were all logged in within a few days of each other. From experience he knew this meant these files were probably generated from a single investigation. The reports were about five years old, around the time of the first Gulf War. He typed in a few more keystrokes and saw that these files had never been accessed by anyone other than himself. He called up and read each head note. As he read he decided it would be worthwhile for him to review the complete files.

72

Fahad quickly jotted down the location of the files. He then returned the program to the search screen. He wished he could delete any reference to the files he had found, but knew the system did not allow this. He figured that the next best thing to do was nothing. Basically, he would hide his research in plain sight.

Fahad had only a general idea of the location but he did not want the guard to know which files he was reviewing. He headed off in his best guess direction. He quickly got to the general location of the files and then began wandering about. Fortunately, he came upon the files sooner rather than later. The files in question were all grouped together confirming his earlier suspicion that these four reports were tied to a single investigation. From his reading of the head notes, he reached for what he felt would be the most promising documents.

He took the first file and opened it. While the information presented was very controversial he had been with the department long enough to know that nothing had come of this investigation, Amani quickly thumbed through the other three reports to see if there was an answer. The information in the other reports was equally sensitive. Fahad then double-checked the author's name and he immediately understood why nothing had come of this investigation. He remembered the author, a fine young inspector, and a man he had befriended, who had been killed tragically in a small plane crash. Akmed Khomani and his chief assistant had been flying from Riyadh to Medina in a small plane. Rumors at the time said that he was following a lead about some dissident group. The plane had gone down en route during a storm and it was about three months later before the wreckage was actually found. Drifting desert sands quite often hid and then gave up its secrets. By the time the wreck was found there was not much to investigate. The desert jackals had gotten to the bodies and the Bedouins had gotten to the plane.

Fahad shook his head. The system both worked for and against the flow of information. The plane crash, most likely caused by sabotage, had ended any further investigation. But the same person who could cause a plane crash could not destroy the files from an investigation once they were archived. He turned to the last pages in the file and began to read:

> *We had been questioning Abdul Yunni for about three hours. We had had very little luck in the way of getting any specific information about the source of cash that had been financing the United Islamic Front. We decided that we needed to apply a little more pressure to our subject. Our subject had stood up well to level two interrogation.*" Fahad knew that level two included psychological as well physical torture, nothing permanent but none the less very unpleasant. *"We decided that because the man we were investigating was a public figure we needed to go to level four immediately.*

Fahad paused, knowing that level three consisted of severe torture that usually left permanent damage. Level four used drugs. Fahad continued reading the report.

> *About an hour after administering the medication Abdul Yunni began to crack. His specific words or rather his screams were, Hazim Aziz is the source of our cash. Without his support our organization would have failed years ago. He has also been our main contact to the rest of the Islamic movement. Because Mr. Aziz is a senior government official and because it is not uncommon for someone to give false information even under level four we continued our aggressive questioning. We wanted to be sure.*

Fahad knew what that meant.

> *After several hours more my partner and I decided that Abdul Yunni believed what he was telling us. We did not know if his information was true or not but we knew that Yunni believed it to be true. Before he passed out he gave us this lead. Next week in Medina, Hazim Aziz is scheduled to secretly meet with a Jordanian Islamic party leader. Khalil and I will need to go to Medina next week and check out this lead.*

This was the last entry. Fahad closed the file. As he re-filed the reports he knew he had to be careful, very careful.

73

As we left the offices of the Hellenic Sea Lines Kate turned left immediately as we hit the sidewalk. I had no choice but follow her. "Slow down, what's the hurry?"

"Sorry I didn't know I was walking too fast. I just wanted to get away from there. That's all. Sometimes when I get concentrating I don't realize I am practically running."

"Well let's just say you had a slow run going."

"Why the charade in there anyway?" Kate asked.

"Two reasons. First, I cut you off originally because I think the room was bugged. Second, you were the professional and I wanted you to ask the questions. Besides I was concerned Mr. Hrawi wouldn't be forthcoming. So I did a little good cop bad cop. It worked, I think he told us more than he would have otherwise, but he thought I was a boor and you were nice."

"He did open up, you were probably right." Kate continued. "So what we know now is that after a number of rather remarkable happenstances Melina Fokina, now Christakos, controls the world largest oil tanker fleet."

"You are the expert. How long can she run the company as an estate administrator?"

"At a minimum, eighteen months. More likely than not two plus years."

"Over two years is a long time."

"Yes, given that time frame and given she knows what she is doing it really means forever. You know there seems to be a lot of coincidences." Kate added.

"I was thinking the same thing. I'm not a big believer in coincidence either. I think we need to see if there is a current tie in or a link of some sort from Melina to our friend Kemal."

"I was just going to suggest that."

"I need to go back to where I am staying and report this back to Washington. We need to move on this. How can I get a hold of you quickly?"

Kate took out a piece of paper and wrote down a series of telephone numbers and circled the top one. She pointed to it and said, "This is my pager number try it first."

"Thanks," I said. I don't know how long it will be but I will call you as soon as I can."

"No problem, I am going to do some more research, it fits great with my series. I am going to take the tube back."

"I need to take a cab. I'll miss you."

Kate smiled, "Me too."

She started to walk away. "Wait!" She stopped and turned around. "Be sure and make some story for you editor, what's his name?"

"Jamie O'Doul"

"About me so if somehow Hrawi follows up on the interview he doesn't draw a blank when my name is mentioned."

"Don't worry. I will take care of it. Bye" She turned and waved and was gone.

74

The regularly scheduled meetings for the day had all ended. Unknown to Kemal Kanuni's secretary there had been one more meeting set for today.

"Please see that no one disturbs me for the next hour or so," said Kanuni.

"Yes Mr. Chairman, I understand completely."

"Very well," Kanuni said as his secretary closed the main door to his office.

Kanuni heard the call to evening prayer coming from the main downtown mosque. As he did Akham Bizhanov silently entered his office through his private entrance. "It is good to see you again, my old friend."

"It is also good to see you," responded Bizhanov. "May we speak freely?"

"Of course, just speak quietly my staff assumes I wanted to be alone at prayer time."

"It seems you have certainly been successful at creating the illusion of being a man of God."

Kanuni smiled and spoke. "They can be such simpletons. An otherwise rational cognitive man can be reduced to committing almost any act in the name of God."

"Why did you call for me?" Bizhanov asked in a low voice.

"I need you to return to London. I have a job that requires your special talents."

"Ah, London," Bizhanov said, "a city where most of the police do not carry guns. Such a place can make my job so much easier."

"Your task will not be easy but it is essential for my plan." Kemal continued, "An international conference will soon take place. The kings of Jordan and Saudi Arabia will meet in London."

"What do you want me to do?"

"I need you to kill the Saudi King as well as the Crown Prince."

"What of the Jordanian King?"

"He is irrelevant."

"Do you know if there will be any more than the standard amount of security?"

"I don't think so. Both men are scheduled to be in the city for medical reasons. A quiet low profile meeting will take place. But because of their health, particularly the Saudi king's, the conference is being downplayed."

"I see. Still killing two will be much more difficult than one."

"I assumed that to be the case. However I have great confidence in your abilities." Kemal continued, "One thing will help you, the meeting will not be held at either embassy."

"Neutral ground, that is better. Accidents are so hard to arrange in an embassy. I may need some help. Is that an issue?"

"Do what you think is necessary. I just don't want any unnecessary people involved," Kemal said.

"Okay. How do you know about the meeting?"

"Abdul Aziz's has been instrumental in keeping me abreast of things."

"Is there anything else you can tell me?" Bizhanov asked.

"Yes, the conference will be held at the Dorchester in six weeks." Bizhanov said nothing. Kanuni waited for the man to absorb all he had been told and then began again. "Let me know right away if you will need any special equipment. I can always move whatever you might require under diplomatic tags. However, large items usually take longer than one would think."

"I will let you know my plan within a couple of days. Is that time enough?"

"That will be fine." Kemal replied. "Thank you. Now I must ask you to go. Prayer time is ending and I need to leave."

75

"Three minutes," the bodiless voice announced.

In three minutes Kemal Kanuni would address the citizens of the league live on both television and radio. Many of those citizens lived without the benefit of a personal television. Nonetheless most of those wouldn't miss the address. The countries comprising the league were still technologically backward in many ways. The countries were not backward in the people's desire for a better life.

"Two minutes," the voice from the production booth announced. Kemal shook his head. He looked around to make sure everything was ready. His plan was entering a critical phase and he needed no surprises. Kemal preferred the medium of television. He believed visual images to be the most effective at reaching the emotional needs of people. What was essential now was the undivided support of the population. Radio, however, did have its advantages. Via short wave, it could be heard worldwide without worrying whether the news services would pick it up. He needed to reach a small but specific worldwide audience

The studio was set in the style of the region. Behind the Chairman were the flags of Bir and all its member countries. To his right were the council members including Vice-Chairman Hakim and the Saudi observer, Abdul Aziz.

"One minute." Kemal looked around and smiled to relax everyone. He needed no mistakes, certainly none caused by nervousness.

The voice broke in, "Four, three, two, one."

76

"May Allah be praised." Kemal began the speech that would mark the beginning of the next phase of his plan. "I am most pleased to announce to you that the first of our great oil bounty has moved through our just-completed pipeline. It is now, as I speak, being loaded onto tankers ready to move this great bounty to market. Today we resume our march to destiny. I want to thank my Council for helping me ensure that the pipeline was completed early. With their support I was able to take the necessary actions to bring this project to a timely and fruitful conclusion. Now we, along with our Islamic neighbor to the south, the home to Islam's most holy sites, have under our combined control over sixty-five percent of the of the world's readily accessible supply of oil. Allah has been most generous to our great Turkic people."

Kemal paused, took a drink of water and continued. "My fellow citizens, I must caution you to guard your expectations. While our wealth is great, it will be some time before the fruits of our new wealth become readily apparent to you, my fellow countrymen. It will take time for our oil money to flow into the country. But in time, it surely will. It will be a testimonial to our greatness that while we wait, we thank Allah. You can be assured that I will ensure that our schools, hospitals, roads and power and sewer plants will be equal to any in the world. Your lives will be lengthened and improved. Your children's lives will be admired by the world. You will be proud of your Turkic heritage and our league, Bir."

Again, Kemal paused. "Our lives will be better because of this you can be sure. But please remember you will have to be patient. I know this is something you all can do. And while you wait, I may again ask your help from time to time. Mostly what I will ask from you will be modest in nature but there will be some things that will be large and will require additional sacrifices. I will ask these things of you because it will allow me make us all even greater, today and in the future for us and our children and our children's children.

"As I leave you, let us all pause and thank Allah for his great gift and also please ask Allah to help me help you. Goodbye until later."

The bright studio lights faded, changing the emphasis from Kemal to the flags. The camera crew lingered for just a moment on the flags, then back to Kemal, again with the lights changing now to a subtle glow. The radio announcer completed his description of the speech scene. The picture faded and the camera light went off.

The speech was seen or at least heard in many different parts of the world. Akham Bizhanov turned off his television set. A knowing smile crossed his face. He knew some of the little things that Kemal would ask of his people. He wondered what the big ones would be.

Melina Fokina, sitting in her London office switched off her short wave radio. Big things were still to come, but it was good to get moving again. She reached for the phone to make a call.

* * *

"Well, how did the speech sound to you?" the central Asia editor asked.

"It seemed it could be taken in any number of ways," Jamie O'Doul replied.

"I agree. This fellow Kemal Kanuni is someone we should know more about."

"Kate O'Hara is currently in the process of doing a five part piece on Kanuni."

"What good timing for her. Do you mind if I take a quick look at it before you run it?"

"I don't; but let me check with her first."

"On second thought, there is no need," the editor responded. "I will do some digging on my end and let you know what I find. Well I've got to run, talk to you later."

"Okay," Jamie O'Doul said as he put the phone down and turned back to the copy in front of him.

77

Mr. Hrawi entered Melina's office with a worried look on his face. She looked up from shipping tonnage reports. "Mr. Hrawi, is there something I can do for you?"

"Mrs. Christakos, I am concerned that our expansion plans are overly aggressive. Since you assumed control of the company you have been acquiring tanker capacity at an incredible rate. Your deceased husband was an aggressive businessman but I believe he would have questioned your approach. I hate to question your actions, but I am very worried. Our economic leverage is now enormous. If anything unforeseen occurs in the world market, we could easily fall into bankruptcy."

"Mr. Hrawi, you only look at one side of the equation. Look at it another way. If something unforeseen occurs we could control the supply of the world's oil."

"But you are taking enormous risks with the company. For example, instead of having our ships flagged in a number of countries, an action that minimizes risk, you have flagged all our ships and the ships in our subsidiary lines in Turkey. You have concentrated our risk."

Melina gave him a weak smile. "Mr. Hrawi, I have a plan and I need your help." I can assure you that I would do nothing to jeopardize this great company. Please continue to do the fine job you have been doing. I will let you know of my plan shortly."

"As you wish, Mrs. Christakos," replied Mr. Hrawi and left the room.

78

It began as a trickle. Then it grew to be a small stream and eventually a great river flowing deep and strong. However, rather than water, what flowed in this case was money, lots of it. And as the money flowed, it transformed itself into oil futures and oil option contracts.

Winslow and Son Ltd. did not have many clients nor did the firm need very many. In fact, except for those few loyal customers who had been with the firm prior to its purchase by Hans Schmidt, the firm only had three clients -- the Oil Ministry of the Kingdom of Saudi Arabia, the Bir League and the Hellenic Sea Lines.

The Oil Ministry of Saudi Arabia was now using Winslow and Son Ltd. as a clearing-house for all of its petro-transactions. The Saudi's main customers were the remaining members of the original seven sisters, those companies who first discovered oil on the Arabian Peninsula. The three remaining sisters wired all of their payments for crude oil through the firm. Winslow and Son Ltd. in turn rewired funds to various locations upon instructions from the oil ministry itself. Some of the money was wired directly into the Saudi Arabian treasury for immediate use, but much of it was being directed into investments. In the past, all of this surplus money had been invested in United States treasury paper or similar paper offered by certain members of the European Union, primarily the United Kingdom and Germany. Now things were being done differently.

The firm had begun investing heavily in oil options and oil futures contracts. Under normal circumstances this change of investment policy would have been noticed in the transparent world of international finance. However Hans Schmidt was careful not to allow this to happen. He had the ability to do this because he now had a new, not yet fully understood, source of money, namely the new oil money from Central Asia and he had lots of it. For this reason there was virtually no material effect on the international interest rate marketplace. To his credit Hans Schmidt succeeded in his deception. It was true that interest rates did rise but they did so only modestly. The movement of interest rates during this period did not seem out of the norm.

The third major client of the firm, Hellenic Sea Lines, had also changed its method of doing business again aided by Winslow and Son Ltd. In the past the shipping line would not have considered taking ownership in the product it transported. Even with the availability of insurance the risk was simply not worth the return. Hauling crude oil across the world's oceans was deemed to be challenge enough. It was common practice in the industry for the shipping line to transport cargo owned by someone else. On daily basis millions of barrels of oil would change hands from producer to consumer without ever being owned by the shipper. In a departure from common industry practices the Hellenic Sea Lines was now taking ownership of the oil it was shipping, most of it from non-OPEC sources. Purchasing this much crude was very costly. Winslow and Son Ltd. issued the necessary letters of credit. It did so with the money it received from brokering central Asian crude.

79

Hazim knew he was playing a most dangerous game. But dangerous games gave the biggest rewards. He knew he should not be going to London but the risk was well worth the return.

Melina Fokina was a most attractive woman, as well as intelligent, which added to her allure. She was his son's age; in fact, they knew each other. He was not quite sure how well. Had they had sex also? He wondered. Not that it mattered. What mattered was that he felt young again when he was with her. That woman knew more ways of having sex than he could ever have dreamed.

When they had been together he had found her grasp of business to be impressive, for a novice. They often talked of oil tonnage and tanker capacity. Whether or not she understood the politics of the oil business he could not tell. If he were to guess in this area she also was a novice. It was a fact if one didn't know how to deal with politics in the Middle East one would be bankrupt within a short period of time. With skill he might get both the business and her.

He wondered how much sex he could have with her once he was President of the Islamic Republic of Saudi Arabia. The mullahs could be so uncompromising when it came to the sex-for-fun game. He would certainly have to marry her.

80

The encrypted cell phone rang, "Hello." Melina answered. There was a long pause as she listened. "Kemal, I understand. Yes, both Akham Bizhanov and Abdul Aziz are now in London."

"You will be very busy very soon. Do you have any questions? Again, my love, I want to thank you. As you know you are essential to the coordination of all our plans."

"I miss you but I know we will be together soon."

"As do I."

She put down the phone and took a deep breath. She wanted to think clearly, to keep her emotions compartmentalized. Looking back at the clock she realized it was getting late. She still had to finish reading her shipping reports, which had grown longer with the size of her fleet and the amount of oil under contract, and meet Hazim Aziz for dinner.

81

I had paged Kate and was waiting for her to call me back. As I waited, I sorted through the faxes that had piled up while I was out. It always amazed me how it felt like so many more of them arrived when I wasn't in as compared to when I was in. I knew this really wasn't the case but it sure felt like it. There was one rather long fax that I was reviewing again. As I re-read it I was impressed the research department had done such a good job in a short time. I suspected that a lot of nights were involved

"First Hakan Kanuni, and then Kemal Kanuni have over the years developed extensive contacts in both their home of Kazakhstan and in Turkey. The reason Kemal Kanuni's influence reaches to Turkey is contacts from his mother's side of the family. He is related to the head of the State Police in Kazakhstan *and* the Chief of Staff of the Turkish Army."

"The religion of this part of the Middle East is predominately Sunni-Moslem. However, the Turkic branch of Sunni Islam is not as conservative as that found in Saudi Arabia. The Turkic region in general considers the teachings of the Shiite branch of Islam to be false."

"Ethnically, the League is Turkic. It is not Arabic. This means a great deal in the historical context. Turkey was the heart of the old Ottoman Empire. The empire was comprised of conquering people as compared to the Arabs who in many cases were conquered people.

The Ottoman Empire was a member of the Axis along with Germany and Austria Hungary during World War One. Turkey was stripped of its empire when it lost the war. Had this not happened Turkey today would control the world's oil supply since the Empire controlled the Arabian Peninsula as well as Iraq."

"It has been rumored that there are many in Turkey and to a lesser degree in the other countries of the Bir League that still see dream of returning to the power and glory days of the past."

"It is anticipated that once the oil from Central Asia reaches full production the Bosporus will rival the straits of Straits of Hormuz in terms of oil tonnage. As it is today all shipping to Russia's southern ports along with Ukraine, Georgia, Bulgaria, Romania and the Danube River traffic must also travel through these narrow straits."

I shuffled the faxes until I got to my favorite; I called it the rumor fax. Officially, it was called the *Forward Looking Report.* The data presented was brief.

"Sources indicate the Hellenic Sea Lines has altered it business model. It has recently acquired substantially more cargo capacity, while re-flagging its entire fleet under the Turkish flag. More significantly the company appears to be buying oil. It is unknown at this point, what the company is doing with the crude it has purchased."

"Sources have indicated the Kanuni's have begun calling the League of the Bir, *"Vatan"*, meaning mother country in Turkic. These same sources a trying to determine if there is significance to this change or it is merely a cultural idiom."

I made a mental note to ask Kate if these events meant anything to her. Unfortunately I would have to wait, as she still hadn't called. The old two-edged sword, I was getting a lot done which felt good but not hearing from her was starting to feel worse. Philip had brought me the Brits file on Akham Bizhanov and as I waited I read it. Not that there was much there, just about as much as in our files.

> "In the West he could have easily been mistaken for a professional athlete. He stands slightly over six-feet-one inches. His weight of two hundred-fifteen pounds is all muscle. He has received training as a "freedom fighter from the Libyans. However, we can't find any occasion where he acted as an Islamic freedom fighter. Our best sources indicate he is in actuality an expert killer who sells his services to the highest bidder."

Quite the charmer, someone you would want to run into in a dark alley. I wondered if there was a connection to Kemal or Melina. The phone rang.

"Hello, Logan residence."

"Hi, it's me."

"Hi, we need to get together. Can I come over?"

"Sure, I would like that."

"I'll grab a cab. See you soon."

"See you." I hung up the phone and grabbed my coat as I headed out the door. I was really looking forward to working with Kate. Rationally I knew I would have to be careful. I would never do anything to compromise national security, or to endanger her in any way. On an instinctual level, working with her felt right and that was a scary feeling. Maybe I was lucky or maybe it was fate.

As I left the building to hail a cab I thought I saw someone look quickly away from me as I made casual eye contact. Most people in London will look at you and smile as you pass in the street, at least in the right neighborhoods and this was one of them. This man was wearing a raincoat and carrying a magazine. Seeing someone wearing a raincoat in London is hardly unusual but very few Englishmen carry magazines, they are by and large newspaper types. I picked up my pace and moved quickly toward the corner a more likely spot to find a hack.

The sidewalk traffic grew thicker as I reached the intersection. By chance a cab had just left off a fare; as quickly as his light came on, it went off as I got in the car. I gave him the address and he pulled away. I searched the crowd. I could not tell if the man was still there or whether I had indeed been followed. I made a mental note to be more careful.

82

Several times on the trip over I doubled checked to see if I was being followed. From what I could tell this was not the case. But in case I was wrong I had the driver let me out several blocks away. I didn't want to lead whoever it might have been directly to Kate's door. I walked off in the wrong direction and made several patented agency moves to lose a tail. It took about half an hour for me to begin to feel comfortable that had anyone followed me I had lost them in my maneuvers.

I got to Kate's flat and rang the bell.

"Who is it?"

"Your friendly visitor from America," was my reply. She buzzed me in and I headed upstairs to her flat. The door was open when I got there. I knocked. "Come on in, I am in the kitchen." I entered and followed my nose to the kitchen.

It was a typical English flat kitchen, small with enough electrical plugs and switches for a commercial eatery. Kate was putting away some groceries. "Hi again." She said as she put the last of the items away. She had done more than grocery shopping while we were apart. She had changed into Levis and sweatshirt. Casual but it looked good on her.

"Hi, did you have a chance to find out anything else?"

"Not much really. I just read some more financial reports, to get a handle on the company."

"What kind of shape is it in?"

"All the reports covered the period before Christakos death, but very good, rock solid. Good balance sheet and highly profitable income statement."

"Credit," I asked?

"The company has very little debt and the highest credit rating."

"I got a fax from Washington with the information I hoped you could help me with."

"Sure, I'll try."

"It seems that since Mrs. Christakos has taken control of the company, the company has changed some of the ways it has previously done business."

"What are they?"

"She has had the entire fleet re-flagged."

"To where?"

"Turkey."

"That's a different choice. I would have expected Liberia or Panama."

"What do you think it means?"

"Not much really. Ships are generally registered in countries that have the loosest shipping rules allowable under international law.

"Such as," I asked.

"Maintenance requirements and liability issues that sort of thing."

I still couldn't quite understand why Melina Christakos had taken this action. "What if there is some kind of international incident? Does the country of registry mean anything?"

"In that case, yes, the registry country could have a distinct advantage given the right circumstances."

"What kind of circumstances?"

Kate paused before answering. "Suppose there was an oil shortage, like back in 1973. The country where the ships are registered could require the shipper to idle the fleet as part of a political power play."

"I see." I felt I had a grasp of this topic I brought up the other issues.

"What about the company increasing its fleet? Any thoughts there?"

"Based upon the numbers I looked at the company certainly can afford to add more capacity. There is more supply coming on line from Central Asia. Maybe it wants have plenty of capacity for this new supply. Do you know how much capacity?"

"Sorry the fax didn't say. The indication was a lot."

"What happens if there is too much world-wide shipping capacity? A glut if you will?"

"The Hellenic Sea Lines has a lot of financial clout. From my research it appears it can weather a downturn better than most other shippers. Anything else?"

"Yes, the company is now buying oil not just shipping it." I could tell Kate was surprised to hear this.

"That is unusual."

"What reasons would the company have to do this?"

"I can only speculate. But the obvious one is control. If you own something you control it. There is also the possibility the company thinks there will be an increase in demand for crude. An increase would certainly drive up the value of any inventory being held. The funny thing is usually a company making a play on the future price of oil will trade options or futures rather than the actual product itself."

"Why is that?" I asked."

"It's easier. You can make a lot of money holding paper without all the hassle of holding the underlying commodity."

"She apparently has a lot of new storage space."

"True but still, it isn't worth it. Unless of course there is something else going on we don't know about."

Kate had certainly hit on it. If there was something going on, it was beyond me. Not a good feeling. "Would you like to go out and catch a quick bite? We can kick around some more ideas."

Kate smiled, "I'd like that. There's a pub around the corner. If we go now I'm sure we can find a quiet corner."

83

As promised the pub was nearby. Also as promised we managed to find a private table. We sat down. I ordered a pint and Kate a glass of white wine. Kate picked up the thread of our conversation and was trying several scenarios to try and find a logical reason for the company to take the actions it had based upon the current world financial condition.

I've always been able to listen and comprehend a conversation while at the same time observe the situation around me. I considered this to be an asset in my line of work. Women whom I've dated have accused me of listening with only half a brain and that it certainly wasn't a gift to do this. What they thought usually didn't matter because I've decided I am what I am and I've long-since given up on trying to improve myself to satisfy others. Kate either didn't notice my eyes wondering about the restaurant or didn't care. I figured she noticed and chose to accept it.

When we first sat down, I noticed a young woman had entered the pub just after Kate and me. It wasn't unusual for a single woman to go to a pub. What was unusual was that by the time our meals were served she was still alone. This seemed slightly out of the ordinary even in the progressive environment of London. Additionally as she sat there she acted as if she was busy reading the paper. My guess was she was really staking someone out. It didn't take the power of Einstein to conclude we were her targets. I kept my eye on her as I turned back to Kate.

"I can't get the accident out of my mind. One minute Charalamambos Christakos is alive and powerful. The next minute he is dead. In a twinkling money goes from being important to nothing."

"I know what you mean. You can't take it with you, though it seems deep down many people seem to think they can."

"Sad isn't it, both of his children also dead? It is the end of the line. It makes you question your priorities. Money is important but it is only money."

"I couldn't agree with you more." I had been looking at Kate but quickly shifted my eyes back to the woman. I caught her quickly averting hers. I was now pretty sure this person was staking us out. The other choice would be that this attractive woman could not keep her eyes off me, Nice, but not realistic. I did not want Kate to worry about being followed, so I suggested, "Let's take a walk. Its lovely out and I thought we could do Kensington Gardens."

"I'd like that."

"So off we go," I said as I helped her with her chair.

84

As we walked towards the park I checked to see if we were still being followed, unfortunately I couldn't readily tell. I didn't want Kate to know, so it was difficult for me to look around too much without raising her suspicions. "You know a lot more about business than I do could you explain some things to me?"

"I will try. What do you want to know?"

"Tell me about futures and options, specifically oil contracts."

"Wow! That is a lot to ask. I am no expert but I can give you the basics I know." We continued to walk along. "Do you understand how treasury bills are priced?"

"Sort of."

"Just as the prices of government obligations are set in the marketplace by the laws of supply and demand, so is commodity contract pricing. Thus a significant change in the supply or demand of commodity contracts would affect their prices. In the world marketplace the effects of anticipated changes in the price of oil are much more dramatic than changes in government financial instruments. Simply because oil is the wheel on which the world's economy turns."

"I have heard terms like in the money and out of the money. What does it mean?"

"In simple terms, a commodity contract, or for that matter any investment type contract, is considered out of the money if it is unlikely under expected market conditions to be exercised."

Usually this kind of conversation put me to sleep, but Kate had a way of making it seem simple and easy to understand. "Where do these contracts come from, where can I buy them?"

"Typically, you can get them through the major brokerage houses of the world. In prior years there were very few out of the money contracts being issued. I understand these institutions have begun issuing them at the urging of the G-7 countries, the United States, Japan and Europe, I understand the idea being to provide the world markets with a complete spectrum of oil-related financial instruments. Thus, if there was some kind of unexpected oil dislocation..."

"Such as an oil embargo?"

"Such as an oil embargo the world markets have a mechanism in place to deal with such shocks."

Kate continued to fascinate me. I was amazed how she could take such an arcane subject and bring it to life. "Out of the money options and futures contracts are complicated instruments based upon a very simple concept. To me it is more like gambling than investing. Brokerage houses write and sell contracts, thus making a profit with the full knowledge these contracts will only be enforced if the price of oil rises dramatically. The price of crude would only rise dramatically if one of three events take place. One, there was a dramatic increase in the demand for crude. This is only likely to happen if there is an increase in the worldwide demand from both industry and individuals combined with extreme worldwide weather conditions. Two, global supply might dramatically fall. This is highly unlikely, particularly in light of the amount of crude being pumped in central Asia."

"What is the third thing that can happen?" I asked.

"Unintended consequences, new products are susceptible to unexpected results and new financial products are no exception. It is a given that many forget, even those in high places, that high profits require high risk, even if those risks are not fully understood."

"What would happen to the brokerage houses if these contracts came into the money?" I asked.

"I am guessing, but I suspect they would find themselves in a difficult position. Do you remember portfolio insurance?"

"I vaguely recall the term."

"Investors were sold a bill of goods. Wall Street salesman took an abstract idea from the world of economics and tried it in real life. The idea was that risk could be eliminated by properly structuring an investment portfolio."

"What happened?"

"It failed miserably. And it failed for such a simple reason. Financial theory assumed there would always be willing buyers in the marketplace. It turned out during the Exchanges collapse of 1987 at least in the short-run, there were no buyers."

"Thanks that helps a lot." By now we were almost to the park.

85

Kate was speaking as we crossed Old Brompton Road. "Every time I take the Piccadilly line, it is as if those pictures from the Blitz come to life. You know, those showing the citizens of London bedding down for the night in the Underground."

"I know what you mean. In fact I wouldn't be surprised if they are still using subway cars from the days of World War II." As I talked I continued to be on the lookout for unwanted company.

"Oh, why is that?" Kate asked

"Well, it could have something to do with the wood floors and those funny straps that hang from the ceiling."

Kate laughed. I was finding it hard to concentrate. Two separate people had followed us. I really liked her and her laughter didn't help. In fact, it only made it worse. We stopped outside Queensgate. "Well, I guess we better turn here or we will miss the Gardens." The light changed and I took Kate by the hand. As I hoped she didn't pull away. As we turned and headed in I saw the lady from the pub. She apparently had been across Old Brampton Road and now was trying to cross the street to follow us without being killed by traffic. I picked up the pace a little hoping to lose our guest without alarming Kate. "You know, when I first came to London one of the first things I did was go to Hyde Park. I had been cooped up all day and I needed to burn off some energy. It was the first time I saw professional dog walkers. They seem to thrive in that part of London. There were men and women walking five or six dogs at time and getting paid to do it. It was simply amazing. Then, when I finally get to the park, I notice these little mailboxes everywhere. Only then I realize these boxes are not for mail. So I decided maybe getting paid to walk dogs wasn't so bad but getting to make deposits in those little boxes was."

86

The Gardens were filled both with flowers in full bloom and people witnessing their beauty on this exceptional day. It was said that the British were avid gardeners. Whether or not that was really true could be debated. What could not be debated was the beauty on display here. Kate and I strolled slowly and talked. We moved along with the crowd toward the giant statue of Prince Albert. As we walked and talked I would occasionally look back to see if our new companion was still with us. I'd been followed before and I didn't like it, but figured it came with the territory. But now, here with Kate, my dislike was turning into discomfort.

"Besides being a spy, where is home? Or can't you say?" Kate asked.

"Well, I'm not really a spy. I'm a government employee who works in security with the NSA."

"That's nice, but you are changing the topic."

"It's not the job, its just habit. I suppose I don't let people get too close to me. I tell myself that I hope I am being conscientious about my job and not just a cold fish."

"Well, I will call you a cold fish if you don't talk," Kate insisted.

"I'm originally from San Francisco. One of the reasons I like London is it reminds me of home."

"What part of the City did you live in?"

"My family lived in the Sunset District. I figure I am a member of the last normal generation to be raised and live in the City."

"What do you mean?"

"Well, I had a normal or what they call today a traditional family. My father worked downtown for Bank of America. He commuted to work everyday on the Muni, the public transit system in San Francisco. Therefore, we only needed one car. My mom stayed at home and raised the three of us. I have a brother and a sister. They are both married and have great kids. But they moved from the Bay Area. After my generation the City filled up with non-traditional types and the families kinda moved away."

"Are your parents still alive?"

"My mom is. I'm lucky. She is in pretty good health and still lives in the home I was raised in. Of course, mom gives me a bad time for not being married yet. She wants more grandchildren to play with. See what I mean about a traditional family?" While I was answering her questions I looked around to see if we had shaken our tail. I could immediately see we hadn't. In a way it was both good and bad. Bad that Kate was in some danger, but good to see one's adversary. It was much more dangerous to be followed and not know it.

Kate started to ask another question when I interrupted. "It's my turn, Ms. Reporter."

"Sorry. Sometimes I just fall into my professional mode, particularly when I find someone interesting or I care about someone."

"It's my turn for twenty questions. Tell me everything about yourself. Leave no detail out and of course you need to do it in fifteen minutes." In the short time we had been together I had come to love her smile and was hoping to see it again.

"Well, I'm a native Californian also from San Diego."

"I thought so. I recall you telling me you had attended San Diego State University. I didn't know San Diego State had a big journalism school."

"It doesn't, but then I didn't take journalism though I considered it at the time. There certainly was some appeal to it. It might have been all those outside classes with the students and the teacher sitting around under the trees having discussions while I had to sit in a stuffy classroom learning about dry accounting stuff like debits and credits. But as you can see today my dad was right on insisting I took a practical major with all the associated self-discipline lessons."

"Why is that?"

"I have a great job and good career while so many of my friends have struggled ever since college finding themselves."

"So that's how you became a business reporter. But how did you end up here in jolly old England?"

"My ear for languages that I told you about put me on the international circuit. So even when I'm not using that ear I'm often assigned out of the country. But it is my turn, so tell me again how you became a spy?"

"At Cal I majored in computer science. After I hurt my knee in the Army the NSA recruited me. I figured the government didn't want to waste all the money it spent on my education. The idea of doing something for my country or at least repaying my college obligation is why I agreed to work for them."

I quickly looked around to confirm we were still being followed. "Kate don't look around but we are being followed and have been since the restaurant." I was pleased to see she wasn't scared. "We need to move quickly out of the Gardens. It's getting late and a little hard to see. It's a good time for us to lose our friend. I want you to follow me and do as I say. Can you do that? No questions asked?"

I admired her look of determination. "I can. Can I ask you something, before we make our move?"

"Okay"

"Where are we going to go?"

"I thought we could check into a hotel."

"I like my place better."

"Whoever is following us will know where you live."

"Not if we get away." I couldn't argue with that logic. "My flat is near and more importantly there is a back way in."

"What about your roommates?"

"They are on holiday and I don't expect them back for a couple of days. Besides, even if they were there, they might need some bothering. I am just kidding."

"Okay, but only if I say so once we get near there. Agreed?"

"Agreed."

With that understanding we walked slowly toward some large hedges. As we approached the bushes I saw our pursuer being bumped by a small child. I pulled Kate behind the bush and we ran out of the Gardens, crossed the street dodging several cars and headed in the direction of Kate's flat.

87

We had hardly gotten in the front door when Kate asked, "Who do you think was following us?"

I closed the door quickly behind us and before she could do anything I reached over and grabbed her hands. "Don't turn on any lights." I said quietly. I then tried a little distraction as I thought about how to answer her question. "I like it your place. It has that lived-in look." I could see my attempt at humor or rather distraction hadn't worked. "I don't honestly know. Is there anyone you can think of that would be following you?"

Kate thought for just a moment and answered, "No not really. I write business stuff. No one tracks you down for that."

"In that case it has to be me. I mean someone following me."

"Have you had this happen before?"

"Yes a couple of times, but not in several years."

"So it has to do with your current investigation then," Kate said.

I wasn't sure of this but she had made a good point. "Could be, but there is also the chance it has to do with another case I just worked on. The case had to do with the illegal transport of nuclear materials. Bad guys play for keeps when it comes to the bomb."

I motioned for Kate to follow me as we went room to room to make sure the windows were closed and that no one had already broken in. We then went to the living room and sat together in the dark on the couch.

"You know, this is kinda scary," she said.

"No, actually it isn't kinda scary, it is just plain scary."

"How long do you thing we will have to sit here in the dark?"

"Honestly, it would be best if we kept the place dark all night. But I don't think anything is going to happen. I really think we lost them."

"Good, in that case we don't have to make life difficult. Would you like a glass of wine or a beer?" Kate asked as she felt her way toward the kitchen.

"I have never gotten used to the taste of warm beer and it would be better to keep the refrigerator door closed so wine would be great. Red wine if you've got it, I don't like warm white wine either. Anything really will do though." I could hear Kate opening and closing drawers as she fumbled in the dark for the wine, corkscrew and glasses.

"Why don't you put something on? The CD player is on the table next to the couch," Kate called out as I heard the cork pop.

"Okay but I will keep the sound low. Want to hear anything in particular?"

"Surprise me."

I found her music collection. I cupped my hands around my small flashlight and searched for some jazz. I eventually found a Miles Davis tape and put it on.

Kate had returned and handed me a glass. "Cheers."

"I hope you like jazz," I said, taking the glass.

"Perfect. Great background music."

We sat back down together on the couch, and both sipped the wine in silence. I spoke first.

"Listen Kate, I really like you and wouldn't want anything to happen to you. If everything is clear by morning, I am going to leave and not contact you again until after my job is over."

"Sorry, that isn't acceptable. We agreed to do this together and together it will be."

"I agreed before this."

"That's irrelevant, I'm in the game, like it or not. I know we have only known each other a short time but I feel very close to you and safe with you. I don't want to put a bunch of pressure on you but I feel I've been waiting for you my entire life."

I had hoped for something like this but reading women was not my long suite. Rather than say anything, I put down my glass and reached over, put my hand behind her head and pulled her close. We kissed and she responded in what I thought was the most sensual way I had ever experienced. We sat on the couch holding each other and the music played softly in the background. I knew our situation could be perilous, but I hadn't felt such peace in a long time. I didn't want this night to end. As I sat there and began to drift off I could hear Kate breathing ever so quietly. She had fallen asleep.

88

"Hazim how nice to see you. Your call was totally un-expected but I am so glad you did," Melina said to Hazim Aziz as they met in the study of her London flat. "Martha would you please bring Mr. Aziz his usual and I will have martini."

"Melina, thanks for inviting me to dinner here. It is so much easier, no press and all their endless questions."

"Yes, the press here can be a problem. No such problems like that at home though," she said laughing. Aziz smiled. "Please sit down. So tell you why you are in London."

Before he could begin, the housekeeper brought the drinks, his was eighteen-year old scotch and her's was a vodka martini. Aziz grasped the glass and took a long drink. "Ah, I see you remember how I like Glenfiddich. Well to be perfectly honest, I came to see you."

"I am flattered."

"Now Melina no need to toy with me. We have a great deal in common."

"Oh you mean besides you have all the oil and I have all the tankers to move the oil?"

"That too. But my dear you love power and I have a lot of power. I will soon have much more. I am sure that is of interest."

"I hope the King and his brother won't take offense to your plans."

"When the time is right, it won't matter what those two think, unless it is how fast they can get out of the country."

"I see. How can I be of help?"

"I would like you at my side, when the time is right."

"That is an interesting proposition. I would of course have to be free to come and go, to run my business."

Waving his hand, "of course, of course."

As Melina sat in her chair she crossed her legs. The dress she had chosen had a long slit up both sides. As she sat back she saw Aziz's eyes look at her with lust. She slowly finished her drink before she spoke. You must tell me more. Yes Martha."

"The dinner is ready, miss."

"Thank you Martha. Reaching out her hand to take his, "Come Hazim, let us see what Gerard has prepared."

"Didn't you steal him from the Countess of Hampton?"

"Steal is such a harsh word. Let's just say the Countess ran into some sudden money problems and could no longer afford Gerard. I simply stepped in and saved the poor fellow's job."

"Well I am glad you did, he is an excellent chef."

"That was one of the reasons I hired him."

"What is the other?" Aziz moved toward the dinning room.

"A perfect meal is an ideal appetizer to the rest of a perfect evening."

89

The last of the dinner dishes had been cleared and after dinner drinks had arrived. Melina waited a few more moments. She could tell Hazim was ready to speak. She held up her hand and finally spoke. "Sometimes the servants linger to pick up gossip. I wanted to make sure they were all the way down the hall and into the kitchen. I understand you have made all the final arrangements. I congratulate you."

"Thank you, but as you undoubtedly know my son Abdul has been instrumental in helping me."

"I see. Let me ask you a question. I don't want to break the mood but I am really quite curious."

"Remember my dear, didn't curiosity kill the cat?"

"I will take my chances. I have been following the price of oil. It has been remarkably stable. How did you do this?"

"Very carefully. Suffice it to say, the options and futures contracts were out of the money and rather dramatically so. This prevented any noticeable market distortions. A rather brilliant plan if I don't say so myself."

Melina tipped her glass in Aziz's direction. "Thank you. Now tell me more about me in your life."

90

Hans Schmidt sat in his office. It was one of those cold, rainy and blustery days in London. A late season storm had rolled in from the North Atlantic. His secretary, Lucy Morgan could not understand why Hans, usually a taciturn man, seemed so happy. "May I get you some tea, Mr. Schmidt?" she asked as she entered his corner office.

"No, thank you, but thanks for asking," came his reply. "Please, just bring me the latest shipping manifests from the Hellenic Sea Lines." Hans was a thorough man and he wanted to make sure the actual shipping documents agreed with the information on his computer.

"Yes, Mr. Schmidt. Right away, sir."

As Lucy left, Hans swung his chair to look out the window. It was time or almost time. Oil was starting to move and so was the money. Not only were Winslow and Son Ltd, going to be the clearinghouse for both the Saudi petrol-dollars and the Hellenic Sea Lines, it was also going to be responsible for brokering the new oil from central Asia. He knew the influence the firm would have and Abdul Aziz would have with all this additional business.

The phone rang. It was his unlisted private line. Reaching slowly for the instrument, he wished not to answer it but knew he had no choice. He was not worried about what the call would bring; it was only that he did not want this moment to pass. Finally, after several rings he spoke into the receiver. "Yes, Melina, we are ready on this end."

91

I awoke still sitting on the couch. Kate was no longer next to me, but I could hear someone presumably her in the back of the apartment. It wasn't the start of my typical day. One, I slept the entire night without waking up, a rarity between job stress and my knee. And two and somewhat more amazing. I had awakened in a woman's apartment, not only that a woman who appeared to be in love with me.

As I head off for the bathroom I heard Kate call out to me. "I left some stuff on the counter for you to use. Leave your clothes out for me. I will wash them while you take a shower." Having someone care was real nice. I did my morning bit and put on a towel and followed my nose to the kitchen. I could smell coffee being brewed. I could tell it was good American stuff, not that dishwater stuff the Brits try to pawn off as coffee.

"Good morning, I like the towel. Your clothes should be ready in a couple of minutes," Kate said, "I don't have much to offer, but I do have fruit and muffins."

"Thanks. Sounds just right."

"Have you had any other thoughts or guesses about who might have been following us?" Kate asked getting right to the point.

"I think I know how to narrow the list down, but before I do I'd like to wear my clothes. Do you think they're ready yet?"

"Should be." She reached over and reached into a combination washer dryer located in the kitchen I had not seen before and handed me my things.

"Thanks, I'll be right back." I headed for the bathroom changed and returned grabbing my cell phone on the way. "I think I can eliminate one of my two choices for who might have followed us."

"Good, knowing is better than not knowing."

I dialed Amani's cell number as I walked in the direction of the living room. It was later in the workday in Saudi Arabia so I figured my chances of reaching my friend were pretty good. The phone rang a couple of times before I heard his voice.

"Hello, Fahad Amani."

"Fahad, Mike Williams, how are you?"

"Mike so good to hear from you. I am doing only okay. I am ass deep in some old files doing research."

"If this is a bad time, I can call you back later."

"No please don't I could use the break. At least for a few minutes"

"Remember the Yemeni smuggling ring we stopped."

"Yes"

"Have any of them or any of their associates been freed or escaped from jail?"

"You have to be alive to escape. Most of them were hanged as traitors. The few who escaped the executioner are still locked up. Why do you ask?"

"I have been followed and you know they swore vengeance on the two of us."

"Everyone swears vengeance and I haven't been followed. I would be very surprised if your being followed had anything to do with the smugglers."

"Good to know, it narrows my search. It sounds like you are busy so I'll let you go."

"Mike, while I have you on the line let me run something by you."

"Go ahead."

"You see I have this problem."

Amani went on to fill me in on his suspicions and concerns. "Let's not talk much longer." I was concerned about our conversation being intercepted and privacy was definitely something that was needed. "I will do whatever I can to help you. Please give me two ways to contact you at any time or place." Fahad had anticipated my request and quickly gave me the information. "I will be in touch."

Kate who had voluntarily kept her distance while I had talked to Fahad joined me in the living room. "Who was that?"

"Fahad Amani, a Saudi, I worked with him on my last job. He has worked for their National Security Force for the last eight years."

"National Security Force?"

"If this were the United States the National Security Force would be viewed as a combination of the FBI and the US Marshall's Office. Prior to being asked to join, one was only *asked* to join the agency; he had been a major in the Saudi Army. You know how large the Royal Family is?"

"Yes"

"Well he is one of the few NSF members who is not somehow related to the Royal family. He's very good at what he does. Of course he'd have to be not being related and all."

"Like Hazim Aziz, the current Saudi Oil Minister."

"I didn't know that."

"Not only that he isn't even one hundred percent Arab. His mother's family is Turkish. They came as traders when the Ottoman Empire ruled the Arabian Peninsula. After Saudi Arabia gained its independence following World War I most of the family returned home. However, his great-grandmother had fallen in love and chose to remain behind to be with the man whom she would eventually marry."

"Interesting information but how did you know it?" I asked.

"Research for the series I am doing."

The Turkish connection intrigues me. "What else do you know about this guy?"

"Normally a position of such importance is reserved only for members of the extended royal family, but because of its importance, ability has more influence than lineage. For example, Sheik Yamini who led the 1973 oil embargo also wasn't of royal heritage. Aziz is considered to be the third most important person in the country. Indeed, if the country were not a monarchy, he might even be its head."

I wanted to think about the possibilities in the information Kate gave me. I also needed to deal with that fact that we had been followed. My choices as to who was involved had narrowed considerably.

"Kate I think whoever is following us is associated with my current investigation. That is the only logical explanation. Fahad ruled out my other choice."

"Kemal Kanuni," Kate said simply.

"Yes."

92

Fahad put down his phone and returned to his research, he needed to check out one more thing. He needed to read the crash investigation report. As expected it was brief but a couple of lines at the end of the report caught his attention.

> *"All parts of value had been stripped from the plane including the radio, engine and windows. The main fuselage, wings rudders and flaps seemed to be in good condition and in working order. It appears the plane's occupants did not die inside the plane as there was no sign of blood in the cabin."*

Department policy precluded the copying of reports unless approved by a senior minister. Fahad didn't want to draw attention to his investigation, at least not yet. Note taking was permitted and this case was all he needed.

Amani took his research items, placed them in the "to be filed" bin waved to the guard and returned to his office. On the way he passed by Mustafa Zell's sitting at his desk. He tapped him on the shoulder indicating he should follow him.

Amani closed the door and turned to Zell, "Mustafa I have been down in the archives following up on the lead you gave me."

"The one about Abdul Yunni?"

"Yes"

"You found something of interest?"

"It seems under interrogation Abdul Yunni implicated the senior oil minister as a clandestine supporter of the banned fundamentalist United Islamic Front."

"Amazing, I presume the report is believable."

"Completely. What is more interesting is what happens next. Akmed Khomani and his chief assistant flew from Riyadh to Medina in a small plane to follow a lead given to them by Yunni."

"And the plane crashed," Zell filled in the ending.

Amani echoed him, "And the plane crashed." Fahad then pulled out his notes and showed them to Zell. Mustafa read them and returned them without saying anything. "Mustafa I find two things interesting. One it appears both men survived the crash and two the engine of the plane was missing. I can't imagine how anyone without some kind of heavy equipment could lift an engine completely out of a plane. Bedouins don't carry heavy machinery. What do you think?"

Zell nodded, I have never known any Bedouin to bring his power tools with him."

Fahad continued. "I can only assume the plane was forced down somehow. Maybe a fuel line problem or even fuel sabotage, something like that. Once on the ground whoever caused the accident was waiting. Akmed Khomani and his chief assistant were killed immediately or captured and possibly interrogated and then killed. The same people also then removed the engine to hide any evidence of sabotage."

Zell nodded, "That's a reasonable explanation fitting the facts."

"If I am correct or close to being correct we both may be in danger. If someone by chance saw either of us follow the junior or senior Mr. Aziz they would without a great effort be able to tie us together. The fact I was in the archives is on record."

"I presume you put other non implicating reference material in the "to be filed" bin."

"I did, but still."

"What should we do?"

"Do nothing special, act normally. I will make some contacts and talk to some friends."

93

"You know we're in this together," Kate said. "I know I don't have security clearance and I also know I am a reporter. But it is my life, it is your life, it is our lives together. To solve this problem we are going to need to be open and maybe just maybe we will get lucky. Because as far as I can tell, we know jack, it's just that someone thinks we know a lot more than we do or at least thinks we might know something. Do you trust me and are you willing to take a chance?"

I knew she was right. I had to make a field decision. There was no time to run this by the bureaucrats in D.C. The time was now. "Okay, I will tell you what I know and you will do the same and we will see what we can turn up. I was originally asked to go to Istanbul as an observer on a diplomatic mission to check out the new players on the street in central Asia. When I went Hakan Kanuni was still alive and the Chairman, his nephew Kemal Kanuni was Vice-Chairman. I have to admit I really impressed with Kemal Kanuni in the sense of the power and magnetism of the man. For some reason, just an impression really, he struck me as someone who to really understand, you needed to disassociate his words from his actions."

Kate had begun making notes. She looked up and said, "How so?"

"I believe that if you listen to what he says, you will conclude certain things about him. If you follow his actions you will conclude something else. At least that was what put in my report."

"What else did you report?"

"I told my ultimate boss, Joann Davis, the National Security Advisor that I believed Chairman Kanuni was cold and calculating about all aspects of life, including religion."

"The kind of personality you describe is exceptionally dangerous, given a position of power." I saw no reason to contradict her.

"Kate, what, if anything, did you come up with on the character front?"

"More confirmation of the same kind of the same thing, some names also, Eileen Wright and Katrina Fokina."

"Katrina aka Melina Fokina?"

"The very same."

"So we've learned that even amoral characters can have soul mates."

"Do you know if they stayed in contact after graduation?"

"It appears they did, at least up to the time that Kemal returned home. After that, I have been unable to determine."

"No knowledge doesn't mean no contact. It just means a lack of information."

"Exactly." I waited for her to finish making some notes. "I think we have made a good start." Kate looked at me with a somewhat doubtful look. I noticed it and began again. "I can see from your expression you think we haven't done much, but think about it."

"Humor me."

"We have two things going. We have a reasonable confirmation of my gut reaction about Kanuni character. From the public's point of view he appears to be a popular charismatic leader who is deeply religious and as such is committed to helping his people."

"Go on." Kate nodded.

"Two we have tied Melina Fokina at least in the past to Kemal. There are indications these ties still exist."

"How so?"

"We know she at least for the reasonably near future has complete control of the Hellenic Sea Lines. In that role she has re-flagged her entire fleet in Turkey, a country very much under Kanuni's influence."

"Don't forget she has also added a substantial amount of shipping capacity," Kate added.

"That's right and the timing is remarkable, just about the same time, Kanuni's oil fields from Central Asia are set to come on line." I stopped again to let Kate complete her note taking. "There is one more thing. There have been a lot of rather untimely deaths."

Kate leaned back in the chair and thought for a moment. "Let's see there was the entire Christakos household. Who else?"

"Don't forget his uncle. He conveniently passed away just in time for Kanuni to become Chairman. He wasn't the first. There was a guy by the name of Dax Salyan.

"Who?"

"He was essentially the Bir League's opposition leader to the Kanuni's, particularly to Kemal. He died in a plane accident over the Black Sea. Conveniently it seems at a place so deep that it was impossible to examine the wreckage."

"It seems that anyone who gets in their way has the life expectancy of a dead person. Where do you think we go from here?"

"We need to get some more facts. See if we can tie Melina in some way to Kanuni today, more than just some coincidences, like re-flagging the fleet. See if we can place them physically together in the recent past. If we do that I believe we can at least fairly assume they are working on some plan."

"How do you propose we do that?"

"I want to go our Embassy and make a few calls. They have the needed secure phone lines there. I need to talk to a few old friends. I will call so they will expect us."

"We can take the tube. It will be the quickest way to get there. While you make your call I'll finish getting dressed. I'll be ready to go in ten minutes," Kate promised as she left the room.

Before calling I stepped to the window to see if we were still being watched. I didn't see anyone obvious, but only amateurs were obvious and I didn't think we were dealing with amateurs.

94

Much to my surprise, Kate was indeed ready within ten minutes. "Before we go, remember we still may be followed so keep your head up."

"Thanks for the reminder. Should we take a cab instead, in that case?"

"I don't think so. For all we know, your phone could be tapped or they could intercept my cell and as soon as we called for a cab, they, whoever they are, would substitute their person for a regular cab driver and we could find ourselves being chauffeured about by the very people from whom we are trying to escape. Are you ready to go?"

"Yes, as ready I'll ever be." Kate replied as she moved to pickup her laptop.

"Let me carry that for you."

"Thanks," Kate said

As I picked up the laptop I said, "I can see why you let me carry this. It's heavy."

"I know. My mom didn't raise any fools. The extra batteries I carry add to the weight."

We locked the door and made sure all the windows were tightly secured. I also saw Kate leave a note for her roommates saying she was going out of town on assignment and that she would call them when she had a better handle on how long she would be gone.

"Smart move with the note, good idea not alarm your friends, besides if someone talks to them, they should be safe because they would really know nothing."

95

It was a short walk from Kate's flat down old Brompton Road to the South Kensington underground station. The station was busier than one would be expected for what was in essence a suburban subway station because it served as a transfer station for both the Piccadilly Line and the district lines that circled London. Kate stood in line to purchase the appropriate tickets while I waited and watched. I didn't see anyone suspicious and began to relax just a little.

"Here you go," Kate said as she handed me my computer card. "Did you see anyone?"

"No, but please stay close."

"That is an order I am more than happy to follow."

We headed off in the direction of the Piccadilly line. As is typical in most underground stations, the district lines are found one level down and the other lines, in this case the Piccadilly Line, is a level below that. We took the escalator to the lowest level and followed the crowd as it wound around toward the platform. The platform was standard Underground. There is a small area on which to stand as one waits for the next train. Kate directed us towards the end of the station closest to the tunnel entrance. She explained it was easier to get a seat if we got in the end cars. Naturally most people hang back from the edge. There are no barriers, and generally people like to stay back from the onrushing cars. However, as the arrival of a train becomes more imminent, the platform fills to over- capacity and those in the front of the crowd are pushed closer and closer toward the tracks, the only thing between them and the onrushing train is a little white line with the words *mind the gap* painted above it. Because we had arrived early, we found ourselves among those lucky ones being moved closer and closer to the edge of the platform.

The crowds grew heavier and we became separated. I could feel the hot air blast that was the first signal of a train arriving. I briefly looked at the overhead sign to confirm the train's arrival, then quickly looked back to locate Kate again. But she was gone, nowhere to be seen. The hairs on the back of my neck stood up. I didn't like this at all. I began to force my way through the crowd, pushing people aside as I moved in the direction where I had last seen Kate. I could hear the train start to thunder into the station. As I moved toward where I hoped Kate was, I heard a scream and knew instantly it was Kate. I was now frantically shoving people aside. I could hear the train begin to screech to a halt. I had gotten almost to the edge of the platform when I saw her. Kate's arms were moving about in a vain effort to try to regain her balance. She was on the edge of the platform and was about to fall in and there was nothing I could do. The train was going to hit her. Suddenly, a hand reached out and grabbed Kate's flaying arm.

To my immense relief the hand caught Kate's arm and managed to pull her back. I was stunned. The lady who had tailed us all day yesterday was hanging onto Kate! The train screeched to a halt filling the entire platform. As the crowd moved to enter the train, I pushed my way through and gathered a sobbing Kate into my arms. As I stood there holding Kate and starring at her savior the last of the passengers pushed crowded into the train and as quickly as train arrived it vanished down the tunnel. We were not on it, but Kate was alive.

It was now quiet enough to be heard. "Who are you?" was the only thing I managed to say.

The lady held up her hand and reached into her pocket. I was instantly wary. However, before I could react, she pulled out some identification. She handed me the folder identifying her as Maggie Smith an inspector with Scotland Yard. The relief on my face must have been evident as she motioned to us to follow her out of the station. A car was parked outside the station and she held the door for us to get in

I helped Kate into the back seat got in beside her and took a deep breath. We had a guardian angel but how and why?"

96

Still silent, Inspector Smith started the car and pulled into traffic. Only after we had gone a couple of blocks did she speak.

"I wanted to get away from the station for safety reasons," the Inspector began. "Now that we are away, I will sort this situation out for you as best I can. Mr. Williams, several days ago your boss Director Brown, contacted my superior, Philip Logan, I understand you and he are friends. As a personal favor, the director asked that someone from Scotland Yard mind after you. You see, he had received rumors from unknown sources out of the Middle East, specifically Amman, Jordan, that American government officials were being targeted by unspecified Islamic groups for, let us say, unpleasant experiences. Obviously, your superior put enough stock in the rumors to ask us for help. Lucky for you, what?"

"Lucky for us."

"I was one of two people assigned to look after you. I had the day shift and Guy Blackwell had nighttime duty."

"I made both of you yesterday. How long before that had you been my guardian angels?"

"We received the request from your government a couple of days ago. Philip didn't want to tell you for security reasons."

"So you were not following me, I mean watching after me, any time before that?"

"No, we weren't." I thought I had been followed earlier on my way back to Philip's place, but I hadn't been sure. I was now sure.

Kate had been starring out the window as we talked. I turned to look at Kate and in a quiet voice said, "You've had a couple of minutes are you ready to give us your side of the story?"

"Well, there's not much to tell," Kate began. "The platform was crowded and Mike and I got separated as the train we were going to take approached. Nothing seemed out of the ordinary. I could feel the crowd pushing me forward in the direction of the approaching train. I could see the crowd settle down all around me, but not exactly where I was. I still felt pressure to move closer to the edge of the platform. I began to resist, but the more I resisted, the stronger the pressure seemed. I felt the rush of air signaling the train's arrival. At that moment I felt a push. A man, possibly judging by the strength of the shove, pushed me into the path of the train. As I was about to fall from the platform I felt someone grab me and pull me back."

Both Inspector Smith and I listened in silence as Kate described the events from her perspective. During the silence I noted we were heading in the direction of the U.S. Embassy. "Well, Inspector, it appears to be your turn."

"Once we arrive at your Embassy, I will provide you with what I know. I would appreciate it if you would have the Marine Guard wave us into the compound upon our arrival. I don't believe we have been followed, but there is no point in taking unnecessary chances this close to the fort."

Within minutes we arrived at the front gate of the Embassy. The car pulled into the driveway and, as it did, a Marine guard came over to the vehicle and the inspector rolled down the window. I leaned forward as the Corporal lowered his head to question us.

"Corporal, my name is Mike Williams." I handed the Marine my identification. "I am a member of the NSA and would appreciate it if you would allow us to pull into the compound. The driver of the car is Inspector Maggie Smith of

Scotland Yard." The Inspector handed her identification to the guard. "The young lady in the back seat is an American citizen. Her name is Kate O'Hara. Someone just attempted to kill her and we need a few moments alone to talk to her." The Guard looked confused, as this was not your typical guard-duty situation. Confusion led to hesitation and at this point I certainly didn't want to be trapped in the car half in and half out of the embassy compound. I decided to help the guard make a decision. "Corporal, if you want, by all means please contact the Ambassador. He will vouch for me and Ms. O'Hara." I figured that last little push would get us inside the compound. As I had hoped the Corporal handed back the identification cards and waved us into the compound.

After parking, Inspector Smith turned to me and said, "I thought the touch about ringing up the Ambassador was well done."

"It did get our butts out of hanging half-in and half-out of the compound, didn't it?"

"Quite right."

"Okay, please tell us what you saw."

"Both of your descriptions are similar to mine. I followed you down into the underground station. As you became separated I decided to stay closer to Kate here. I figured you could take care of yourself better than Ms. O'Hara. Fortunately for all of us, I was correct. I could see that the crowd around Kate was still being pushed ahead as the train was pulling into the station. As has been previously noted, this was a most unusual occurrence. As I watched, it appeared that one man was causing the commotion. As I moved forward I could see this man reach out and push Kate so she would fall into the path of the train. I didn't have much time to see what he looked like but he was definitely Middle Eastern, Arabic, Turkish. I managed to grab onto Kate and we all know the rest of the story, at least to the point where we all entered the compound of the American Embassy."

"Did you see him leave?"

"From the corner of my eye, as I grabbed for Ms. O'Hara I could see him move quickly toward the station exit," the Inspector responded.

"So we have no idea if he was working alone or with others."

"True, disconcerting but true. What do you two intend upon doing now?"

"Well, I don't think either of us know for sure. We'll need to sort some things out. Originally we had intended to go to the Embassy to make some calls and then follow up on any leads."

"I suggest that you stay here at the embassy until you hear from me. Considering the turn of events, I will need to talk with my superiors before I can offer you any additional help." She handed me her card as she spoke. "Here is my card. It contains my cell number, so if you decide to ride off somewhere, you can always reach me."

I took the card and placed it in my pocket. "Thanks for all your help. Kate and I need to talk about things. I will let you know what we intend to do." I wrote a number down on my card and handed it to the Inspector. "You can reach me anytime at this number. I think your job is done here, at least for a while." As I spoke, I motioned for Kate to get out of the car. Kate and I got out. I put my arm around her as we walked in the direction of the embassy's private entrance.

97

I placed my left hand on the pad by the door. Within seconds it opened, and Kate and I entered. We walked into a rather ornate reception hall. To the left there was a modestly appointed study where I escorted Kate. Once inside I closed the door. In the far corner were two leather, winged chairs. I motioned Kate to sit in one and I took the other.

"How are you doing?

"I think I am still slightly in shock. You know, it's not everyday that someone tries to kill you. I'm still young enough to think that I'll live forever or at least for a very, very long time. I suspect my view of life will never be the same. But I am okay."

It was an honest assessment but I was still concerned, "Look at me. Are you sure you'll be all right?"

"Yes, as sure as someone in denial can be."

"Kate, I love you. Before the incident today I thought I loved you; afterwards, there's no question in my mind. I can't imagine living life without you. I hope you feel the same about me but I understand what an emotional jumble you must be in right now."

"You know, it's kind of funny. The only thing I'm really sure about is how I feel about you. You make me whole and I never want to lose you. I can't tell you how happy I am that we have found each other. It must be one of God's jokes. I could do a piece on it. Couple finds love in near-death experience or how a subway trip changed my life forever."

"Kate, I love how you can joke, but on a serious note, how do you want to proceed? It's just a question. No right or wrong answers."

"Part of me wants to run and hide somewhere with you. I know that's not real. The other part of me knows that we have to find the answers. If we don't, our relationship will suffer maybe not today but eventually. I need you. I trust you. But I'm scared."

"I'm scared, too. I think we've stumbled onto something big. I wish we could head for the south of France and forget the whole thing. I can't do that and now I know you can't either. It's who and what we are. We need to take this thing to a conclusion." By now Kate had risen from the chair and was pacing about. In each step I could see her become more confident and self-assured.

Kate spoke at last. "You're right. Just help me out and I will help you." Her energy was infectious. I was also up moving towards her. We embraced and clung to each other. I had never held anyone with such intensity in my entire life.

98

"Let's go" I grabbed Kate's hand and headed out the door in the direction of signals. Signals was the communications section of the working Embassy. "I need to make those calls I mentioned earlier."

"Who are you going to contact?"

"I want to talk to the stations chiefs in Ankara and Astana."

"Where is Astana?"

"It's the new capital of Kazakhstan. I want to find out if there is any current connection between Melina and Kemal. If there has been I am going to work on the assumption there is some kind of plot."

"A plot can be bad but it doesn't necessarily mean a threat to the United States or world peace."

"True. I also think I want to give my friend Fahad Amani a call."

"The Saudi inspector?"

"Yes."

"Why is that? Haven't we figured out who was following us?"

"Yes, but I have this gut feeling."

By now we had arrived at our destination. Again I placed my left palm on the keypad to gain access to the room. Kate and I entered and the door closed automatically behind us. "Kate, of all the sections of the embassy this one is the most heavily protected from electronic eavesdropping. From here we can make contact anywhere in the world. It's manned by three NSA employees twenty four hours a day seven days a week."

We approached the Maria Ventura the deputy NSA director for the embassy.

"Maria," I pointed to Kate, "this is Kate O'Hara she's helping me with an investigation."

Maria shook Kate's hand and turned to me. "Clearance?"

"Field promotion."

"I see." I had a reputation for being a little unorthodox when it came to procedures. I had heard jokes behind my back. I was described as a cowboy, the kind that shoots first, keeps shooting, and then if anyone is left alive, ask the questions. Some thought of me as rash. I preferred decisive. My lack of conformity would have been a problem but I had record of success that mitigated the issue.

"Kate would you mind standing in the back of the room?"

Kate looked at me and I nodded that it was okay. "Maria I need to make some calls, what desk is available?"

"Take mine."

"Thanks." I headed for Maria's desk sat down and entered my identification code. Within a few minutes I had contacted both station chiefs, faxed them a picture of Melina Christakos and asked them to see if there were any facts or reasonable rumors of Kemal and Melina meeting within the last several months. Both chiefs thought they could get me the information by day's end.

My next call was going to be to Amani in Saudi Arabia. I had the feeling that somehow the Saudis were involved in all this. Before I could put the call through to his cell number Maria came up to me and told me Fahad was on line two.

99

"Hello Fahad, this is Mike Williams."

"Mike, how are you?"

"Fine Fahad. How about you? After all these months then twice in one week, you must have finally realized how much you missed me."

"A good friend such as you is always missed."

I knew something was wrong, I could tell it in his voice. I was wondering if it had something to do with his suspicions about Hazim Aziz. Still wishing to keep it light, "Is this a social call or do you want me to tell you the right horse to wager on at Ascot next weekend?"

"If it were that, I would be telling *you*, rather than the other way around." It amazes me how even in a time of apparent crisis and urgent communication, it was necessary for this round of small talk to take place. It was an Arab custom and would never change under any circumstance. Had it been a German on the phone, the conversation would have been over and everyone would have been out the door at least ten minutes ago. "The reason I am calling is that I recall you mentioned that you had a college roommate who now works for Cisco Systems."

"Ah yes, Mr. Big Bucks. Joe Clinton, the king of the ISO, incentive stock option." Really wanting to get to the point, I asked, "Do you need help with your investment portfolio?"

"Civil servants, even in Saudi Arabia, do not have investment portfolios," Amani replied. "The problem I am having is that the Force ordered some very sophisticated computer-switching gear and software from Cisco and we can't get delivery. As I recall, your friend is an executive vice president with the company."

"Yes, he is," Mike said. "Why can't you get delivery?"

"According to our procurement officer, Cisco says we are late with our payments. We have not yet paid for items we ordered six months ago."

"Wow, Fahad, that's hard to believe. Hasn't your country always had a policy of timely payments?"

"Yes, it has been a point of honor for the King. That is what worries me. I can't believe the country is out of money, so I was hoping you could find something out about this problem on the QT, out of channels, of course, for me."

"Fahad, sure I'll make a few calls. It may be a few days before I can let you know what happens, time zones and all. Is that alright?"

"I appreciate any help. When you do call please call using the numbers I gave you the last time we talked."

"I will. Before you go, I need to ask you a question. As a matter of fact I was about to call you when you called me."

"What can I help you with?"

"I remember hearing that Hazim Aziz was part Turkish."

"That is the case. His mother's family was originally from Turkey."

"Do you know if he or any of his family has any contact with Kemal Kanuni or the new Bir League?'

"Why yes, his son Abdul Aziz is a Council observer with full voting rights I understand."

"You are sure?"

"Oh yes, this is common knowledge."

My head was racing. My gut was correct. There was a link between the Saudi's and Kemal and that link went at least as high as Hazim Aziz, the senior oil minister. I needed to talk to Kate about this and about the money thing.

"I will phone you back as soon as I hear anything about the money question you had. Until then good-bye."

"Good-bye, Mike. Good luck or should I say good hunting?"

100

I rose from Maria's workstation. "Thanks, I am expecting a couple of calls from Ankara and Astana. Please patch them through to my cell when they come in."

"Sure and good luck."

I headed for the door and Kate followed me. "We need to talk. There's a conference room down the hall." We walked in silence until we entered.

Kate asked, "Did you have any luck with the station chiefs?"

"They will check it out and call us back."

"What else?"

"I was about to call Amani when he called me instead."

"Oh"

"He wanted to me to check on something for him. Apparently the NSF can't get delivery on some equipment it ordered from Cisco."

"Why?"

"Get this the Saudi Government is a deadbeat."

"What?"

"According to Fahad, Cisco is telling him they haven't been paid in six months. He wanted me to check with my roommate, a mucky muck there to see if it was true."

"That would be amazing if true." Kate checked her watch; "If you call right now you can probably catch him before lunch on the West Coast."

She waited while I called. Within minutes I had managed to get a hold of Joe Clinton and had confirmed the rumor.

I put down the phone and looked at Kate. "It's true. Do you think this is possible?"

"I don't know but I know where to look."

"Good, we should follow up on that next. I have one other tidbit for you."

"You are quite the fount of knowledge today."

"It seems that Abdul Aziz, Hazim's son is an observer, a voting observer I might add, to the Bir League."

"So we now have a direct link from Kemal to someone high up in Saudi Arabia."

We fell silent thinking about the implications of what we had just discovered.

101

Maggie pulled out of the embassy compound and headed toward Oxford Street and headquarters. As she drove back to 10 Broadway she took out her portable Dictaphone and began to speak:

"Per request of the American government I was assigned discrete protective detail for NSA officer Mike Williams. I expanded the assignment to include his associate, Kate O'Hara. Ms. O'Hara is a business news journalist. Make a note; I need to find which paper she works for. I followed Williams and O'Hara, who according to their statements are collaborating on an investigation, to the Kensington underground station. They said it was their plan was to take the tube to the American embassy to continue their research. At the station an unknown male assailant of apparent Middle East origin attempted to murder Ms. O'Hara. I managed to prevent injury to Ms. O'Hara."

"Conclusion: By extrapolation one would have to conclude that Mr. Williams and or Ms. O'Hara have some very important and dangerous information. I believe they are unaware of exactly what this information might be as they did not appear to be evasive when I asked them this question. Clearly, the attempted murderer knows the information already. No need to capture someone to gather the information. Rather, this is a case of trying to suppress knowledge. The logical conclusion is that, together, the Americans know something worth murdering for, whether they know it or not. It is further reasonable to assume that Ms. O'Hara has some knowledge or access to knowledge unknown to Mr. Williams that would make her rather than Mr. Williams the target."

Maggie put down the tape recorder as she pulled into headquarters. She parked her car and quickly headed for the identification section.

102

As Maggie Smith entered the identification section, a cubicle farm filled with computer equipment, she began to search out her friend and senior sketch artist, Ambrose Blair. By common acknowledgement he was the best in the U.K., having helped put away a number of the most notorious members of the I.R.A, and she needed the best.

She found him at his workstation fixing a cup of tea. "Ambrose, I need your help."

"Well, Maggie, it's good to see you, too," he said without looking up.

"I am sorry to be pushy but I just witnessed a crime and I want to describe the perpetrator while his face is still familiar to me."

"I understand, just teasing. I figured you needed something quickly or you would have asked me for some tea first. Well, then, let's have a go at it."

Ambrose pulled out his sketchpad and began working as Maggie gave her description. He asked a few questions and with each answer filled in more detail. Finally, he turned the picture toward her.

"Is this the person?'

"Yes. It never ceases to amaze me how accurate you can be based upon what I think are so few clues."

"Good let's take it to the computer." They walked a short distance to the picture recognition station where Ambrose took his sketch and scanned it into the bureau's system. The software would make an initial review of the picture and then as part of the process would prompt Blair to make any refinements necessary to enable the system. The file would then be downloaded into face recognition software. The software would convert the picture into an electronic file format. This particular electronic file would then be compared to other files in the identification database, an enormous electronic file that contained electronic pictures from all the old mug-shot books in the world. For the last ten years worldwide law enforcement and other security agencies had cooperated to make their files available to each other. This meant she would be able to search data from here in the United Kingdom, Interpol and the American F.B.I.

"How long?" Maggie asked.

"A couple of hours, at least."

"I am going to grab something to eat and file my report and be back. Once the match comes up, please ring me at my cubical," Maggie said as she got up from her chair to leave.

"No problem, Ms. Smith," Ambrose replied.

She had taken about three steps toward the door when she heard Ambrose call her name. "I think you should stay. It seems we have a match."

Maggie was surprised that a match had come up so soon. What it meant was that the man she described was probably on file with either domestic security sources or Interpol. The program was structured to look at the closest files in geographic terms before searching further a-field. It wasn't, of course, that the computer cared where the file was located; it was just easier on the police and cheaper to talk to someone closer to home when conducting an investigation than someone halfway around the world.

Maggie hurried back and as she arrived at Ambrose's workstation a picture was coming up on the computer screen. As the picture appeared a paper copy was being automatically printed at the same time. "Ambrose, that's him, the man who tried to kill Kate O'Hara."

On the computer screen was a picture from Interpol with a name underneath —Yussof Dakkak. A description printed next to the picture: This man was between 30 and 35 years of age and Turkish by birth but now traveled under a Kazakh passport. The biography went on to report that he was a hired killer with no ideological preferences. Money, not love or causes, was clearly his motivation. According to sources, he could kill in any number of ways but preferred firearms, particularly sniper rifles. While she read the computer screen the data was also being printed on a color printer.

She grabbed the picture and shuddered; "Ambrose, this is one bad guy."

"It sure looks that way."

"Thanks for your help. I have to talk to Philip Logan about this. Can you send this picture to the American Embassy?"

"Surely, no worries."

"Thanks. Send it to Mike Williams' attention. He and Kate O'Hara need to be warned about this fellow. Waving as she left, she said, "Thanks, Ambrose. I owe you."

"If I were paid a pound for everyone who said that, I could retire a rich man," he called back as she disappeared out the door.

103

"So, Yussof, tell me what happened. You look uncomfortable. Don't worry. Just tell me what happened."

Yussof Dakkak looked at his employer.

"Well?"

Dakkak had not realized he had not yet responded. "Mr. Bizhanov, as you instructed, I followed the American, Mike Williams. During the time of my assignment he appeared to team up with another American, a lady by the name of Kate O'Hara. She is a reporter with the *Washington Post*."

"I have read some of her articles. She seems to understand business and international finance quite well. Go on," Akham commanded.

"Upon your instruction I made contact with all our usual sources. It seems that both Mr. Williams and Ms. O'Hara have a common assignment, to investigate Kemal Kanuni. I can only surmise, but it is logical to assume that they somehow met and in so doing learned of their mutual projects. I reported this to you. You then further instructed me to do whatever it took to delay their investigation. Unfortunately it seems the subway accident I attempted was not successful."

"What happened?"

"As I pushed her into the path of the subway train, a woman managed to grab onto her and save her at the last minute."

"And who was this woman?"

"I believe she works for either British intelligence or Scotland Yard."

"So you failed because of a woman," Akham Bizhanov remarked sarcastically.

Trying to defend himself, Yussof replied, "It is only a setback, an inconvenience it was not a failure. I can assure you I will kill both of them. I am embarrassed I did not do a professional job. That will not happen again. I am sure you, the person I consider the ultimate professional, can appreciate my embarrassment.

Akham enjoyed toying with some of his operatives. "I am forced to agree with you, but it will be a failure if you do not kill them and do so straight away. I am sure you know your life will not be worth camel dung if you don't fulfill your assignment. I am also certain you understand what I mean?"

"Completely, yes I do."

"Then go and do not fail."

Yussof rose quickly and left the room. He knew the consequences and had no intention of failing again.

104

"Prime Minister al Shariff, I wanted to see if my staff has been responsive to your requests. I know there are times they have been viewed as rude."

"Quite the contrary, Mr. Aziz, your staff has been nothing but helpful, attentive down to the smallest of details. In fact since your ministry has been in charge of coordinating this conference we have had very little to do."

"Does this represent a problem to your government? Is your King concerned about his safety or is there something wrong with the accommodations I have chosen?"

"Of course not Mr. Minister. The Dorchester is an excellent choice. I am certain my king will be able to meet with His Highness and the Crown Prince as well as following his physician's recovery orders at that location. I hope the same can be said for the King and his medical needs."

"I thank you for your concerns. The King will be in the best of care. I personally have seen to it as well as to his and his brother's security."

"Speaking of safety issues, my head of security has mentioned to me certain concerns. I would appreciate it if your counterpart would contact his over these concerns."

"But of course, Khalid, I will see to it right away."

"Thank you, I don't want to seem impertinent but I must stress how important it is to our government that we confer with your security chief as soon as possible."

"I completely understand. I will call him as soon as we ring off."

"Again, thank you."

"Goodbye Khalid," Hazim Aziz said as he returned the phone to its cradle and left for his weekly massage.

105

"Father, I wanted to make sure there were no last minute problems," Abdul Aziz asked.

"Everything is going as planned. The Jordanian Prime Minister has made certain security requests, except for that, nothing."

"We anticipated that."

"Yes we did. We are slowly dealing with their requests, very slowly," the Oil Minister replied.

"And by the time we have dealt with them all it won't matter."

"Exactly. I am sure everyone will remark how unfortunate it is that bureaucracies move so slowly."

"What exactly is al Shariff's complaint?" Abdul asked

"He is particularly concerned that so many sessions are outside. As I recall his term was lack of a "controlled environment," Hazim Aziz replied.

"Do you think he will back out of the summit?"

"Not a chance. We have the money and they need it," Hazim Aziz said.

"I will contact our friend and let him know everything is going according to schedule."

"I understand. That is acceptable. Just to let you alone know, I plan to send several last minute revisions to the Jordanians as the meetings approach. By the time the meetings begin I suspect the Jordanians will be thoroughly frustrated. They I am sure will wonder how I could have the ability to pump gas let alone run the Oil Ministry."

"Well, this is the first time you, or any of your subordinates have run a summit," Abdul laughed.

"And I suspect the last," Hazim added. "I plan that by the time they get to the hotel, their attention should be focused on the Oil Ministry's incompetence rather than anything else. Don't be concerned as to what happens next just trust me everything will work out. I have planned well. Things may seem to be out of control to you. Remember they won't be.

"I will keep your word in mind father," Hazim said as both men hung up.

106

The silence hung heavily in the air. We sat in silence in the conference room each with our own thoughts. Finally I spoke. "You know we have learned a great deal."

"How's that?"

"We know something big is going to happen." I thought it was a more than reasonable assumption considering a hit man was chasing us.

"True, we just don't have a clue as to what it is," Kate responded.

"Agreed, but someone does."

"Isn't that wonderful? Killed because some nut case thinks we know something."

"I know, I know but let me continue." I was wondering whether it was better to be killed by mistake by someone who thought you knew something as compared to being just killed by a mistake.

"Shoot, oh sorry, bad word, go right ahead."

I was pacing now, "We have established a link between Kemal Kanuni and the Oil Minister of Saudi Arabia. In addition, we know the Chairman is not what he appears to be. A reasonable guess would rate our friend as someone completely untrustworthy."

"Okay, I will buy that but so what? He is not someone to be trusted. There are a lot of untrustworthy people out there," Kate pointed out.

"That is a point well taken. By untrustworthy I mean he has portrayed himself a man of peace and a man of the people. Suppose he is neither."

"If the League were a country then I would say he wanted the job of dictator."

"Why?"

Kate looked in my direction and answered. "My guess, he wants the oil money and probably power that goes with it. But this is all speculation. We do know as a fact that Melina Fokina Christakos has had and maybe still does have some kind of relationship with Kemal." By now Kate had joined my pacing, walking in the opposite direction. I figured if anyone saw us they would have had quite the laugh. "Melina controls oil shipments."

I jumped in. "Saudi Arabia and the new League have a lot of oil that is shipped to America and Europe." Fortunately my impulsiveness didn't seem to upset Kate. She continued.

"The common ingredient is oil. If we could get a confirmation of Melina and Kemal being seen together recently, I think we could safely assume they're involved in some manner."

I checked my watch, hoping to get a call from one of the two station chiefs. "What about this issue about Saudi Arabia not paying its bills?"

"I have been wondering about that myself. How could a country like that have any cash flow issues? It's not like they can't just pump more money. I need to think some more about this. I think it would help if we could get back to my place." Kate raised her hand as I began to object. "I know we have this almost being killed thing going on. But we are a lot safer now with the Embassy knowing what happened as well as Scotland Yard." I had to concede that point to her. "I could help you a lot more if I could get back to my place or the office where I could do some real research."

I somewhat lamely objected, "Anything you might need is available here."

"But my computer and all my information is at my place or my office." I could see this was going nowhere and before I could think of another argument, there was a knock at the door.

"Come."

Maria stuck her head in. "There's a call for you."

"Who is it?"

"The station chief in Ankara."

I grabbed the phone from her workstation and waved to the operator to put the call through. "Mike this is Franklin Adams." Adams was actually the assistant station chief. That meant he was head of counter intelligence in Turkey. "I hear you had a question about Kemal Kanuni."

"I did, do you have something?"

"Possibly, I think so. Ever since the League was formally recognized by the U.S., we have been monitoring the Chairman. First we followed Kemal's uncle until his death and since then we have been tailing Kemal. My main man in Istanbul says one of his local operatives might have seen something. It was late on Friday and two men and a possibly, I repeat possibly, a woman entered the Chairman's offices through a side entrance. It is our understanding the Chairman was in the building at the time."

"If it was a woman, the woman could have been his aunt." I responded, thinking this information was just too thin.

"I agree. Still I thought letting you know couldn't hurt."

"You're right. I appreciate you getting back to me so quickly. Is there anything more you can tell me about the men?"

"No, the only thing he said was that both appeared to be from the area, the Middle East, and one was a large and powerful man."

"And the other man?"

"Average, was the description."

"Franklin, if by chance you learn anything more, please let me know as soon as possible."

"I will"

Looking at Kate, "One of our informants in Istanbul saw three people late on a Friday night enter the building where Kemal has his offices. He apparently was in his offices and maybe one of the three was a woman. It could have been Melina or it could have been a hooker for all we know."

"We must get back to my place. I need to check something out." Kate was being very insistent. "This slow pay thing has to fit in and I need to pull some numbers."

"Do it here."

"No, it will be faster at my place."

'I am worried about your safety."

"Bring along a Marine if need be, but I am leaving." With that Kate got up and started for the door. I knew it would be useless to try to stop her so I followed.

107

Thankfully it was an uneventful ride back to Kate's flat. I had managed to get a car and driver from the embassy. I felt much safer with an armed driver and one of those special embassy cars that had bullet proof everything. I hoped Kate did too. "Pull over here," Kate told the driver. We got out and the driver got out with us. "A little backup isn't a bad thing." was all he said. I agreed with him. As it turned out the extra precautions weren't necessary. Apparently no one had entered the apartment since we'd left. A quick reconnoiter proved no one had tried entering the flat in any less conventional manner. As the driver and I played junior G-men Kate went straight to her computer and booted it up. "I need to check a couple of things," was all she said.

After I thanked the driver and he left, I entered her bedroom where her computer was set up. "What are you looking up?"

"A couple of things. First I want to check out some monetary figures. Then I plan to see if I can learn anything more about Melina's background."

I headed for the kitchen and for the first time noticed how hungry I was. We hadn't eaten in hours. "Do you mind if I find something to eat?"

"No, go right ahead."

"Thanks, I'll be right back. Do you want anything?" There was no response. Obviously Kate was into it.

I rummaged around and managed to find the makings of a sandwich along with a cola. Food and drink in hand I headed back down the hall.

"Mike, I want you to read this before I move on."

"What do you have?"

"It's a little more on Melina, from her college records; the information substantiates our earlier suppositions. It seems here in England they keep more personal information than we do at home." I read over her shoulder. I could see she had been an exceptional student. She had graduated with honors in economics with a minor in international business. Her mother was Egyptian and her father was Turkish. It appeared that her parents were not divorced because they both had the same surname. However, they did not live together as they used separate mailing addresses. She had received her high school education in Switzerland at one of those private boarding schools where rich girls were sent. The only record of her being into trouble at school had to do with some loud partying. Kate spoke first.

"Turkey and business keep coming up."

"You're right. For ease of investigation, let's assume there are connections and let's assume everyone involved has a pretty good idea of how business operates."

"Sounds fair. I am going to spend some time looking up some numbers. It may take a while."

"I'll go in the other room and make some calls and do a report or two. Let me know when you have something." I headed to the living room.

108

Several hours had passed and I had heard nothing from Kate. I mean I could hear her working but she hadn't called me. I thought it was better not to bug her. From what I had seen she was good and quick at what she did. Any encouragement from me would probably slow the process considerably. I must have dozed off, because the next thing I knew Kate was waking me.

"Mike time to get up."

"I wasn't asleep. I was merely resting my eyes."

"Yeah right."

"Did you find anything?"

"Its more what I didn't find out," Kate began.

"Please explain, you are the resident business genius."

Kate continued, "The basic oil marketplace has been disrupted by the introduction of a new source of crude. The result is that prices have fallen somewhat, really returned to a more traditional pricing level." I must have given her a quizzical look. "Kuwait has only recently returned to its pre War production levels. As far as Iraq goes, it's not producing anywhere near its pre-war capacity. Even if it could the U.N. sanctions are effectively limiting its ability to sell."

"I see, so prices have fallen but not to any dramatic degree."

"Exactly. In addition, it appears that Saudi Arabia is spending about the same this year as it has over the last several years. Right after the war, the Saudis spent more than usual."

"Why?"

"For one, they agreed to pay us to fight the first war and for another they did have some associated damages. I believe that they spent some additional money, mostly with the U.S., upgrading their military capacity."

As Kate listed her reasons my memory finally woke up, "On all counts you're correct. But to my knowledge most of those contracts were over about three years ago."

Kate nodded, "That's exactly what my research has shown."

"So Kate, why would they become deadbeats?"

'I don't know and I haven't found anything. You know it is more than a little frustrating. I usually can find things pretty quickly."

"Let's take another tack and assume the facts are correct. Let's follow the money and see if by doing that we can figure out the "Why".

"That makes sense."

"Do you know anything about that trail?"

Kate smiled. Gosh I love her smile. "Yes I do. It seems the money flows through a small and heretofore unknown London based financial house, Winslow and Sons, Ltd."

"Wow, if my memory isn't playing tricks on me, I recall that the Hellenic Sea Lines uses Winslow and Sons, Ltd. as its clearinghouse."

Kate smiled again, "You recall perfectly well. It seems their monetary volume has increased exponentially. They don't seem to have a lot of customers."

"Apparently just the right one."

Kate laughed, and said, "Hey, I was going to use that line."

"Too bad. Kate, I think we need to pay a visit to Winslow and Sons, Ltd. What are your thoughts?"

"I agree. It couldn't hurt and it'd probably really help." I hoped she was right on both counts but I had my worries about the first part. She then added, "I think we ought to learn a little more about the company before we pay them a visit."

"I thought you would never volunteer."

109

Yussof Dakkak was not about to fail twice. He had to assume that he had been compromised. Based upon that assumption he asked a man he knew from a prior operation, a man by the name of Murphy, a member of the Provo Wing of the Irish Republican Army, to follow Williams and O'Hara. Dakkak was now listening to that report.

"As you asked I followed Williams and O'Hara."

"Where are they now?"

"Back at her place. They have been there all day since returning from the U.S. Embassy."

"Do they have any extra protection?"

"None that I see, but when they came back from the embassy, the driver, my guess a Marine, entered the apartment building with them. I suspect he was there to ensure their safe return. Those two will be much more careful in the future."

Dakkak grabbed the cell phone a little harder upon hearing Murphy's comment. "You are probably correct. I will relieve you in the morning. If anything comes up in the meantime, you know how to reach me."

As Murphy continued to watch the Kate's building in his rear view mirror he answered simply, "okay," and flipped his cell phone off.

110

I was learning that Kate could be a bit compulsive when it came to her work. Even though I thought we had made substantial progress she still wasn't satisfied. I could hear her typing away at her computer. She had been at it for several hours. "Mind if I order some take out?"

"Thanks that would be great. There isn't much to eat in the place as I am sure you found out at lunch and I don't feel like going out or cooking." There was no need to tell me. I could see it in her eyes on the couple of occasions I had dared to enter her bedroom now clearly a research inner sanctum. "I am going to flip on the tube, do you mind?"

"No just keep the sound down, thanks."

I grabbed the remote and began channel surfing. Sadly not only was it the wrong time of the day for any decent sporting events it was also the wrong day of the week so I had to settle for the news. I flipped to the BBC saw a reporter standing at what appeared to be Heathrow.

"Good afternoon, this is Nigel Homersmith of the BBC Home Service reporting from Heathrow Airport outside London. In the distance you can see a Royal Jordanian Airbus 310 just arriving." Homersmith turned away from the camera and pointed toward the cobalt and white plane with red and gold striping in the distance.

"The King of Jordan has just arrived for his annual medical check up. As many are aware there have been rumors about the monarch's health over the last several years. There have been some reports that he has been treated for cancer. It is anticipated that the King and his entourage will motorcade from here to the Jordanian Embassy where he will be staying."

"It seems to be London's time to play host at hospital for foreign heads of state. The King of Saudi Arabia and his brother the Crown Prince are scheduled to arrive within two hours time. The Saudi King is also coming here for what has been described by the Saudi Embassy as routine medical procedures. It is widely accepted that due to health reasons the King has turned over the day-to-day running of the country to the Crown Prince. As well as running the daily operations of government the Prince is the leader of the Saudi military, the National Guard."

"The Prince has been described as a man of many talents. By many accounts he has needed every one of those talents in balancing the different interests within the Royal Family."

"Islamic fundamentalists supported by a faction of royals have grown increasingly vocal over the last several years in part aided by a resentment of American troops being stationed within the country. Saudi Arabia is home to the most holy sites in Islam, and as such is the keeper of the faith for those in the Muslim World. Many consider the presence of Western troops an abomination.

However there are others in the royal family who would prefer closer ties to the West particularly the United States. Those members believe Saudi Arabia needs protection from other less friendly countries in the region. This would include an essentially leaderless Iraq but most importantly Iran. Sunni Saudi Arabia considers Iran and its mostly Shiite population to be a bunch of heretics to Islam."

"Reportedly, no individual speeches or news conferences are scheduled for either King. However, the Jordanian Embassy has released the following statement. "His Highness King wishes to thank Her Majesty and her government for the consideration she has offered him over the years in respecting his and his family's privacy when it comes to personal matters."

"From sources in the Middle East the BBC has just recently learned that there is a strong possibility that the two monarchs will meet in an impromptu summit located at the Dorchester Hotel. This world-class hotel just off Hyde Park has reportedly been preparing for this meeting for several months now. We will be taking you now to Leslie White who is at the hotel. She will bring you all the details from there. Leslie."

"Thank you Nigel. I am standing outside the Dorchester where within a couple of days the Kings of Jordan and Saudi Arabia will meet in a long planned but until today secret summit meeting. The hotel was chosen as a neutral site. Both delegations will stay here. However, because of health reasons both monarchs will stay at their respective embassies and will travel to the hotel as conference needs dictate."

"From our sources we have learned that the topics to be discussed will be broad ranging. Nonetheless the brunt of the discussions will undoubtedly center on the stability of Jordan, its large Palestinian population and associated instability caused by its large refugee problem. The Gulf Wars particularly hurt Jordan economically as Iraq was its main trading partner and supplier of oil. Saudi Arabia has pledged to aid in rebuilding Jordan's economy while at the same time has agreed to supply any necessary oil at the same prices negotiated with the Iraqis. Now back to the studio."

I flipped around the channels to see if there was anything more on this meeting. There was nothing. It was time to phone Washington.

111

"Jazel, Mike Williams."

"Hi Mike, how are things going?"

"I believe I am making substantial progress." No need to use the "we" word. I had no doubt that Jazel Hammiby, Under Secretary of State for the Middle East knew I had an unofficial partner. It was just easier not to bring it up, for both of us.

"Good, good. What can I do for you?"

"I have just seen reports from the BBC saying that Kings of Jordan and Saudi Arabia are meeting in London for a long planned but heretofore secret summit meeting. Is there anything you can tell me about this?"

"Very little really. I just saw those same reports. We are certain that both men were originally coming to London for health related reasons. Coincidentally the timing of their visits was such that it was easy to set up a conference."

"Why didn't we know about it?"

I could sense a rising frustration Hammiby's voice. "Good question, this lack of information is very frustrating. In my opinion we have relied way too much on electronic surveillance and not enough on human intelligence. I know you are with the NSA and electronics is your thing, but there are times when nothing, nothing beats feet on the ground."

"Jazel, you are preaching to the choir. I agree. Do you have a guess at least why we were so out of the loop?"

"Mike, my best educated guess is that the conference was put together outside the usual channels."

I was surprised to hear her suggest this. "I don't follow."

"Summits and conferences of other levels are typically handled through a country's foreign ministry. Our sources within those ministries in both Jordan and Saudi Arabia are pretty good. Those sources gave us nothing. So logic would tell me that another branch of government was responsible for the meeting."

"Do you have a guess?"

"Not really. All I can offer is that whoever it was or whatever ministry it was it had to be a powerful one. Otherwise the foreign ministers would have had a fit and would have taken over the process."

"Makes sense." I have a feeling I know which ministry it is but I think I want to keep that to myself for a bit longer. "Any sense which country initiated the meeting?"

"Again we are in the dark. But if I were to place a bet it would be on Saudi Arabia."

"Why?"

"Our sources are better in Jordan."

This was about the closest I was going to get to a confirmation of my suspicions. But it was good enough for my purposes. "Jazel, thanks for the input.

"You're welcome. It wasn't much."

"More than you think, good bye."

112

Kate must have heard me speaking and came out to see what was happening. I relayed the news story to her as well as my telephone conversation with Jazel Hammiby.

"Interesting timing," was all she said.

"I know, I was thinking the same thing myself. It could mean a great deal or nothing at all." We had too many random facts. There was nothing to tie anything together. "Are you done with your research?"

"I've gone about as far as I can on everything but checking out the investment house. I just needed to get up and walk around before I start up again."

"Once you get that last bit of data, have you thought about how we are going to get in the front door?"

Kate said, "I figured it would come to me as I did my research."

"Anything I can help you with?" I hated waiting though I knew I had no choice.

"Yes, why don't you order dinner?"

"You want anything in particular?"

"No just surprise me." Great a real opportunity to screw up.

113

"Maggie have you had any luck with finding this Yussof Dakkak character?" Philip Logan asked as he entered her office.

"No, Mr. Logan, unfortunately I have not. I don't mind telling you my lack of success is frustrating."

"Quite, though it is the nature of investigative work."

"I know but I can still be frustrated. I hadn't really expected to find out an exact name such as Abdul Hire a Killer, 312 S. Exeter Street, Leeds but I had hoped to find *something*. I anticipated that I could at least narrow the list down to a number of groups that could be real possibilities. Philip, it's as if Yussof had decided on his own to kill an attractive American newspaperwoman using a subway train as his weapon of choice. Not the most common choice of weapon but one that might give him the award for Most Unusual Weapon Used at the annual assassins awards banquet."

Logan laughed, remembering again how sarcastic Smith could be when frustrated, the greater the frustration the more the sarcasm. "Maggie, logic would dictate that a lack of information means that the information isn't widely known. A small group and not your garden-variety terrorist organization has to be involved or, maybe even more likely, a single individual."

"I agree. That's what worries me. If someone or some group were after the Americans there would be no reason to think they would stop after failing once."

Logan spoke, "I agree. Since you haven't found the perpetrator and it seems likely whoever it is will try again I think our best bet would be to provide them with protection. It's less efficient but better than doing nothing."

"I'll see to it,"

114

I went to the refrigerator to see what phone numbers were listed for take-out places. I looked over the list and found a Mexican restaurant listed. Wondering what English Mexican food tasted like, I ordered two combination plates and salsa.

"I ordered Mexican. I hope that's okay?"

"From Felipe's?"

"Yeah. What did you find out about Winslow and Sons?"

"Here it is," she handed me several pages.

"Can you give me a quick summary?"

"It can be real quick. Winslow and Sons Ltd. Investment Bankers is a small investment company founded in 1875."

"That's it?"

"That's it. I can't figure out anything else about it or who owns it. Other than Hans Schmidt is the president of the company. Hans is not a British subject. My guess he is German or Austrian.

"Not much, what else?"

"We were not suffering from brain fade. The Saudi government appears to be using the firm as its clearinghouse as well as the Hellenic Sea Lines."

"Okay but…"

"But … I think I have found another player."

"Who?"

"The Bir League."

"My God," was all I managed to say.

"I agree. It does shed another light on things doesn't?"

"I'll say." We heard a knock on the door. "Probably dinner," I went to check and thankfully, it was a Hispanic looking man holding a bag. It wasn't likely a bomb so it had to be dinner.

I brought the food in and Kate had set the table. "Want a Corona?"

"I would love one, where did you get it?"

"We expats have our ways."

"Well, I am glad you do," Regardless of how bad the meal tasted I could always wash it down with a good beer. "Let's let things roll around in our heads and we can pick it up after dinner."

"Sounds like a plan."

115

We ate dinner in silence, each of us mulling different ideas. We finished about the same time and cleaned up, "You know the food wasn't bad."

"Hmm," was all Kate said.

"Let's see what we can summarize. We can put it all on that white board you have in the hallway. Maybe once we see it written down we will be able to sort something out more easily."

"I like that idea."

I moved the board into the living room and began to list various pieces of information we had discovered. I wrote down Hellenic Sea Lines to start. "Kate what do we have here?"

"Several things."

"Likes?"

"Since Melina Christakos has been in charge the Company has made some significant changes to its operations."

"Such as?"

The company recently re-flagged its entire fleet to Turkey. Prior to this action the ships had been registered in all the usual countries including Panama, Liberia, Malta and U.A.E."

"Anything else?"

"Yes, the Company has started to purchase the oil it transports."

"Is this unusual?"

"I think so."

"Why?"

"Well, it consolidates risk rather than diversifies it. Now if a tanker is lost, all the risk is with the company, rather than the owner, the insurance company and the shipper."

"Why would one do it then?"

"The only reason I can think of at the moment is control. You now have complete control of the product."

"So I can make sure I understand let me summarize where we are at this point. We know that Melina Fokina has come to run the Company through a most unusual set of circumstances. I would speculate but am not positive those circumstances are or were beyond her ability to initiate. Therefore someone, of whom we have no idea, wanted Melina Fokina to run the Hellenic Sea Lines. We also know that the tanker company moves a lot of oil around the world, oil that it now owns. Most of the oil is non-OPEC. For other unknown reasons she has caused the company to re-flag all its ships putting them under Turkish control. Lastly, we know that the company uses Winslow and Sons, Ltd. Did I miss anything?"

"No, that is pretty much it." Kate nodded.

"Kate, what else do you have?"

"Two things. For all the changes that have been instituted since Melina Christakos has taken over took one has remained constant."

"Its customers."

"Precisely. The Company still moves a great deal of oil, most of it from non-OPEC sources."

"What is the second thing?"

"What I have is very technical. I have facts but no truth."

"Give me the facts and hopefully between the two of us we can figure it out."

"Basically, interest rates are not acting the way they're supposed to. Interest rates for both U.S. Treasury paper and various European countries paper are too high. Based on historical patterns there is no market reason that interest rates for these kinds of instruments should be rising. I was curious so I investigated. I mean I really spent a lot of time on this."

"What'd you discover?"

"I found funds that normally would be invested in the government paper market are now being diverted into the oil options and futures marketplace. However, the strange thing is that the contracts being offered are "out of the money contracts"."

"Please give me the Simple Simon definition again."

"Someone or a group of someones are investing in oil-related contracts that will only have value if there is a meltdown in the oil marketplace. Because the contracts are risky, they don't cost very much, so without spending a fortune, if something does go wrong the contract holder or holders will control a lot of oil. Incidentally, the contracts apply to both non-OPEC and OPEC related oil."

"In spy school we were told to always follow the money. Can you tell where the money is coming from or going to?"

Kate paused for a moment. "No, all I can determine is that many contracts and hence a lot of money is being handled through Winslow and Sons, Ltd." I was still writing on the white board after Kate had finished. "Let's review what I put down so far. Money or a portion of money normally being invested in government securities is being diverted to oil contracts that are in today's terms worthless. Can you tell how much is being diverted?"

"The level of interest rates suggests that not all the money is going into option contracts or futures contracts," responded Kate. She smiled; this was a question she hadn't thought of. Two minds were sometimes better than one.

"So we don't know where the spare money is going, correct?"

"Correct."

"Let me make a few more notes on the board." I went over and purposefully blocked Kate's view. I wanted her to see it all at once. I wrote quickly and stepped away. "I want you to look at these words and then tell me immediately what comes to mind." In the center of the board I had placed the name Kemal Kanuni. Under the name I had written four lines, Charismatic, Enigmatic, Motives and Goals.

"After the first I would add natural-born leader, dynamic. After the second I would add unknown quantity, could be a force of good or evil. For the third word, completely unknown but based upon what we have learned about his character what he says may not be what he truly believes or means. As for the last word I would add either an Islamic Gandhi or Turkic Alexander the Great.

Kate concluded after a moment. "Yes it's quite possible that his name belongs in the center."

116

We were sitting in silence staring at the white board hoping to tie the information together when the phone rang.

Kate walked over to the telephone.

"Ms. O'Hara, this is Maggie Smith of Scotland Yard. If Mr. Williams is there, may I speak to him?"

"Of course. Mike, it is for you. It's the lady from Scotland Yard."

"Hello, Ms. Smith. This is Mike Williams."

"Mr. Williams, we have been able to identify the man who almost killed Ms. O'Hara. His name is Yussof Dakkak. According to Interpol he is an experienced, very experienced professional killer. It seems he has no ideological preferences; his only god is money. He is between 30 and 35 years of age and is Turkish by birth but now travels under a Kazakh passport. According to sources he can kill in any number of ways but he prefers firearms, particularly sniper rifles."

"Thank you for this information. Do you know where he is?"

"No, sorry we don't."

"I see. Well, thanks again."

"Mr. Williams, good luck."

I hung up the phone and turned to Kate. "Scotland Yard was able to identify the man who tried to kill you in the tube. His name is Yussof Dakkak. He is a paid assassin, Turkish, but now travels under a Kazakh passport."

Kate paused and said, "Seems like we could add one more thing to the white board."

"What is that?"

"Turkey and Kazakhstan. In both places Kemal Kanuni has a tremendous amount of influence. This isn't the only thing that appears to tie to these two countries."

I wrote down Turkey and Kazakhstan and in parenthesis, *Bir.* "I think it is time that we went to Winslow's office. What do you think?"

"First thing in the morning, let's do it."

117

Kemal was returning from mid-day prayers. He walked slowly nodding in the direction of the imam who was at his side. In this part of the world it was important to incorporate religion into one's daily activities. Kemal was seen daily in the presence of a number of different mullahs. As they approached the door to his private office, Kemal bowed slightly toward the imam in deference. The teacher smiled and walked away. Kanuni waited for the man to turn the corner before he placed his right hand over the optical scanner next to the door of his office. Within seconds it swung open. In the far corner of his office behind a screen was a bank of television screens and computer monitors. The televisions and computers were hooked to satellite dishes on the roof of his office building. The televisions were on continuously. Each set was tuned to either a world news channel or a financial news network. One of the computers was up-linked directly to the computers at Winslow and Son Ltd. The other was hooked continuously to the internet. This computer also had the capacity to make completely confidential telephone calls either just audio or also visual.

Kemal smiled as he scrolled through the figures on his screen. He was seated at the computer that was online at Winslow and Son Ltd. His plan was unfolding just as he had envisioned. Hans Schmidt was a competent player in the world of international finance who took directions well. Kemal could see that the directions given to him by Hazim Aziz were flawless. Aziz had been able to position the market as they had planned without causing any appreciable market distortions.

118

The purpose of the opening session was to read prepared texts by the two monarchs. Both speeches contained the same theme. The speeches contained promises of openness and a desire for frank and business-like discussions, with the usual words of warmth and friendship. To facilitate the meetings each delegation had taken suites on the terrace overlooking Hyde Park.

A great deal of the work of a diplomatic gathering occurred between meetings. This was a time when aides could meet and talk off the record. It also allowed these same aides to report any developments back to their leaders. It was between the first and second sessions that the Prime Minister of Jordan and his chief assistant met.

"Salim, I want you to meet with your counterpart. We need to deal with this Fundamentalist movement. You and I both know that the Jordanian Islamic Federation is supported by and therefore controlled by the Saudis. This group is not yet a major force, but I fear that given enough time and money, most particularly money, they will have to be reckoned with. We know the Saudis have plenty of money. We have seen how governments can be destabilized. I want to prevent that from happening at home. Our King needs time not only to deal with the Palestinian refugee problem but to heal our country's wounds and move us forward out of being a third world country. I fear he will not have that time if these Fundamentalists become more powerful. I want you to see what the Saudis can or will do about their Islamic Front. Do not tell anyone else about this. This subject must be kept most confidential."

"Yes, Khalid. I will let you know what I can find out."

119

The phone rang. Yussof Dakkak, who had been cleaning his weapon, answered it. "Hello?"

"Mr. Dakkak, this is Mr. Murphy."

"Yes, Mr. Murphy, do you have anything else to report?"

"Yes. I am at the investment house. I have to do a little more research. I don't think it will take long. I will then complete your report and will fax it to you."

"Again, thank you, Mr. Murphy. I, of course, will be sending you a check as soon as I get your report."

Yussof knew he had to move quickly. The Americans were visiting Winslow and Sons, Ltd. He could complete his assignment there. Fortunately, the offices weren't far.

Kate and I stood opposite the offices of Winslow and Sons, Ltd. As I began to walk, Kate grabbed my arm and said, "Please wait."

"Why?"

"Well, for one, I need to review our cover one more time and more importantly I want to see the operations. I don't want to rush. That includes observing any traffic going and coming to these offices." The offices of Winslow and Sons, Ltd were located at the corner of Old Broad Street and Liverpool Street across the street from the underground's Liverpool Street station.

We watched the comings and goings of business activity from the tube station across the street. Being situated on the corner, the building had a rounded exterior such that its front door opened onto both streets. From our vantage point we could see anyone entering from either direction. The building itself had that proper English look of old money and was indistinguishable from the buildings around it. As we watched I was reasonably certain no one in the building would notice us. Street traffic was heavy and included the full gamut of English vehicles additionally pedestrian traffic was also heavy. Both sides of the street had people from all walks of life. Bankers and stockbrokers dressed in their Savoy Road finest, clerical workers dressed in a coat and tie of significantly less quality and people from all over the Commonwealth wearing their native garb.

"I've seen enough; let's go inside and see what we can find. Remember we are doing a story on the Hellenic Sea Lines. You are approaching the story from the shipping angle and I am doing it on the financial side."

"Got it"

I wanted to take her hand but figured it would be bad form for co-workers to be holding hands. We waited for the lights to change before we headed across the street. As was common in London we had to wait at a pedestrian island in the middle of the road protected only by some ornamental railing, which appeared to have been installed before the Great War, and one of the few things in downtown London that had probably survived the blitz. This island was similar to many others found in London except this one also had a statue of some hero of the empire long forgotten and longer dead. Once across the street we walked quickly to the front of the building. I opened the door for Kate and at the same time made sure my gun was safely tucked out of sight. What we found inside was a modern financial office. A glassed-in corridor about ten feet wide ran in both directions from the front door paralleling the streets outside. Across from this corridor was a large glassed-in room. Against the walls ticker tapes ran reporting the results of the day's trading through out the world.

In this room were a number of workstations, each with several glowing computer screens. Kate turned to Mike and whispered, "There is no one here, unlike any other investment company I have ever been in."

"What do you mean?"

"Look around. There are a few employees down on the floor. Some are sitting at their desks making trades but most seem to be milling around. Besides, in any other brokerage-house normally this hallway would be filled with customers intently watching the ticker tapes. We're the only ones here."

"It looks like you were right about the business having very few customers." As I finished a young lady approached us. She had come from what appeared to be private offices at the far end of the corridor.

"Hello, my name is Madeline Ross. Is there something I can help you with?"

"Yes, I am a financial reporter with the London Bureau of the Washington *Post*." As Kate spoke she handed the young women her credentials. "I am doing a story about the Hellenic Sea Lines; well, actually, I am doing a story about the new owner, Melina Christakos." Kate nodded in my direction. "Mr. Mike Williams is a colleague doing a parallel story but he is approaching it from the maritime side. I was wondering if we could speak for a few minutes with Mr. Hans Schmidt? We don't have an appointment but I would really appreciate it if you could see what you could do."

"I will check for you. While I am checking, would you care to come with me? I can have you wait in the conference room." Ms. Ross indicated a door down the corridor and began walking in that direction. As she opened the door to the conference room she asked, "May I offer you something to drink?"

We both declined. "Please make yourself comfortable, while I check with Mr. Schmidt."

While we sat in silence, I checked out the conference room. I could see Kate reading the ticker tape. It was a typical business conference room with a large teak table that could seat at least fourteen in oversized leather chairs. At the far end of the room was another door, through which Hans Schmidt entered.

Good day, Ms. O'Hara, Mr. Williams."

Kate returned to her place at the conference table after we all shook hands.

"My assistant tells me you are doing a story on the Hellenic Sea Lines and you have come to ask me some questions."

"That is correct, Mr. Schmidt," Kate responded.

"Well, you must certainly be aware that all of our client's business activities are totally confidential."

"Of course, I understand that. What I really wanted to talk to you about was of a more generic nature. I wanted to get your take on the oil marketplace. It seems that many contracts for oil futures and oil options are being purchased. I find it quite unusual especially since these contracts are so far out of the money."

"Well, I don't see what this has to do with the Hellenic Sea Lines."

"Well, for one, the Hellenic Sea Lines moves a substantial amount of the world's oil and for two the shipping company has begun to purchase its cargo rather than just transport it."

"I see. All right then but I do have only a few minutes."

"Thank you, I appreciate it," Kate said.

As this exchange went on I had sat silently observing Hans Schmidt. It now seemed an appropriate time for me to speak up. "Yes, thank you very much for your time. Let me give you a brief idea about my part of this story. It has to do with the logistical aspects of the oil transport business. I initially have two questions. How many gallons will a tanker carry and at what associated cost? And why would a transport company take ownership of its product?"

I thought Hans Schmidt looked annoyed before he answered, "I am not at liberty to speculate on the plans of a client. Most certainly a fine company such as the Hellenic Sea Lines would have a good reason to take a particular course of action. Regarding tonnage, the largest tankers, the VLCC kind, will carry over 2 million gallons of oil. The cost, of course, varies depending upon the market."

"Well, there must be some cost range?" I could see that Schmidt was getting a little frustrated with my line of questions. So I decided to back off a bit. I didn't want him to terminate the interview before Kate had a chance to ask her questions. "Any help you could offer would certainly be appreciated."

Hans Schmidt replied, "I will have to get you that information. Please leave your card with my assistant."

"Thank you." I hoped a little sucking up would improve his temperament. I also figured he would enjoy talking to Kate more than me anyway, unless I misread his leer.

Kate began immediately. "We understand that confidentiality is a given in your business and we would not presume to put you in a conflicting situation. I did want to ask you some questions about the mechanics of oil trading here at your firm."

For the next fifteen minutes Kate questioned Hans Schmidt on a number of issues. She asked him how options contracts were written at the firm, how futures were priced and how money was collected; first, as it related to the initial contract payment and the subsequent covering payments. Additionally, she asked about the company's trading desk and if the investment house had any strategic partnership the company used in dealing with the oil marketplace. Finally she asked him questions about the sources of world oil, its demand and the anticipated supplies in light of the new crude coming from Central Asia. During the entire interview Hans furtively kept looking at his watch.

"Ms. O'Hara, if you ever decide to give up your job with the newspaper, please come and see me. I am sure we could find a position for someone as knowledgeable as you," Hans said to bring their meeting to a conclusion.

Kate smiled and said, "We appreciate you giving us some of your valuable time. Again thank you very much."

"We at Winslow and Sons Ltd are always happy to meet and talk with the fourth estate," Schmidt replied as he showed us out of the conference room and guided us towards the main corridor. "I am sorry to run, but I have a conference call to make. The exit is just up head."

We exited the building and headed back in the direction of the underground station I waited until we were away from the building before asking, "Kate, what did you think?"

"I think the President of the investment firm doesn't know much about the oil marketplace. He is technically weak in the arena of options and futures. He seems a little over his head regarding the entire process."

"In crude terms, he doesn't know shit from shinola?"

"Pretty much. Though he did accidentally confirm that the Hellenic Sea Lines happened to be a client. Not that there is much value in that since it was something we were pretty sure of. The other thing we were pretty sure of was the low number of clients using this investment house. I would say our observations confirmed this."

"Agreed, though there was something else you determined; something I think was very valuable."

"What's that?"

"That someone else is orchestrating whatever is going on. He is only a front man. You said so yourself. He is weak technically but more importantly, strategically."

"You can always hire technical help though."

"Right. But not strategic help."

Kate looked at me and said, "You're right."

"Let's head back to your place." I pointed in the direction of the Underground station. "I want to update our white board and see if we can determine who the investment firm's few clients might be."

120

We approached the corner to wait for the light to begin our two-part street crossing. The light was red. As we waited I became uneasy and to assuage those feelings, I reached into my coat pocket to release the gun's safety. I took comfort in the cold steel. I was glad I had decided to bring it with me. As the light changed and Kate began to cross the street, I realized that if someone out there wishes us harm I don't want to be standing on a pedestrian island in the middle of a busy thoroughfare. I reached to grab Kate deciding it would be safer to take a cab back. Unfortunately, she was quicker than my thought process and had gotten far enough in front of me that I couldn't reach her.

I raised my voice enough to attract her attention but hopefully no one else's. "Katie, please come back. I would rather take a cab home. My knee is really bothering me." Thankfully she began returning to where I was standing as the rest of the pedestrian traffic began to clear.

It was then that I saw movement from the pedestrian island in the middle of the street. Someone was bent over and partially obscured by the statue located there. Anyone hiding or lurking around a statue on a traffic island was someone looking for trouble. We must have been followed and somehow I had missed that fact. Looking more closely, I thought I could see a hand reach down and back for something. I didn't know if it was a weapon but I sure didn't want to find out either. Within a moment I had my answer. A gun appeared. I had to do something and quickly. Kate was completely exposed and I was only slightly better off.

I tried to keep my voice as calm as possible, "Katie, dive to your right and then roll! I then dove to my right and rolled over. As I dove I prayed Kate would react. As I flew through the air I managed to reach into my coat pocket and pull my gun. As I hit the sidewalk hard, I could feel chips of concrete fly up and strike me in the legs. Good, I thought. Our actions surprised the gunman. Apparently our assailant had only enough time to lower his gun to shoot, thus striking the concrete where I had just been standing. No doubt a few seconds later I would have been dead. I came up on one knee in firing position. I fired quickly three times and then rolled again. More bullets flew by. On my second roll I managed to come up behind a lamppost offering at least a little protection. I was sure I was the primary target and not Kate. That wouldn't last if I missed a second time. I knew he had only one chance left. From the angle of the bullets impact I could tell the killer had protected himself from low angle shots. My only option was to expose myself and go for the high angle shot. If I missed, I was dead as well as Kate. Knowing I had no choice. I rose from behind the lamppost aimed and fired off three more rounds. I decided to run right at the shooter and hopefully surprise him. As I approached the statue, I could see blood. At least one of my shots had found its mark. However the gunman was still alive and began to rise to his feet. I lowered my weapon and fired my remaining rounds. The killer sagged to his knees, both arms at his side. His right hand released the gun he had been holding and he fell on his face motionless.

I waited knowing if there were any accomplices I would be dead in a moment as I was out of ammunition and very exposed. Thankfully he was alone as there was nothing but silence. I walked toward the body and as I did Kate joined me.

"Are you okay?"

"Shaky, but okay, I am a veteran at this kind of thing now."

I rolled the body over to see his face. Kate touched my shoulder. "That's the man who tried to kill me in the underground."

"Then according to Scotland Yard this is, or rather was, Yussof Dakkak." Sounds began returning. I could hear crowd noises and the wail of a police siren approaching.

I looked at Kate examining her to see if she had been hit but didn't know it as sometimes happens. "Does it hurt anywhere?"

"All over, I'm not used to diving onto concrete. But I'm really only a little bruised. How about you?"

"I'm okay." We held each other. We did not say anything for several minutes. I was contemplating life and mortality and life with each other. I presumed Kate was doing the same thing.

121

The passage of time had returned to its usual speed by the time the police arrived. An assortment of law enforcement vehicles, including an ambulance, swarmed onto the scene. In this case thankfully, the police ambulance would become a hearse. The body of the former Yussof Dakkak would go from here to the central London crime lab for an autopsy. From my discussions with Philip I knew the London police and Scotland Yard shared forensic lab space. As far I was concerned this was a good thing. I would get help from either Maggie Smith or Philip at Scotland Yard without questions. I couldn't count on that from the London police department.

As Kate and I stood on the pedestrian island, someone who appeared to be the lead investigator approached us. He was a short man wearing a well-loved raincoat. I had seen this type before and if I were to guess he was a career man long on questions and short on imagination. I whispered to Kate. "We need this to go smoothly. We can't afford to be tied up for hours dodging answers to his questions."

"Can't we just tell him to talk to your friend Logan?"

"That might work eventually but not after some time spent bowing and scraping. Don't say anything. Let's have him do the speaking. That way we can see what his attitude is. I will do as much of the talking as possible. If he talks to you act dazed and out of it."

"That won't be hard." We waited for the investigator.

"Can you explain what happened here?"

There was no particular inflection or tone to his voice. I thought this was a good sign. "Hello officer, my name is Mike Williams. This lady is my friend Kate O'Hara. As you might have guessed we are both Americans. This man," I pointed in the direction of the body, "attempted to kill us."

"I see. Some of the witnesses I talked to said you used a gun in a professional manner."

"I did use a gun to defend myself."

"How is it you happen to be carrying a firearm, you being an American and all and private firearms being illegal in the United Kingdom?"

I believed the key to getting out of here quickly was to keep it honest and keep it simple. I needed to develop a bond with this man. I began to slowly reach into my jacket pocket and as I did I spoke. "I have a permit. May I show it to you?"

"Bloody good idea, let's see."

I handed him my permit. He took it. "A gun permit for an American a bit unusual what?"

"Yes I understand that is the case but as you can see it is perfectly legal. I am a member of the United States National Security Agency and because of that I have been issued a permit to carry a weapon here in the United Kingdom"

"I can see that. You haven't finished telling me what happened."

"This man," I again pointed to the corpse, "well it wasn't the first time. Earlier he tried to kill Ms. O'Hara by pushing her into the path of an underground train." As I spoke I hugged Kate. "You can confirm this with Maggie Smith of Scotland Yard. I shot him in self defense."

"How about you miss, what can you tell me?"

I continued to speak. "Ms. O'Hara is a reporter based here in London for the *Washington Post*. As I'm sure you can imagine she is a bit dazed over the whole thing." While I was introducing her to the policeman Kate was handing the officer her identification. The policeman silently took both pieces of identification and walked to his car.

"How do you think it is going?"

"Hopefully, he will call this information in. Everything should check out and we won't be under suspicion and that will be that."

Within a few minutes the inspector returned. "I contacted Ms. Smith and she confirmed the information you gave. It appears that today was your lucky day. Apparently our dead friend over there is not the kind to miss. I also talked to my fellow investigators. It seems there were several eye witnesses to the shooting and they confirm that you two were the targets. I have no need to detain you any further. You are free to leave. Of course, you should not leave the country until we talk again." As the inspector spoke he handed the identification cards back to Kate and me. "I will have one of my men take you where you want to go." As he said this he pointed to a nearby unmarked vehicle. "Oh, by the way, Ms. Smith requests that you contact her as soon as possible."

I took Kate by the arm and we walked supporting each other in the direction of the police sedan.

122

Kate and I got into the back seat of the police car. "Where can I take you?" the policeman asked.

"Kate, rather than immediately going back to your place, I would like to go by the embassy first. Is that okay with you?" I was concerned about pushing her too hard after the latest incident.

"Whatever you think is best. They do serve drinks there, right? At any hour?"

"If you know the right people they do."

"Well, I have it on good authority that you're on first-name basis with the President. Is that high enough up the food chain?"

I laughed. "Under normal circumstances, yes, but in special cases like this it is really better to be on a first-name basis with the head bartender." I turned to the driver and said, "Please take us to the United States embassy."

We sat in silence as the police car slowly moved through traffic. The driver pulled up to the front gate and rolled down his window as the sentry looked in. He immediately recognized us. "Mr. Williams, we should stop meeting this way. Who is your chauffer?"

"Hi sergeant, our driver is a member of the London police. He has kindly taken us here after some fellow tried to separate us from our lives."

"Second time?"

"Second time, same guy. But there won't be any more times. He was perforated, folded, spindled and mutilated." I turned to Kate, "I think it is safe to get out. Let's leave the good policeman to his duties." We thanked the driver for his courtesy, and headed quickly across the courtyard toward the private entrance. We entered the building and headed to the elevator. "We are going to the basement."

"Back to signals?"

"Yes, I need to check on some things with Washington." The elevator doors opened and we entered the elevator car. I punched in my access code. "Do you remember the lady on duty the last time we were here?"

"Marissa? Maria?"

"Maria. She and I go back a long way so she cut me some extra slack about you being downstairs. If she isn't on duty we're going to have to do things a little differently. Unless of course, there is something you haven't told me, I presume you lack top secret clearance."

"Well, I was worried about my clearance, but the elevator car looks like it is at least seven feet tall and since I am five eight, I figured my clearance was okay."

"Very funny, newspaper lady, but this is a problem and I want you to know this before we go in. If you remember, when we enter there is a Marine guard seated behind a desk. On a table next to the guard's desk is another security checkpoint. We will be required to sign in on the electronic screen. I will sign in, as will you. You will sign in using the name of Ann Wells. Your security code is 980-b22-qu#1. I need you to act like you've done this 100 times and it is as natural as going to the library. Once our clearance is approved we will be able to use the equipment. Do you think you can handle this?"

"What about my signature, won't the machine know I'm not Ann Wells?"

"Not to worry Ann Wells is a code that allows access without signature recognition provided the security code is correct and my signature and security code are correct."

Within moments the car's descent ended. "I have to enter an exit code or we will be enjoying our stay in this elevator for a long time."

"Why is that?"

"Extra security feature, punch in the wrong code or no code and the car become a jail cell. This extra feature was added after the Gulf War I in response to terrorist threats.

"What are we going to research?"

"There are a number of things I need to confirm. Once I do, I'll go over them with you. Then we can look up anything else we think is necessary. There is no time limit down here. The guards couldn't care less if we spend twenty minutes or twenty hours. Any more questions?"

"None."

"Then let's give it a go." I turned and punched in my exit code. The doors opened. I looked around to see if I could spot my Maria, but there was no such luck. We approached the guard.

"Hi, where is Maria? I thought she worked this shift."

"Usually does but she phoned in sick, there is a nasty flu bug going around."

"I see, well I'll be sure and breathe through my ears."

The guard smiled at my humor as we signed in silently and waited for the clearance process. Within minutes we were granted access and I led Kate to the most isolated computer workstation in the room. "This spot should give us the most privacy. Thanks for coming with me. I need to access information that I can only get from the embassy's secure computer network access capability."

"Listen to me, Mike. I was so scared today I still can't believe it. But I wasn't afraid for me. I was afraid for you. So whatever we can do to solve this, whatever we can do to get our lives back, I want to do," was Kate's response. "I think I am beginning to love you."

I was pleased but stunned. I had the same feelings yet just didn't want to express them. I was silent, suffering from male syndrome disease. When confronted with the unexpectedly emotional, stay silent. Kate reached over and touched my hand as if to say, it's okay. You don't have to say anything. With a renewed sense of energy and urgency I sat down at the terminal, typed in several codes as the software prompted me. I turned to Kate. "At the same time I left for London, Jazel Hammiby, Under Secretary of State for Middle Eastern Affairs, formed a working group to sort through any available data on our friend Kemal Kanuni. I can access their work from here. The NSA has developed the ability to retrieve real-time data from anywhere in the world. So if a working group is halfway through a report or whatever, I can access their work at whatever stage of completion they have reached from anywhere in the world."

"That is impressive."

"Yes it is, let's just hope the group has turned something up." I turned back to the screen. I could see that the program had finally gone through all its security protocols and we could start getting some information. "Let's see what the group has come up with."

I scrolled through several screens. "We're in luck. We've caught the group at just the right time. They have just finished their information gathering stage but haven't gotten to the point of drawing any conclusions. I like to look at reports at this stage. It keeps me from having my thoughts pre-influenced by other's opinions."

Kate pushed up next to me to get a better view of the screen. I tried not to be too distracted. "Wow, they seem to have pulled together a lot of information."

"Let's go to their summary." We read together in silence. I pointed to the screen. "See here, it seems Washington has also discovered that Kemal Kanuni and Abdul Aziz are cousins."

"I see that. Look further," Kate commanded. "They also have discovered that Hans Schmidt is an East German ex-Communist and it appears he knows less about international finance and commodities trading than your average Communist."

"Which isn't one whole hell of a lot is it?"

"That information makes sense. Remember how I mentioned to you how little I thought he knew about the investment business and oil trading?"

"Yes, I do."

Changing the point of research, Kate asked, "Do they have any other data about Winslow and Sons, Ltd?"

"Let me check." I clicked through several windows. "Good, they have something. They've traced the ownership to a Netherlands Antilles corporation. They also found out that this offshore corporation is owned by a trust. They have had no luck so far tracing down the trustees or beneficiaries. It seems, though, that there is a lot of communication between the company in London and the Middle East, specifically Saudi Arabia."

"We know the Saudi's are a client. They could also be the owners. That wouldn't be uncommon or unexpected."

"Good point, let's assume for our purposes that is the case."

Kate leaned back in her chair and thought for a moment. "Let me have a look, to see if there is anything else I can glean from the numbers." I slid my chair back to make room for Kate.

Kate pulled closer to the monitor. She put her chin in both hands and began to stare at the computer. "These transactions seem to involve just a few sources. See this in here?" Kate pointed to the monitor. "These transactions involve the Hellenic Sea

Lines. From what I see here my guess is that Winslow and Sons has been financing the oil that the shipping company has been purchasing."

"Based upon everything else we have learned this doesn't come as much of surprise."

"I agree."

I turned to Kate. "Do you have anything else you would like to look at?"

"Yes, as a matter of fact I'd like to check one more thing. Can your computer pull up international current account information?"

"Our computers can pull up any data you would like. But what is international current account information?"

"Financial information that tells how any country is doing paying its bills in the international marketplace. For example, the U.S. is always short. We are constantly borrowing money from abroad. Some like to say the reason for this is that America is such a great international investment opportunity; others say we are spendthrifts. I prefer the former and hope it isn't the latter.

"I think I can find that information, with your help."

We moved our chairs so we could sit next to each other and jointly worked through the computer until we found what Kate was looking for. I then backed away so she could have room to study the data. I made notes as she studied the screen for almost forty-five minutes. Occasionally she would make a note on a pad of paper she had dug out of her purse. Finally, she leaned back. "Did you learn anything?"

"As a matter of fact, I did. You can concentrate for the longest time without getting up. I on the other hand have to move around or my concentration wanes. But the real question is did you learn anything?"

"I believe so but before I say anything I want to check some numbers when we get back to my place."

"That works out just fine. I want to get back also." I checked my watch, startled to see the day had almost slipped away. "We need to fill in more detail on the white board. I think we are getting very close to figuring this thing out." To exit the room we had to reverse our entry process. We punched in an exit code rang for the elevator.

123

Dawn broke on the second day of the conference overcast and dreary. The weather report indicated that the entire day would be like this. It was going to be a gray day that matched the Prime Minister's mood. The information or more precisely the lack of information in Salim's report had not help his mood. He was tired and had not slept well since the conference had begun.

Turning back to Salim, "Your report could be titled the *not-a-report, report*. You haven't been able to get anything at all from the Saudis on the fundamentalist movement, either in Jordan or Saudi Arabia?"

"Unfortunately true Mr. Prime Minister."

Khalid took off his glasses and rubbed his eyes. "Don't you think this lack of information is unusual? You know how diplomats love to gossip."

"It is unusual and in my opinion it can only mean the Saudi Oil Ministry is controlling all aspects of this conference as tightly as I have ever seen anything controlled."

Rising from his chair Khalid walked to the window and looked out. "How could anyone live in such a climate? It was no wonder that the British conquered the world. It wasn't really world conquest and the pursuit of riches they sought; it was just sunshine."

"Maybe you should use that someday as a joke at one of their receptions. There is one good thing about this weather."

"What is that?"

"At least there will be no outside receptions. The weather will keep everyone inside."

"Your point is well taken Salim. I have never felt comfortable with the number of outdoor receptions. One can never have adequate security outside, but the Saudis have insisted, really pushed for one being scheduled for each day of the summit."

"Salim thank you I appreciate your efforts."

"I am sorry they haven't borne fruit."

"Please keep up your efforts and hopefully we will learn something useful. Unfortunately now I have to get back to my desk. I must face that mountain of faxes and memos."

124

When we got back to her place Kate went immediately to her computer. As the machine booted up she called out to me, "Why don't you see what you can fix us to eat? I'm famished. I'll bet you are, too."

"I'm hungry but I'm also thirsty. Do you have something to drink?"

"There is some red wine in the cabinet next to the stove and there may be some white wine in the fridge," Kate called back. "I will have whatever."

Mike carried two glasses into the living room as Kate was making some notes. "Just as I suspected."

"What's that?"

"I wanted to confirm the figures we got from your computer with data I had pulled up about a year ago. Here, I will show you." Kate proceeded to pull out her notes from today as she grabbed a paper off the printer. She placed the papers on the table. "One year ago, Saudi Arabia was a creditor country. It had substantial sums invested in U.S. treasury bills and notes. It also had billions tied up in various European paper, mostly English pounds and German marks. Today, the country appears to be broke. Its investments are gone and it is several months behind in its obligations."

"What about production and prices?"

"Production levels are up and crude prices have been stable."

"Any major projects going on in the country?"

Kate typed feverishly. "No, nothing, it has been a quiet year. The money is gone and it has to have gone somewhere."

I walked to the white board. Under Winslow and Son's Ltd, I wrote down the following names: Bir, Saudi Arabia and the Hellenic Sea Lines.

"Don't forget to put Saudi Arabia off to the side and put a dollar sign under the name with a question mark next to it."

"Good idea."

We stared silently at the board. Kate finally spoke up. "You know, this is very frustrating.

I believe we have most of the parts here, but I can't tie the pieces together."

"I feel the same way. Please look up two more things for me?"

"Sure, what are they?"

"Please see when the cash flow at Winslow and Sons increased. And then compare that to the increase in option contract sales."

Kate headed back to her computer saying, "This may take some time."

"Okay" I had intended to head to the kitchen but continued to sit on the couch staring at the white board in front of me.

125

Akham Bizhanov sat on the floor next to his bed in the flat he had taken for his London stay. He was wearing a blindfold. In a case in front of him were parts of a sniper rifle. He sat there silently practicing the weapon's assembly in total darkness. As he worked the rifle, he considered the task ahead. Originally, he had hoped to have Yussof Dakkak help him. It would have been easier to do the job with two of them. But then Yussof went and got himself killed. It was unfortunate because it would make his job more difficult but not impossible. He knew he could get at most three possibly four shots off before he would have to flee. Every shot would have to count. For Yussof, it only meant that he had met his end a few days earlier than Akham had planned. Akham quickly reached into the gun case and assembled the gun. The weapon was a Brugger and Thomet category 3 sniper rifle with silencer. NATO forces used the weapon extensively. As a matter of fact this weapon had recently been borrowed from just such a source. This bolt-action gun used subsonic heavy bullet ammunition with pin-point accuracy up to 200 meters distance. There was no question in Akham's mind about the use of a silencer. Its use had the potential of reducing both range and accuracy, but it was an essential element to his escape plan. Akham was no one's martyr. He fully intended to go on living and after the assassinations he intended to live very well. While it probably would not be necessary to put the gun together in the dark, he had wanted to be totally familiar with this weapon.

Today was overcast with just a hint of rain. He had been informed all the outside events had been cancelled because of the weather. However, the forecast for the rest of the conference was for good weather that meant the remaining outdoor receptions would be held. He had had already checked out several possible sniper locations. Two were satisfactory and one was excellent. Akham had decided to go to his first choice location tomorrow and if everything was right, complete the task. If tomorrow did not work out, there was still the day after.

126

Maggie Smith looked in the mirror. She had just come off an eighteen-hour shift of police paperwork. Her assignment *de jour* was the file on the Irish Republican Army's Sean Murphy. All other things equal, he was a charming rogue with a wonderful gift of the blarney about him. The only problem was that all things were not equal and this "freedom fighter" had killed or rather was suspected of killing a newspaper reporter in Belfast who dared question the worth of the Provos. The newspaper reporter happened to be a Catholic and happened to work for a Catholic newspaper, which she supposed proved that Sean and the rest of his cohorts were not really prejudiced. They would kill without regard to race, creed, color or national origin.

She supposed she could look on the bright side. Even though it was paperwork, it was more than report writing. The problem was that she had found nothing new to add. She had spent hours trying to learn something, anything about the IRA terrorist. She had come up empty. She had contacted friends, enemies and informants, the latter group, of course, fit neither category but were at least interesting. An entire day wasted and a damn long one at that. She hated that. At least she would now have the chance to take a long hot bath and then get some much needed rest. It would have been nice to come home to someone. It was hard to have a love life when one was a cop. The hours the job demanded were simply boyfriend killers. There were always interested police officers but most of them didn't interest except for Philip Logan. Still and all she loved her work.

* * *

About six weeks ago the Hyde Park Residence was one of three flats that Exeter Trading Company of the Isle of Man had rented for three weeks. The Exeter Trading Company consisted of a post office box located in Douglas on the island. Akham Bizhanov had paid by postal order thus avoiding any opportunity of being traced. It happened that this week was the middle of the three. He had taken three flats mainly because he wanted to obscure his trail and because there still had been some uncertainty about the actual site of the summit at the time. The three-week time period was for the same reasons. He liked this flat not only for location but also the fact that management did not require guests to turn in their keys upon leaving the building. Last week and this he had made a number of trips to the different flats bringing in groceries etc. A lived in look made people less suspicious. The flat he had rented at the Hyde Park Residence would give him the best firing field. This is where he would go today.

127

I awoke on the couch, staring at the white board. It appeared Kate had fallen asleep in front of her terminal. When I went into her room she opened her eyes and began to speak as if she never stopped to rest.

"I got an answer to the two questions you asked. The cash flows to the Winslow and Sons and the futures and option contracts all began about the same time, about a year ago."

I motioned for her to follow me to the living room. "Just about the same time the Saudi economics began to change."

"Precisely,"

"So what do we have?'

Kate pointed to the white board. "We have learned that certain abnormal financial transactions have been disguised and laundered through the investment firm for over a year now. What we haven't been able to do is figure out is why. We do know that vast amounts of Saudi money have probably been used in whatever is going on. We know that Winslow and Son's Ltd. Gets its money from only three sources – The League, the tanker company and Saudi Arabia. We have tied Melina and the Hellenic Sea Lines to Kemal Kanuni at least on a personal basis. We also know Hans Schmidt is a front man for someone in the Middle East."

I picked up the discussion. "We also know that Kemal and the Saudi Oil Minister are related. I think we need more information. I know just who to get it from, I began dialing Fahad Amani's cell phone. There were the usual international call noises and then a subtler, but nonetheless comforting, sound of an encryption device. Within a couple of moments, the instrument rang. It only rang twice.

"Hello?"

"Yes, Fahad, it's me. Can we talk?"

"Yes, but for no more than three minutes." I immediately set the timer on my watch.

"When you called me earlier there was something important with which you needed help. I presume it has something to do with your government."

"It most certainly does. We don't have time for details but suffice it to say I became suspicious of Hazim Aziz and his son Abdul Aziz. I did some investigating and in the process have learned that our Oil Minister is deeply involved in the Islamic fundamentalist movement both in my country and in Jordan."

"That information is incredible. Are you sure?"

"The information is accurate. What it means I cannot say. It could mean that Mr. Aziz is plotting something or that he is in the process of saving my country from a plot of some kind."

We were getting short on time. "On another matter I confirmed the cash flow question you had for me. From our research it seems that for the last year or so the flow of your country's money has changed dramatically."

"I see"

Looking at my watch I could see our three minutes were almost up. "Who could make such a decision?"

"One of only four men."

"Who?"

"Obviously the King or the Crown Prince acting on his behalf. The other two are the Finance Minister or the Oil Minister."

"Thanks" I could see that only seconds remained. "I will call again." I hit the end button certain that Fahad would not be offended but rather would be grateful to me for so abruptly ending our call.

I quickly related to Kate what Fahad had told me.

Kate, now fully awake, responded with excitement in her voice. "That information ties all the players together! I am certain Hazim Aziz has been directing the activities of Winslow and Son's Ltd. It makes total sense. He is one of the few people in the world who could figure out and keep track of such a complicated series of financial maneuvers."

"Fahad doesn't know whether Aziz's involvement with the Islamic fundamentalist movement is to help or hurt the present administration. My guess at this point is that he is no friend of the government."

"I agree. Taking this one step further, I am guessing he is involved in a plot of some kind with Kemal himself."

I had noticed how easily we had picked up each other's thoughts and had been able to move the thought process forward. I again moved to the white board and added more information. As I wrote, Kate again spoke. "Okay, we have a plot. What is that plot? What are your thoughts?"

"The obvious I suppose. It has to have something to do with the oil supply. How about an oil shortage?"

Kate paused before she answered. "An oil shortage itself has been done before with mixed results. There has to be something else or another part to their plan."

Together we fell into silence. I felt we were close to figuring this Rubik's cube of a puzzle out.

128

Hazim Aziz settled back into his seat in his limo and took a deep breath. He glanced around at the verdant British countryside as he sped toward the airport. This land was so different from home. All this greenery was foreign to him and after just a short time away from home he longed for his native desert. It was unusual for such a high-ranking government official as he to leave a summit meeting in progress, but that could not be helped. Hopefully, the King and his other ministers accepted his explanation. Thankfully, most of them were technically ignorant so his excuse of unexpected ground pressure differentials in the old fields around Dhahran and his need to visit the site was acceptable. Even if they were skeptical it didn't really matter much. In one or two days his years of planning would come to fruition. Praise be to Allah.

The military was ready. It had taken years to find enough loyal officers, those who were either not members of the royal family or were fundamental believers. Now all it will take is one phone call and the young colonels will mobilize their troops. As he had decided they would arrest or kill, it really didn't matter, the old guard generals and Royal family members. As soon as his informant could tell him that the King and Crown Prince had been killed, he would have his units seize control of all the major public installations around the country including the television stations.

Seizing control of the government after killing the King and more importantly the Crown Prince was the easy part compared to the next portion of his plan. He was into the game of his life with unbelievable stakes. If he succeeded he would be the undisputed leader of the Islamic world. If he failed, well, he simply could not afford to fail. There was one more call to make during his *coup d'etat*. As long as Kemal Kanuni had oil wealth, he would be a problem. His oil wealth and vast numbers of people would easily overwhelm Saudi Arabia as well as the other Gulf States. That could not be. Hazim Aziz had no intention of playing second fiddle to anyone.

He had to deprive Kemal of his source of income. The newly completed pipeline transporting crude from Central Asia was the easiest place to make this happen. Properly placed charges would render the pipeline useless while at the same time looking like an accident. Without oil, Kemal's plans would be dead in the water. Once Kemal's oil was cut off, Hazim would call due all the notes being held by Winslow and Sons, Ltd. Securing the oil being shipped by the Hellenic Sea Lines. Hazim would not only gain control over the non-OPEC oil, he would also gain control over the very beautiful Melina. He smiled to himself as he thought of this. Indeed, this might be the most truly elegant part of his plan.

Unbeknownst to anyone but Hazim, he had made sure that the Saudi oil contracts and futures arrangement would be the first triggered once the world crises struck. His plan was to stop the crises before Bir's contracts were triggered. He would use the vast amounts of Saudi wealth to bail out the world's brokerage houses. Thus he would ensure both the financial ruin of League and the support of the Western world for his new regime. Without this last move the West would have been loathe to do anything but figure out how to get rid of him. They would not have that option when he was finished. A great contentment came over him as he closed his eyes to sleep.

129

It hit me like a lightning bolt. Could it be possible? Yes, it was possible, and because it was so subtle, success was indeed likely. I knew I would never have discovered the plan without her. We needed each other to discover the plot. I knew I needed her now more than ever to stop the plan.

Kate had seen the subtle shift in the numbers. She first saw the upward trend in the interest rates of U.S. Treasury paper. She couldn't readily explain why there had been fewer buyers in the marketplace. In searching for the answer she had also discovered that the same phenomenon was occurring with Euro paper. She had reasoned that if there were fewer buyers in that marketplace, they must be in another marketplace. After grueling hours of research she had found that there was a marked increase in the number of out of the money oil future contracts and oil options being sold. I knew I would never have been able to decipher all the data that Kate had. Had it not been for her background we would have been lost.

Still, while Kate could find the financial irregularities, she never would have been able to tie them together. The NSA had found Kemal Kanuni's fingerprints in the most unusual places. It was from the research in Washington that we found enough about Winslow and Sons to believe the company was controlled by the Saudi's. It was my friend Fahad Amani who unearthed the fact that Hazim Aziz was deeply involved in the Islamic Republic movement in Saudi Arabia and in Jordan. We also got hints from him of Saudi Arabia's dire cash flow condition. The Washington group had learned that Hans Schmidt was an old East German Communist who hated the United States and knew nothing about the finance or investment business.

Kate had answered the simple question, where did all the money go? However, the answer was far from simple, in that it didn't matter as much where; but *when*. Kate had pointed out that whatever had been planned was going to have to happen soon. The world markets could not be fooled much longer about the Saudi money or more exactly the lack of Saudi money.

Unfortunately we hadn't been able to conclusive tie Melina and Kemal together in the recent past. But in my opinion it was a safe assumption.

Separately, but at roughly the same time, we had both learned that Kemal Kanuni wasn't the person he claimed to be. A thoughtful yet charismatic, moderate Islamic leader he was not. I believed and with good reason that he saw himself as above any law and the writer of new laws for others and a follower of none, someone who could only be described as an Islamic Messiah or a Turkic Alexander the Great.

The plan was brilliantly conceived. Fully over 65% of the world's oil supply was within the grasp of Kemal Kanuni, not to mention that he controlled untold billions of dollars of oil contracts. What still was unknown was the trigger mechanism. What we needed to figure out now was what would cause the dominoes to fall? How was Kemal Kanuni going to control the Saudi oil production?

Kate spoke, "I have been watching your eyes. They have been going back and forth like mad. You've figured it out haven't you?"

"I think so. Correct me if you think I have missed something or have gone over the top." I quickly went over my thoughts of the last several minutes with her.

"Mike, how is Kemal going to do this? The Bir is an economic League, it isn't a country."

"True but he is immensely popular there. He just won a League-wide popular election to serve as Chairman and he did so overwhelmingly."

"Now that you mention it, I do recall."

"You also have to remember that he has extensive family contacts and associated influence in the largest countries in the League, Turkey and Kazakhstan. My guess is everything is already in place for him to be "The Godfather.""

"I can't disagree," Kate said. I think you have it. Kemal Kanuni has the ability to ruin the West. He has us two ways. He has the ability to control our oil supply. If he can't break us with oil he can get us financially. I believe he controls enough financial instruments to ruin all the major brokerage houses in the western world. These investment houses will easily fall and, like dominoes, the major banks will follow. The U.S. Treasury and the European Central Banks will be powerless to do anything. They will just have to watch their world crumble around them. The question I have for you, wonder boy, is the obvious one. How do we stop this plot? We must stop it before it starts. In my opinion, if it starts, there's a high likelihood it will cascade into worldwide crisis."

"Kate, you're right, we need to discover the trigger mechanism and then stop it from happening."

130

We sat on the couch each with our own thoughts. Kate was the first to break the silence. "This plan is brilliant. It is subtle and I think will succeed if we can't figure out how to stop it. We don't have much time either"

"Are you sure?"

"As sure as anything else. Look we stumbled on it. We were lucky and it took the two of us together to figure it out but we did. Given more time someone alone will undoubtedly stumble onto the plan. Wait long enough and everyone will know that Saudi Arabia has run out of money. The only reason that hasn't happened yet is that the League's new oil money has masked that fact. The market has yet to digest all the cash flows. But it will. It always does. It's a ponzi scheme and from what I can tell the money has just about run out."

I listened to Kate and tried to find a flaw in her logic, something she missed but I couldn't.

"I agree."

"You know, for this thing to work, something very unsettling must take place in the world," Kate thought out loud.

"I don't disagree but tell me why."

"Well, for one, the world needs to be distracted."

"Meaning?"

"The second part of the plan is to bankrupt the world's investment firms, right?"

"That's correct."

"So the world has to be worried about something else or there is a possibility that the U.S. government and the European

Union might be able to inject enough liquidity into the world's financial system to save the investment houses. If everyone is distracted there won't be enough time to stave off disaster."

Considering the possibility, I asked, "How much time will be needed?"

"Very little really. As a guess I would say less than thirty-six hours."

I changed the direction of the conversation. "Let's assume that Kemal Kanuni devised this plan. Is there anything he could directly do?"

"No I doubt it other than dreaming it up in the first place. I wouldn't think so. Neither do I think his girlfriend Melina Christakos could do anything to trigger the plan."

"Agreed. That leaves us with Saudi Arabia and Hazim Aziz." I rose from the couch. I needed to pace, over the years I had found moving about helped me think. It allowed me to focus. Kate watched and waited. "That has to be it. There can be no other choice. It's Saudi Arabia. Something is going to happen in that country, something big like a coup or an assassination of the King himself or possibly the Crown Prince, who has taken on an a much bigger role in the government as his brother's health has failed. Hazim Aziz seems to be at the center of this."

Kate exclaimed, "It will be an Islamic fundamentalist revolt! Whether Aziz leads the country or someone else does it won't matter. Everything we know about the region will be turned upside down. Look at Iran and the consequences of the Ayatollah."

"This maybe a stretch but once things begin moving anything might happen. Don't count our friend Kemal out. He may also have plans for who is in control in Saudi Arabia."

"Can you imagine one man in control of all the oil in the Middle East, except for the oil in Iran?"

"Kate, not only the Middle East but much of Central Asia as well."

"My God! What a disaster."

"Unmitigated. I need to contact Washington immediately. I should probably also let Amani know what we have discovered. That will give us a little edge there."

"Mike, it could happen right here in London. The King of Saudi Arabia and the Crown Prince are meeting with the Jordanian King at the Dorchester."

"That would be distracting. A clean sweep, the government of Saudi Arabia would be in disarray. Jordan would be destabilized. Israel would be brought into play, what a perfect backdrop for a Fundamentalist revolt."

"Anything else we can do?"

"Yes. We need to get some local help as well. While I make my calls why don't you contact Maggie Smith at Scotland Yard and bring her up to speed. When you do, ask her to let Philip Logan know what we have discovered."

"Okay, I will do it in a minute."

"Why the wait?"

"If I am going to save the world I need to get out my Wonder Woman suit. Do you want to be Batman or Superman?"

Kate was perfect. She knew just what was needed. The situation was dire but we both needed to think clearly and not panic. "I've always been partial to Superman. I figure, how could you go wrong with Lois Lane?"

131

The morning sunlight in all its glory streamed into his hotel suite. He had gotten to bed late, actually early in the morning and now, to his incredible bad luck, unfortunately had forgotten to close the shades and now he was awake with no hope of going back to sleep. Khalid shook his head trying to put some coherent thoughts into it. With what appeared to be such a nice day it was highly likely that today's social events would be held outside. He grabbed his day sheet from the nightstand to confirm. Just as he had thought both the luncheon meeting and the evening reception were to be held on the hotel's outside terrace. He didn't like the security risks but there was nothing more he could do. He had complained to no avail. His philosophical side said that all he could do was pray. God willing, the prophet would protect his Highness.

He reached for the telephone and dialed. "Salim I need to talk to you can you come over?"

"Certainly, Mr. Prime Minister, by the way, how do you think it went last night?"

"I am a bad one to ask. You know how I hate diplomatic meetings. The higher up the food chain they are, the worse they get. Summits to me consist of long meetings where nothing actually ever takes place followed by social functions that go to all hours of the night. It's always the same. First there is the reception that follows the last official session of the day. At this function you are required to stand around and talk to the same people you have dealt with all day long. This is one of the few times in my life that I wish I were an infidel. At least non-

Moslems can drink their way through the evening, dulling the boredom from excruciating to tolerable. Following the reception comes the dinner. That is a function filled with too many courses of overly rich food."

"Mr. Prime Minister I suppose if you keep a good attitude during this process you will surely see paradise, as this is so hard for you."

"Salim I hope you are right and thanks for listening. Even those diplomatic events wouldn't be so bad if after them I didn't have to return to our Embassy to catch up on my other favorite thing, semi-meaningless official paperwork."

"Kahlid, I will be over shortly. I do have some good news."

"What is that?"

"I have found a store that sells excellent coffee. I will have some delivered."

"Thank you for your consideration. That will give me something to look forward to." Still shaking his head, he rose from the bed and made his way slowly toward the bathroom.

132

Maggie tested the water. It seemed to be just right. She was about to get in when the phone rang. She looked down the hall at the instrument with a look of hatred on her face. No, she was off-duty and she needed this time to herself. The phone stopped ringing as the answering machine picked up. "Maggie, this is Kate O'Hara. It is terribly important that I speak to you. I phoned headquarters and they said you might be at home. Please pick up if you are."

"Bloody hell," she said aloud. There was no way she could relax without at least talking to the American. Not bothering to grab her robe, she walked down the hall naked to answer the phone. "Hello, this is Maggie."

"I am so glad to have gotten a hold of you." The voice said at the other end of the line.

Guardedly responding, she asked, "Why is that?" Maggie at that instant knew she would regret that she had asked. She listened quietly as Kate told her the story. "What do you want of me?"

"I was hoping you could go to the Dorchester and see if you could persuade the Kings, their aides or whoever is in charge to keep their Highnesses inside and off the terraces. Mike and I were going to see if we could spot the sniper. If we got lucky we also hoped you could send some of your able co-workers to the rescue."

Maggie knew she had no choice but to agree. How could she say, *I would love to save the free world but I am off duty and am taking a bath?* "Very well."

"Thank you. Mike also asked that you contact Philip Logan and bring him up to speed."

Maggie depressed the receiver and waited for the dial tone. She dialed the number to headquarters. She was going to need backup quickly.

133

"Did you get through to Inspector Smith?"

Kate answered,"Yes I called Scotland Yard and they forwarded me to her home. I told her what we have discovered. However, I'm not sure that she completely believes me. She did believe me enough, though, to send the police to the Dorchester."

"Thanks, Kate. At least that is something. With the police going to the hotel I don't think it would do any good for us to go there. If anything happens at the hotel, the authorities will be on the scene. Instead, pretend you are the killer."

"Okay. First thing, I am not suicidal and I am not a zealot."

"Agreed. The killer wants to survive the assassination. How would you do that?"

Kate paused. "I would need to kill from a distance."

"How?"

"We are assuming that the murder is to take place here, correct?"

"Correct."

"Then I would try poison or some kind of explosive device."

Mike nodded and then added, "Or I shoot them."

"Not a hand gun?"

"Too difficult to get away. No, I would say a rifle, say a sniper rifle."

"Maybe even one with a silencer."

I nodded and held up my hand. At this moment I needed to review the results of our conversation, to figure out if we had arrived at a conclusion or a dead-end. "A bomb or poison would take place at the hotel and the police can handle that. I say we concentrate on the shooter aspect. A sniper could work, but he would have to be outside. An inside sniper makes no sense. He could never get away. That would mean some kind of outside reception at the hotel. It is most unlikely that their royal highnesses would take a stroll in Hyde Park."

"The Dorchester has a number of exclusive suites with terraces that overlook Hyde Park," Kate added. "As a matter of fact, I've had the privilege of experiencing the terrace gardens. They are lovely, open and very exposed. There are enough buildings around the hotel that are tall enough to offer a clear view of these outside venues."

"What type of buildings?"

"All kinds. A few hotels, apartments and one or two office buildings," Kate enumerated.

I rubbed my chin and spoke, "It has to be a hotel. Anything else wouldn't work."

"Why?"

"Office buildings or apartments would be too hard to get into, too much chance of someone catching on. Hotels rent rooms as a business, much easier. See what you can find about hotels." Kate headed for her computer and began to punch away. "Let me look up the hotels that also front onto Hyde Park that are near the Dorchester. What is the range of a sniper rifle?"

"No more than 200 meters, relatively close."

"It looks like the only possibility is Hyde Park Residence. It isn't a hotel per se but rather one of those buildings that contain flats and apartments that are rented out like hotel rooms."

"Same difference," I shouted and hopped up. "That's where we are going. With luck maybe we can stop the shooter. That way we can keep the police out of the bucket-and-sponge business."

Kate shook her head as she and I headed out the door.

"What?"

"You certainly have an interesting way of putting things sometimes."

134

Akham Bizhanov looked out the window of his hotel room. The London sky was blue and there wasn't a cloud to be seen. Undoubtedly the summit's outdoor events would go on as originally planned. The conference was scheduled to end tomorrow. If everything worked out as he hoped, today would be the day; regardless he wouldn't alter his routine, fewer suspicions that way. He had paid for his room with cash through tomorrow. It was the kind of hotel where no one questioned the use of cash.

He slowly walked about the room making certain he had left no clues behind. He did this every time he left a location. As he was about to leave he gathered up his bags. He had two of them. One, a black nylon over the shoulder garment type bag, was, as it appeared to be, a bag to carry his clothes. The other was an inexpensive nylon briefcase-type, also black. He wore a worn blue sport coat, white shirt and tie with a pair of inexpensive gray slacks, the type of business uniform worn by many as they traversed the streets of London going to and from work. He had also lightened his hair and cut off his mustache. While the outside of his briefcase was made of the same indistinguishable black nylon found in every other brief, the insides were unique. He had the bag custom-fitted to carry his sniper rifle, scope, silencer and ammunition. The job was so masterful that from the outside the bag had the same weighted-down-with-too-many-papers look that so many others had.

* * *

As Kate requested Maggie called Philip Logan's office.

"Philip I got a call from Kate O'Hara."

"Who?"

"Your friend Mike Williams' girlfriend. You know the lady newspaper reporter."

"Oh right. Is anything wrong?"

"She was calling for Mike. He thinks there is going to be an assassination attempt at the Dorchester Hotel either today or tomorrow."

"Unbelievable, did he say how he knew this?"

"No, they apparently didn't have time."

"All right, I will do some checking on my end, make some calls. Keep me apprised. Better let Lord Alex know."

'I will." After she hung up Philip, Maggie immediately dialed again. She asked for Logan's boss, her section head, Lord Alexander Chamberlain. Lord Alex was a rather tweedy anachronism well past retirement. Maggie quickly told her story and thankfully during the conversation only had to repeat herself once. Lord Alex agreed to send whoever was immediately available from the anti-terrorist unit to the Dorchester Hotel.

Immediately after making her call Maggie threw on some clothes. She wanted to arrive at the hotel when or hopefully before the unit from headquarters arrived. As she quickly dressed she considered what to do. The antiterrorist unit had a lot of experience. Though most of it had to do with the Irish Republican Army, but then bad guys were bad guys. She gathered up her coat, checking to make sure her gun was in the pocket. Even though English Bobbies carried no firearms the same could not be said of the members of Scotland Yard. She knew it would have been suicidal not to be armed. Scotland Yard's work was just a tad more dangerous. Maggie slammed the door as she left fumbling for her car keys. With luck she could be at the hotel within a few minutes.

135

The delegates had just returned from their morning break. Generally the individual sessions were designed to run no more than two hours. The first session of the day generally began at 8:00 or 8:15 a.m. and ran until about 10:00 a.m. The mid-morning meeting followed. Today, the mid morning meeting was scheduled to be shorter than usual. The delegates were scheduled to convene again at 10:15 a.m. and would break for lunch, a formal affair, at 11:30 a.m. The lunch was set to start at noon today. The location was the Saudi delegation's official suite, more specifically the outside terrace off the suite.

"Salim, have you been checked everything out?"

"I have. There is nothing more we can do. The views from the terrace are magnificent. From the balcony there is a view towards Hyde Park."

"It will make a nice setting for the Kings to meet. What can you see in the Park?"

"Mostly lawn and trees, the view is somewhat obstructed, as there are a number of other buildings in the area with views to Hyde Park and of course back at the Dorchester."

"Remind your men to watch the buildings."

"I have done so and I will do so again, Mr. Prime Minister. We have been assured that security teams have secured all the rooms facing the hotel."

"Thank you. I know I repeat myself, but until we are safely home I will be this worrying old woman driving you crazy."

Salim nodded, "I understand. You might feel better if you came upstairs and saw the site for yourself. Do you expect anything of substance to come from this short session?"

"No not really." Khalid al Shariff was about to get up when His Highness King of Jordan rose to speak. The Prime Minister turned to Salim, this is unscheduled."

"We have met and visited for several days now and I have enjoyed meeting with you all. In particular I have been honored to talk with his Royal Highness King and Prime Minister Fahd bin Abd al-Aziz Al Saud and Crown Prince and First Deputy Prime Minister Abdallah bin Abd al-Aziz Al Saud. The insights they have brought to our humble conference and to me in particular have been most invaluable. For this I am eternally thankful. I am equally thankful that they have been most generous to the Jordanian people. Without their and the Saudi people's support my country would have suffered terribly. That is why I feel compelled to raise an issue that has not been put on the agenda. Tomorrow the conference ends and I would believe it to have been a failure had I not broached this topic."

The King paused rather dramatically at this point and reached for a glass of water. He took a rather long and slow drink before resuming his speech.

"Our people occupy a region of the world that has been long on strife and short on peace. The citizens of both our countries and those of the entire region should be able to live in peace. Since the Kuwaiti War there has been peace or at least the nearest thing we could find to it. Now, I believe this fragile peace has the gravest potential to be threatened. The cause of my concern is the newly formed League of Bir. As we all know it has quickly progressed from a simple trading group to a united entity. It has done this under the leadership of Kemal Kanuni. This country has both money and the manpower to be a major influence in the region, yet we have not been able to open a dialogue with him. We have tried and have been unsuccessful. I am using this meeting to ask my Saudi brothers to join with me in inviting President Kanuni to a tri-party summit next month in Amman."

During his entire speech Khalid noticed the King did not refer to his notes once. Clearly, this was an area about which His Highness felt very strongly. So strongly that he had taken the unusual and bold step of extending an invitation without the usual diplomatic maneuvering. The Jordanian King remained standing for almost a minute after his speech. The Prime Minister had seen him do this before when emphasizing a point. As the King sat the murmuring and comments among the delegates began. The rotating chair of the meeting happened to be the Deputy Saudi Oil Minister. The Oil Minister, it seemed, had had to rush home to deal with some oil field emergency.

"Mr. Prime Minister, I take it from everyone's actions this speech was not expected."

"You take it correctly."

"Should you do anything?"

"No, let's see what the Saudi's do."

It took several more minutes for the Chairman to return order to the meeting. "I recognize Prince Al Bin Faisal."

"His Royal Highness, has offered us a great opportunity. I for one would like to ask that we adjourn at this point so that we may confer before our luncheon meeting."

The young delegate quickly sat down and looked at the chairman, who gaveled the meeting to a close.

136

Bizhanov exited the underground at the Marble Arch station. Though not as convenient as a cab he preferred the anonymity of the tube. From there he took the subway to Park Lane and the flat. As he walked he observed the Dorchester Hotel. He could clearly make out the terraces. He would have to wait until he got to the room before he knew if there were any inconvenient obstructions in the way. Awnings or umbrellas are nothing to the flight of a bullet, but he had yet to develop x-ray vision.

He walked the few steps up to the lobby, pressed the button and was admitted. The young girl behind the front desk waved to him and without a second thought returned to her paperwork. Again, rather than waiting for the elevator, he chose to climb the stairs. Walking the stairs would take extra time but his chance of encountering anyone was much less in the stairwell.

He eventually climbed the entire flight of stairs. There were a total of seven units on his floor. When he'd first checked in, the clerk told him he had been charged a little less for his unit because it did not have a view of the park. Little did the clerk know that he would have paid extra for this particular flat. He walked slowly and nonchalantly down the hall toward his apartment. He really did not expect a problem, but had trained himself to be careful. He encountered no one and quickly unlocked the door, gathered up his things, entered and shut the door behind him.

137

The flat was brightly lit even with the curtains partially drawn and without any lights on. Bizhanov quickly locked the door and did a quick search of the premises to ensure no one else was here or had been here. Akham hung his garment bag in the front hall closet, and then proceeded to the kitchen table where he removed his gloves and opened his briefcase. The case was designed to open completely. The double zipper wrapped around the entire bag. He had had it designed this way for ease of use. After some practice he had found that he could knock down the gun and place it in the bag and have the bag zipped in under thirty seconds. Thus Bizhanov, from the time he fired his final shot to the moment he left the apartment, could be gone in less than a minute.

He unzipped the case fully, first putting on a pair of surgical cloves before beginning work. Like a surgeon he quickly yet carefully assembled the sniper rifle, attaching the scope and silencer. Making sure that his scope was properly adjusted; he went to the window that overlooked the Dorchester. The assassin stood back from the window. From that undetected vantage point he could clearly see the terrace below. For the first time he could see there were minimal obstructions, as had been promised. He practiced shooting the weapon several times including testing the trigger mechanism, each time slightly adjusting his scope and the trigger action. Satisfied that all was perfect, he then loaded the weapon. Bizhanov then placed the weapon and additional bullets carefully next to the window and went to get a chair to sit on. He checked his watch. The lunch meeting would begin soon and he wanted to use the facilities before then.

138

Because the mid-morning session had broken early the waiters had been instructed to hurry. The lunch was scheduled to begin at noon, but it was now likely that at least some of the delegates would be arriving early. They had about fifteen minutes to compete all their preparations. The setup was a standard conference informal arrangement. Eight-top tables were situated to provide the most shade possible without using umbrellas. To do this the tables had been located in the northeast corner of the terrace allowing for shade from the hotel itself as the sun moved from east to west. Because the tables had been located in the northeast corner of the terrace, the refreshment bar had been set up on the southern side of the terrace. The remaining open portion of the terrace was thus fan-shaped with the base of the fan located between the luncheon tables and the bar and with the edges of the fan consisting of the outer walls of the terrace. The outer walls of the terrace were about four feet high, high enough to keep anyone from accidentally falling over but not so high as to interfere with the view. As the waiters hurriedly completed their tasks, the first delegates began to arrive

139

Kate and I hopped out of the cab and stood on the sidewalk in front of the Dorchester Hotel. The trip had reminded me of Disneyland's Mr. Toad's Wild Ride. When we flagged down the cab outside her flat, Kate had offered the driver an extra fifty pounds if he could us to the Dorchester within twenty minutes. He definitely took our request to heart and got us to the hotel with a couple of minutes to spare. "Well we made it here and in one piece, my guess that for an extra 100 quid he would have run-down his own mother."

"Mike quit your whining, I know we had a couple of near misses but that's better than one or both of the Kings to have a near or no miss experience."

"I hear you, still..."

"You just don't like to be in the passenger seat, that's all, now what do we do next?"

"Let me get my bearings." The front door of the hotel was back from the street with a drive approach and fountain situated between Park Lane and the lobby entrance. Behind us was a cabstand with at least ten cabs in it. I could see there was nothing of note here. "It's almost eleven-thirty. Let's take a quick walk down the sidewalk."

"What are we looking for?"

"A sniper." We walked down the sidewalk looking alternately between the hotel and the buildings around it. We walked until we spotted where the terraces were located.

"What about there?" Kate had pointed in the direction of the Hyde Park Residence.

"If it were me, the top floor of that building would be my first choice. See those last three windows on the far right? That's where I would want to shoot. Let's go see what we can find."

"Okay," with that we ran off in the direction of the hotel.

140

We entered the hotel lobby. There was nothing special about the layout of the room. The front desk was on the right side of the lobby. Behind the counter was a small office. To the immediate left of the counter area was a set of stairs with the elevators on the far left. As Kate and I approached the front desk, I said, "You do the talking. I think he," I pointed to the clerk who moments ago had been sitting in the small office watching television, "will more easily answer your questions than mine."

Kate nodded in agreement and approached the front desk.

"Excuse me you have such a lovely hotel here. I was wondering if you might have any rooms available?"

"Yes mum, we do. But I don't see any luggage and this is a respectable establishment."

Kate, feigning astonishment said, "Oh no. We left our luggage in the taxi. No sense in lugging it into each hotel we look at."

"Very well."

"Might you have anything on the top floor?"

"I'm afraid not. Those units are booked months in advance."

"Oh, I see. I was hoping one would be available. Do you have any pictures of rooms on that floor? Or would it be possible to see one? You see, if we like one, we could book it now for our next trip."

"I am not allowed to preview rooms that are already occupied. Management considers our guest's privacy as paramount.

Sorry. I can get you a brochure, though. I just need to get one from the office."

"Thank you. If you would, that would be wonderful. Take your time. We are in no hurry."

The clerk turned and walked into the office. As he started to rummage through the drawers Kate, called to him, "Never mind. My husband has changed his mind." With that, Kate and I bolted for the stairs and were out of sight before the clerk had time to turn around.

As we approached the top floor, we slowed, not wanting to be caught off-guard or sound like the thundering hordes arriving. At the same time I motioned for Kate to move over as close as she could to the far wall. "Better cover" As I got to the landing I looked to see if anyone was in the corridor.

"Anyone there?" Kate whispered.

I looked up and down the hall "No one, not even hotel staff." By now Kate was next to me. "There are only two possibilities." I pointed to the two doors at the far end of the hall. "It's one of those two flats. We are going to have to choose one and see what happens. Any last thoughts?"

"None."

"Then stay behind me and next to the wall. If anything goes wrong, run like and hell and get help."

"Okay, just don't let anything bad happen to you."

"I'll do my best. Let's give it a go."

141

Maggie brought her car to a screeching halt in front of the hotel, threw open the door, got out and bounded up the steps into the hotel lobby. "Madam, Madam, and may we help you?" Maggie could hear hotel security call to her. She believed time was short and she needed to find whoever was in charge. As she entered the lobby she caught her breath. The manager was nowhere to be found. Smith continued to look around the lobby for help. Finally she walked quickly to the somewhat bored looking concierge, thinking she would make the list for the most unusual requests.

Maggie heard the sound of a police siren wailing in the distance.

"Excuse me, my name is Maggie Smith. I am an inspector with Scotland Yard." Maggie presented her credentials to the young man. "It is desperately important that I speak with the hotel manager."

All hint of boredom erased, the young man behind the counter inquired, "Is there something I might help you with? The manager is quite busy." Exasperated, Maggie practically shouted, "You can bloody well get me the manager immediately or he will be a damned sight busier than he has ever been in his life." Not used to being talked to in that particular tone of voice, but certain that he needed to ring the manger, the concierge complied. "Templeton, I have a police woman out here who insists on talking to you immediately."

Maggie could not hear the other end of the conversation, but could see the young man's head nod up and down. "I will take you to our manager, Templeton Wainwright. Please follow me." They began to deliberately cross the lobby when the first contingent from Scotland Yard arrived. Maggie indicated by a silent hand signal that they should reconnoiter the lobby and wait for her.

The young man saw the activity and quickened his pace perceptibly. They arrived at an unmarked door and entered. Maggie could see that the concierge was by now completely rattled. They entered a small reception office where a secretary would normally sit. Glancing at the condition of the desk, it was easy to conclude the secretary was taking a lunch break.

"Mr. Wainwright, this is the inspector from Scotland Yard," the concierge announced and then quickly left the room.

"How may I help you?" Templeton Wainwright rose from behind his desk to greet her.

"Mr. Wainwright, here are my credentials. We at the Yard have good reason to believe that there will be an assassination attempt on the lives of the Kings of Saudi Arabia and Jordan. Furthermore, we believe that the attempt will take place today, certainly no later than tomorrow." Returning the documents to Maggie, he said, "What can I do to help you?"

"For starters, where are the royal parties now?"

"They should both be on Terrace B. The Saudi's are hosting a luncheon reception."

Completely alarmed, Maggie asked, "Is that one of the roof top garden terraces?"

"Yes it is."

Maggie instantly knew the answer to the next question but chose to ask it anyway. "I don't suppose there is any cover there?"

"No, not really. We pride ourselves on having a beautiful and unimpeded view of Hyde Park."

"I need you to take me there immediately. I saw your security where is theirs?"

"I am not certain, but I presume with the royal parties."

Turning immediately in the direction of the door, Maggie spoke "We must get to the terraces as fast as possible." She strode out of the office with the hotel manager chasing after her. Reentering the lobby, she signaled for one of the squad to remain in the lobby and for the rest to come with her. "Is there a private elevator?"

"Yes, follow me. I will take you to one that goes directly to the penthouse."

To the casual observer, the five people crossing the lobby to the elevator banks made for an unusual ensemble. It was not everyday you saw three of Scotland Yard's finest being commanded by a rather attractive woman following a middle-aged hotel manager, particularly at the Dorchester.

142

The hotel manager pushed the call button and simultaneously inserted his passkey into the lock. The door to the left opened immediately and the four from Scotland Yard and one terrified hotel employee entered.

"Ms. Smith, this car will take us directly to the penthouse suites. Off the suites are the private terraces. I have to assume that the Kings' security details are there now."

"I only saw hotel security when I got here. I didn't see anyone when I arrived. Is that common?" Maggie asked.

"I hadn't really paid attention. Just let me think. No, not unusual for this particular summit. For others we have had in the past, yes. As I recall the delegations always seemed to have a few extra security people present in the lobby and other public areas."

The elevator had almost reached its destination. Maggie turned again to the manager. "I need your help when we get out. As soon as we all get off, every security man will have us in his sights. I need you to make sure they don't shoot us before we can save them. I also need you to get the Saudi and the Jordanian security chiefs to come speak with us. Do you think you can do that?"

"I will do my best," replied Templeton Wainwright.

The car was slowing to a halt and the doors were about to open. Maggie turned to her subordinates. "Draw your weapons, but hang back in the car. I don't want to provoke anyone. We don't know who the killer is and we certainly don't want to do the job for them. Right?"

"Right, ma'am. If we did I would certainly think the PM would have our guts for garters, what?"

"That would be mild. Let's just say life on the Falklands would seem a reward. Let's be ready men."

The doors opened and Maggie and Templeton Wainwright stepped out.

143

As Smith stepped out of the car she could see the reception had already begun. The two Kings and the Crown Prince along with their closest aides were talking. Because of the configuration of the terrace, the members of the royal party were located on the outer edges of the terrace. This part of the patio offered both the best views of Hyde Park and the most room for all the guests and diplomats. The elevator was positioned in the vestibule of the suite. This area was the most heavily guarded, obviously on the theory that any intruder would enter by way of the elevator or the nearby stairwell door.

"Ms. Smith, I see the head of Jordanian security, Almed Nassir."

"Who is that standing next to him?"

"I don't know."

"Please wave him over here." Smith could see that the man was alarmed and had signaled to his staff. Maybe he could see her men behind but still in the elevator car. Whatever the reason, some of his men had withdrawn their weapons and were aiming them at the elevator and its occupants.

The hotel manager managed to get Almed's attention. He was coming in Wainwright's direction. As he came towards them he repeatedly glanced back over his shoulder and in the direction of the lift. From the way he was looking Smith believed security chief could now clearly see that her uniformed men in the elevator. Thankfully no one on the terrace had yet noticed anything unusual.

Wainwright called out, "Mr. Nassir may I talk to you for a moment?" The security chief had stopped about three yards away from Wainwright and Smith. "Mr. Nassir, I would like to introduce you to Ms. Maggie Smith of Scotland Yard." As Wainwright spoke, Maggie was displaying her credentials to the Jordanian security chief. "I will let her tell her story." The hotelman, obviously relieved to be able to pass the responsibility to someone else mopped his forehead with his handkerchief and stepped away from Smith.

Maggie began, "Mr. Nassir, for your information, there are three of my associates in the lift. They are armed. I would like your permission to allow me to bring them into the penthouse."

"Why should I?"

"Scotland Yard believes there will be an assassination attempt on the lives of the Kings and or the Crown Prince. I am here along with my men to help you protect them."

"The only unexpected people I have seen today are you and your men," countered Nassir.

"I understand but we have received compelling information. All I ask is that you move the Royals inside the penthouse and out of the open. I believe there may be a sniper or snipers in one of the adjoining buildings."

"Thank you for your offer. Please come with me. I want you to personally ask the Royal party to move inside. They will move if you ask and there will be less political fallout. Please have your men wait in the lobby."

Almed Nassir immediately turned and began walking toward the outside patio. Maggie quickly fell in behind him. The lowest level staff members were situated in the penthouse. They and the working hotel staff fell silent as the security chief and Smith passed by. On the terrace itself were higher-level delegates, their level of importance increasing the closer they were situated to the kings and the crown prince.

144

French doors divided the terrace from the actual penthouse. The doors were opened in an apparent attempt to ease the flow of people. As Smith passed through the French doors she had her first opportunity to investigate any sniper positions. A quick appraisal told her that there were two or three potential sites, but the best was to the right. She slowed her pace as she scanned the building, picking out the location she would have chosen. The top floor corner windows gave the best field of fire. There was no doubt in her mind, if there was a shooter, the shooter would be there. Maggie stopped and motioned for her sergeant. This brought Nassir flying back to her. "No, no he cannot come out on the terrace."

"Mr. Nassir, I must talk to my men and there is no time for petty politics. I need him to go to that building." Maggie pointed as she spoke. "I believe if there is a sniper that is where he or she will be."

The sergeant arrived in time to hear what was needed. "Yes Ma'am, I'll check it out." He spun around and was gone before Almed Nassir could agree or disagree.

"Mr. Nassir, let's go meet your boss." She was in no position to command this man, but she didn't care. If it were going to happen today, she believed the time would be now.

145

I had had Special Forces training, but it seemed like a long time ago. The most value it had been to me lately was in impressing women. Of course, under almost any circumstances that was a good reason for such training. Now it was for real, I hoped it was like riding a bicycle, something you never really forgot how to do. Within the next few minutes I would again find value in this training.

"I am going to have to pick the lock. Stay against the wall right there back and out of the way." I pointed to where I wanted Kate to wait. "If our shooter is in there and he hears me, I don't want you hit when he shoots the door."

I whispered to her. "Once I get in I will call you. If you don't hear from me or something happens to me trying to pick this lock in get out as fast as you can. Get downstairs and get help. Do you understand?"

Kate nodded. Her eyes like saucers.

I took out my tools and began to fiddle with the lock. I was being as quiet as humanly possible. Nonetheless to me it sounded like I was dragging a ball and chain across a concrete courtyard. The fixture lock was a simple one and I managed to open it quickly. I then drew my weapon, nodded to Kate, opened the door and in one move rolled across the floor and found cover behind a couch. The apartment appeared to be unoccupied. The shades were drawn at least in the rooms I could see. I could also see no light coming from under any of the doors or from down the hall. Damn bad luck, I had chosen the wrong one, it had to be next door. I normally would have left Kate in the hall for safety reasons. However, it was likely that a trained killer was in the unit next door and I didn't want Kate to be standing in the hallway with a killer on the loose.

"The coast is clear. Come in," I said in as loud a whisper as I dared. I hoped it was loud enough for Kate to hear, but not the bad guy next door. Within a few seconds Kate joined me. "The sniper, if there is one, has to be in the unit next door. Look quickly around and see if you can find something that can be used as a weapon."

"What are you going to do?"

"I am going to call the police for back up. Then I am going to look out one of the windows to see what, if anything, I can see of the unit next door."

As I pulled out my cell phone, I heard Kate rummaging in a nearby closet. Just as I was about to dial I heard another distinctive sound. One I hadn't heard since my days of Special Forces training. It was the sound of a high velocity rifle being silenced.

146

"Excuse me, what did you say?"

"I need to talk to whoever is in charge, immediately," Smith responded. "I simply don't have time to discuss this with you or to negotiate with you."

The Jordanian security chief said, "Khalid al Shariff, our Prime Minister is over there." The Security chief pointed toward the edge of the terrace.

Smith could see a group of four men standing together about thirty feet from her and Almed Nassir.

"Over there?"

"Yes,"

"I recognize Jordanian King. I assume the other two are the Saudi King and his brother the Crown Prince."

"That is correct."

"Well they are perfectly positioned for a shooter." As she spoke Smith looked up at the corner window. Just as she looked, she saw a window open. It was too soon there was no way the sergeant had somehow gotten to the room in time. Maggie began to run and shout at the men.

"Move! Get down!" Maggie shouted. The men stared at her in confusion, frozen, too confused to move. Again, looking back at the room, she saw a long object. It had to be a rifle barrel.

By now Almed Nassir had also seen the rifle and began shouting in Arabic.

Maggie and Nassir's shouts finally caused a reaction. The Jordanian king, the youngest man in the group moved quickly toward Smith. Unfortunately, the Saudi king was old and en-feebled. He could no more move quickly than he could fly. By now the King of Jordan was parallel to Abdul bin Saudi. The angle was such that the Saudi king was shielding the Jordanian monarch. The Prime Minister and the Crown Prince had begun to drop to the terrace deck.

Maggie was almost there. She knew the sniper would get off at most three shots, but most probably two. She was about to dive onto the old man when a bullet struck him in the chest and spun him around. Pieces of tissue and blood flew everywhere.

Almed Nassir had gotten to the Prime Minister and the Crown Prince and thrown himself on top of them. "Stay down and don't ..." he began to order when a second shot rang out. Skull fragments of the Security chief immediately covered the men he had protected as the bullet exploded his head.

Seeing the kill Maggie altered her course. With luck she could get to King of Jordan before the next shot was fired. She confronted the king and began to push him to the ground. He at first resisted but then understood. He collapsed on the floor under her as another bullet struck.

People began shouting and some even screamed.

147

The Jordanian king tried to get up. As he did he began to thank this unknown policewoman for protecting him, but for some reason he could not move.

"Your Highness, are you alright?" Nassir asked as he ran towards his monarch. Blood was everywhere, along with human body fragments. "Have you been injured?"

At first the King could not even speak. By now however some control was returning to his body and with it, pain. He knew he had been hit in the upper chest. He needed to move, he needed to breathe. He spoke to the woman still on top of him but received no response. He then began to push her but nothing happened. He tried again, and then as if by magic, the woman was off of him and he was being assisted by his security chief, Almed Nassir.

Nassir bent down over the fallen King and quickly examined him. "Your Highness, you have been hit. Your wound does not appear fatal, but staying out here could very well be. Put your arm around me. We are going to make a run inside. Do you understand?" The security chief lifted and pulled the king to his feet.

"Yes, yes, but what happened?"

"When we are safe I will give you a full report." As Jordanian Monarch struggled to his feet, he looked down at the British policewoman. Nassir saw him looking. "She is dead, let's go."

Half-dragging, half- running the two men struggled for cover. They made it inside the hotel suite. Once inside the penthouse the King continued to look in the direction of the fallen officer.

"She protected you with her body," Nassir said. "The impact of the bullet meant for you was slowed by her body. That is why you are alive. Now please lie down. The doctor will look at your wound."

148

Panic and terror continued unabated on the terrace. While some delegates had sought cover there were others frozen in place by what had occurred. All it seemed were shouting and screaming. Chaos reigned. In the confusion, one man, a lower level Saudi representative from the oil ministry, reached for his cell phone. The delegate pressed a speed dial number and within a few seconds the call was completed. "It is done. I believe His Highness is in Paradise. King of Jordan and the Crown Prince have survived."

"Your Highness, your brother has been shot." Khalid al Shariff was telling the Crown Prince.

The tall man had struggled to his knees and was looking in the direction of the king. "Yes Mr. Prime Minister I see that. Do you know his condition?"

"No."

"I must go see."

"You can't it may not be safe. Please remain behind this wall. I will go check."

"Thank you for your offer. But he is my brother and my responsibility." With the Prince stood and began walking towards the fallen man.

As they walked the Jordanian Prime Minister placed his body between the King and the building from where the shots were fired. "That is not necessary Prime Minister al Shariff. I am sure the shooting is over. Come and if you would please help me with my brother."

Both men knelt and examined Abdul bin Saud. The Crown Prince reached to his neck to see if there was a pulse. "I believe he is still alive. I think there is a faint pulse. Come help me get him inside. With luck and by the grace of Allah we can save him."

The two men were about to lift the monarch when two young delegates came and picked up the fallen King and brought him into the hotel suite.

149

I had no time for phone calls as I sprinted towards and out the door. I turned down the hall and was prepared to kick the shooter's door down. I quickly examined the outside of the door to see if there were any weak spots. This door, as compared to the one I just picked open was subtlety different. It looked like it had been re-enforced. Damn, I was never going to be able to enter by kicking the door down. My only hope for immediate entry was to disable the lock. I was going to have to shoot my way in. I took off the safety to my weapon and discharged the magazine into the door and its locking mechanism.

Smoke, incredibly loud noise and wood splinters filled the hallway. I had obviously lost the element of surprise. As loud as it was just seconds ago, it was now incredibly still. In that stillness I heard another round being fired. I knew I was too late for the dignitaries. All I could do now was to capture the shooter. There was no point in me rushing into the flat. Most likely all I would succeed in doing was to get myself killed. I knew there were no external escape routes on that side of the building. I decided to back from the door and wait for the shooter. He or she was trapped. The only way out was through the door in front of me. Local law enforcement would arrive within minutes. If I can keep him in the flat until they arrive then at least we can capture the assassin. I dropped to one knee, reloaded and waited.

As I pulled back down the hall, I saw Kate poke her head out of the door down the hall. I immediately waved for her to get back inside. It was at that instant bullets began to fly around me. I was safe for the moment, but pinned down. No doubt the killer would try to escape during the next barrage.

Just as I expected, a second wave of shots rang out. I returned the fire hoping to slow his escape. The assassin was making his getaway. He probably didn't want to be around when the cavalry arrived. I tucked backed down and waited for the bullets to stop. The killer would have to turn his back to me to get down the stairs. In that instant I would have my chance.

In a flash the shooter was out the door and leveling a field of fire to escape behind. Smoke and noise filled the small hallway, a din so loud it was overwhelming. I raised my head and saw Kate step out behind the killer. His back was to her as he was shooting in my direction. She lifted an object high over her head and brought it down on the shooter. It was a cricket bat and she was using the killer's head as a ball. The shooter dropped his gun and staggered under the blow. Because Kate was substantially shorter than the killer she had insufficient leverage to knock him out. However, she had bought me some precious time.

I came out from where I had taken cover, my gun reloaded and aimed at the killer. I recognized him immediately it was Akham Bizhanov. I didn't want to kill the man I needed to capture him. I needed to know who had hired him. He could answer all our questions. "Don't move." I ordered. "I will kill you if I have to." Recovering, Bizhanov lunged at me. "Stop!" He didn't. With that I had no choice I took aim and fired. All the shooter and I heard was a click. My damn weapon had jammed. In that instant Akham Bizhanov was all over me. We fell to the floor clutching and tearing and grabbing at each other. Fists flew and legs kicked. Each of us tried to use our hand-to-hand combat skills. However, the space we had was simply too small for anything other than the most primitive fighting methods. We rolled around the hallway kicking and biting, I was trying to subdue the man, hold him until help came. Bizhanov was fighting like a man possessed; he was fighting for his life, fighting to escape. Finally Bizhanov managed to squirm free and in the moment of freedom kicked me hard in the head. I was stunned and lay motionless on the carpet. I could see Bizhanov but at the moment could do nothing more than watch him. If he went for his gun, I was dead. But Bizhanov must have concluded that this was his best chance to escape and he might lose that if he stopped to shoot me. He scrambled to his feet and moved quickly toward the stairs and potential freedom. He was about to descend when Kate, who had been lurking in the doorway, flung her cricket bat at Bizhanov's feet. The bat hit him in the right ankle. As he had already taken his first downward step, the bat caused him to trip and tumble down the stairwell. He rolled down crashing head over heels until he came to a stop on the mid-flight landing.

Astonishingly, Bizhanov wasn't killed or badly injured, just mildly stunned. In fact, both the assassin and I shook off our injuries at the same time. Bizhanov continued down the stairs as I chased him. He was about a half-flight ahead limping slightly. The limp was the only outward appearance of injury from his tumble. I hoped his whole foot would just fall off.

I chased the killer. At each landing I got slightly closer. I could see the limp was definitely slowing Bizhanov down. I had almost caught up with him by the time we approached the first floor. We jumped the last half-flight of stairs into the lobby. As soon as I landed, I made a leaping grab to haul down the shooter. I managed to grab hold and pull him down. I fully expected another desperate fight as before, only in a different location. I prayed I was up for it. It was then I heard the unmistakable metallic sound of a semi-automatic weapon being cocked. I looked up and saw an English police sergeant, wearing a Scotland Yard windbreaker.

"Don't either of you chaps move. I will kill you if you do," the sergeant commanded.

150

hank God help had arrived. I shouted to the sergeant, "My name is Mike Williams. I am a U.S. government official stationed at the U.S. embassy here in London. I have diplomatic immunity." This was a half-truth. I had no current immunity, but if need be I could get it. But if the half-truth kept me from being killed by either the sergeant or Bizhanov I would worry about the details later.

I knew it couldn't look good. The assassin and I lay sprawled on the floor of the Hyde Park Residence. An assassination had just taken place and shots had been fired in this hotel. The good sergeant would easily conclude that one or both of the men sprawled before him were guilty of something.

"I must speak to Maggie Smith. It is urgent."

"How do you know Inspector Smith?"

"I was the one who first phoned her with the information that sent you here."

"I'll have to check before I can do anything."

"No problem. Check all you like."

Still training his weapon on us the Sergeant pulled out his radio and called. He was becoming very agitated. He eventually signed off.

"Inspector Smith is dead."

"My God, what happened?"

"It seems she was hit while shielding the Jordanian king from the sniper. You may be telling me the truth and maybe you are not. I am going to take you both in for questioning. The higher ups can sort this thing out."

"Sergeant, we don't have time. This man must be questioned and I must contact my government."

"All in good time."

As the sergeant was about to take both Bizhanov and myself to headquarters Kate, limping badly, hobbled into the lobby. "Sergeant, my name is Kate O'Hara. What this man is telling you," Kate was pointing at me, "is true."

The sergeant glanced up and a look of recognition came over his face. "You are that lady reporter, aren't you?"

"Yes. I am surprised you recognized me."

"My hobby is to follow the American stock market."

I spoke up. "May I get up?"

"Okay."

"I need your help. I must get this man," I pointed towards Bizhanov still lying on the floor, "to your interrogation center. He has information I must have. Will you take me there?"

"What about me?" Kate interjected.

"I don't want you to go there. I don't want you involved in this part of my job. I will tell you what I find out."

"All right."

I could see she was disappointed. "It may not be pretty. Sometimes getting information quickly can be a little draining to the subject." I hoped I could frighten the killer. A frightened man was usually easier to get information from. I doubted what I said would make a difference in this case. Bizhanov was not the kind to frighten easily.

"Please stick around and see what else you can learn. Then meet me at the embassy. With luck I should be there by 4:00 p.m."

Kate looked doubtfully at me, "More like 4:00 a.m. would be my guess."

Shrugging towards her I turned back to the man from Scotland Yard and asked, "Are you ready to help?"

"If it helps find Maggie's killer I would escort you into hell," came the sergeant's reply.

We wrestled Bizhanov to his feet and dragged him outside to an awaiting police vehicle. We climbed in and were off to Scotland Yard. I hated leaving Kate but this was something I needed to do alone.

151

The call from the terrace at the Dorchester was a local call. There was just too much danger in sending an unencrypted international call. Had anyone been able to trace the call they would have found that it had gone to an investment house in London, Winslow and Sons, Ltd.

Hans Schmidt put down the receiver. Though the results were not as successful as had been hoped they were still acceptable to move forward. Years of planning and preparation were at last in motion. The West, in all its capitalistic decadence, would soon learn a major lesson. Hans smiled. The lesson was certain to be a long and painful one.

He needed to call Reuters and leave an anonymous tip that the kings of Saudi Arabia and Jordan had been killed. He would then call CNN to confirm the Reuters report. Hans glanced at his watch. The U.S. markets were just opening and the markets here were not due to close for another hour. Plenty of time for the oil markets to begin their meltdown.

But first he needed to call the oil ministry in Saudi Arabia. Hans grabbed the telephone receiver, pushed the speed dial code and waited to complete the first of his calls.

152

Hazim Aziz heard his private cell phone ring. Quickly hitting the send key, he spoke into the unit. "Yes?"

There was a few seconds delay before the voice at the other end of the line responded. The encryption process caused this delay. "The winds from the north blow and are cold even in summer."

"But the desert will warm those winds."

Both men were satisfied. The proper code was given.

"What news do you have for me Schmidt?"

"The old lion is dead." Hazim closed his eyes. The old king had been sent to his just reward. Only Mohammed and Allah knew what that was. "What about the Crown Prince?"

"Unfortunately he appears to have survived"

"That is most unfortunate, still the other news could change the world," a suddenly more cautious Hazim replied. "Is there anything else?"

"Indeed there is. The Jordanian king was wounded but appears to be still alive."

"That will make it more difficult for our followers in Jordan. However, it will not change our plans."

"What about the Crown Prince?"

"Fuck him. It is now or never"

"I was just double checking"

"Just proceed as we have planned"

"Very well"

"I will be in contact." Hazim ended his call. It was time for the "go" signal. But with the Crown Prince still alive time was even more important than before. He needed to make only one call. His supporters would move once they heard the announcement from the oil ministry. He paused and looked at the receiver in his hand, curious how a telephone and not a gun would be his weapon. The modern world was different from the ancient one only in its tools. Putting all other thoughts aside, he began to dial.

153

Kate gave her statement to several Scotland Yard officers several times. Eventually they brought her to the embassy where she cleaned up and began her wait for Mike. The television had excited reporters on every channel. Kate walked to the set and turned up the volume. A reporter on the exchange floor was making a report.

"It began as a normal day on Wall Street. It certainly will not end that way.

There is no place in this world that lives, breathes and reacts to rumors more than Wall Street. So when word leaked out about an assassination attempt in London on the lives of the king of Saudi Arabia, its Crown Prince as well as the king of Jordan, the stock market reacted quickly.

The stock market hates instability and the Middle East is the capital of instability, having only been in a state of relative calm for the last few years following the initial Gulf War. So when something happens involving that region of the world, a knee-jerk reaction always occurs in the markets.

Of course, this particular rumor is true. Both CNN and Reuters have announced that the King of Saudi Arabia is dead and King of Jordan has been wounded at a reception at their summit meeting in London. The exact condition of the Crown Prince is unknown. Based upon sketchy reports he is presumed to be gravely injured. Except for the announcement, there has been no other hard news. While the traders are somewhat concerned over the situation in Jordan, because of Israel and the Palestinian refugee problem they are considerably more concerned about the situation in the Desert Kingdom. While it is true that there is an extensive royal family and thus a large pool of potential candidates to ascend to the throne, the actual line of succession is ill defined. A king is generally chosen after an extensive period of family negotiations. Presumably, the royal family will meet and in some form of consensus and compromise choose a new monarch. Who will run the country in the meantime is anyone's guess.

Here in America the initial yet somewhat muted reaction of the market was to sell and move the money to safe investments like U.S. Treasury paper. However, now that it has become known that it was more than a rumor, the market has begun to sell off in earnest. Trading floor veterans are reporting a great deal of uncertainty and confusion. Sell orders have swamped any buy orders, with prices falling dramatically. It is anticipated that the market's circuit breakers might be invoked shortly."

"Now back to the studio. Bradley"

"Thanks Charles for bringing us that breaking report." Turning to the camera the host continued.

"After the 1987 stock market crash, the stock exchanges implemented a new set of trading rules. These rules, or circuit breakers, cause trading to be halted when certain conditions are met. That is, if the Dow or SP drops so many points the exchange will suspend trading for a period of time. This out of balance rule also applies to individual securities. That is, if many more sell orders are being received than buy orders or if there is some dramatic news relating to a particular stock, trading in that stock will be halted. The stock market basically creates a time-out."

"Let's now go to Riyadh for more breaking news"

"If there was any doubt about the possibility of trading restrictions being applied, that doubt ended with the announcement a few minutes age from the Saudi Oil Ministry. Everyone has expected an announcement, which came with slightly more than an hour left in the trading day. The expectation was that the government would make a statement saying that it was not changing the present oil policy. That expectation was dashed when the announcement was made that the Saudis are immediately cutting oil production. No official reduction amount was given. The unofficial amount, which in Saudi-speak was the equivalent of an official announcement, was in the range of 2,500,000 to 3,000,000 barrels per day."

"Thank you. We are now going to Chicago and the CBOT."

"If uncertainty is the current watchword on Wall Street, it is chaos here in Chicago. The CBOT, the Chicago Board of Trade is in a state of shock, a melt down if you will. Many, but not all, of the out of the money oil contracts previously sold by the brokerage houses were now very much in the money and in play. From my discussions with floor traders here no one knows who is making the money on these contacts. Everyone knows who isn't though and that is the major brokerage houses including those owned by banking holding companies. They are in deep trouble. There is blood in the water, lots of it and everyone knows it.

* * *

There it was the plan. It was masterful, Kate thought. The U.S. was under economic attack. She needed to talk to Mike.

154

Hazim was watching the television broadcast. The West's financial markets were melting down. The West and all its decadence would be ruined. Islam would emerge triumphant.

As he had planned, the first oil contracts to come into the money were the Saudi contracts. They were generating billions. Kemal's contracts had not yet reached the point where they could be sold. Hazim had laddered the contracts and, of course, had put in his contracts on the prime spot of the ladder. Hazim had made sure that if any of the contracts were going to go bad, they wouldn't be his. If everything went as planned, Kemal would make his money; if not, the Turk's money would come up short. Aziz knew that once the world knew the Crown Prince was still alive some of the chaos he created would subside. In that case Kemal Kanuni would be coming to him in need of money.

155

It seemed like the ride back to Scotland Yard took forever, I knew that in actuality we had arrived quickly. I was just anxious to get what I could from Bizhanov, report back to Washington and meet Kate at the embassy. We pulled into the underground garage. Two additional officers were waiting for us to arrive.

"We are taking the prisoner to Interrogation Room B. why don't you meet us there in a couple of minutes? The sergeant can point you in the right direction."

I knew there was no point in arguing besides I needed to make a pit stop and get something to drink, not tea. I stopped to let nature do its thing. When I returned to the hallway the police officer handed me a Coke and told me to follow him. I followed him through an elaborate labyrinth of hallways in the bowels of Scotland Yard until I found myself looking at a door marked Room B.

"Here we are and good luck.'

I thanked the sergeant for his help and stepped into the room. The room Bizhanov was in, euphemistically called Interrogation Room B, looked like a typical hospital operating room. Strapped to a gurney in the middle of the room was the assassin. Scotland Yard had done a terrific job of prepping him for interrogation.

The man was about to give a great deal of information unwillingly. Scotland Yard had a hastily thrown-together dossier with various facts most of which I already knew. There was one interesting point. The Yard believed he had from time to time been in the employee of Kemal Kanuni. I was going to find out if what Scotland Yard believed was or was not true.

Standing in the room when I entered was Philip Logan.

"Mike"

"Philip"

"Quite the day, did you know this son of a bitch killed Maggie Smith?"

"Anyone else?"

"Not yet but we still don't know whether the Saudi King will make it.

"Let's get started."

"Agreed."

We approached a now wide-eyed Bizhanov. I could tell the drugs were beginning to take effect. I knew that over enough days anyone would crack under this technique. Philip and my challenge was to compress days into hours.

The process was grueling. The drugs and the electric therapy took its toll on both the enforcers and the victim. No doubt given the choice, everyone would rather have been the enforcer as compared to the victim, as the toll was much higher for the person being persuaded to give up information. Modern techniques aimed to avoid permanent damage to those under interrogation, but even given that I hated the entire process. It was a necessary evil. I had to have the information locked in the man's head.

What we managed to learn was astonishing. Kemal Kanuni was involved in a conspiracy with Hazim Aziz. Bizhanov didn't know the specific details but their plan was to work as partners to control the world's oil supply. It didn't matter that Bizhanov knew little of the actual plans I already knew about their plans to destroy the Western world's banking and brokerage institutions. He did also confirm the missing piece of information about Melina being involved with Kemal. What I hadn't known before was that Hazim Aziz intended to overthrow the Saudi government in the process. Apparently Aziz wanted to create an Islamic Republic in its place. Hazim Aziz was going to be President and his son Abdul was going to be his Chief of Staff.

I filled Philip in on some of the missing details. "Philip I have to go, is that a problem?" Seeing Kate again aside, I had to make a secure call, making it imperative that I return to the embassy.

"No I am going to stay awhile longer with our friend here and see if I can't get some answers to some old questions I have. You know glean the finer details from Akham Bizhanov."

"I am sure those finer details will undoubtedly yield many good results."

"Let's hope so"

"Philip, I presume you can arrange a ride for me?"

"No problem. No doubt you have a lot to report back on. I'll walk you to the transportation section. At this hour they will have you back in no time. Besides, this old boy here could use some rest before he starts singing again."

156

Just as Kate suspected it was late when I finally got back to the Embassy. I found Kate sleeping in a chair in the small sitting area off the private entrance. I gently shook her awake. Wordlessly, I motioned for her to follow. I needed to get to the communications center. Every lost minute made my skin crawl. I had to contact Washington. As we got into the elevator I turned to Kate and asked, "How you doing?"

"Fine just a little tired, that's all."

"Sorry I took so long but the wait was worth it. Bizhanov confirmed there was a plot involving Kemal and Aziz."

"Anything new to report on Melina?"

"Yes, he confirmed she is in the game too."

"I thought so."

"Did you learn anything else after I left the residence hotel?"

"Nothing there but I did check the financial wires and television reports. The worldwide markets all reacted badly, actually badly would have been good, they all cratered. If we can't stop this soon, the depression of the 1930s will look like a mild recession. It is also being reported that there is a big meeting scheduled for tonight. Apparently all the heavy players are scheduled to be there or check in by phone." Kate looked at her watch. I could see her doing some quick math. "The meeting is probably over or close to it by this hour."

"That makes sense. Is there anything they can do?"

"Maybe"

I didn't like the way Kate said maybe. It really sounded more like no.

"Mike, is another war a strong possibility?"

"Kate, I don't know." I suspect she didn't like the way I said, I don't know.

The elevator car stopped. I punched in my security code. As the doors opened I took Kate by the hand and said, "Let's go, we don't have a lot of time."

"Agreed"

157

National Security Advisor Joanne Davis sat bleary eyed at her desk. She had just gotten out of a hastily called meeting and was reviewing the transcript hoping to find something she could use. She was on the team that had been scheduled to meet shortly with the President to review any available options.

"Present at the meeting or available by telephone: the chairman of the Securities and Exchange Commission, the President of the New York Federal Reserve Bank and Treasury Secretary Wong," Also listed were the heads of the leading independent brokerage firms, major world banks. "Attending via conference call was the chairman of the Fed, the head of the Bank of England and the chairman of the Bundesbank, The chairman of the Bank of Japan and the head of the Chicago Board of Trade."

Secretary Wong began. "Thankfully the day has ended with no one cashing in their contracts. We know we won't be so lucky tomorrow or the next day. For that reason among others the President has asked us to present him with a list of options to deal with this situation. I thought the best way to begin would be for each of you, to give us a three-minute briefing. Mr. Lowenstien would you please begin?"

Samuel Lowenstein, Chairman of the Board of Merrill Lynch reported first. "At this hour we are still unsure of the condition of Abdul bin Saud. He is said to be hovering between life and death. That fact combined with the subsequent announcement from the Saudi Oil Ministry has had a chaotic impact on the financial markets. In no particular order of importance, mainly because I don't have the vision to prioritize the situation nor do I believe I need to, the following are my observations:

1) The NYSE and Nasdaq may not be able to open for trading tomorrow. My guess is that if they do, they will close in less than half an hour.

2) If, as we suspect, the holders of the oil futures contracts present them tomorrow, and I can't imagine why they would not, our brokerage house and I suspect everyone else's will not have the ability to honor those contracts. Noon tomorrow is when we will run out of funds. I assume we are no different than anyone else.

3) If we and the major banks run out of funds, the U.S. Treasury, the Bank of Japan and the European Central Banks will have to become lenders of last resort. They will have to bail us out. There is no option.

4) The strain on the United States and the European Economic Community's credit worthiness will be intense. Our governments may not be able to fill the world's liquidity demands without creating hyperinflation.

5) If the cut back in oil production lasts for more than 45 days, the odds are 65% we will have a severe recession, 35% we will have something more profound.

6) Other non-financial considerations include that Israel will come under extraordinary pressure.

7) Congress will either demand that President Espinoza declare war to get the oil flowing again or face the real possibility of impeachment."

Samuel Lowenstein examined his note cards to see if he had missed any points. He found he had not, thanked the Treasury Secretary and sat down.

"Thank you, Mr. Lowenstein. Mrs. Roth, would you proceed?"

Davis scanned the remainder of the transcript. Miriam Roth, Chairman of the Board of Citigroup, presented observations similar to those of Samuel Lowenstein. In fact, all those attending echoed his remarks.

Davis placed the transcript back on her desk and looked at the clock. It was time to meet the President.

158

I headed straight to the secure phones. I need to talk Joanne Davis. She and the President must know about the plot. Thankfully Maria is on duty and just waves to Kate and me.

* * *

Seated in the Oval Office the National Security Advisor was listening to the President's briefing when the President's Secretary tapped her on the shoulder. "Ms. Davis I have a phone call for you from Mike Williams, he says it is urgent."

"Thank you, Mrs. Scott." The entrance of the President's secretary though not uncommon was rare enough to cause Joint Chiefs Admiral Duncan Evans to pause. He had just begun presenting the current military assets available in the region. "Excuse me, I am sorry you were interrupted Chairman Evans but I must take a call from Mike Williams."

"Who?"

"Mike Williams he works for me. He has been on assignment, personally requested by the President to investigate the new Head of the Bir League, Kemal Kanuni. Mr. Williams had earlier expressed concern about Mr. Kanuni. He may have something more definitive. He says it is urgent."

"Joanne, you may use my private office to take this call."

"Thank you Mr. President."

* * *

"Joanne, Mike Williams"

"Hi Mike what have you got for me? It better be pretty good you just pulled me out of a meeting with the President."

"Joanne, this is better than good." I went on to explain about Kate's involvement, Bizhanov's interrogation, concluding with the plot between Hazim Aziz and Kemal Kanuni.

"Mike you need to tell the President what you have told me. He needs to hear this first hand. I am going to put you on hold and get him. But first give me the particulars on Kate O'Hara so I can pull up a quick bio."

* * *

Davis returned to the Oval office. "Mr. President I am sorry to interrupt again. But the call was incredible in nature. You must hear for yourself what Mike Williams has learned. If it is all right with you I am going to put him on the speaker?"

"Please do."

159

"Mr. President, this is Mike Williams calling from our embassy in London."

"Go ahead Mike. May I call you Mike?"

"Of course, Mr. President."

As the President began to speak, Davis handed out a bio of Kate she had just printed out.

"You are on the speaker phone in the Oval Office. In addition to myself and National Security Advisor Davis, also present is Jazel Hammiby, Under Secretary of State for Middle Eastern Affairs, Secretary of State Robert Wright and Chairman of the Joint Chiefs Admiral Duncan Evans and Federal Reserve Chairman Raymond Kelly. Please continue."

"I have just come from an interrogation session of Akham Bizhanov, the man who shot the Saudi king and wounded the King of Jordan."

The President cut in, "I presume the information you received is accurate."

"Sir, as accurate as our drugs can make it. In fact, the information may be false but the interogatee believes it to be true. In this case I believe it to be true."

"Continue," the President commanded.

"Bizhanov has told us that as part of Kemal Kanuni's plan to create an Islamic super state with himself as its head there is to be a coup in Saudi Arabia. Hazim Aziz, the current oil minister, is the leader. He will proclaim an Islamic Republic with himself as its president. Kemal Kanuni has a small cadre of close associates. One of its members is Abdul Aziz, the son of Hazim Aziz. Incidentally, Kemal is related to both men."

"Mike, this is Jazel. Were you able to find out when this revolution is to take place?"

"No, Jazel. I did find out that Hazim Aziz has been working on this plan for years. He hates the West and all it stands for. To this end he has developed a group of young army officers who are both loyal to him and an Islamic revolution. From what I can tell, the Saudi Royal Guard Regiment consisting of three light infantry battalions has not been compromised. I would assume therefore that those would be the only army units that could be counted on to stop this revolt."

Everyone around the table nodded in concurrence. The President spoke again. "We will of course work through this on our end. Is there someone you can contact who would be of value?"

"Yes, Sir. His name is Fahad Amani. I will contact him immediately. I will also provide him with the necessary contact information so that he may reach the NSA directly."

"Please proceed Mike. And please instruct the communications officer there to maintain a direct line to the White House."

"Yes, Mr. President."

160

As instructed I informed the embassy communications officer of the President's request. I then turned to Kate and filled her in on his conversation.

"What are you going to tell him?" Kate inquired.

"I'm not exactly sure. That's why I haven't put the call through yet. I can't ponder this too long, though."

"I suggest you keep it simple and let him work it out."

I asked the communications technician to reach Fahad Amani. Within moments the call had gone through and I was speaking with my old friend.

161

"Fahad its Mike"

"Yes Mike what can I do for you?"

I filled him on all I knew about Hazim Aziz's plot. There was mostly silence from his end of the line. When I was done he thanked me. "Before you go can you tell me anything more about the King?"

"Just that his life hangs in the balance. It is up to Allah. The doctors have done all they can."

"I see, I will pray for him."

"Thank you. I must go know. Hopefully when this is all over we will have great stories to swap. Until then, peace."

"Good luck"

Amani signed off and put his secure phone on standby. He would need help, so he rang up his assistant and told him to meet him in the main cafeteria.

"So it is revolution." Mustafa Zell said. "I know we had suspected for some time that something was afoot. But I would never have guessed it was a revolution."

"Have you noticed anything unusual? Such as troop movements, calls not be answered, that sort of thing?"

"No Fahad, if anything it seems quite the opposite."

"Mustafa, that makes sense. Listen we need to remain calm. If we lose our heads, figuratively speaking, many others will lose theirs not so figuratively speaking."

"What should we do?"

"Two things, While I try and find the whereabouts of Oil Minister Aziz you will need to find our boss, General Saud bin Faisal."

Hopefully he will have command of enough loyal troops to stop this thing."

"Once I find him what should I do?"

"Contact me"

"Okay"

162

"Kate tomorrow is going to be brutal."

"You mean later today?"

"Yeah you're right later today."

"I need to get a few hours of sleep. I won't be worth a damn if I don't. Let's find a quiet corner and get some rest."

Kate and I managed to find an empty conference room. I fell asleep almost instantly on the floor. As I drifted off I could hear her flipping television channels.

I awoke about three hours later feeling a little better. I stretched after I got off the floor. Kate was sitting in a chair. She looked liked she was half dozing half awake. "Sleep okay?'

"Yes, just a bit stiff. I'm not as young as I used to be and sleeping on the floor was never my best thing." I stopped talking and pointed to the T.V. The reporter was standing in front of Winslow and Sons, Ltd.

"As had been widely anticipated, with the start of the business day in London oil contracts have begun to be redeemed. Thousands of contracts representing millions of dollars are flowing through this boutique investment house behind me.

Also as anticipated, the Western governments and Japan have been forced to intervene on behalf of the world's financial institutions. The purpose, of course, was to acquire the funds necessary to shore up the banks and brokerage houses. With each round of borrowing the U.S. Treasury, the Bank of Japan, the Bank of England and the Bundesbank have found it ever more costly to borrow. As the day has worn on the value of all these countries currencies has begun to fall causing even more pressure on the world banking system.

I turned the sound down and looked at Kate now fully awake. "Michael I'm scared."

163

In just a few hours he would go on TV and announce to the country and the world that he was the newly appointed President of the Islamic Republic of Saudi Arabia. He smiled at the thought of being appointed, having appointed himself to the job. He wished he could make the announcement sooner but his army units would not be able to secure the country until that time. Until then Hazim was in constant communication with his fellow conspirators and nothing unusual was going on. No suspicious questions were being asked. All was as it was supposed to be.

The operation would be tricky, particularly with the Crown Prince still alive. Adding to the urgency was information from his operatives in London who had told him the Prince was planning to fly home within the next few hours. The plan was for some of his units to take control of all the centers of communication, telephone and cellular, TV and radio. That would be the easy compared to the next part. The remainder of his forces would have to locate, isolate and round up the Royal family before the army or national police could rescue them. Conveniently for Aziz most of the family was waiting together to see if a new king would have to be chosen.

Within hours of capturing them he would hold a series of Islamic court trials. The Royal family would be found to have grossly violated Islamic law. The sentence would, of course, be death, which would be carried out immediately. He would not make the mistake that the Bolsheviks had made. Russian reds and whites never would have fought if Lenin had immediately executed the Tsar and his extended family.

164

Once Williams was off the line, the President turned to Joint Chiefs Admiral Duncan Evans and asked, "You were just beginning to tell us what assets we have over there that we can use immediately"

"Sir, we have some heavy tank units and light infantry brigades. As you know, our tanks as requested by the Saudis are located in a central staging area away from Riyadh. Driving them into town might cause quite a stir."

"What can we use them for?"

"They can be rather easily deployed near the airport or the capital's power installations."

"Not both?"

"No. To do the job right they can only cover one or the other."

"What about the light infantry?"

"Sir, they can be anywhere important in the country in less than an hour."

"Any other assets?" National Security Advisor Davis asked.

"Yes, our best strike force in the area is the 2nd Marine battalion out of Camp Pendleton in California. Fortunately for us they are currently deployed to the region. That makes them are our best option for a surprise action. With their helicopters they could be having afternoon coffee with the Royal family before the Royal family knew they had invited them. Give them a go order and in half an hour they can be lifting off from our fleet. The Navy has had them as guests for about six weeks.

They should be completely stir-crazy by now. They could use a little excitement."

"Admiral Evans, please return within forty five minutes with an action plan. Within the hour, based upon that plan, I will instruct you to take action. I know forty-five minutes to stop a war and prevent an economic catastrophe similar to the one that occurred with the fall of Rome isn't much but it is all we have. And yes I know God had a week to create the world."

"Yes, Mr. President." Admiral Evans immediately left the Oval Office.

165

Fahad Amani and Mustafa Zell agreed to meet again in an hour. Hopefully it would also be with General Faisel. In the meantime the inspector's task was to find the location of the oil minister. He made several inquiries to learn that Hazim Aziz was indeed in the capital at the oil ministry.

He called over to the ministry and asked to speak to one of his minor associates, a man he had known slightly from school. A made up story about the Crown Prince was sure to get him through.

"This is Ali. May I help you?"

"Yes Ali, this is Fahad Amani, do you remember me?"

"Yes Fahad, I do, what can I help you with?"

"I wanted the oil minister to know that I have learned the Crown Prince will be arriving within the hour and I need to speak to him about it."

"I can give him that information. However, he is unavailable and will be so for the remainder of the day. He has been tied up all day on the telephone."

"Is that usual?"

"Not that it is your business, but no. However, these are not usual times."

"Is there any way I can get in to see him, just for a few minutes to talk to him, perhaps later in the day, just before he goes home?"

"I am afraid not. He is scheduled to go to the State television station shortly, something about an address to the people."

"Must have something to do with the King's health."

"Well it was good talking to you anyway. Please pass my information onto him when you have chance."

"Goodbye it was good hearing from you again also."

Amani had gotten all this data by just being pleasant and spending some effort with a low- level staffer he had vaguely known from his school years. It always amazed him how much valuable information was available from people in low places if you treated them well.

Amani looked at his watch. He figured that if something were going to happen, the Oil Minister would make some announcement over public radio and television. So while he waited to meet again with Mustafa, he thought he would have just enough time to go over to the national TV headquarters and observe what was going on.

166

When the inspector arrived at television headquarters he could see there was more activity than usual. Technicians and staffers were scurrying about.

"You guys seem extra busy today, anything going on?" Fahad asked one of the nearby technicians.

"We are. The oil minister had scheduled a public announcement for later this evening. Then the ministry phoned and told us he had moved it up. Now we only have a couple of hours to get ready."

The station employee began moving off, "Glad I am not in your shoes. Good luck." Looking at his watch, Fahad realized he had better hurry to his meeting with Mustafa. The hour was almost up and he had agreed to meet Mustafa again in the cafeteria.

167

Fahad hurried as fast as he dared. He didn't want to attract any unnecessary attention. He reached the hall and spotted Mustafa.

"Did you have any luck?"

"Yes."

"Thanks be to Allah."

"We are to meet the General in half an hour at his headquarters."

"That long? I just came from the TV station. Something is going to happen and is going to happen soon. My guess is that Hazim Aziz will be announcing a change of government."

"It will take us almost that long to get there."

"Let's go then, Mustafa. I will drive."

168

Hazim Aziz was a patient man, very patient. Still, time for him was practically standing still. He had almost made all the calls he could make and double-checked all that could be double-checked. There was only one call left to make.

"Has the Crown Prince left yet?"

"He has been delayed. It seems that unexpected mechanical difficulties have grounded the plane indefinitely."

"Good, then he will be there for many more hours?"

"No, not hours, the British have offered him the use of one of their Royal Air Force planes and he has graciously accepted their generosity."

"Is there anything you can do?"

"Only a little."

"A little may be just enough."

"I will see what I can do."

169

"Admiral, thank you for being prompt."

"You are welcome Mr. President." The Chairman quickly outlined his plan.

"Admiral quite impressive I must say particular for such short notice. I am sure we all could do better if we had more time, but that is a commodity we do not have."

"Agreed, Mr. President."

"Then let's do it and May God have mercy on us."

The admiral took his leave while the President turned to his National Security Advisor. "Joanne, you know this will only work if the Saudi's cooperate."

"Yes Mr. President. Unfortunately, the entire Royal Family is meeting waiting to see if they will have to select a successor for Abdul sin Saud. We have been unable to get through to anyone over there."

"Keep trying."

"I will, Mr. President. Sir?"

"Yes, Joanne."

"I could try Mike Williams. He may have had more luck on the ground than we have."

"Use my office"

170

"Thank you sir" National Security Advisor Joanne Davis picked up the phone. "Communications get London on the line. I need to talk to Mike Williams again."

"Yes, ma'am."

"Mike, Joanne. Did you get through to Fahad?"

"Yes." I filled my boss in on my conversation with him.

"Good work. I have to get back with the President and let him know. It seems the rest of our communication lines are blocked."

"Doesn't surprise me, probably the beginnings of the *coup d'etat.*"

Davis again returned to the Oval Office. "Mr. President, I have talked to Mike Williams. Fortunately he had been able to make contact with Inspector Amani. According to Williams the inspector is fully aware of the implications of the entire situation. As a matter of fact, he and his assistant are on their way to General Faisal's headquarters."

"Who is Faisal?"

"A General and a member of the Royal family. He commands the King's private guard and National Police Force."

"Is he loyal?"

"We can only assume so."

"Damn I wish we knew for sure."

"As do I. Since we've had no luck through our normal channels, our best hope is these two Saudi policemen."

"Thanks, Joanne. The troops are going in regardless, with or without help. I am afraid many more troops will be needed and many more American lives will be lost without help."

171

Fahad and Mustafa raced against time as they sped toward the general's headquarters.

"Mustafa at best we have only a couple of hours. I am sure of it."

"I am forced to agree with you. Before I left I heard some of the men talking about a special broadcast they had heard the oil minister was going to make shortly."

"Then it is H-hour"

"H-hour, that's what it was called in those old World War II movies I loved to watch."

"Why do you like them so much?"

"That's easy. The good guys were true and noble; the bad guys were evil. No middle ground. And good always triumphed over evil."

"Fahad, if it were only that way in the world. LOOK OUT!"

"Thank you I was lost in thought. I would have missed the camp if you had not yelled."

The car with the two policemen approached the front gate of the compound. Like all military bases throughout the world this one had a guard shack with a barrier preventing unauthorized entry. Fahad slowed to a stop, rolled down the window. We are here to see General Faisal. We have an appointment and he is expecting us."

"I will check, please wait. This may take some time."

The two men sat in the car. "I hope nothing is wrong this seems to be taking too long."

Zell pointed to the guard returning. "We will soon find out."

"The general will see you. Please follow the main road." The guard pointed in its direction. "Someone will meet you when you get to the headquarters building."

"Thank you." Fahad engaged the car and headed toward headquarters.

172

We sat in silence. "Kate, you know waiting is so much harder to do than almost anything else."

"But waiting it's all we can do right now, correct?"

"Correct. At least here in the basement we will have a front-row seat to the day's events.

To pass the time I pointed to a screen in the upper corner of the bank of TV screens. "Saudi TV may be the first place we see anything."

Kate smiled at me. "I love you. I know you have done your best regardless of what happens."

I reached over and squeezed her hand, saying thank you without words. This is a crazy world. It is falling apart and this wonderful person is in love with me.

"I love you too."

173

The two Saudi policemen were met at the front door and then ushered into General Faisal's office. The commander rose from behind his desk and walked toward them.

"Please be seated."

The general was a distinctive man over six feet tall, ruggedly handsome, who bore a striking similarity to the original King Faisal, his great uncle. He addressed the inspector the tone of his voice not revealing anything. "Zell here told me a most amazing tale. Had I not known his family for many years I would have thought him insane. But because of his family I know he would not make up such a story. I also understand that Hazim Aziz is an ambitious man. As you know his background is Turkic and it is possible that what you say is true. Do you have anything more you can tell me?"

"Yes, general." Fahad went on to describe what he had heard; first about the oil minister's telephone habits and then about what he had seen at the Communication Ministry.

The general appeared to mull over what had been said. "A reasonable explanation would be an attempted take over. Yes a coup attempt seems likely. Thank you men. I appreciate your loyalty. Now I am going to ask more of you. I will be sending a squad of my most loyal troops with you. Go back to the television station. Prevent Aziz from going on the air. You must do so at all costs. Any questions?"

"May I ask what you will be doing?" Amani inspector inquired.

The general sighed deeply. "I am totally certain of the loyalty of only a small number of troops. I am going to take those men with me to protect the Royal Family."

"Sir, we need more men. There are more places we must protect — the airport, communication centers, the power plants."

"I know but I have only so much to work with."

"What about contacting the Americans?" Fahad suggested.

"Yes, I suppose we have no choice, but how sad. We must ask an Infidel to help us save our king and country. I am sure the price we will eventually have pay for their help will be quite steep."

"Can we afford not to pay it?" Mustafa inquired. With that, the general merely shook his head no.

"Go. I must make arrangements. A young major will be waiting for you at the gate. He will be the one wearing the armored personnel carrier. You can't miss him."

174

At last it was time to go to the television station. Hazim glanced at his notes again for the umpteenth time. The speech he was about to give would rally the Saudi people to his cause. Tomorrow, a new day, a new era would begin. The triumph of Islam was at hand; only it would be he and not his nephew Kemal who would be its new leader. He would be an Islamic Messiah, the new Alexander, not Kemal Kanuni.

"Mr. Minister are you ready?"

"Yes"

175

Following the armored personally carrier as closely as he dared Amani raced back to the communication Ministry building, Zell turned on the car radio to check on any special announcements.

"Please stand by. There will be an important announcement from the Oil Minister." To kill dead air the announcer speculated that a new king might have been selected and if that was the case that was what the message was going to be.

"I wish it were the selection of a new king."

"So do I. Look we are almost there."

The small column had chosen to approach the building from the rear, assuming that by now the building was under rebel guard. With luck there would be fewer troops in the back.

"Mustafa it looks like we were right. It looks like only a single squad is patrolling the rear entrance." Amani slowed the car down as the policemen approached the guards.

"Fahad I sure hope this works."

"If not we will be the distraction. Got your gun?"

"Yes, you?"

"Yes" As the car stopped Amani rolled down his window. "Lieutenant, why are you patrolling the building?"

"It is an army matter and none of your business."

"Internal security is my business."

"I said move along."

Fahad could see the soldiers were becoming agitated. They were going to have to leave soon or come out shooting.

Without cover that second option was a sure ticket to Paradise. He wanted to go to Paradise, but not today.

Then it happened. Gunfire erupted all around them. Rebel troops were going down without any resistance. Only the lieutenant was left standing. Fahad swung his gun up quickly and then there were none. Silence, not gunfire, was all they heard. The young major yelled. "Let's go" The security officers got out of the car and raced with the army squad into the building.

176

Kate was amazed. There in front of her were banks of television screens showing broadcasts from networks all over the world. In addition to the standard commercial networks being shown, there were also images being projected from other sources. To her left were two rows of monitors showing real-time satellite projections. I had explained to her that the top row showed images from satellites in geosynclines orbit. The bottom row came from satellites that could be directed to focus on certain parts of the world. It was that row of TV screens that now had our attention. Satellite command had redirected two birds to the Middle East. With the repositioning of those two spy satellites, space command had now made it possible to get continuous coverage from specifically chosen areas from that part of the world. To Kate, this setup was impressive, but what was the most amazing were the real-time pictures coming in from high altitude drone planes. By command of the President, several hours earlier as a precautionary measure three-camera drone planes had been launched. They were now in position high over Saudi Arabia. These three drones were up and broadcasting. Their cameras were focused on the airport, the Communications Ministry, and the site where the Royal Family was gathered for their meeting. These drones could stay aloft for hours and the pictures they brought back were better than those from helicopter-cams. I also told her that, if need be a cruise missile could be outfitted with a camera rather than a bomb. The picture clarity was outstanding at least while it lasted. Kate was going to see the television show of a lifetime.

I tapped Kate on the shoulder and pointed to the screen showing Saudi television. A special announcement notice had just gone up. English subtitles streamed across the bottom of the screen. "Looks like it's show time for our friend Hazim Aziz."

The spy satellite, had taken up a wide-angle camera position. In that way command and control would know if something were happening in the country outside of Riyadh. Whether or not they could do anything about it was another question. The general assumption however, was that this event was going to be played out in and around the capital.

All at once it seemed the screens began showing a great deal of activity. There had been a small skirmish at the back of the Communications Ministry building. "Kate the good guys just won one."

"How can you tell?"

"They are the only ones still standing."

"How do you know it's the good guys?"

"I recognize my friend Fahad. He is the one on the far right." I pointed to another screen. "Kate please take a look at that picture. Look in the distance it looks like an American Light Infantry Brigade is moving in the direction of the TV station."

"What about there?"

"That's the heavy stuff." American armor could be seen on another of the screens. MI-AI battle tanks and Bradley fighting vehicles were moving in the direction of the airport.

"Good move. We need to get control of the airport."

"Why's that?"

"It is the key to additional man power. If we can control the airport we can get extra help in and Hazim will be unable to. He will have to play with the hand he was dealt. And with our troops in the picture, I'll bet his hand just got a whole lot weaker."

No pictures had come in from the third drone. Kate turned to me, "Do you think the third plane is down or the camera isn't working?"

"I think everything is okay. Just wait." Almost as if on command the screen came to life. I pointed to the screen and told Kate, "This drone must be looking for the Royal Family." Its cameras had focused on the government buildings in the center of the city, the area is known as Qasr-al-Hukm. "Looks like this is the spot."

Unfolding before our eyes was a column of troops moving against the buildings. We could also see a much smaller group already there.

"Looks like the rebels have a lot more men than those defending the location."

"Don't worry it takes fewer men to defend." Still I was worried.

In the next few minutes it became hard to track the action. The rebel troops guarding the TV station had just discovered that their comrades in the rear of the building had been killed. With that Kate pointed out that she could see some of these troops leave their positions outside the building and instead rush into it.

Another screen was showing U.S. tanks taking up strategic positions around King Fahd International Airport. No fighting had yet taken place there.

"It is unlikely anyone will have much luck there against us."

"Why is that?"

"Too much firepower. I wish I could say the same for the defensive position around the Royal Family."

177

Fahad and his small group were in the building. Fahad turned to the major. "The studio is on the second floor."

"Let's go." Turning to one of his troops, he said, "I wish I could give you some help, but I can't. Stay here. You are the rear guard. Don't let anyone get by you. Play it like an American – shoot first and ask questions later."

"Yes sir. I will not fail," was the corporal's reply.

The small team raced up the stairs and rounded into the studio corridor when a hail of bullets met them. Two squad members went down right away. A third managed to find cover on the other side of the hallway.

Fahad crawled up to the major as bullets were flying everywhere. The squad had taken up position just outside the corridor. "We have to get into that studio. Is there anything I can do?"

"Yes. See if they would like to surrender." It was then that they heard rifle fire from downstairs. The major turned and said, "Looks like we are trapped between them."

"We have a chance if we can get into the studio. We can stop the broadcast and there is a chance we can save ourselves," Fahad offered.

"Agreed. This, I think, is our only option. There are five of us left. Four of us have hand grenades. We will all toss them at the same time. As soon as they explode we race down the hall firing away. Hopefully, we will make it to the studio."

"I am ready."

"Then let's go." The major signaled his remaining troops with the plan. Seconds later the hand grenades exploded with a thunderous sound. Fahad saw one of the soldiers go down as he tossed his grenade. The four remaining men rose and entered the hall screaming fiery blasts from their automatic weapons.

178

The rebel troops were moving in force against the government buildings. A real-life game of capture the flag was unfolding before our very eyes. The small band of defenders was falling back.

"They are losing troops they can't afford to lose. It will be just a matter of time before they are overwhelmed."

"Mike is this position critical?"

"I think so. The game is being played here, regardless of what happened to my friend Fahad at the TV station. The revolt will succeed or fail here. Look you can see the attackers bringing up light artillery pieces. That's it. If the defenders don't get help soon they are doomed and with it I presume the Saudi Royal family."

Just as the rebel's artillery was about to come to bear, there was a blinding white flash. We could see nothing but smoke.

"Mike what happened?"

"I'm not sure." As the screen finally cleared, we could see what had happened. The artillery pieces lay overturned and mangled. The troops attending the pieces were in worse condition. "Kate the U.S. Marines have landed. Look there. You can see their gun-ships."

"I see the helicopters."

We watched in fascination as the battle began to turn. The Marines supported by aerial gun ships were pushing back the rebels. Soon they were being overwhelmed and routed.

I turned to Kate "Looks like the cavalry rode over the hill just in the nick of time." I then saw Kate cover her mouth. I immediately returned to viewing the screens. It was Saudi TV. They saw Hazim Aziz begin to announce that he had taken control of the government when a bloody man appeared from camera right.

"It's Fahad."

"Mike he is aiming at Hazim Aziz." There, on live television, we saw the Chairman of OPEC and would be new Islamic President of Saudi Arabia become a former human being. Hazim sprawled across the desk he was sitting behind, killed instantly by the bullets fired from my friend's weapon.

The screen immediately went dark.

179

Kemal Kanuni had been watching television and getting reports all day. He saw Hazim Aziz gunned down live on Saudi television, his anger rising each time something had gone wrong. So when Hans Schmidt phoned him to inform him that his oil positions had become worthless, Kemal's closest aides feared an eruption that would have made Vesuvius mild by comparison.

Later they would speculate that it was the presence of Melina Fokina Christakos and maybe it wasn't.

He merely turned to them and quietly asked, "Please leave. We need to be alone on this bad day." But from that day forth his reputation grew. He was considered by many to be a truly remarkable leader. One they believed some day would indeed lead all the Islamic people of the world.

Once his staff left, he turned to Melina. "We should never have trusted Hazim. He simply didn't have the balls to pull it off."

Quietly Melina replied. "Well, he had enough fucking balls to be willing to screw us."

It was then that Kemal realized that as mad and frustrated as he was, she was even more so. "I won't make that mistake again. But all is not lost."

"How so?"

"Your tanker fleet exists and is intact. Your debt position is greatly reduced. Your business is out of any danger."

"Well, a fucking lot of good that will do us now."

He knew he would have to calm her down or she might do something rash. "Listen to me. This is a setback but I am not going to let it stop us. I will threaten the Saudi's with the recognition of Abdul Aziz as the rightful successor leader to the Islamic Republic of Saudi Arabia."

By now Melina had begun to return to her normal, rather Machiavellian, self. "Of course, and they will pay you not to do this."

"I think I can get them to pay enough that our setback will not be that long. Besides, we are young and we have time. And at the end of the day I will recognize Abdul anyway."

"What about Akham?"

"The Brits have him. If they ever let him go, which I doubt, I will make certain permanent travel arrangements for him."

"What of Abdul? Do you think you can trust him?" Melina tested him.

"Only so far as I can see him. I have decided that he will only be the potential president while in exile. When his exile ends, so will he. I will make sure the only leader needed at that time will be me."

Melina looked at Kemal and spoke. "My love, I know things will work out. Our time will come because we have been written off. It is a very stupid mistake."

"And a very dangerous as well."

180

"Mr. President, in conclusion," National Security Advisor JoAnn Davis summarized the events of the past few days. "We were lucky, very, very lucky. By the will of God or the luck of the Irish we managed to preserve the status quo in the Middle East. The Saudis are again grateful; for how long we don't know, but we preserved only the status quo. The King survived but is in very poor health. The Royal Family has named the Crown Prince Regent. He will remain in that role until the King can re-assume his duties. I believe his regency will be good for America. He is man whom with whom we can deal. The extra power of the regency should allow him to keep the Wahabee faction of the Royal Family in check for at least a while."

"What about the oil situation?"

"Good news there also, the announcement from Riyadh renouncing their earlier production cuts had the desired effect. Oil prices have returned to normal. As a result, our financial system, though bent and battered remains intact, our banks and brokerage houses sadder but wiser.

"What about this Kemal Kanuni character?"

"Kemal Kanuni still runs Bir, though he lost a fortune pursuing his scheme. Basically we ended up with his money and the Saudis kept theirs. But I believe we will have to deal with him again. He has undoubtedly learned from his mistakes and that, I fear, will make him an even more dangerous adversary in the future."

"Do you have any further comments or recommendations?"

"My recommendation for the future, Sir, is that we develop an energy strategy that prevents us from relying on the good graces of foreign governments, any foreign government, but especially those in unstable parts of the world. We really have no choice. We must stop giving lip service to energy independence. We must act and do so quickly."

"On a final note, I recommend a blue-ribbon panel be formed to study the effect on our and the world's economy of the forces of consolidation in our financial industries. I am terribly concerned that there are too few financial entities on a world-wide basis and that when one of them sneezes, we and quite possibly the rest of the world will catch a cold."

"Thank you for your report, Joann."

"Thank you Mr. President."

181

Kate was hurrying to finishing up her column. She was going to meet Mike at her flat for dinner and was running a little late

> In retrospect it is apparent that the world's investment houses had taken a good idea to an extreme and had issued too many options and too many futures contracts. Upon review it is also apparent that the amount of new money flowing from the Kazakhstan oil fields was not fully understood by the international financial community. In the long run world markets are very efficient. Efficiency is an economic term. The term refers to a marketplace where there are willing buyers and willing sellers and all financial information is known both to the buyers and the sellers. In the short-run, markets are anything but efficient. Because it was spread over many suppliers, no one seemed to notice that the government of Saudi Arabia had significantly slowed down its payment process for ordered goods and services. In business parlance, the Saudi Government was aging its customers. Of course the plan would have failed had there been no coordination between the firm's three clients. Competition in the world's markets is assumed to eliminate this kind of collaboration. The market thus assumed nothing like this would be possible.

Kate knew her roommates, June and Maureen, would be gone and she was grateful. Not that it really mattered, but Mike was special and this night was special and she did not want to share him with anyone right now. She took one last look at her column before filing and it and heading for home.

182

I walked up the steps to Kate's flat. For first time in weeks I was relaxed. I had nowhere I had to go or better yet no report I had to file. I knocked and Kate opened the door. "You look great. Can I come in?"

"Thanks and yes."

I headed for the refrigerator. "Mind if I have a beer?"

"Not at all, please bring me something."

"I hunted around and found two Newcastle's. I opened them and took them into the living room. "Here you go."

"Thanks."

"Did you file your story?"

"I filed my story. They were pretty happy with the exclusive I gave them, so when I asked for time off, they had no choice but to agree. How about you?"

"Since all I..."

Kate interrupted me. "Don't you mean we, dear?"

"It is truly we, but to the Washington powers that be, it is still I. So let me continue. As I was saying before I was so rudely interrupted, since I/we saved western civilization they had no choice but to agree to pay for a two-week vacation in Bermuda. We are booked on the British Air 8:00 pm flight tomorrow. First class, I might add."

"It will be a little dull, you know, just the two of us with no world to save," Kate kidded.

"I'm really looking forward to two dull weeks with you."

Made in the USA
Charleston, SC
15 June 2010